THE ST. PAUL CONSPIRACY

MCRYAN MYSTERY SERIES

ROGER STELLJES

The St. Paul Conspiracy by Roger Stelljes

ISBN 978-0-9835758-0-1 (ebook)

ISBN 978-1-679181542 (paperback)

ISBN 0-87839-234-3 (hardcover)

First edition September 1, 2006

Never miss a new release again, join the new release list at www.
RogerStelljes.com

ACKNOWLEDGMENTS

A book, especially a first book, doesn't see the light of day without the help of many people. First, my appreciation to Corinne for her help and guidance in bringing the original print version of *The St. Paul Conspiracy* to press.

Many thanks to my college roommate, Jeff, and lifelong friend Jim for their invaluable editing assistance. I also wish to extend my gratitude to local authors Jack Uldrich and Michael Hachey for their editorial suggestions and insight into writing in general and the book-publishing business in particular.

Thanks to family and friends: Tim, Mike, my parents, Chad, Matt, my wife, James, Sue, Marla, Carla, Steve, Barb, and Dawn for their time, feedback, and encouragement as they read various drafts of the manuscript. The next round is on me.

Of course, I'd be remiss if I didn't thank John Sandford, Vince Flynn, Steve Thayer, Tami Hoag, and the many other great Minnesota authors who inspired me to take pen to paper.

Finally, I'd like to thank my wife for her infinite patience in frequently answering one constant question, "Mom, why is Dad on the computer again?"

Never miss a new release again, join the new release list at www. RogerStelljes.com

1

"I'M IN."

HALLOWEEN

The van turned left off of Grand Avenue and northbound onto Grotto, stopping mid-block at the alley. A man jumped out, quickly ducking between the back of a dumpster and a building on the right side.

Ten fifteen p.m., no moon, nothing but the stars. Fifty-seven degrees with a light breeze—balmy for the last night of October in Minnesota.

He looked east down the alley between Summit and Grand Avenues. The left side was residential housing, early twentieth-century Victorian mansions converted into condominiums—a fashionable trend in St. Paul. To the right was a combination of alternating businesses and red and brown brick apartment buildings, hip because of their location along the popular Grand Avenue. At the far end of the alley to the right was a hot nightspot, Mardi Gras, which specialized in Cajun food and Creole music. Revelers in costumes of all kinds would be in and out all night.

The van pulled away, turning right on Summit and disappearing from view. Dressed head to toe in black, the man invisibly picked his way through backyards, around garages, over fences and under trees to the other side of the block. Within five minutes he was looking through a gap in a hedge at the backside of the condo.

He had done this many times, for many years, but rarely in his home country. He worked alone, although there was the usual need for technical assistance. When he did this for the government he stalked his prey for weeks or months at a time, getting to know their every move, learning about the people they saw and when they saw them, getting the layout of where they lived and worked. Did they have pets? Lovers? Family? He would probe, follow, observe, determining the perfect place to strike. That had not been the case this time.

There hadn't been weeks; there had barely been three days.

The mitigating factor in his favor was that his target, unlike most in his career, didn't consider herself one. In fact, she wasn't concerned about security at all. She had no security system. She left a key under the front steps mat and followed a routine schedule, always working at night and never home until after 11:00 p.m.

Claire Daniels, investigative reporter for Channel 6. She was good, the best in town and would be until she left, which was to be soon, a network job in the offing. Having watched her on television for the last few years, he understood why.

And then there was her beauty.

Like many female television reporters, Claire was stunningly attractive. She had blonde hair, blue eyes, and a curvaceous body she worked on relentlessly. The man had watched her workout at the club three times now—aerobics, treadmill, Stairmaster, bike, weight machines. There was no messing around as she worked with feverish intensity with excellent technique, sculpting her body to absolute perfection.

Claire was the desire of every man in town. She had desires of her own, and currently it was Minnesota's senior United States senator, Mason Johnson. The two were dating in the loosest sense of the term, meeting late at night, usually at her place, usually when the senator's wife was in Washington, DC.

Even if he had only three days to prepare, the whole situation provided the perfect cover.

Through the gap in the hedge, he could see her place which was part of an old mansion, now subdivided into expensive condos. She had the last condo to the north. He was looking at the rear entrance, across the narrow driveway and through the side door of the one-car, tuck-under garage.

The man darted across the driveway to the side door and quickly pulled out a key, a duplicate of the one left under the mat on the front step. The key slid smoothly into the dead bolt, giving a light click as the door unlocked. He slipped inside, quickly removed the key and quietly shut the door. Fetching a towel out of his small backpack, he cleaned and dried his shoes. With the towel again stashed in the backpack, the man moved through the garage to the back door and up the stairs, which took him into the kitchen. At the top of the stairs, he stopped and listened. Silence.

Moving through the kitchen took him to a hallway that led into the living room. The drapes were pulled over the large picture window that looked out to St. Albans Street. Just before the front door, he turned right and took the steps up to the second level.

There were four rooms on the second floor. Along the back was a spare bedroom that Claire used for storage, a bathroom, and a second bedroom she used as an office down on the end. The front was a single open bedroom, thirty-five feet by fifteen according to the blueprints filed with the city. An arch divided the bedroom from a sitting area.

He went into the first spare bedroom, directly into the closet that faced into the hallway. Hiding in the left side of the closet, he kept the door open enough so he could get out without having to open it further. Through the opening he could see across the hallway into the master bedroom. Thin streams of illumination from the streetlight fought through the window shades to provide a dark outline of the king-sized bed and flanking nightstands.

In the closet, he checked his watch: 10:25 p.m. He tapped his throat mike. "Eagle Eye, this is Viper. I'm in."

"Copy that." Eagle Eye was parked in the Mardi Gras parking lot across the alley from the condo with a view of both the back and front of the condo.

Viper. He'd used this code name as an assassin for the agency. It gave him a certain comfort level, put him in the right mindset for this little operation.

He sat sideways, so he could peer around the sliding door. If Daniels and the senator held to their schedule, they'd arrive within the next hour.

Forty minutes later his earpiece came to life. "Viper, Lexus in the alley, just turned in. It's her." Viper heard the garage door hum to life. The senator wouldn't be far behind. He shut off the mike and took out his earpiece, securing it inside his collar.

He could hear Claire as she came up the backstairs from the garage and walked quickly through the kitchen to the front door. The front door opened. Viper heard quiet talking. The door closed and then silence for what seemed like five minutes. Then he heard movement up the stairs, rough and halting, as if only a few steps at a time. There was heavy breathing, and Viper imagined them slowly working their way up the stairs, warming up for what was to come.

Suddenly, they appeared in the doorway to the bedroom, Claire already down to her bra and panties. The senator stripped down to his dress pants. As they moved into the bedroom, she reached with her right hand and hit the light switch, turning on the left nightstand lamp.

Viper could see their profiles, as they finished undressing each other and fell into bed. He looked away, as a professional should. But he could hear them, especially Claire, and he couldn't help himself. Daniels had the effect on him that she had on others. She was intoxicating, making love to the senator in a hushed breathy moan, the vertebrae in her back visible as she arched, moving in perfect rhythm. He envied the senator, his hands on her small buttocks, moving with her in stride, making love to the incredibly beautiful reporter.

Hidden in the closet, invisible, Viper watched as Claire became the aggressor. She picked up the pace, moaning louder, back arched more, moaning louder, head leaning farther back, moaning louder, writhing passionately.

And then she came, exhaling loudly.

Half an hour later, the lovemaking long complete, they lay on the bed, enjoying a little pillow talk about nothing in particular. She talked about the live report she gave in front of some local government building; something about a city spending a little too lavishly on its employees. The senator related a story about how he had just managed to avoid the check scandal when he was in the House of Representatives.

At 1:15 a.m., the senator rolled out of bed and began to dress. All the while, Claire lay on her side, naked, watching him. She had not rolled over and gone to sleep. There had been no half asleep admonition to lock the door. Viper could see it in her eyes. She wanted him to stay. The senator finished his tie in a nice Windsor knot and walked over to the bed, leaning over and kissing her good-bye.

Mason Johnson walked out of the bedroom, turned left, and headed down the stairs. A few seconds later, Viper heard the front door open and close. After a brief moment, he heard the dead bolt lock into place.

Viper turned his gaze towards Claire. She was rolled over now. He could see her back, once again making out the little vertebra of her spine. The nightstand light oddly remained on.

The spare bedroom was carpeted, which helped to cover his approach as he slithered out of the closet and to the wall, putting his back to it and sliding towards the hall. The condo was quiet. The only sound was the hum of the furnace, starting up to keep the condo's temperature constant. It provided just enough ambient noise to cover his approach.

His watch said 1:37 a.m. Timing was important.

He sprang across the room, jumped on the bed, rolled her over, and clenched her throat. Viper saw the horror in her eyes. Frantically, she reached for his hands, but he was too strong. She flailed at him, striking his face, shoulder, and arms, all the while kicking her legs, wiggling her hips, trying anything to get away. She tried to scream, but only gasps and croaks made it through his grip. He coldly looked in her eyes through his mask while pressing the life out of her.

After a minute, the flailing and struggling slowed and weakened. As he tightened the vice on her throat, her eyelids fluttered, then her eyes rolled back in her head, and he felt her body go still underneath him. Removing his left hand from her neck, he checked her pulse with his right.

She was dead.

Pushing off her and standing up, he checked his watch, 1:39 a.m. He took his mask off and massaged his jaw. Daniels was strong, and he'd been hit hard, but she was tired, and he was too quick. There had been no time for her to react or scream. She never had a chance.

Viper carefully searched the condo. He had been through it once already the previous night, but he'd been ordered to search again. For the next hour he methodically worked his way through the bedroom, sitting room, office, hallway closet, built-in buffet, and spare bedroom. Next, he moved to the main level and eventually to the basement.

The information about his employer was not to be found.

He headed back upstairs to her bedroom. Was there anyplace he hadn't looked? He searched the television cabinet. It was stocked with CDs and DVDs, but not with what he was hunting for. The computer was ignored; it was already searched and now monitored from afar.

He checked his watch, 2:30 a.m., time to get moving. Viper made a last trip to the master bedroom to look at Claire. What a shame, such a beautiful woman. He flipped off the light switch and headed for the stairs, sliding his mask back on in the process. He made his way to the garage, where he found the Lexus. A quick look inside didn't reveal the documents. How about the trunk? He triggered the latch on the driver's side door and popped open the trunk. Empty other than a flashlight, a pair of boots, and a window scraper—typical accouterments for the coming Minnesota winter. Viper shut the trunk and moved to the rear door.

"Eagle Eye, Viper. I'm at the rear door."

"Copy Viper. Go."

Out the back door, through the hedge and down the alley Viper went. The pickup point was a parking lot between an apartment building and the Kozlak Foodmart. Viper moved his way to the side of a garage across the alley from the parking lot.

The black van turned into the parking lot, approaching from the other side of the alley. As the van turned toward him, the sliding door opened. Viper sprang from the side of the garage, across the alley, over the guardrail and into the van while it was moving. Once inside, he asked, "How'd Bouchard come out?"

"It's done."

2

"YOUR DAY JUST GOT WORSE."

Many St. Paul residents started their morning at the Grand Brew, a cup of coffee to get the workday started. For Michael McKenzie "Mac" McRyan, a fourth-generation St. Paul detective, it was his way to start the day. Not only did he love the coffee, it was making him a little dough. Two childhood friends owned the Grand Brew. Mac had invested a little money six years before in exchange for a small piece of the action. That "small piece" was turning out to be a nice, and ever-growing, supplement to his detective's salary.

Mac grabbed his coffee and looked at his watch, 7:30 a.m.—day of paperwork ahead. He had cleared a murder the day before, a stick-up gone awry. It took Mac and his partner a week to put the case together and find the stick-up guy, a nineteen-year-old kid they identified from a surveillance camera. They hauled the kid in, and he went quickly.

Mac's partner was Richard Lich, or better known within the department, and often to his face, as "Dick Lick." Mac frequently wondered what in the world Lich's parents had been thinking. Dick was a veteran cop with money problems; two divorces would do that to a guy. That being said, when motivated, Dick was a good detective. He had an easy manner with people and a quick wit. When he was on his game, Lich was a good complement to Mac's blunt, if not occasionally abrasive, approach to matters. Problem was, as of late, Lich had checked out. Mac hoped he would snap out of it soon. He could use the help.

Mac jumped into his Explorer, put his coffee in the cup holder just as his cell phone vibrated. He took a look. Just like that a seemingly slow and easy day turned busy. His captain was looking for him.

"McRyan."

"Peters. St. Albans, between Summit and Grand, cleaning lady found a body." Mac wrote down the address. "I called Lich. You'll be there first. Keep me advised and keep your cell on." *Click.*

Well, good morning to you too, Mac thought. Captain Marion Peters was a good guy, an old-guard cop that Mac and the rest of the McRyan clan knew well. The gruff manner had more to do with last night than the body on St. Albans. The University Avenue Strangler had struck for the fifth time.

The University Avenue Strangler. *Good grief*, Mac thought. It wasn't a cop moniker. That was a media creation and cornball as hell, but that was the media. If you have a serial killer, which they did, the media had to give him a name. A name made for great headlines in the *Pioneer Press* and *Star Tribune*.

Four women, now five, had been killed, strangled, sexually assaulted and dumped into vacant lots in the vicinity of University Avenue. The signature item identifying the killer was a balloon left behind, marking the body like a buoy. The balloon was always the same—a smiley face. "Have a Nice Day."

Of course, with a serial killer, people, including politicians and especially the media tend to go into a panic. Mac saw it on the morning news shows. The media in full glory, hyping the murder of another innocent victim for ratings, providing "Team Coverage" and "Exclusives you'll only see on Channel 12." City council members had already been on the tube reassuring everyone that the police would find the killer. Undoubtedly, Captain Peters's gruff mood had something to do with the latest murder, the media swarm, and Mac suspected the hysterical calls from city politicians demanding something be done. As if it was that easy.

Mac pulled out onto Grand and headed east to St. Albans with a murder to work on. He was thirty-two years old, six foot one, and one hundred ninety pounds. He was ruggedly handsome, with blond hair and icy blue eyes. His short hair formed around a taut face, with a square jaw and a dimple the size of the Grand Canyon in his chin. He had three crisscrossing scars under his chin, the result of stitches from hockey-related cuts. He worked on his wiry, strong body frequently and was proud of the fact he remained in "game" shape, no heavier than his college hockey-playing weight.

Mac had taken a somewhat circuitous route to being a cop, considering his family. Growing up, all he ever wanted to be was a detective just like his dad, the famous Simon McRyan. It didn't hurt that his grandpa and great-grandpa, several uncles and cousins—all of them were cops. It was the family business. As a kid, his two best friends were his cousins, Peter and Tommy. All three were going to be like their dads, St. Paul cops.

But then Mac turned out to be a straight-A student and a great high school hockey player, garnering an athletic scholarship to the University of Minnesota. After four years, he graduated again with straight As and had captained the Gophers to an NCAA Championship. He was engaged to the prettiest and smartest girl on campus. His road to life was paved for something other than police work.

So, while Tommy and Peter joined the police force after college, Mac and his fiancée enrolled in law school. He graduated summa cum laude, second in his class. He had a job lined up with Prescott and Finnerty, a prominent law firm with a $100,000 starting salary. His lovely wife, also a lawyer, would make equally as much in another law firm. With his name recognition, perhaps politics would follow. He was set for a wealthy life with a beautiful wife.

Then two weeks after the bar exam, while standing on the eighth tee at Somerset Country Club, his life changed forever. His cell phone rang. Peter and Tommy had been killed in the line of duty, shot as they responded to a bank robbery.

Mac was a pallbearer for both, the only one not in a police uniform. As he stood by one casket and then the other at the cemetery, he looked to his family, more than twenty of his cousins and uncles in uniform, laying it on the line to protect their families and city. Listening to the priest speak of the commitment his two cousins had made, he felt selfish and empty. What has he done that compares to Peter and Tommy? Why has his lot in life been different? The athletic and academic success, the law degree, marrying the pretty girl—did that mean that being a cop was for someone else? That his family and their sacrifices were beneath him? That he shouldn't feel the same sense of obligation that four generations of his family had?

A week later he joined the police force.

His mother, always relieved that he had been going down a different and safer path, nonetheless understood. It was the McRyan way.

His wife never forgave him. He ruined the perfect life she thought they would have. It took seven years, but the perfect marriage eventually came to an end. He'd gotten the final divorce papers in the mail the day before.

Joining the force also brought the unspoken pressure for Mac to measure up to his father, the revered Simon McRyan. His dad died in a freak deer-hunting accident fifteen years before when Mac was still in high school, hit in his heart by a stray bullet from a far-off hunter. They never found the person who'd fired the shot. Mac had been with his father, holding his hand as he died.

Simon McRyan was the standard by which all other detectives in St. Paul had been and —to a certain degree—still were measured, and Mac wanted to measure up. He didn't want to be known simply as Simon McRyan's son. He was proud of his father, thought about him often when he grabbed his badge and Glock 9mm. But every day Mac operated under the shadow of Simon McRyan, cognizant of its existence, aware that, as his father's only son, he had much to live up to.

Mac turned left into the parking lot for Mardi Gras, knowing it would be a good out-of-the-way place to park, and saw two squads in front of the condo. The yellow crime scene tape was already up, twisting in the breeze. A crowd of locals was gathering.

There were five other McRyans of Mac's generation who were cops. One of them, his cousin Patrick, stood on the porch of the condo. He came down the steps to meet Mac.

"What say you, Paddy boy?"

"It's not good, cuz."

Mac furrowed his brows, knowing the tone of Patrick's voice. "What's going on?" he asked quietly, as they walked towards the condo.

"Our dead body is Claire Daniels."

Mac stopped abruptly and looked at his cousin for a minute, "The reporter?"

"Yeah."

"No shit?"

"Yeah, I always wanted to see her naked, but not like this."

"Where is she?"

"Upstairs."

"Is forensics on the way?"

"They'll be here any minute."

As he headed up the front steps, Mac stopped and asked, "Any media yet?"

Patrick rolled his eyes. "Not yet. They're all probably still over at the serial killer site giving Riley hell, but I gotta think the newsies'll show pretty soon."

"All right. I'm going up and take a look," Mac said, as he fished out some white rubber gloves out of his pocket and turned to go inside.

Claire was living pretty well, Mac thought when he walked in, noticing the furnishings. To his right was a large living room with nice furniture, mission-style chairs and tables with an expansive leather couch, probably from Room & Board or Pottery Barn. He noticed that the condo looked in order, very neat and clean. The stairway up to the second level was to his immediate left.

At the top of the steps, a uniform cop, Bonnie Schmidt, waited for him. As Mac got to the top of the steps, she nodded towards the bedroom. A white blouse lay on the floor at the top of the landing. Mac kneeled down to it and took a quick look around. He walked back down the steps and took a look at the living room; everything was in order, immaculate.

He walked back up the steps. "Was the blouse here when you arrived?"

"Yup. Cleaning lady said she picked up a pair of slacks on the landing. She was about to pick up the blouse when she looked into the bedroom, saw the body, and you know the rest," Schmidt said.

Mac left the blouse and turned into the bedroom. He carefully sidestepped the bra and panties lying on the floor. Claire Daniels lay on the left side of the bed, flat on her back, her arms spread out, her left leg straight and the right hanging over the side of the bed. Mac walked to the left side of the bed and crouched. He immediately saw the bruising on the neck. The cause of death was pretty obvious. Strangulation. The killer probably had been straddling her on the bed, pressing down on her windpipe.

She was naked, and Mac wondered if sex had been involved. It might explain the blouse on the landing, the scattered underwear. Forensics would find out soon enough. Mac took a moment to look around the room. Odd. Other than the blouse on the landing and the panties and bra on the bedroom floor, no other clothes lay strewn about. He saw no apparent signs of a robbery. Things seemed tidy. Mac walked over to the dresser. There was a jewelry case on top. Using his Bic, he flipped it open and immediately realized she had some valuable pieces. But each slot and drawer was filled with jewelry. If someone rummaged through it, they put everything back just so.

Mac heard some commotion on the steps, looked back and saw that it was forensics. "Hey, Mac," said Linda Morgan, a young nerdy crime-scene tech Mac really liked. "Paddy told me Claire Daniels?" Linda said conversationally.

"You heard correct," Mac replied, standing with his hands on his hips. "Best I can tell, the killer put his hands on her throat and squeezed. You can see the bruising. Strangling, I'm thinkin'."

"Anything else?" Morgan asked.

"I'm sure you'll check for sex, and I think you'll find it," Mac answered. "It feels like that happened here."

"Why do you say that?"

"It just feels like it. The blouse on the floor. Bra and panties here. I haven't spoken with the cleaning lady yet, but there were slacks down on the landing. Seems as if Claire was in a hurry to get them off. It just feels like something like that happened here."

"Well, if she did, we'll find out." Linda put on her glasses and reached for some rubber gloves to start evaluating the body. Another tech Mac didn't know was getting the fingerprint kit going.

Mac grabbed his cell phone and hit the speed dial for Captain Peters.

"Peters."

"McRyan. Your day just got worse." Mac said neutrally, "Our homicide is Claire Daniels."

Silence. Then, slightly stammering, Peters asked for confirmation. "The TV reporter? From Channel 6?"

"Yes."

"Cripes, what's next," Peters sighed. "Mac, do you need some help over there?"

"Yeah, some extra units'd be good. We're going to draw a crowd." He thought for a moment. "If you got any extra people to spare, I have a feeling we may need to do some door to door here."

"Okay. I'll get some bodies down there. You run it. But listen, son, the shit's going to hit the fan with this. If you get stuck, ask for help. If the media are not there yet, they will be soon. They'll be all over you. Don't say a word until we talk. Got it?"

"Yes, sir."

"Dick Lick there yet?" Peters asked caustically, knowing Lich's approach to things as of late.

Mac stifled a chuckle, "No, sir."

"Whatever you do, Lich doesn't talk to the press. He always loves to talk. It's your case. You run it, and he follows." There was a brief silence, and then, "Look, if Dick pulls his head out of his ass, don't be afraid to use him. He's been around. If he's set right, he knows what he's doing. But you lead. I'll let him know that." With that Peters clicked off.

It was his case for now. This was going to be a major case, and Peters was giving him the chance to take the ball and run with it. Mac planned to do just that.

Mac watched forensics as they started to set up, unpacking gear from their fishing-tackle boxes. Black lights, cameras, plastic bags. He walked out into the hall and up to Schmidt. "Cleaning lady?"

"Down in the kitchen."

Mac headed down. As he came to the bottom of the steps, Lich walked in. In his early fifties, Lich was pot-bellied and bald. He owned a collection of old, faded suits, replete with coffee stains and the occasional burn hole from one of his cigars. His choice that morning carried a couple stains. Lich, as Mac often said, was a piece of work.

Lich was divorced, so he and Mac had that in common. He had been cleaned out, which they didn't have in common. It was a point Lich frequently made. His ex cleaned him out and left him without a pot to piss in.

"Mornin', Mac. Your cousin filled me in." Just then Lich's cell phone went off, and Mac figured it might be Peters. He didn't want to be there while that conversation took place. Instead he headed for the kitchen. The cleaning lady was sitting at the kitchen table with a uniform cop named Jones. "Lich'll be a minute," Mac explained to Jones.

The cleaning lady was hunched over, looking anxious and just a shade from terrified. Just then Lich came in and whispered to Mac, "Peters says you lead."

Mac nodded, "Let's get after it then."

The cleaning lady, Gloria, had arrived at her normal time, 7:00 a.m. She had gone upstairs to grab some clothes for the laundry. On the way up the steps, she had picked up the slacks on the landing and saw the blouse at the top. As she bent over to pick up the shirt, she glanced around the corner and saw Daniels lying on the bed. She then immediately called 911.

After listening to the summary, Mac asked, "Did you and Ms. Daniels ever talk? Have a conversation?"

"Sometimes. She was friendly, always letting me make coffee for myself, as long as I made some for her. Sometimes I would bring rolls. She was a nice lady."

"Did she ever mention anyone who might be after her? That she was concerned about? Was there ever any hate mail lying around? Disturbing phone messages? Anything like that?"

The woman's eyes were wide with innocence. "No."

"How about people she saw, dated? Ever talk about any of that?"

"We never talked about things like that. I didn't know her like that. I might see her in the morning and say, 'You have a date last night?' She would just kind of smile and nod."

"Was she seeing anyone right now?"

"She might have been, but I don't know who it was."

"Is it 'might'? Or do you know?"

Terror edged into her eyes. "I think she was seeing someone. Yes."

"Why do you think so?"

"When she's dating someone, she gets up really late. She works late and I think her dates are late."

"And if she's not seeing anyone?" Lich asked.

"Then she's a pretty early riser, has coffee, reads the paper, exercises. But if she had a date, it seemed like she liked to sleep in late."

"Anything else that tells you she was seeing someone," Mac continued.

"No, just that she seemed to be sleeping in late."

"And you don't know who she's seeing?"

"No. She never said. If he ever stayed the night, he was gone before I ever got here."

"How many days a week do you come?" Lich asked.

"Three."

"Three?" Mac asked. "Seems like a lot for someone who lives alone."

Gloria said, "Ms. Daniels, she liked things perfect."

"Neat freak, huh," Lich said.

"Not so much that as just a perfectionist," Gloria answered. "Just the way she was."

"When you arrived here this morning, did anything seem out of place, you know," Lich asked, and then pointed up, "other than the obvious?"

Gloria vigorously shook her head. "No, everything seemed pretty normal."

"How'd you get in?" Mac inquired.

"Front door. I have a key."

Mac went to look at the front door for a second. There was a dead bolt, fairly new. He examined the lock and the door. It was clean, no scratches, no signs of forced entry. He walked back to the kitchen.

"Gloria, is your key for the dead bolt?"

"Yes."

"Was the dead bolt locked this morning?"

"Yes."

"Is that a new lock?"

"It was put in a few months ago."

Mac looked past her to a stairway going down the back. "Is the back entrance down those stairs?"

The cleaning lady nodded.

Mac and Lich went down the steps and looked at the back door. Unlike the front door, the knob was very old. There was a dead bolt, but it wasn't locked. Through the door was a single-car garage with a garage door and a dead-bolted side door to the left. This dead bolt was newer looking. As with the front door, there was no sign of forced entry.

"Wonder if the same key opens both?" Lich said.

"Let's see."

They headed back up, and the cleaning lady confirmed that both doors had the same key. Mac did some quick mental gymnastics. No evidence of forced entry. No evidence of robbery. Maybe somebody had a key?

Just then a couple of other younger detectives from robbery homicide showed up. Mac chuckled. Bill Clark and Al Green looked like a couple of IBM guys. They were tall, with short black hair, blue suits, and red ties.

"I must not have gotten the memo."

Green and Clark at first looked blankly at him. Then they looked at each other and just shook their heads, "Fuck you, Mac," Green replied. "The captain ordered us down here to give you a hand. So, what do you need, smart ass?"

Mac chuckled and gave them the rundown on what they had so far, which wasn't much. "Let's start door knocking on all these brownstones and checking the apartments across the street. Use some uniform guys, and I'll get Peters to send some more down." Mac was also thinking the newsies would be there soon, and he would need to control them and the crowd. The media would go nuts with one of their own dying.

"Bill, grab Paddy. He's up for detective. Take him around with you. Al, grab another uniform and start knocking on doors. If you come across something, let me know."

With that Green and Clark headed out to start the canvas.

Mac and Lich headed back upstairs. Morgan was jotting down some notes as another tech took a few more pictures of the body. A third tech was dusting for prints. "Linda, got anything for us?"

Morgan stared at her notes a minute, biting her lower lip. "Body temp indicates preliminary time of death as between midnight and 2:00 a.m. Cause of death is pretty obvious; she was strangled. He got on top of her and basically pressed the air out of her, with his hands on her neck, thumbs straddling her windpipe, fingers around the back. Strong sucker, whoever did it."

"Sex?"

"Yeah, she'd had it all right. I'll be able to tell you a little more about that once we examine her downtown."

"Will you be able to get DNA?" Lich asked.

"We should."

Mac thought for a moment, "She had sex, but ..."

"It looks consensual. I've taken a quick look. There's nothing to indicate rape. There's no tearing around the vagina that I can see. We'll know more after the autopsy."

"Are you saying he—we're assuming a he—killed her after sex?"

"Not necessarily. I might know more when we get back and examine her. Could be that she was into something weird, sexual asphyxiation, something like that. I don't see any tools or props around here to suggest that, though. It could be she said he was a bad lay, and he got pissed and killed her. Heck if I know right now, but we might be able to do better after we examine her."

"All right. Are you going to move her now?" Mac asked.

"In a bit. We need to take more pictures and do a few other things."

Lich appeared to be mildly interested for a change. "What do you think?" Mac asked.

"No signs of forced entry. At this point, nothing points to a break-in, so it seems like it was someone who knew her."

Mac couldn't argue with that. No forced entry made it more likely it was someone she knew, which would narrow the field of suspects. They headed down the steps. Lich reached the bottom and was looking at the front door. Mac slipped by him onto the front porch and looked out at the street as a Channel 12 news van pulled up. "Ahh, shit."

"You knew they'd get here sooner or later. They'll soil themselves when they find out it's Daniels," Lich replied lightly, morbidly amused by the situation.

Mac turned back towards Lich, who was standing, hands on hips looking out to the street. Mac's eyes wandered down to the floor mat in front of the door. He kneeled down and flipped it up thinking, *She wouldn't* ... but she did.

"Well, lookey there," said Lich, "I didn't think people did that anymore."

"Might explain no forced entry," Mac thought. Lich called upstairs for forensics to come and get a picture. Just then Mac's cell phone chirped.

"McRyan."

"Peters. You and Lich need to come down and fill me in. The chief'll be in on the meeting. It's 8:40 now. Be here by 9:00."

Peters clicked off. Downtown was ten minutes away. Mac looked at Lich. "We have an audience in twenty minutes."

"The chief?" Lich asked.

Mac nodded. Lich chuckled lightly.

"Bet he's had half the city council on the horn yelling at him this morning. Now this. I wouldn't miss it," Lich replied.

Mac snorted, "Well let's get going then. I'd hate to deprive you of the show."

"REAL POLICE."

Viper yawned. It had been a long night. After a couple hours'
sleep, he was back to monitor the situation. Sitting in the back
of a blue van parked on the northeast corner of Summit and St.
Albans, he looked back at Daniels's brownstone one hundred fifty
yards away through tinted glass. A crowd had gathered, and a
number of uniformed cops controlled the situation, putting out the
yellow crime scene tape, keeping people to the other side of the
street. It was 8:15 a.m.

Viper took another drink of water, avoiding the coffee the rest of
his crew swilled. He rarely drank coffee. It was bad for the system,
and he was a self-professed health nut, except for the occasional beer
or glass of wine. He would have to watch it though, or he'd have to hit
the can, and he didn't want to leave the van. He wanted to make sure
events started and stayed on the proper course.

A couple of detectives, a young blond-haired one in a sharp blue
suit and an older bald guy in a rumpled shit-brown suit, were talking
on the front porch of the condo. Suddenly the young detective looked
down and flipped up the mat. The key. Viper figured they'd find it.
That was fine by him. No evidence of forced entry, meaning someone

had a key or easy access to one. The senator, when they found him, would have to admit he used it. His prints would be on it.

Viper trained the binoculars on the young cop and watched him reach for his cell phone. It was a brief call, thirty seconds at most. He looked to the bald detective, said something, and pointed away from the condo. They walked down the steps and looked to be leaving. Then they stopped, turned and climbed the steps to the neighbor's condo to the right of Daniels's. The young detective pointed in a few directions, and the other detectives nodded. Directions given, the younger detective and the bald one left the porch and headed to the south and out of sight.

Viper thought a little more about what he had just seen. It looked like the young cop was in charge of the situation. He couldn't be much over thirty years old. Yet, he seemed to be the one giving directions, with everyone else nodding when he talked. The bald guy, much the younger detective's senior, hadn't said much at all. Viper wondered why such a young cop would be calling the shots on a high-profile case like the death of Claire Daniels. He would have someone make a call. Maybe they caught a break.

As Mac walked through the door and into the St. Paul Public Safety Building, the intensity of the day hit him in the face. Faces were taut, voices low and serious. It was not St. Paul's finest day, and all eyes were on the department. The desk sergeant saw Mac and Lich walk in and directed them up to the chief's office.

Charles Flanagan had been chief of the St. Paul Police Department for eight years. At fifty-four years old, he was a thirty-three-year veteran of the police force who worked his way up from uniform cop to chief. He was a tall, slender Irishman that seemed to have aged ten years in the last month, largely due to the serial killer. His once bright red hair had turned gray.

Chief Flanagan knew police work but, to put it charitably, the politics and public relations aspects of his job were not his strengths. His saving grace was that he had the complete and total support of the force, unusual for many big-city chiefs. He was, as Mac's Uncle Shamus liked to say, real police. The chief always stood behind his men. While that made him popular with the rank and file, it occasionally made him some enemies at City Hall, enemies now making his life miserable. Mac had known him for as long as he could remember. He had been with Mac, Shamus, and Pat Riley, another St. Paul detective, when Mac's dad was shot and killed.

Mac and Lich walked into the chief's outer office, and his secretary led them in. As they entered, the chief looked up. He walked to Mac, shook his hand warmly and said, "Mac, it's nice to see you, boyo."

"Good morning, Chief. Nice to see you as well." The chief's appearance told Mac what kind of day it had already been. The suit coat had been jettisoned, the tie and collar loosened, and his shirt-sleeves rolled up. There were three coffee cups on his desk, all half empty. If Mac didn't know better, he got a faint whiff of cigarette smoke, although a quick scan failed to reveal an ashtray.

"Lich, how are you?"

"I'm fine, sir. Thank you for asking."

"Well, boys, the shit's hittin' the fan. We'll be speaking with the media soon," Flanagan said, wincing. "I know you probably don't have much, but Peters, Sylvia, and I need an update. So," the chief said, pointing to Mac, "give us what you've got."

Mac pulled out his notebook to give the basic rundown. He finished with, "Forensics preliminarily puts time of death between midnight and 2:00 a.m."

"How'd the killer get in? Were there any signs of forced entry?" asked the chief.

"Not so far," Mac replied, explaining about the new door locks and key they found.

"Anything missing?"

"Doesn't seem to be," Mac answered. "The house isn't ransacked in any way. She had jewelry in her bedroom, some fairly expensive pieces, which appear to be undisturbed. So, at this point, it looks like whoever got in was let in, or had a key. Maybe a boyfriend."

"Do we know anything about who she was seeing?"

"Not yet. We'll need to get down to the station and talk to the people she worked with. Maybe we'll learn something there."

Sylvia Miller, the department spokeswoman, piped in. "The media knows that it's Claire Daniels. I've already been getting calls, and they, being the media, want to know when we'll have something to say. What can we offer at this point?"

Mac was about to speak, but he first looked to Flanagan, who nodded. "I know the heat's on, but I don't think we should release much. She was found dead this morning in her condo. I'd give them the usual bullshit that an autopsy will be performed. Indicate that we'll be questioning people in the neighborhood, people she worked with, that sort of thing. Beyond that ..." Mac shook his head.

"We're getting hammered here, with the serial killer and then this," Miller pleaded. "Can't we go with more, the strangling, time of death, the sex information ... any of that?"

"Not yet," Flanagan answered. "It's way too early. I don't want us to get hung based on speculative information we'll have to retract later. I don't wanna compromise the investigation."

"I understand that, but information'll get out on a case like this," Miller pushed. "The media pressure'll be immense. One of their own is dead here. We need to throw them a bone, or we're gonna get skewered."

"Damn it, I fuckin' know that!" yelled Flanagan, who then caught himself, obviously regretting the outburst. After a quiet moment and an exhale, he said more calmly, "I'm sorry. I do appreciate your situation, Sylvia. But we must let the detectives do their work. If we catch the guy, we'll be fine. If not, I'll take the heat." Flanagan then turned to Mac. "This is your case to run. But be smart. You need help, boyo, ask, and keep Peters in the loop. And, son, all media requests go to Sylvia for now."

"Avoiding the media is fine by me," Mac replied.

"That goes for you too, Lich," added Peters, his tone just a bit accusatory.

Mac smiled inside. Lich liked to talk.

"What'd I do?" pleaded Lich with his arms held open.

"Dick," said Flanagan, "you have a rep for leaking. Not here. Keep your mouth shut." It was not a request.

"Yes, sir."

"Okay, boys, go to it."

Mac and Lich left the room.

Once they were gone, Miller, always evaluating the public perception of things asked, "Chief, isn't McRyan kind of young to be handling this?"

The chief gave Miller a long, severe look before answering. "You know his background. He's got four good years as a detective. He'll be fine. From your perspective, he should be someone we want in front of the camera. People will recognize the name."

"That's all true, but this isn't a public service announcement. This is a murder case of a well-known reporter on top of a serial killer. This is very high-profile. McRyan doesn't look very senior. People might wonder, is all I'm saying."

"Your concerns are noted," was Flanagan's terse reply.

With that, Miller and Peters got up to leave. The chief asked Peters to stay.

With the door closing behind Miller, the chief asked, "She have a point on Mac?"

"No," Peters responded without hesitation. "Mac's fine. He's young, sure, but smart. Lich's fine too if he's with it, and I made sure he was properly motivated this morning. Mac doesn't concern me."

The chief considered it for a minute. "Real police. It's in his blood."

"Yes, sir," Peters replied. "He's a natural at this. He's level headed, a natural leader, he wants the responsibility. Plus, he's smarter than hell."

Chief Flanagan thought it over. "You know, he reminds me of his old man."

Peters smiled. "Me too, Chief."

"Well, screw them all then," Flanagan said. "We let the real police do their job."

4
_____

"CLAIRE'S DEAD."

Mac and Lich got back in the Explorer and drove to Daniels's place. Mac was jacked. It was not often he got a case like this. Lich, catching the mood of the moment, put it right, "This type of case—bring it home, and you're set, Mac. Screw it up, and you might get night watch down in the jail."

As they pulled onto Grand and were a few blocks away from Daniels's place, Lich chirped, "Media's in heaven. They'll have a field day with us today."

Mac couldn't argue with him, it was going to be rough, especially for the chief and Sylvia Miller.

"What's the plan, boss?" Lich said with just a touch of wry sarcasm.

Mac caught the tone. "You gonna be okay following my lead on this?"

Lich chuckled. "There'll be no problem, Mac. I haven't exactly been busting my hump lately, but I'm with you on this. No fucking around."

"Thanks."

"So, what's on our agenda?"

"Check out the condo. Then we'll head down to Channel 6 and

talk with her colleagues. Her mother's been notified. We'll have to talk with her as well, although word is they weren't close."

As they approached Daniels's condo, the media horde became evident, with television trucks and microphones everywhere, people running back and forth. To avoid it, Mac dumped the Explorer in an open spot along Grand, half a block away. He and Lich got out and made their way towards the condo, casually winding through the news vans, and ducking under the crime scene tape.

Mac saw a uniform cop and said, "Go get me Clark and Green," and to Lich, "Let's take a closer look around the condo."

As Mac entered the bedroom, forensics was getting ready to transport the body. Morgan had nothing additional to give them; they would have to wait for the autopsy. On his first time through, Mac had gotten the feeling that very little was amiss, but he wanted to look around and get a feel for Daniels.

The bedroom was really two rooms. There was the area where her bed, dresser, and closet were located. Claire must have slept on the right side normally, as there was a phone and an alarm clock on that side of the bed. The drawer on the right nightstand was filled with the usual stuff one might expect, including a notepad and pen to take messages. The drawer on the left side held a brass tin that contained condoms, which was interesting, for, if nothing else, she was prepared.

He took a look at her closet, a deep walk-in. Claire had been a clotheshorse, which was not surprising for a television reporter. There were a couple of boxes with personal effects, some family pictures, and a high school yearbook from Bristol, Ohio. Mac took out the yearbook and thumbed through it. Bristol was a small town as Claire's graduating class looked to be about fifty students. He found Claire, with a last name of Miller, so she must have been married at some point or changed her name. Her graduation picture certainly indicated that she must have been the object of many a Bristol boys' dreams.

Mac left the closet, and went to the other side of the bedroom through a wide archway into what was a large sitting room. When she was home, Claire obviously had spent most of her time here. The room was tastefully furnished with a plaid love seat and chair combination. There was a large entertainment center and collection of DVDs and CDs. Claire was a Meg Ryan fan, owning copies of *Sleepless in Seattle, When Harry Met Sally, You've Got Mail,* and even *Kate and Leopold.* There was also a run of movies that had some of the hotter scenes around. She owned *Sliver, Body Heat, 9½ Weeks, Basic Instinct,* and a few Andrew Stevens and Shannon Tweed B movies, flicks one would typically find in a frat house. There were even two porno flicks, which he found mildly amusing, something he would have expected to find in a couple of his buddies' places, but not here.

There were also a number of DVD copies. Upon closer inspection, Mac saw that they were DVDs of her TV work. Each was indexed and well organized, indicating the story she had reported and the date. She also had some videotapes of her work in Denver and Salt Lake City.

A door from the sitting room led into the hallway. On the other side was an office. She had an L-shaped desk with a glass top. A desktop computer sat on the left corner, a tower of CDs to the right, Forensics would go over the computer with a fine tooth comb.

There were a couple of filing cabinets. A quick inspection of the desk revealed she was, again, very organized. Mortgage, investments, insurance, vehicle information—all segregated in colored folders with typed labels. There was little else in the office of interest. It didn't look as if anything had been disturbed or was out of order. As he finished, Lich came in and just shrugged his shoulders—nothing of interest found downstairs.

They walked back down the hallway to a built-in cabinet. It had bookshelves on top, a drawer and cabinet on the bottom. The cabinet had spare towels, washcloths, and some bathroom supplies. The drawer had some decorative washcloths and towels, probably for when Claire entertained. There were a few books, trinkets, and a wood Roman numeral X on the shelves.

A tour of the spare bedroom revealed a junk room, with some old clothes hanging in the closet and a few pieces of exercise equipment.

They walked back into the master bedroom. Lich spoke first. "Gotta be someone she knows, because, best as I can tell, nothing's out of place."

"You may be right," Mac replied, unable to argue with the premise. He headed down the steps. As he reached the bottom, he saw Clark and Green walking up. Mac tilted his head up in greeting as they approached.

"Nothing so far," Green said. "We've gone through the apartment buildings across the street. There are a couple of apartments where people didn't respond, though, so we'll have to go back."

"Okay, keep at it. Lich and I are heading down to Channel 6 to talk to her work people. If you get anything, give me a call."

Nobody had anything to add, so Mac and Lich headed out. Word spread that Mac was lead on the case, and the media had identified him. As he and Lich headed towards the Explorer, a throng of reporters approached and started shouting questions. "No comment," and, "You'll have to work through media relations," was all Mac would say. Lich, on his best behavior, said nothing.

There were two US Senate dining rooms. One was for use by current members, their families, as well as any former senators. The other dining room, a small one, was only for current senators. It was perhaps the most exclusive restaurant in Washington, if not in all of the country.

Senator Mason Johnson was having a late lunch with the junior senators from Wisconsin and Iowa. They were discussing various issues involved in a farm bill before the Agriculture Committee, of which all three were members. The Republican senator from Iowa had sponsored the bill and was explaining to his esteemed Democratic friend from Wisconsin his displeasure with other Democratic senators who were, in his terms, "fiddlin" with his bill.

Senator Johnson was hearing their conversation, but he wasn't really listening. Rather, he was enjoying his tomato-basil soup out of an exquisite fine-china bowl and thinking about Claire.

As he was finishing his lunch, a senate page approached their table. He had a note for the senator. "Come back to the office right away—Jordan." Jordan Hines was Johnson's best friend and chief of staff. *Hmmm*, he wondered. *What could be so important?* Johnson excused himself and made tracks for his office in the Russell Senate Building.

The senator was conflicted. He knew his own marriage was over, although he had not discussed divorce with his wife. While he was only forty-four years old, he had been in Washington for fourteen years, six as a congressman and eight as a senator.

His years in Washington had taught him one immutable truth about his job: it was demanding on a marriage. There were long hours at the capital, traveling, raising money, as well as spending time in the home state. His wife was a good woman, intelligent, attractive, but not one to stay home and be the dutiful senator's wife. In their many years in Washington, she had become a force in a number of political causes, some of which differed from his own political philosophy. The time she spent on her career and the time required for his strained the marriage. He had brought up the issues with Gwen, hoping she would understand the importance of what he was doing as a senator and would give up some of her work to be there for him. However, the more he brought it up, the more strained things became. He couldn't remember the last time they had spent a night together or made love. He needed her love, her attention and affection. Instead, he often found himself alone at the end of the day. They had simply drifted apart.

Then he met Claire. It was early September, at a birthday party for a political supporter back home. He was standing next to the bar, having a gin and tonic and talking to a group of friends when he saw her walk in. She was wearing a black strapless dress and, while very tasteful, it left little to the imagination. Then she flashed that smile he had seen on TV. She was stunning. While he had noticed her, as every other male in the joint must have, he didn't make any sort of a move towards her. It was another half hour, and suddenly someone grabbed him by the arm. It was his friend Conner Lund, and with him was Claire Daniels.

"Mace, Claire wanted to meet you."

It was not often that he was made uncomfortable, even intimidated by anyone, and in particular a woman, but Claire had that effect on him initially. It was her beauty. She was the most attractive woman he had ever met. However, once he met her, shook her hand and spent a few moments with her, he liked her immediately. He found her to be warm, funny, and intelligent. They talked for what seemed like hours, both within a group of people, as well as by themselves. There were numerous times each of them broke off to converse with others, but somehow they always ended up back together. At the end of the night, as everyone was leaving, he found himself standing next to her, waiting for the valet to bring up his car. He wondered how he could somehow mention seeing her again. She made it easy. As the valet pulled up her car, she mentioned she was going to be in DC in a couple of weeks. She wondered if they could get together for lunch. Of course, he said, just call his office. He didn't even know if he was scheduled to be in town, but he decided he would make sure he was.

Sure enough, two weeks later, Claire showed up on his calendar. She was going to stop by the office to say hello. However, it was not going to be around lunch, but at 5:00 p.m. He figured she was busy but would stop by to say hello, probably on the way to the airport.

She stayed for five hours. They talked about everything going on in Washington. She had interviewed for a position with CBS, working in the capital. The job would start in January. She was excited about the opportunity. While she loved Minnesota, she was growing bored with local news and she wanted to work on a larger stage.

Toward the end of the evening, the topic of the senator's wife came up. He had only told Jordan about his marital problems. For whatever reason, he told Claire everything. She just listened. She didn't judge him. She didn't lecture or argue about his wife's desire to have a career of her own. She just listened.

At the end of the night, he walked her to the door of his office. He felt like a teenager on his first date. There was nobody around; he probably could have kissed her good night. He was attracted to her, yet he wasn't sure if she was attracted to him. He'd never cheated on his wife, and he held back. Well, not completely. "I'm going to be in the Cities in a week. Maybe we could get together for a drink?"

"I'd like that." She left him her home number and leaned up and kissed him on the cheek.

Claire was all he could think about for the next week. On Friday, he got into town and immediately called her. They agreed he would stop by her place for a drink. When he got there, they were in bed within fifteen minutes. She was everything he dreamed she would be. She was an energetic, aggressive, even wild lover. He'd never been with anyone like her. He felt twenty-four, instead of forty-four. She made him feel like a man again.

As a senator, he always made frequent trips home. He loved his state, and it was good politics to be seen at home, lest it appear you become more a resident of Washington, DC, than Minnesota. Having met Claire, he made it a point to get home each weekend. He made the trips home three-and-four-day weekends with plenty of political events to cover the visit. But most late nights were spent with Claire.

He would have to talk to Jordan. Hines knew all about Claire. He was the only one he'd told about it. He didn't know if what he had with Claire would last. He wasn't sure long-term relationships with a woman like her would work. She had a career of her own and was not the type to be the supportive, stay-at-home wife to a senator. But she made him feel alive again. He wanted to spend as much time with her as he could to see if it might work. But if nothing else, he knew that his marriage was over. It was time to have that conversation with his wife. He thought she might be having the same feelings. Maybe it wouldn't be so bad.

Then there would be the political fallout. He and Jordan would have to plot out how best to handle the divorce from a political standpoint. It wasn't unheard of for politicians to get divorced. What he didn't want was a scandal. If he did it soon, with four years left in his term, any short-term political damage could be repaired, especially if the divorce was handled right. As he entered the lobby to his office, the receptionist indicated Jordan was waiting for him inside. As he walked into his office, Hines, with a concerned look on his face, motioned for him to close the door. The senator closed the door and asked, "What's up?"

"Claire's dead."

5

"WE ALSO LEARNED SHE'S A HORNY LITTLE MINX."

Mac and Lich spent the afternoon interviewing people at Channel 6. First up was Station Manager Mary Carpenter. Carpenter hired Daniels three years earlier from a station in Denver, where she had worked for two years. Prior to that, Daniels worked in Salt Lake City. According to Carpenter, while it wasn't officially announced, Daniels had taken a network job in Washington.

Carpenter was unaware of anything special or unusual Daniels was working on or investigating. In fact, when they heard she had been found dead, Carpenter immediately asked around, but nobody seemed to know much of anything. It hadn't been unusual for Daniels to work the background of a story unbeknownst to Carpenter and then bring it to her or a news producer.

Mac asked, "We'd like to get a list of stories she's worked on, as well as a list of anybody who sent threatening letters, e-mails, messages, or things of that nature."

"We're already working on it," replied Carpenter.

Interviews with the rest of the station staff were similar. Daniels was well-respected, worked hard, and was the total perfectionist. As with Carpenter, all were unaware of whom she was dating.

Tim Mullany was Claire's most frequent cameraman and her

closest friend at the station. They had worked together since she came to Channel 6. He was a fifteen-year veteran at the station, had worked with numerous reporters over the years, and stated that Daniels "was easily the best I've worked with. She was a total perfectionist. Yet she did it in a way, the perfectionist part, that wasn't offensive." Smiling, Mullany continued, "She was here three years and had a lot to do with the work ethic picking up around the station."

"Was she seeing anyone?" Mac asked.

"I'm pretty sure she was."

"Do you know who?"

"That I don't know. Claire kept her dating private. She never told me about the people she dated, and I never really asked. It was none of my business."

"She made it into the tabloid pages a lot," Lich said.

Mullany nodded, "Claire was someone that people were interested in. She was a beautiful woman, and she dated some fairly well-known people in town, an athlete or two, some fairly prominent business people. She tried to be discreet about it. I kind of admired that."

Joe Elliott came to the conference room next. He was the sports anchor for Channel 6. He started at the station at the same time as Daniels and the two had dated briefly. If Daniels made the men's hearts skip a beat, Elliott made the ladies swoon. He had been a college linebacker at Indiana and didn't appear to have let the years get the better of him. He looked like he could go out and play now. Mac got right to the point, "I understand that you dated Claire Daniels a while back?"

Elliot smiled, "Yeah, we came to the station about the same time. We didn't really know anyone and kind of struck up a friendship."

"It was more than friends though?"

"Yeah, I was certainly attracted to her right away, and I had just gotten divorced and was looking to get back into the swing of things. Claire was at the right place at the right time."

"Why didn't it last?"

"I certainly had no intent of getting into any sort of relationship at that point. And our relationship, if you want to call it that, was pretty intense, but wouldn't have lasted."

"Intense how? Sexually intense?"

Elliott cringed, looking as if he wanted to stop the conversation. "I wish I wouldn't have used that term. Claire was, is, my friend, and I can sense where you're going with the question. I'm not sure what nature our relationship was or took has anything to do with what happened to her. I mean, it was two and a half years ago."

Mac leaned forward in his chair. "I wouldn't ask the question unless we thought it was relevant. And you're right as to where I'm heading. As uncomfortable as this is, I need to know if she was into anything kinky or out of the ordinary."

"Does this have something to do with how you found her this morning?" asked Elliott, going into reporter mode.

Mac stayed neutral. "Again, I wouldn't ask unless it was relevant."

Elliott looked away at a picture on the wall for what seemed like a couple of minutes, thinking about what he wanted to say. "Claire was no repressed Catholic school girl, that's for sure. She wasn't promiscuous, but she liked sex, a lot. Told me she always had, from the time she was a freshman in college. Said she even made a sex tape with an old boyfriend her junior year. She used to joke she'd end up like Paris Hilton if that thing got out. And she exuded sexuality. It was almost intimidating when she came onto you, like a sexual freight train, this pulse you would get from her."

"Was she into anything kinky, weird, anything like that?" Lich asked.

"Weird, no. Kinky, a little. She wasn't into anything like whips, chains, anything like that. But she was intense, energetic. I'd even say a little wild. I used to say, 'And women say men are loud.' I mean, you knew when she had an orgasm."

"You said I was right about kinky. How was I right?"

"She liked different positions mostly. I remember she told me once about a shirt her friend had which showed these two little devils, male and female, in all kinds of different positions. She said she wanted to try them all. We tried a few, but nothing too crazy. It was fun. She was fun. Like I said, she was something in bed, almost perfect at sex. I mean, she could really get you going." Elliott seemed to smile at the memory.

"Why did it end?"

"People at the station found out, so we ended it. We were new to the station, and we both felt it didn't look right."

"Did you remain friends?"

"Yes. We actually became really good friends. In fact, I just recently became engaged, and she bought my fiancée and me this wonderful gift for our house."

Mac shifted gears. "I haven't had a chance to speak to her family. Claire had been married, right?

"Yes."

"Must have been before she came here?"

"Yeah. She married a guy named Kevin Daniels out in Salt Lake City. It didn't work out, lasted maybe a year and a half, and that was it."

"Why didn't it work?" Lich queried.

"It was her career. She didn't want to stay at home and have babies, and he wanted that from her. She always said it was a big mistake. He wasn't a bad guy. He probably thought he could change her, convince her to do the family thing." Elliot shook his head, "But that wasn't Claire then and never would have been. She was ambitious and intense about her career. Shit, I've never seen someone so intense about everything she does."

"Perhaps that explains the DVDs," Mac said.

"DVDs? What are you talking about?" asked Elliott.

"When we were looking around her place, we saw she has this cabinet full of DVDs of her work."

"That'd be Claire," stated Elliott, nodding and smiling. "She was very vain and a complete and total perfectionist. She was like a football player. She'd watch film of herself all the time. It's why she was so damn good at what she did."

∾

The rest of the senator's afternoon schedule was cleared. There wasn't much on it, mostly lobbyists who would be more than happy to accommodate him and speak with him another time.

He couldn't believe it. He'd been with her just the night before. She was fine when he left. The first question he asked was, "When? How?"

"She was found dead in her condo this morning," Hines replied. "The media doesn't have much, but I spoke with a few people, and apparently someone strangled her. They think sometime last night, although the police haven't released anything official yet."

Johnson and Hines sat in silence for a number of minutes. Hines broke the silence. "You saw her last night?"

"Yes."

"What happened?"

Johnson didn't like the tone of the question. "What do you mean, what happened?"

"Easy. What did you and Claire do?"

"What do you think we did?"

Jordan knew what that meant. However, he was not only the chief of staff, but a former prosecutor, and he suspected now that his best friend might end up being a suspect.

"Did you use a condom?"

Johnson jumped out of his chair and screamed, "What?"

Hines put his hands up immediately to say, "I'm not asking what you're thinking." He put his finger to his lips and looked towards the door.

Johnson composed himself. "What do you mean you're not asking what I'm thinking? You're asking me if I used a condom. Yes, Claire and I had sex. I did not use a condom."

"So, you left semen behind."

It was a statement, not a question, and in that instant Johnson knew exactly where Hines was going. Not only had his lover been killed, he might be a suspect.

"I did." Johnson responded in a soft voice, "But, Jordan, man, I didn't kill her. I swear to God. She was alive and well when I left."

"What time did you leave?"

"Around 1:30 a.m."

"Did anyone see you leave?"

Johnson immediately bowed his head, running his right hand through his thick black hair. "Yes."

"Was it someone you knew?"

Johnson exhaled, "No, it was someone walking along the sidewalk. I looked outside before I left to see if anyone was out there. I waited until after 1:00 a.m., so someone from the bar crowd didn't see me. I didn't see the guy, but I obviously missed him. He passed by me right under the streetlight."

The senator realized he was in a pickle. Suddenly a ton of thoughts flashed through his mind all at once. If this got out, what would his wife say? What about the political implications? Could he survive? He didn't kill her, but it would probably come out that he was seeing Claire. "So what's gonna happen?"

"We'll have to see. Assuming they find the guy who saw you, the police may want to interview you. How much they want to talk to you may depend upon cause of death, what time they think she died, who else she might have been seeing, who might have an axe to grind—that sort of thing."

"What do we do now?"

"We call Lyman."

~

Late in the afternoon, Mac and Lich left Channel 6. They drove in silence along I-94 heading back towards Daniels's place. As Mac hit the Lexington Parkway exit and headed south towards Summit Avenue, Lich piped up, "So what do you think we learned?"

"Well, we learned she's really well liked and respected," Mac replied. "She doesn't appear to have any enemies at the station. She was serious and committed to her work. To the best of anyone's knowledge, she wasn't working on anything that would cause someone to want to kill her. Nobody's aware of anyone she was currently seeing."

"We've also learned she's a horny little minx," Lich added, obviously enjoying the more salacious details acquired that afternoon.

"I was wondering how long it would take you to mention that. Elliott obviously enjoyed the fling they had," Mac said. "But we learned she was passionate, maybe a little kinky, but not into anything unusual."

"Elliott neutered the details," Lich replied dismissively. "I imagine at some point he'll be going through them in his mind again, probably to great delight."

Mac couldn't disagree, although he didn't respond as he turned left on Summit and drove past the Victorian mansions and majestic cathedrals that dotted the avenue's landscape. He zoomed by the sprawling Minnesota governor's mansion on his right and stately William Mitchell College of Law on the left. Three more blocks east, Mac pulled into an open spot along Summit, a block short of Daniels's place on St. Albans. As they got out of the truck, Lich remarked, "I can't believe how warm it is."

It was remarkably warm, Mac thought. It was 5:00 p.m. and still sixty degrees, which was extremely warm for November 1st in Minnesota. Might not want to mothball the golf clubs just yet, he thought.

They walked to the corner, turned right on St. Albans towards Daniels's condo, and stopped to take in the scene. The crowd had thinned some, but the news trucks and reporters were milling around. While Lich was standing with hands on hips, looking towards the news media getting ready for their 5:00 p.m. live reports, Mac saw Green and Clark standing on the porch to Daniels's place. Mac grabbed Lich by the elbow and nodded his head towards the two other detectives.

In a couple of minutes, they had threaded their way through the crowd, ignoring the many questions. The yellow police tape finally held the media back. Mac and Lich climbed up the steps to the porch. "What's the status around here?" Mac asked. Clark gave them the rundown, all the people they interviewed and buildings cleared. "What about across the street?" Mac asked.

Clark answered. "We missed four units in the one right across the street. That was one of the first places we went, so the people may be back by now."

"Okay. Lich and I can run over there quick before we have to head back downtown. Which units?"

Clark gave them the numbers, and Mac and Lich headed across the street. The three-story brown-brick apartment building rested on the southeast corner of Summit. It was one of many desirable red-and-brown-brick apartment buildings between Summit and Grand.

At the first apartment, there was still no answer. They would have to come back. Mac jotted a note on the back of his business card and slipped it under the door. At the second unit, Mac and Lich found a couple of women in their mid-twenties just home from work having a beer. One was a heavier-set brunette still wearing her blue business suit. The other was an attractive, petite blonde, wearing a tight T-shirt that showed her midriff and blue jeans. She made eyes at Mac imme-diately, which he tried to ignore, although it was difficult. Her name was Carrie. She said that she and her roommate had been at the Halloween party at Mardi Gras the night before. They left the bar around 12:30 a.m. and walked home along St. Albans and came in the back door along the alley. They hadn't seen anything and might not have even if they were looking as both admitted to having a really good time at Mardi Gras. It looked like they were ready to get a good start today, as there were a couple of empty bottles sitting on the coffee table. After five minutes, it was apparent that they knew noth-ing. Yet, every time Mac got up to leave, Lich kept the conversation going.

As they finally left, Mac asked. "How come you kept that going?"

"Just trying to get you laid. She was attractive as hell and ready to be had," Lich said, smiling. "Hell, she was throwing herself at you. They know nothing about the case. You should step back and get yourself a little."

Mac appreciated Lich's concern. He wasn't the first one to make the comment in the last few months. It had been a while. His buddies kept telling him he needed to "Get back on the horse."

In the next unit, they found a couple of William Mitchell law students. They had ignored Halloween altogether, having studied until 10:00 p.m. at the law school. Then they came home, had a beer and hit the rack around 11:45, after watching Letterman. They hadn't seen anything and didn't even know that Daniels lived so close.

Lich and Mac moved on to the last unit, which was on the third floor along the front of the building. They knocked on the door a couple of times. No answer. Mac slipped a business card under the door with a note to please call him. He and Lich turned to leave, were ten feet down the hall when they heard the chain unhook and the dead bolt turn open. They turned to walk back as a Hispanic man who appeared to be in his late thirties or early forties opened the door. "What can I do for you?"

"St. Paul detectives," Mac replied as he and Lich flashed their identifications. "What's your name, sir?"

"Juan Hernandez. What's going on?"

"There was a murder in the neighborhood, and we're wondering if you knew anything about it?"

"No kidding? Where?"

"It was across the street, in one of the condos on St. Albans. The victim was Claire Daniels—you know, the reporter from Channel 6. We're asking everyone who lives in the neighborhood if they saw anything," said Lich. "And by the way, can we step inside?"

"Oh, sure."

Mac, Lich, and Hernandez stepped inside his apartment into the living room, which was sparsely furnished with a couch, chair, coffee table, and TV. There were few if any personal furnishings displayed. Lich, looking around, asked, "Just move in?"

"Yeah, just a few days ago," Hernandez replied. "When did it happen, the murder?"

"We think last night?"

"Oh, my," Hernandez replied, putting his hand to his chest. "What time?"

"We're not sure," Lich lied.

"Hmpf." Hernandez walked over towards the porch looking out onto Summit Avenue. "Is her place the last condo on the end?"

The way he said it caused Mac and Lich to share a look. This guy was leading somewhere. "Yes. Why do you ask?" Mac inquired.

"Well, I was having trouble sleeping last night, so I went out for a walk around 12:30 a.m. Thought maybe the fresh air would clear my head. So, anyway, I was walking up St. Albans and ran into someone in the street."

"Who was that?" Mac asked neutrally.

Hernandez hesitated. "You guys probably won't believe this."

"Give it a shot," Lich said.

"Mason Johnson," Hernandez blurted.

That got their attention. "What? Mason Johnson? Senator Mason Johnson?" Mac replied, disbelieving, his heart skipping a beat.

"Oh, yes, I'm sure," Hernandez replied confidently.

Mac shared a quick look with Lich that said, *Oh, boy, the case might have just gone nuclear.* "What time?" Mac continued.

"It was 1:30."

"You're sure?"

"Oh, yes. I thought it odd to see him so late like that on the street, so I looked at my watch. It was 1:30."

"Where did you see him on the street?" Lich asked.

"He was coming down the steps of the condo, and he turned and walked right by me on the sidewalk. I even said hello to him, and he said hi back," Hernandez said, remaining self-assured. "I don't think he expected to see anyone on the street at that hour. He kind of ducked his head when he saw me coming. But he said hello, walked by me, and got into his car."

"What kind of car?" Lich asked.

"Lexus, I think, white. He'd parked it down the street a ways. I kind of turned to watch him after he went past me. He got in the car and drove away. I remember thinking it was the darndest thing to have seen him on the street like that."

"Mr. Hernandez, you're sure?" Lich asked, a little unbelieving.

"Oh, yes. It was him. He's on TV a lot. You couldn't help but recognize him. I mean, he's a pretty recognizable guy. You say Claire Daniels lived in that condo, huh?"

"Yes, sir," Mac replied.

"Kinda late to be leaving there." Hernandez stopped for a second and put his finger to his mouth, and then quietly said, "Hmmm. I thought the senator was married."

Mac was thinking the same thing and gave Lich another quick look, "Mr. Hernandez, we need you to come downtown and give us a statement." Viper was parked on the north side of Summit Avenue, across the street from McRyan's Explorer. That had been mere serendipity, as they were parked there when McRyan arrived in the late afternoon. They tried to move the van around all day, never parking in the same spot for too long. They even changed vans around noon, from the dark blue one to white. It wasn't unheard of that a murderer would be watching the police work at the crime scene and get noticed. Viper wanted none of that, so they changed vans and locations throughout the day.

Viper wanted to make sure the crime scene developed as planned. If the police investigated properly, they would find what Viper wanted them to find. He checked on McRyan, and the word was he was a good young cop. So far, so good, as the young detective and his tubby partner were following the trail of breadcrumbs he left behind.

As he rubbed his eyes and yawned for what seemed like the hundredth time, he heard one of his crew exclaim, "*Beautiful.*" Viper knew what that meant. He moved over to the window and saw McRyan and his partner approaching the Explorer, along with a Hispanic male.

"Well that didn't take long," remarked Viper, a smile creasing his tired face.

6

"EVER HEARD OF CHAPPAQUIDDICK?"

While Lich was taking Hernandez's statement, Mac made a call to Linda Morgan for an update. The Daniels case had been on the fast track, everything else, other than the case of the serial killer, was pushed aside. Morgan confirmed that the cause of Claire Daniels's death was suffocation by strangulation. While measuring time of death was a tricky thing, they had been able to narrow it down to between 1:00 and 2:00 a.m. She'd had sex, but there was no vaginal tearing. Rape was not indicated. They would be able to get DNA from the semen, but it would take a little time. There were prints from the scene, which had yet to be matched. *That may quickly change*, Mac thought.

"When will the autopsy be done? When can I have the official results?" Mac asked.

"Tomorrow morning."

"Anything else? I'm on my way to meet with the chief."

"Nope. We'll have the autopsy done and the results to you in the morning. Any ideas on who might match the semen or prints?"

Mac thought for a moment, he would have to run things by the chief and Captain Peters first, "I might have something for you on that later."

"Who?"

"Can't tell you yet. I gotta run that one by the powers that be. All I'll say is, it could be tricky."

Mac could hear the excitement in Linda's voice, "Let me know as soon as you can, okay? It'd be really great to clear this one. Get the media off our asses."

"That it would." Mac hung up on Linda and shuffled over to a pay phone, flipping the White Pages open to the government listings. He found the number for Senator Johnson's office. A staffer told Mac that the senator had been in town until this morning. Last night he was at a fundraiser in downtown Minneapolis that ended sometime around 10:30 p.m. The senator *had* been in town. Hernandez seemed legit.

Just then Clark and Green came down the hallway with a man in a red cardigan sweater with glasses hanging on a string around his neck. Green stopped while Clark took the man into an interview room. Green had an excited look.

"Who's that?" Mac asked.

"Daniels's neighbor, guy named John Chase. You'll never guess who he saw leaving Daniels's place two nights ago."

"Mason Johnson."

Green went blank. "How ... how the hell did you know?"

Mac related the discovery of Hernandez having seen Johnson leaving the night before. Lich approached and Mac filled him in on Chase. Lich checked with Motor Vehicle Records. The senator owned a white Lexus with Minnesota plates. It was registered under Gwen Johnson, his wife, with an apartment address at Galtier Plaza in downtown St. Paul. Mac mentioned his conversation with Morgan and that he had confirmed that the senator had been in town.

"Mac, boy, seems like we got ourselves a prime suspect," said Lich, pulling up his trousers and popping on the balls of his feet.

"We'll see."

"We'll see, my ass. Don't look a potential gift horse in the mouth."

"Well, let's go tell the chief about our prime suspect and ruin his night," Mac said.

With Hernandez's statement in hand, Mac and Lich headed up to the chief's office. This would be an interesting meeting. It would include the chief, Captain Peters, Sylvia Miller, as well as District Attorney Helen Anderson. Mac had to chuckle, for as much as Chief Flanagan loathed the cameras, Anderson loved them. Anderson was something of a publicity hound. While an assistant district attorney would handle the case, the high profile guaranteed Anderson's involvement. She was more a politician than attorney and held hardly concealed aspirations for higher office. She would love the exposure this case would bring, especially if it involved a sitting United States senator from the opposing Republican Party nonetheless. Take down a powerful Republican—now that was the way to rise in the Democratic Party.

Lich, as usual, was lighthearted about the situation, "This should be a circus if the DA's involved, especially when you drop the senator on them."

Mac agreed. "Yeah, she'll want the spotlight."

"She'll pee her pants."

It was 6:30 p.m., and while it was chaotic in the rest of the Public Safety Building, it was quiet around the chief's office as most of the support staff had left for the day. Mac knocked on the door, heard a "Come," and they walked in.

The Department of Public Safety Building was a city government building and, therefore, alcohol and smoke free. So naturally the chief had a lit cigar in his mouth and had taken his bottle of Irish whiskey out, with himself, Captain Peters, and even the DA having a touch. There was also a woman in a blue suit sitting with her legs crossed on the couch. She had red hair pinned back in a swirl, stylish dark-rimmed glasses, and what looked like a nice pair of legs sticking out from her skirt. She too had a drink in her hand. For some reason, she looked familiar to Mac, but he wasn't sure where he had seen her. Flanagan was digging in his desk drawer. He looked up as Mac and Lich entered and stood with two drink glasses in his hand, "Hello, boys. May I offer you a libation?"

Lich readily agreed. After a moment's hesitation, Mac decided, what the heck, he was done for the day and heading to the bar afterwards anyway. Besides, a drink would help him break the news.

Once everyone had a fresh drink, the chief made the introductions. "As you boys know, that's District Attorney Anderson." He waved towards the couch with his drink, "The young lady over on the couch is Assistant District Attorney Sally Kennedy. Looks like you boys'll be working with her on the case once you have a suspect."

Mac and Lich shook Kennedy's hand. Mac exchanged a look with her, something familiar. The chief then prodded Mac, "Go."

"Well," Mac started, "we may have a pretty good lead."

"Do tell," the chief replied lightly.

"Well, it could be ..." Mac grimaced, "... difficult."

"Spit it out," Peters interjected.

Mac exhaled, "We gotta witness who saw Senator Mason Johnson leaving Daniels's place last night at 1:30 a.m. and another witness who saw him leave around the same time two nights ago. You put that with time of death between 1:00 and 2:00 a.m., and he starts looking pretty good for this."

Silence. The chief pinched the bridge of his nose, and Peters's mouth was agape. Everyone else had a look of disbelief on their face. After a minute, Anderson broke the quiet. "Whoa."

"Yeah," the chief added. "Mac, you better start from the beginning."

"Yes, sir." Mac related what Hernandez told them. He added in Chase and the other information regarding the senator's car and the fact he was in town last night. Then he went into what he learned from Linda Morgan. They had prints from the scene that were different from Daniels's. They had yet to be matched. But they also had semen from which they would be able to get DNA.

That caused Captain Peters to let out a long whistle. "Son, you're telling me we'll get DNA from the semen?"

"That's what Morgan says."

"And prints?" the chief added.

"Yes," Mac replied. "We'll need to see if we can access the senator's prints. I would assume that, as a federal employee, they are on file somewhere."

"They are," replied Anderson. "We can go to work on that if you'd like, Chief."

"I think we'll need that, Helen." Then to Mac, "Seems like your case is moving quickly in a certain direction."

"At this point, yes. We'll have to see the final autopsy report and think about how we'll go about testing the senator's DNA."

"I don't get it," said Peters. "I mean, I've spent enough time around politicians. They always leave themselves a way out. What, he kills her and then just gets on a plane, heads to Washington and acts as if nothing happened?"

"Ever heard of Chappaquiddick?" That caused a chuckle, and Mac turned his head to look at Kennedy, who was smiling herself.

"She has a point," said Mac, picking up on the line of thought. "Think this one out a little, it's not that hard. Senator's married. Maybe Claire says something about his wife. Asks, or better yet, demands that he get a divorce. He says no. She says, 'If you don't tell your wife, I will.'" Mac took a sip and continued, "Senator gets upset, says she can't tell his wife. It'd ruin his career or at least do it a lot of damage. He just wants something on the side."

"He's a senator. It's not unheard of," Lich added.

"Yeah," Mac replied, going on, "but Claire Daniels isn't a woman to put up with that. She's assertive, says she'll do what she wants. They argue. It gets physical on the bed, gets out of hand. He grabs her around the throat. Can't stop himself and strangles her."

"Yeah," Kennedy replied, thinking along with him, "something like that could have happened. He's killed her. He panics. He can't call the police. He can't be seen with her. He's got to get out of there and as far away as fast as he can."

Mac finished, "So, he goes home, composes himself, and heads to Washington, acting like nothing happened."

"Crime of passion?" offered Lich.

"Manslaughter," said Mac, nodding his head agreeably.

"You bet, Detective." Kennedy took a long swallow of her whiskey, leaned back into the couch, and casually said, "He doesn't go there with any intent of killing her. He wants to get laid, nothing more. Daniels, as you said, is getting sick of being his bed sheet."

She was blunt, thought Mac.

"So she says it's either his wife or her. They argue, it gets physical, and before you know it, she's dead."

"Only one fly in the senator's ointment," added Mac.

"Yup," said Kennedy, now looking right at Mac with a little smile on her face, *a nice smile,* he thought, "Juan Hernandez coming down the sidewalk. Bet he didn't count on that."

"No, Counselor, he didn't. Hernandez puts him at the scene at the time of Daniel's death."

"But he's gone too far down the path now. The senator can't go back, so he has to keep going. Gets on the plane. Gets back to Washington. Hopes the guy didn't recognize him. Maybe you and Lich don't find him."

"And you know what?" It was the chief now, making sure Mac and Kennedy didn't monopolize the whole conversation, "if he were some average Joe, he probably wouldn't have been noticed."

Mac jumped back in, "But he's not. We got Hernandez putting him there last night and the neighbor a couple of nights ago."

"And we have samples of DNA and a print that, if they match the senator—" Lich started.

"He's nailed," Peters finished.

"I don't know about nailed," Kennedy replied, putting on the brakes. "We're not even twelve hours into this thing. And we're speculating here. There might be any number of ways this thing could go. But if we get DNA and print matches, it will be pretty tough—"

"—To create reasonable doubt," said Mac, finishing Kennedy's thought. "But ..."

"What?" Kennedy asked.

"I keep thinking about what the captain said. I'm having a hard time believing Johnson did this. He's too smart. It doesn't make sense."

"Politicians aren't any smarter than anyone else, and in some ways they're dumber," the chief replied. "No offense, Helen."

"None taken," though her look said otherwise.

"Can we leak anything to the media? That we have a lead, a suspect, anything?" asked Miller, pleading, looking weary.

The chief picked up on Miller's tone, "I sympathize, but not yet. It shouldn't be long, but we have to wait." Flanagan, moving back to the topic at hand, asked Mac, "When will we have the autopsy results?"

"Tomorrow morning."

Flanagan continued. "I assume we're in agreement that, at this point, our prime, frankly only, suspect is the senator."

Everyone nodded in agreement.

"Okay. Helen, or I suppose Ms. Kennedy," the chief looked at Anderson, who nodded, "tomorrow we'll need to start looking into what kind of access we can get to Senator Johnson's fingerprints." Then he turned to Mac and Lich. "Mac, as soon as you get that autopsy report, you and Lich are back in my office. We need to move very carefully on this one. We're dealing with a senator. He doesn't get favorable treatment, but we don't haul his ass in here without having our shit together. Understood? And not a word to the media about this."

If you were in trouble with the law and you had money, Lyman Hisle was the man to call. His firm, Hisle & Brown, had eighteen attorneys, all very busy. Busy attorneys were profitable attorneys. The firm's offices were on the top floor of the World Trade Center in St. Paul. Hisle & Brown's success had provided for plush office space, large offices, ornate furniture, and art. The offices proved a powerful aphrodisiac when recruiting lawyers and clients to come to the firm.

Twenty years before, Lyman started out doing largely criminal defense work. His success led to a comfortable living for him, and his skills as a trial attorney had not gone unnoticed. Then he took on a sexual harassment case for a former client. Lyman had offered to settle the case for $150,000 prior to trial and was rebuffed by the employer. At trial, Lyman made the harasser look like a monkey in the witness box. The jury returned a verdict of $1.2 million. Following the verdict, Hisle & Associates, as the firm was known then, expanded its practice from criminal work to include personal injury and discrimination litigation, specializing in class-action lawsuits. The judgments and settlements were worth millions to the firm. As the firm's founder and main litigator, Lyman had amassed an impressive fortune. Those lucrative judgments and settlements over a period of ten years allowed Lyman to do two things. One, enjoy an exceedingly high standard of living, and, two, return to the practice he truly loved, criminal law. He was the best in town and only took on interesting cases. The potential case of Senator Mason Johnson qualified.

Lyman had known the senator for years and he was a frequent campaign contributor. The death of Claire Daniels had been on the news all day. That his friend might somehow end up caught in the middle of the case was a shock to the system. Lyman heard the senator's recitation of the facts. He told them to sit tight for the time being; he would call them back.

The quandary for Lyman was how to advise the senator. Maybe a drink would help. He went to the small wet bar in his spacious office. He dropped a couple ice cubes into his glass and poured himself a scotch. Back at his desk, he sat in his leather chair, kicked his feet up, and looked out his thirtieth-story office window south over the Mississippi River. He gave his options some thought. The key was whether the police had the senator's name.

As Lyman saw it, he could have the senator sit tight and see if the police connected him to Claire Daniels, the thought being that there was no sense admitting involvement prematurely if the police did not know he was involved. They might never connect Daniels with Mason. If he was to be believed, and Lyman did believe him at this point, he had nothing to do with her death. The downside was that, if the police did connect him, he looks guilty not coming forward. They would have to call him in. Additionally, it would get out to the media that the senator didn't come forward. It could do irreparable harm to his political career. Gary Condit came immediately to mind. If there were a murder trial, not coming forward would not be good for a potential jury pool.

The other approach would be to come forward voluntarily to the police. A man walking in front of Daniels's place saw him on the street. The police probably had the senator by now, and while reluctant to call him in, they would eventually do so. If they went in voluntarily, offering information they had available, it might prove to be helpful to the investigation. Going this route, Lyman could get them to play ball, keep Mason's name out of the media. Lyman may be a defense attorney, but he had defended St. Paul police officers on numerous occasions. He knew Charlie Flanagan well and could ask for discretion and would get it. Flanagan was as straight a shooter as there was, and he had no love for the media. If they went this way, it could save the senator's career. And if there were a trial, at least he'd be able to say the senator came forward voluntarily. If nothing else, he might look better in front of a potential jury pool.

There was a knock on the office door. Summer Plantagenate, an associate specializing in criminal law, stepped into his office. She assisted him on a number of occasions where he had represented St. Paul police officers. Her last couple of hours had been spent calling her contacts in the department.

"Come in. Care to refresh?" Lyman asked, holding up the bottle.

"Yes." Lawyers. The only bar they ever passed was the one for a license to practice law. Lyman filled a glass with scotch and walked it over to Summer, who had taken a seat in one of the deep leather chairs in front of Lyman's desk. "Have your contacts been of any help?"

"No," she said disappointedly. "I tried every way I know how, but the people I know aren't involved in the Daniels case."

"Have you learned anything?"

"The detective running the case is named McRyan."

"Michael McRyan?"

"Yeah. Do you know him?"

Lyman smiled. "That I do. Mac's fairly young, but he's been a detective for a few years, I think."

"In any event," Summer continued, "he's met with Chief Flanagan twice today. The last guy I talked to told me that he heard McRyan was up meeting with the chief tonight, along with District Attorney Anderson."

"Anything else besides McRyan?" inquired Lyman.

"They're keeping a tight lid on this one. Nobody seems to know anything."

"Hmmmm. Does that seem unusual to you?"

"Yes, a little." Summer took a sip of her drink. "You can usually get something, but nobody involved directly in the investigation is talking."

"Do you think they have our client's name?"

"If I were going to Vegas, I'd say yes."

"Because nobody's talking?"

"Yes. That, and the fact that the district attorney is meeting with Flanagan. That's not something that happens on a normal case this quickly."

Lyman got up and went over to the bar to freshen his drink. He raised the bottle towards Summer. She waved him off. He put the top back on the bottle. He sipped his scotch and looked in the mirror over the bar. He walked back over to his desk and picked up the phone and dialed.

"Jordan? Lyman."

Viper took the elevator up to the office. The boss would be waiting for a status report. Viper had worked for him for over twenty years, and the man always loved his status reports. It wasn't that he tried to quarterback things. Nothing could be further from the truth. Rather, he always wanted to be informed. It's why he had always been so successful, which now made Viper a wealthy man and a loyal one as well. In fact, the boss had looked out for Viper for over the last twenty years. He'd do anything for the man.

It had been an exhausting twenty-four hours, and he was ready to go home and get some sleep. It was always that way with a mission. The excitement, tension, and adrenaline of it kept you going, as if there was no recognition of the time passing. However, once the mission was over, the exhaustion hit. And he was older now, and the recovery time would be longer. Good thing he didn't often have to run these operations anymore. In fact, he thought he was done with them altogether. Then Claire Daniels came snooping around, and he came out of retirement.

As he walked in, the boss was sitting behind his desk looking at some papers. He saw Viper walk in and put the papers into a manila folder. He walked over to sit down on the couch, and Viper joined him. The boss was having a drink. He offered, but Viper declined. A drink might put him to sleep.

"So, where are we at?" asked the boss.

Viper smiled, "We're good."

The boss gave him a long look, "How good?"

"Like I said, we're good. Real good." Viper kept smiling, a tired smile, but he was smiling.

"Ahhh, you're telling me they already have the senator?"

"Yes."

"The police did it all on their own, eh? We didn't have to help them along at all?"

"No. They found our guy this afternoon."

"Hmpf. That was quick," said the boss as he took a drink.

"The kid running the investigation seems to know what he is doing."

"So, this young McRyan seems on top of it?"

"From a distance, yes. He's young, but he seems to have the respect of those working with him. His partner is far senior but seems to work with him without a problem." They sat in silence for a minute. Viper looked out the window towards the Xcel Energy

Center. It was well lit, and the crowd was strolling in. Must be a concert; the Wild were on the road.

Viper broke the silence, "What does your contact have to say?"

"I haven't asked, as of yet, son. I'll be getting to that, I assure you. Whatever I find out, I'll pass along."

"Thank you, sir."

"Do you have anything else?"

"No, sir."

"Then to bed with you. You look tired. Are you getting too old for this sort of work?"

Viper gave the boss another tired smile and headed out. His bed was beckoning.

"WELCOME TO MY WORLD."

Mac pulled the Explorer in behind the bar. It had been a long and exhausting day, yet exhilarating all at the same time. His first truly "big" case and in the first day his prime suspect looked to be a sitting United States senator. "Top that," he thought. He doubted anyone in the bar could.

The bar was McRyan's Pub, the other family enterprise and a true St. Paul institution. The Pub sat on West Seventh Street, just on the southern outskirts of downtown and one block from the Xcel Energy Center, home of the NHL's Minnesota Wild. It was the favored watering hole of hockey fans, and the St. Paul police.

Opened in 1907 by Mac's Great-Grandpa Pat, the Pub had a colorful history of serving drinks before, during, and after prohibition. The during prohibition occurred in the now infamous Patrick's Room, located in the basement and hidden behind what looked like a typical built-in wooden buffet one might find in an older home. A latch inside the middle drawer of the buffet opened the door into a large, hidden room. During prohibition, the police, politicians, and citizens together enjoyed illegal drinks and fun. Currently, the inside of Patrick's Room was adorned with black-and-white photos of that colorful era, while the outside was marked by a plaque denoting the room's colorful history. Patrick's Room was now used for private parties, meetings, and cop poker games.

Mac walked into the left side of the main level, a classic, old-fashioned bar, the counter of which stretched half of the length and width of the room, leaving barely enough room for people to stand three or four deep, as it was tonight. Behind the bar was a long mirror with MCRYAN'S PUB and a big green shamrock stenciled on it. Two retired cops were tending bar, pouring drinks and trading stories with the crowd, which, from the looks of it, was entirely made up of cops. The room was abuzz. There was plenty to talk about with the Daniels murder and the fifth serial killing.

Most nights, when Mac walked in, he went in like everyone else, got a few, "Hi" and "How're ya doings" as he worked his way through the crowd of cops. Tonight was a little different. He got looks, stares, and nods. He was working a big case, one people all around town were talking about. Undoubtedly, the boys would be looking to grill him for the facts on the case, his list of suspects, and, for those cops not involved with the serial killer, queries if he needed any help.

He made his way through the crowd to the bar and ordered a Guinness. He preferred darker beers, especially if he was only going to have a couple before going home. That was his plan, too. Mac took a long swig, saw a couple bar stools open up and grabbed one.

"Mac, boy, mind if I grab a seat?"

Mac turned to find an old family friend giving him a tired smile. Pat Riley was having one of his specials, a Dewers on the rocks. Mac suspected it wasn't his first, and he saw in Pat what he himself might look like in a month if he didn't clear the Daniels murder.

Riles was heading the detail on the serial killer. After seven weeks of investigation, he looked worn down, tired, and tonight, properly drunk. The stress could be read all over his large, round face. A big man, Riles was six three, with a developing pot belly and a large mane of black hair. His face was jowly, and his five o'clock shadow made him look Nixonian. His bushy hair was disheveled, his tie loosened, and his face pale except the dark circles around his eyes. It had been a long couple of months for him.

Any cop in Pat's position wanted more than anything to find the bastard who was killing these women. You lived with it twenty-four/seven. It consumed you, especially the longer it went on. Mac remembered his dad telling him that when he first starts working a case such as Pat's, there was a certain excitement. But, if it went unsolved, the excitement went by the wayside, replaced by stress and pressure. These mounted with time.

Usually, the pressure started with the media. With a serial killer, the media pressure was constant, with daily stories and special reports. And now it was November 1st, a sweeps month for television. Investigative reports would be coming. The media pressure in turn created political pressure. Media stories scared politicians from the mayor down to members of the city council. Mac's dad, Uncle Shamus, the chief, and Captain Peters all said at one time or another: a politician would never, ever, find a better job. They would do whatever they could to keep it, too. Consequently, they all had an innate, almost instinctive ability to apply pressure on the police, the fire department—whomever—to provide cover for themselves.

Naturally, when the media and the politicos got together, the pressure built on the detectives involved. Such was the case with Pat. The serial killer case was getting to him. Mac could see it. He was drinking more, sleeping less, and looking beaten down. No wonder. The case itself brought tremendous stress and pressure. Add media and political attention, and it was understandable why one would be driven to drink.

"Welcome to my world," Pat said wearily.

"It has been an eventful day," Mac agreed.

"Careful what you wish for, boyo. If your thing goes on like mine, it'll wear on you."

"You look beat."

"Shit, this case is kicking my ass," Riles replied, taking a sip of the Dewers. "You watch, it'll do the same to you."

Mac gave a little chuckle, "It's only been one day, Pat. It better not get to me yet, or I'm not long for this line of work." Mac thought he might mention something more about Pat's drinking, but quickly put it out of his mind. It wasn't his place.

"True enough. So, what's up with your case?"

This was tough for Mac. He'd love to tell Pat about the senator and what they had learned about Claire Daniels. About what the autopsy report might say in the morning. But the chief had been clear; he couldn't tell anybody anything about the case. Not the media, not fellow cops, not even his dog. Mac, however, couldn't shut out Pat completely. That wasn't the way it worked either. Quietly, he gave him pretty much everything but the senator.

"So, Pat, quid pro quo?"

Pat took a long sip of his Dewers and said, "Fair nuff." The fifth victim was found in a vacant lot behind O'Neill's Bar by a delivery driver. Like the first four, she had been strangled and sexually assaulted. The killer had used a Trojan condom when he assaulted the victim. Like all the other victims, a smiley-faced balloon had been left as a calling card.

"So, it's number five, eh?" Mac finished.

"Looks that way."

Mac hated to ask, "Anything new?"

"Nada, and that fuckin' balloon," Riles sighed. "Cripes, the guy's mocking us with that damn thing."

"You guys trace the balloon?"

"Yeah. You can buy them at forty-seven different locations in the Twin Cities by last count. No way to trace a specific balloon to a specific package or box. We've had guys go to all the stores, but we've got nothing."

"What about this victim?"

"That's one thing that's a little different this time. This one was a CFO at a local company. The other victims weren't professional, educated type ladies. We got a couple waitresses, one convenience-store clerk, and a gal who worked a drive-thru. This one was a professional. So, that's a little different. The rest is pretty much the same."

They talked for a few more minutes. Pat was running the show on the serial killer case and he already had a few meetings with the chief. The mayor was putting the pressure on about the murders and wondered if increasing the detail or changing the detail leadership would be necessary.

"What did Flanagan say to that?"

"What do you think he said?"

Mac smiled. "Told the mayor to go fuck himself, huh?"

A small smile creased Riles's face. "Yeah. I'm sure there was a certain level of political-speak involved, but that's basically what he said. Of course, he can only do that for so long. We need to bring this sucker home." Pat took another sip from his drink. "Man, do we need a break in this thing." He shook his head and looked down.

They chatted for a few more minutes. Pat was drunk. Mac made eye contact with the bartender and nodded towards Pat and made a steering motion with his free hand. The bartender returned the nod and scampered off. A minute later, Bobby Rockford, a member of Pat's detail, ambled over and offered Pat a ride home. Well, it wasn't really an offer, it was a "try to drive and I'll kick your ass" proposition. Pat, too tired to argue, took the last sip of his Dewers and headed out with Rock.

Mac ordered another beer, grabbed a newspaper and menu from behind the bar and took an open booth by the front window, away from the crowd. His cousin Kelly came over and chatted him up for a few minutes, then took his order for a BLT. Mac flipped open the Business section when he heard, "Mind if I join you?"

Mac looked up to see Sally Kennedy. "Evenin', Counselor. What brings you here?"

"Some friends were supposed to be here, but I'm a little late. They seem to have left." Kennedy took a look around. She obviously wanted to have a drink, but who wanted to drink alone, other than George Thorogood?

Mac offered, "Grab a seat. I just ordered something from the kitchen. Hungry?"

Kennedy smiled her thanks. "No. What're you drinking?"

"A Guinness. Can I order you one?"

"Sounds good."

Mac motioned to Kelly, held up his glass and one finger. A beer was there thirty seconds later.

Kennedy thanked him and took a sip. "Quick service."

"Helps when my cousin's waiting on the table."

Kennedy took a long drink. "I like the dark stuff. Especially if I'm only going to have one or two."

"Exactly," Mac replied. "If I have any more than three or four of these, I start getting full. I'll usually switch over to vodka tonics or something." Mac took a drink and a long look at Kennedy. "I couldn't help but thinking that you and I met before?"

"We have."

"Where?"

She smiled, and it was a nice smile. "Law School. William Mitchell. I knew who you were at the U of M because I went to the hockey games, but you'd remember me from Billy Mitch."

Mac connected instantly. "That's right! Now, I remember. We had a class or two together, I think, maybe third year?"

"Yes, I think that's right. Stiffs and Gifts perhaps?" That was Estates and Trusts to most people.

"Could be." Mac nodded.

"I remember seeing you over at Billy's on occasion as well. I think with your wife."

"Yeah, I was married back then," Mac replied.

Kennedy sighed, "If it's any consolation, Detective, I've been divorced a year myself."

"Ahhh. So, I have joined elite company?" Mac replied ruefully.

That caused Kennedy to smile. "Why, yes, Detective, yes you have."

Mac raised a mock toast, "To the newly divorced, and you can call me Mac. Everybody does."

"Well, then, cheers, Mac. Call me Sally." They clinked beers.

"Sally, let's talk shop."

"Good idea, but where's your partner?"

"Lich? He stopped in briefly, but I think he went home. He's in the newly divorced club as well, and not for the first time, either."

"Man, marriage—not exactly a solid institution is it?"

"Oh, I don't know. There're lots of people who make it work. I'm just glad we didn't have kids. How about you?"

"Kids? No, although it's probably what led to the end of things. He was ready. I wasn't. We had a big blow-up about it, but I refused. Few days later, I come home to find he's cleaned out his part of the closet and dresser. Said he was staying at a hotel. Couple of weeks later, I got papers from his lawyer and, as they say, the rest is history."

"I remember now, you were married when we were in law school, weren't you?"

"Yeah, my ex was a year ahead of me. We're both lawyers. He figured he could continue with his career, and I'd stay home and be the happy homemaker. I was the prosecutor, in a government job making 50K, and he's up for partner in Fitzgerald and Bush, making 150K. We didn't need my salary, so I should just stay home." Kennedy shook her head. Mac could relate to a spouse who didn't value a job where one served the public good.

Mac's food came just then. He took a bite of the sandwich. "You haven't always been a prosecutor in Ramsey County, though, have you?"

"No. Just came over in the last couple of months. I was over in Minneapolis, with Hennepin County," Sally replied, taking a pull from her beer. "Thing was, I kept running into my ex over there. He tries a number of cases. Knows the judges. I knew the judges. Too many rumors going around. Then he started seeing another lawyer I saw all the time, and it got to be a bit much. Ramsey County had a position open, and here I am. But enough about me." Sally's voice went quiet. "Let's talk Mason Johnson."

"Okay. What happens when Senator Johnson comes in?"

"You mean *if* he comes in?" Kennedy responded.

"Oh, he'll be coming in. Question is, how he'll do it. Voluntarily or involuntarily."

"What makes you think he'll do it voluntarily?"

"If I was him, I'd want to get in front of this, especially if I'm innocent, which I'm sure he'll claim to be." Kennedy furrowed her brow. "You disagree?" Mac asked.

"I'm not sure. I see what you're saying. He'd look better if he came in to help." Kennedy took a drink. "Thing is, he may not know if we know about him. He might be thinking, 'Why implicate myself if the police don't know about me?'"

"If that's the case, he's gambling we didn't find Hernandez." Mac took a sip of his Guinness, looked out the window and continued, "But I see what you're saying. He's got to anticipate we'll find Hernandez. He's got to think that maybe a neighbor somewhere saw him. That maybe Claire told someone at the station about the relationship, if there was one. Sooner or later we'd get to him. So, why not come out front. My question is whether he'll seek legal counsel first. If so, how much will his lawyer get in the way?"

Kennedy smiled and nodded. "I'd be stunned if he didn't show up with legal counsel. Good legal counsel."

"Of course, Johnson's an attorney, isn't he? He might just show up himself."

Kennedy waved him off. "You know what they say, Mac. A lawyer who represents himself ..."

"... I know, I know. He has an idiot for a client." Mac chuckled, remembering the old maxim from law school.

It was Kennedy's turn to peer out the window. Then she said, "So how will you handle it if he comes in?"

"I haven't thought about it much—yet. I suppose it depends upon when and where. I know the chief's going to call either tonight or tomorrow. I won't know much until that happens." Mac finished his sandwich and wiped his fingers with his napkin. "Want another beer?"

"I was thinking about it, but it's getting late," Sally said, looking at her watch. "I should get home."

"Where's home?"

"I have a little place over in Highland Park. How about you?"

"I'm up on Summit. I have an apartment on the third floor of one of the old mansions, a couple houses south of the James J. Hill mansion."

"Wow. That's nice. How'd you swing that?" A hint of skepticism in her voice. Where did a detective get that kind of money?

"It actually doesn't cost me that much. Family friend. I help out in the summer, mow the grass, trim the hedges—that sort of thing. I look after the place in the winter. She's a snowbird. She charges me little rent. She doesn't need the money. Of course, I do, so it's a good deal." Mac actually was just fine financially, but he didn't want people to know that. They might start asking how a detective did so well, which was from a combination of factors, both the Grand Brew and the divorce. Mac had received all of the investments. Added to the McRyan Pub dividends and his salary, and he was living quite comfortably.

Getting back to business, he said, "I'll tell you one thing. I'd like to keep my little visit with the senator quiet until we nail this down."

"Press?"

With a sigh, "Yeah, I'm not a big fan of the media, especially television. And with Daniels being the victim, well, this is gonna get ugly."

"You know, Mac, I'm a hockey fan. I had Gopher student tickets when I was at the U and you were playing. You didn't seem to mind the media then."

"That was different. The sports guys weren't like the rest of the media. They like sports and for the most part knew something about it. They were mostly interested in the real story, especially when they were covering college." Mac took a last drink from his beer. "Besides, it wasn't like heads could roll because of them. But the media now?" Mac shook his head. "The newspaper guys are good. They usually take the time to get it right. I've always got time for them. Especially a couple of those old time scribes from the *Strib* or *Pioneer Press* that hang around the crime scenes. They're kind of fun to talk to."

"Guys who have been doing it for forty years?" Sally added.

"Yeah, exactly. But television? I don't know about them. It seems like it's all about entertainment, ratings, looks—less about real news.

You have to tell the story, say about our serial killer, in thirty-second sound bites," Mac said skeptically, shaking his head. "There's no way to do a good job that quickly, and we usually come out on the short end of the stick. And the thing that really burns me is that, with the exception of a couple of them, most don't know shit about police work."

"They don't know much about the law either," Kennedy added. "I agree with you, Mac, but they'll be a fact of life on this case."

Mac sighed, nodded his head and ran his hand through his thick, blond hair. "I'm afraid you're right. It'll be a circus if word about the senator gets out. I'm not looking forward to that."

Kennedy finished her beer, "You're right about that. Shall we?"

"Yup." As they both put on their coats, Mac looked back in the bar to wave good night and saw it immediately. Cops, seven or eight of them, had been watching him and Sally talk. He knew what they were thinking. He could see it in their eyes—Mac's going to get some. Mac shook his head at them and, with his back turned to Kennedy, mouthed, "Fuck you." They all just laughed. He turned to Kennedy, who hadn't noticed, "Where are you parked?"

"Just across the street," Kennedy nodded out the front window, "the Camry. You?"

"Out back. I'll walk you across the street. You never know."

She shared a warm smile. "Thanks."

They walked across the street in silence. Mac stopped about fifteen feet short of her car. She dug out her keys and continued to the driver's door. As she opened it, she looked back, flashed him a smile. "I suspect I'll be seeing a lot of you now?"

The smile, the comment, the way she said that—which could be taken a couple of ways, one of which made Mac's heart skip a little beat. He played it cool. "I suppose so."

Kennedy nodded, flashed him another smile, and got in her car. Mac turned and walked back across the street. He would be seeing a lot of her most likely and that wasn't an altogether bad thought. It had been the longest conversation he had with a woman since the divorce. As he was walking around to the back of the Pub, he looked in the front window through the MCRYAN'SPUB letters and saw his friends, laughing, waving their arms and giving him the look like he struck out. Mac chuckled. He imagined his couple of beers with Kennedy would be the talk of the town tomorrow. Cops—they loved the gossip. He thought about going back inside and trying to stop it before it started, but he knew better. He'd only make it worse.

~

Sally turned into her driveway, hit the garage door opener and pulled into her one-car garage. It was late, 11:30 p.m., but she smelled like a bar—smoky. She knew she couldn't sleep like that. She took a quick shower. The warm water felt good, and she instantly knew she would sleep better.

She got out of the shower, grabbed a towel, and dried her shoulder length hair. Looking at herself in the mirror, she liked what she saw. She was thirty-two and took good care of herself. The Stairmaster in the spare bedroom, used daily, helped. With no husband and a lot of extra time, she spent it on herself. Not that anyone could ever really tell when she was in her business suits, but that was the way she wanted it. The last thing she wanted to attract was another lawyer. But, she was starting to stir. The divorce would always be with her, but a lot of the pain was behind her now. She thought maybe she wanted to start seeing people, wanted to start dating. McRyan. She hadn't spent that much time talking with a man in months, at least a good-looking one, and he was that. Might have to try to get to know him a little better, she thought.

8

"WILL WE GRANT THEIR REQUEST?"

Mac pulled into the parking lot of the Cleveland Grille. Lich had suggested an early breakfast. The Cleveland was a greasy spoon if there ever was one. Breakfasts were fattening and the coffee thick. It had a classic seventies décor with vinyl booths, butt-ugly yellow-and-brown wallpaper, and a speckled tile floor. It was a total design disaster. It was also the best place in town to get breakfast. Mac loved the Cleveland Grille breakfast burrito. It was guaranteed to make lunch unnecessary.

When he walked in, Mac saw a couple of uniforms at the counter getting a cup of coffee to go. They nodded and smiled. Odd smiles?

Mac found Lich in a back corner booth, reading the *Pioneer Press* with a cup of coffee in front of him. "Mornin', Dick."

"Good morning to you." Lich looked up and smiled, a shit-eating grin. "So ... tell me ... how's Sally Kennedy?"

So that's why the odd smiles when he walked in. Mac rolled his eyes. "Christ, that didn't take long." He looked back to find the uniform cops laughing. Cripes.

"Word is you two talked for quite a while last night."

"Yeah, we talked, *about* the case."

"Riiiiiight."

"Whatever."

"Hey, don't get defensive." Lich took a sip of coffee. "I was glad to hear it. Get back on the horse, son. You can't sulk about your divorce forever. It's over and done with. Your ex was a bitch anyway," Lich reasoned. "I'm secure in my masculinity, so I can say this—you're a good-looking guy, Mac. Get out there and get yourself a little. Sally Kennedy? She's a damn fine-lookin' woman. Have at it."

"I need to stop *sulking*? You bitch about your divorce all the time."

"About the financial aspects, sure. The bitch cleaned me out. But I'm better off without her."

Just then their waitress appeared. She was a late forty-something named Dot. She wasn't the prettiest woman in the world, but her ample bosom flowed out of her top that was two sizes too small. She looked at Mac, and then gave a big smile to Lich. No wonder they were here.

"What can I get you, Detectives?" Dot asked.

Lich went first, "Dot, honey, I'll have my usual."

"And you, Detective?" Her smile remained but turned businesslike.

Dot, honey, I'll have my usual? Mac gave a long look at Lich and smiled, and then looked up to Dot. "I'll have a CG burrito, an orange juice, and a cup of coffee."

"Coming right up," Dot replied. She gave Lich another smile and walked away.

Mac didn't say anything right away. Instead he grabbed the sports section, checking out the latest on the Vikings. Dot came right back with the coffee and juice. Mac looked over his paper and saw Dot refill Lich's cup, giving him another very pointed smile and a, "Let me know if you need anything else?" It wasn't directed at Mac.

Mac kept reading for about another minute, then said, "So, ya seen her tits yet?"

Lich let out a rueful laugh, "Not yet, but rest assured, young man, I'm working on it."

Mac cackled. Maybe Lich was right. If at fifty-two, or whatever his age was, he was getting back after it, maybe he needed to as well.

They talked about the case a little, deciding what they were going to be doing for the day. The autopsy report would be ready. Then they would canvass the neighborhood some more and try to catch up with some people they missed. And, of course, they would find out what they were going to be doing about the senator.

Mac finished his breakfast and paid his tab. He left Lich behind so he could make some time with Dot.

Viper awoke at 8:00 a.m. refreshed. Eleven hours of sleep would do that for a person. The boss wanted him at his house by 10:00 a.m. to discuss the status of the Daniels matter as well as a few other things. He imagined the boss was working his contacts to see where the police were at with the case.

The drive out took forty minutes. Viper didn't mind. He owned a Corvette, and he was running out of days to drive it. Soon snow would fall, and Viper would have to break out his Land Rover.

The boss lived on Lake Minnetonka, twenty miles west of Minneapolis. Lake Minnetonka, or "The Lake" as residents who lived out that way called it, was prime home land for Minnesota's elite. The lakeshore held some of the most valuable real estate in the Twin Cities. The boss's house was on a three-acre, pie-shaped lot with three hundred feet of shoreline. The house was an impressive three-story mansion overlooking a tennis court, pool, and, of course, the lake. There was a long, winding driveway from the main road, which circled in front of the house. To the side of the house was an area for guest parking. Viper pulled the Vette into a guest spot and headed inside. A housekeeper took his coat and directed him up to the third-floor study.

The boss was on the phone. He waved Viper in and pointed towards a table containing refreshments and rolls. Viper poured himself a cup of coffee, grabbed a croissant, and walked over to the window. The office offered an impressive view, looking out over a large lawn to the lake. It was even more impressive in the summer when the boats were out. Now, everything was buttoned up for the coming winter.

He heard the phone hang up, and Viper turned to see the boss head towards the coffee table and pour himself a cup. "Come sit," he directed.

They engaged in idle chitchat for a few minutes, and then got down to business.

"So, what does your contact have to say?" Viper asked.

"Well, I have several contacts."

"Yes, sir, but you know what I mean." The boss liked it when Viper had to drag information out of him.

"My source confirms that they have zeroed in on the senator. They have Hernandez and a statement with the senator leaving around 1:30 a.m."

"Anything else?" Viper asked.

"Well, as luck would have it, a neighbor has also given a statement that a couple of nights before the murder he saw the senator leaving Ms. Daniels's place at a similar time, so that's a break for us, don't you think?"

"I do," said Viper, smiling. "Will the police be bringing in the senator?"

"Yes, but they want to keep it quiet," the boss replied, taking a long sip of his coffee.

"When?" Viper asked.

The boss nodded. "That's a good question. My source indicates they'll be contacting the senator soon to request that he come sit down with the detectives investigating the matter."

"Do we think he'll come in voluntarily?"

"I suspect so."

"Why?" Viper asked, not sure he agreed.

"He won't want to draw unnecessary media attention," the boss replied, buttering another croissant. "After all, he didn't do it. He's going to want to say that." He poured himself another cup of coffee. "He looks better if he comes in on his own. In fact, I wouldn't be surprised if he contacts them first."

Viper thought about that for a moment, seeing the boss's point. "If we assume they'll keep their interview with him quiet, they won't bring him downtown."

The boss agreed, "No, a meeting outside the Department of Public Safety Building would allow him to fly below the radar."

"The senator definitely doesn't want the media on this," Viper agreed.

The boss paused for a moment, "So, it would be rather unfortunate for him if the media were to find out about his involvement now, wouldn't it?"

Viper looked at the boss, catching his drift, "Yes, it would now, wouldn't it?"

Mac and Lich met with Linda Morgan. The autopsy determined that Daniels was strangled as they already knew. She also had sex prior to death. They had semen, which had been sent out for DNA testing. Then they would have to match it up. Mac and Lich suspected it belonged to the senator. The time of death remained between 1:00 and 2:00 a.m.

Forensics found no further evidence of forced entry, Morgan reported. The key under the front doormat had two good fingerprints, a thumb and index finger. The prints were not Daniels's. Crime Scene also found two sets of fingerprints in the bedroom. One set was Daniels's and the other set matched those on the key. The DA was still working on getting the senator's prints. Only Daniels's prints were found on the back door.

Mac was most concerned with the time-of-death issue. He'd seen it picked apart in court on more than one occasion.

"How solid are we on the time of death?" Mac asked.

"It looks good," Morgan answered. "We got to her fairly quickly after death. The conditions in her condo were good for preserving her body." Linda considered her answer further, "Is exact time of death important?"

"Maybe," Mac replied neutrally. They talked for a few more minutes, and then Lich and McRyan headed up for their meeting with the chief.

Chief Flanagan's secretary saw them coming and said, "Go on in, but he's on a call." The chief saw them walk in and waved them towards the couch, the phone still pressed to his ear. The leather chairs from in front of the desk had been moved over to the other side of the coffee table and were across from the couch. There was a pot of coffee and some Styrofoam coffee cups waiting for them. Lich poured himself a cup and one for Mac. Mac took his cup and walked around the table and sat down on the end of the couch. He mixed in some cream and sugar and stirred it with a pink straw. Just then, Helen Anderson and Sally Kennedy came in.

Sally passed on coffee, having brought a bottle of Aquafina with her. She sat down on the other end of the couch and greeted Mac. "Good morning, Detective."

"Mornin', Counselor."

It was Lich's turn to stifle a laugh and a grin. He could just hear Lich asking, "Seen her tits yet?" Not that Mac had tried, he barely knew Kennedy, although Lich's reprimand about getting back in the game had him suddenly thinking about her. Her red hair was up again, and she had the stylish glasses back. She looked good in a form-fitting gray plaid skirt suit, white silk blouse, and heels.

The chief hung up the phone and sauntered on over to the group, grabbing one of the leather chairs. His coat was already off, sleeves rolled up. He quickly poured himself a cup of coffee. "Peters should be here in a minute. We'll get started then."

The group engaged in some brief discussion about the upcoming Vikes game. Packer week would do that. Anderson, a Packer fan, was predicting a tough day for the Purple at Lambeau.

After a couple of minutes, Peters came in and quickly grabbed the last chair and poured a cup of coffee.

The chief looked at Mac, "So what's the scoop?"

Mac spent the next few minutes giving everyone the rundown on the autopsy report and discussions with forensics. The last topic discussed was the lack of any evidence of forced entry. It had everyone focusing on the senator.

"Well that last phone call was with Lyman Hisle," the chief stated. "Can anyone guess who his client might be?"

Mac smiled. He knew Lyman well, knew he didn't represent just anybody, "A certain US senator who just might be implicated in the death of a prominent local television reporter?"

"I see that U of M education didn't go to waste," Flanagan replied, smiling.

Sally jumped in, "So, what did he have to say?"

"Oh, that his client, the esteemed senior senator from the state of Minnesota, is guilty. So, in an effort to avoid inconveniencing anyone and wasting hard-earned tax dollars he was elected to protect, what would be the best time for him to turn himself in and save us all the time and effort of a lengthy drawn out jury trial?" Lich replied wryly, causing everyone to have a good laugh.

"No, Dick, although, Lord knows, we could use it," said the chief, still chuckling.

Anderson got everyone back on track. "So, what *did* he have to say?"

"He said his client had some information. That, since we might run across him as part of the investigation, he thought it'd be a good idea to get together," the chief replied.

"When?" asked Mac.

"They'd like to do it tomorrow afternoon, 1:00 p.m., at Lyman's house in Stillwater."

"Why out there?" asked Anderson.

"My guess," replied Sally, "is that he wants to keep a low profile. No media attention. If the senator shows down here at the Public Safety Building, the media'll see him and wonder why he's here."

"Seems to make sense," Peters piped in.

"Yeah, not to mention, if he's trying to keep it from his wife, better if it's not at a hotel, the airport, or even at this condo, where it might look odd if the police showed up to meet with him," said Mac.

"Exactly," said Flanagan.

"Will we grant their request?" Sally inquired.

"Yes," replied the chief. "We play this one close to the vest for now."

"Agreed," replied Anderson, surprising everyone. "We keep it quiet. We don't want to compromise the prosecution."

"Good," Flanagan replied. "We're all on the same page. Mac and Dick, I want you guys to work with Ms. Kennedy to prep for tomorrow's interview with the senator. She may give you some insight as to what Lyman will do. He's apt to have a trick or two up his sleeve, and we may only get one shot at the senator before Lyman intercedes and says, 'Prove it.' So let's be ready," Flanagan said sternly. "And I want the prep work done outside the building, preferably after hours. I don't want any attention drawn to this." Chief Flanagan looked at Anderson, "Helen, I assume that's okay with you?"

Anderson nodded her agreement. The chief continued, "You guys figure it out, but I don't want you seen meeting around here. People'll talk, think we have something solid. I told Hisle we'd keep the meeting quiet, at least for the time being. So, nobody in this room talks about this with the media or anyone else." Everyone nodded in agreement.

"Mac? Green and Clark—do they know about the senator?" the chief asked Mac.

"Yes. They interviewed the neighbor John Chase first."

"This comes from me—they don't talk."

"I'll convey that message, sir." Mac didn't need to worry about those two, and the chief knew it, but he was covering all the bases.

"Dick?"

With his hands up, Lich replied, "I know, I know."

"Okay then. You two and Ms. Kennedy here figure out what you're going to do. And, Mac, you and Lich let me or Peters know if anything develops today."

With that, the meeting ended. Mac, Lich, and Sally walked to the elevator.

"So, how do you guys want to do this?" Sally asked.

"My place is up on Summit, close to downtown," Mac said. "Let's all meet there at 7:00 p.m. I'll order pizza." Lich knew where Mac lived, but Kennedy needed directions.

"Sounds good," replied Kennedy, "I'll see you guys then."

Mac and Lich got off on the second floor, heading to their desks. Kennedy continued onto the main level. Her office at the Ramsey County Courthouse was a five-block walk away.

After they got off the elevator, Lich let out a disappointing sigh.

"What's up?" asked Mac.

"Tonight."

"What about it?"

"Well, I gotta date with Dot. You know, that waitress with the major-league cantaloupes."

Mac smiled, "Dicky boy, Dicky boy, what time?"

"Seven."

Mac thought for a moment. He wasn't even sure they really needed to meet with Sally yet, although she likely would have some insight on dealing with a shark like Lyman. The interview wouldn't be much different than any other, and Lich was actually pretty good on interviews. Lich didn't need to be there. "Look, we're going out to Hisle's place tomorrow afternoon, so we'll have time to talk in the morning, so go ahead."

"You sure?" asked Lich.

"Yeah, but I reserve the right to ask for details, at least about Dot. I can do without details about you."

Lich chuckled. "Thanks, man."

Mac took another look at Lich. He was wearing a brown suit, beat-up black lace-ups, and a faded yellow shirt with a brown-and-tan striped tie. It was not an impressive ensemble. "What're you wearing tonight?"

"Hell if I know."

"Promise me it's not what you have on now?"

"What's wrong with this?" Lich said, looking down at himself nonplused.

Mac rolled his eyes, shook his head, and kept walking, leaving Lich behind to examine his reflection in an office window.

9

"WILL HISLE LET HIS CLIENT TALK?"

L ich was getting anxious. He was nervously tapping his pen on the desk, checking his watch every thirty seconds. Mac took a look at his watch, 4:45 p.m. "So, Dick. What do you and Dot have planned?"

"We're meeting at the Grand Filet."

The Grand Filet was, naturally, on Grand Avenue, not far from Daniels's place. It was a small restaurant that would seem more in place two hours to the north of St. Paul. The Filet had a real North-woods feel, with cedar-planked walls and the best walleye in town. It was perfect for them.

"Sounds good."

"Yeah, the Filet, man. I've been looking forward to it all day."

Mac laughed and thought of Dot's rather impressive rack, "Dick, that is *not* the feast you've been thinking about all day."

Dick grinned. "Fuck you."

"Look, go ahead and bail. We're not accomplishing anything right now." They had been back for a half hour. In the morning they inter-viewed two people that Channel 6 station manager Mary Carpenter found for them. The two had individually threatened Daniels after investigative reports. Mac and Lich ran both men through the drill, but both had good alibis. Neither felt right. After the interviews, the two detectives spent the rest of the afternoon on follow-up canvassing the neighborhood around Daniels's place. It was fruitless. Neighbors hadn't seen anything on the night of the murder or anything unusual in the days leading up to it. A few people still weren't home, and Mac left his card behind with a request that they contact him. The one big piece of news from the day was that the district attorney's office obtained the senator's prints, which had now been matched to the key.

"Have fun with Dot."

Lich gave him a knowing smile, stood up, put on his coat, and headed out with a distinct spring in his step.

Mac smiled to think that Lich looked forward to a date at his age. Good for him. Well, if Lich wasn't coming tonight, he'd better let Kennedy know. He picked up the phone, dialed, and heard, "Hello, you've reached the voice mail of Sally Kennedy. I'm either on my phone or away from my desk ..." He hit POUND and left her a message. It was 5:00 p.m., enough time to get a workout in before getting home to meet with Sally.

~

Sally pecked away at a motion on her computer, a light-rock station playing quietly in the background. She wanted to polish the motion a bit more before finishing. It would be ready to file in the morning. She took a sip of her Diet Pepsi, when there was a knock on the door and she turned to find Helen standing in her doorway. Sally hit the DND on her phone, and Helen shut the door.

"So, with Johnson's prints, he's the prime suspect in the Daniels case, don't you think?"

"I do."

"Are you all set with McRyan and Lich tonight?

"Yes."

"What do you think of them?" asked Anderson, a touch of skepticism in her voice.

Sally gave it some thought before responding. "I don't know yet. Lich's been around, although it sounds as if he'll occasionally talk out of school to the media."

"What about McRyan?" Helen pushed.

"I haven't seen him in action. The chief and Peters obviously think highly of him. I sense you have your doubts?"

"He strikes me as a lightweight," Anderson replied. "I want you to call me tonight after you're done to let me know. I can always press Charlie to make a change."

Sally had to stifle a laugh. Helen Anderson would have absolutely no ability whatsoever to get Chief Charles Flanagan to change a detective on a case. Sally had seen first hand in the past two days—Flanagan ran his department *his* way, politics be damned. She rather liked it, too—doing the right thing as opposed to the politically expedient one. If the chief thought McRyan was right for the case, so be it. Nonetheless, she needed to keep her boss informed. "I assume I can reach you at home tonight."

"No," Helen answered. "Call me on my cell."

"What, a hot date?"

"No," Anderson replied coolly. "Fundraiser."

Mac was late. He'd stopped for a workout at a buddy's gym. He finished by 6:30 p.m., but then his buddy, Joe Ball, went into his stand-up routine. Joe was a classic, ten jokes at the drop of a hat. Mac couldn't tell a joke to save his life. Joe's stand-up routine caused Mac to lose track of time and suddenly it was 6:50. Mac rushed out of the club, got in the Explorer, and raced for his place. He pulled in right at 7:00 p.m. and ran up to his third-floor apartment. He got in and threw his gym bag in the spare bedroom when the doorbell rang. Sally.

Mac hit the buzzer to let her up. He needed to take a quick shower. But first he ran into the kitchen to grab a couple of beers, Grain Belts. As he was walking back in with the beers, there was a knock on the door. He opened it up. *Whoa.*

Since Lich was not going to be at the meeting, Sally had decided a quick shower and a change of clothes would be in order. She was attracted to McRyan and thought maybe it was time he saw her in something a little different than her business suits.

After her shower, she took a look in her closet and tried on a few different ensembles, settling on a pair of tight tan suede pants and a body-forming white-ribbed turtleneck. The outfit would allow appreciation of her figure. She let her fiery red hair down to its regular shoulder length, and put a little curl in it so it fell just over her right eye. Leaving her glasses behind, she popped in her contacts. The outfit was completed with some silver hoop earrings, soft red lipstick, and makeup, a bit more than she normally put on. Her mirror confirmed it—she looked good.

McRyan apparently thought so as well.

Mac's heart skipped a beat, and he did a double take. He almost didn't recognize her. She looked fantastic. "Come in," he said, trying to be cool.

Sally gave him a little smile and walked by him and took off her coat. Mac finally remembered to speak. "I'm sorry. I went to work out. I just got home. I need to hop in the shower quick."

"No problem," replied Sally.

"Before I do that, I should order. Pizza okay?"

"Yeah, great."

Mac asked, "Pepperoni, sausage, mushrooms, what do you like?"

"I love garbage pizzas."

Mac grinned. A woman after his own heart. "I'm on it. By the way, I grabbed a couple of Grain Belts out of the fridge."

"Great. I could use a beer."

"I'm ... ah ... going to hit the shower," he waved his arm around his apartment. "What's mine is yours."

~

Sally walked around while Mac showered. She was pleased her outfit seemed to have the desired effect. Of course, this was a strictly professional meeting, and they needed to prepare for the senator. Nonetheless, she was having some fun again.

Mac had the whole third floor of the Summit Avenue mansion. It was a large space. She was a bit surprised that it was tastefully appointed with a large black leather couch with a matching love seat and two chairs. A big, weathered, antique trunk served as the coffee table. She perused a bookshelf. He had a collection of mystery and military thrillers and was obviously a fan of John Sandford and Vince Flynn. Next to the bookshelf were two large, framed, autographed posters. One was of Kirby Puckett, pumping his fist, having just hit the winning homer in the eleventh inning of Game Six of the 1991 World Series. The other was Bruce Springsteen, the best ever.

At the end of the living room on the right was the kitchen. It was small, had an old gas stove, a small fridge and microwave, but not much else. There was barely room for the sink and cupboards. What caught her attention, however, was the door out to a small deck.

The deck made whatever Mac was paying for the place worth it. The view was panoramic. To the right she had a view over the Mississippi River and the High Bridge. Straight ahead was downtown St. Paul, a perfect view of the skyline, as well as the Xcel Energy Center and Science Museum. To the left was the State Capitol, brightly lit. She imagined McRyan spent summer nights sitting on the deck, having a beer and surveying the city.

She could still hear the water running when she walked back in and sat down on the couch and started thumbing through a *Sports Illustrated*.

~

Mac took a quick shower, put on a pair of jeans, and threw on a black mock turtleneck. Sally had stunned him. She was not unattractive at work. In talking with her at the Pub the night before, he realized that underneath the professional veneer was a very attractive woman. But it was clear how much she dressed professionally and was all business while at work.

He stopped in his office and grabbed his notepad and then walked back out into the living room to find Sally sitting on the black leather couch. Mac grabbed his beer and sat down in one of the black leather chairs. "Pizza should be here in a few. Should we get started?"

"Yeah. Other than Senator Johnson's prints, anything new today?"

"No." Mac mentioned that the remaining neighbors didn't see anything, and that the few people who'd threatened Daniels because of her work did not look good.

"Anyone else you haven't talked to?"

"A few people in Daniels's neighborhood haven't been home when we've knocked. They might be out of town. I left my card. I'm sure we'll hear from them eventually, although at this point, I'd be stunned if anything came from it."

"So, it looks like the senator's the guy?"

"Looks that way," replied Mac, grabbing his notepad and pen. "So, when we meet with the senator tomorrow, do you think Hisle will let him talk?"

Just as Sally opened her mouth to answer, the doorbell buzzed.

The pizza was a Classic Supreme with everything on it but anchovies and black olives from Classic Italian Pizza. Mac grabbed a cutting board from the kitchen on which to set the pizza. Plates, forks, and napkins were grabbed as well, along with two more beers. The spicy aroma of hot pizza made both of them realize it was getting late and they hadn't eaten. The pizza didn't stand a chance. Once it was devoured, they got back to business.

Mac started pretty much where they left off. "So, when we meet Johnson tomorrow, do you think he'll talk or be a mute?"

That was the $50,000 question. Would Hisle let his client talk? "Were this a run-of-the-mill murder case, probably not," Sally said.

"But this isn't your run-of-the-mill murder case, is it?"

Shaking her head, "No, it's not."

Mac took a pull from his beer, leaned back in his chair and looked at the ceiling. "So, in this case, you think he'll talk?"

"Some." She said this thoughtfully.

He lowered his head and looked straight at her, "How much is some?"

"Part of that will depend on what he, meaning Hisle, knows about the case."

"Meaning, how much the good senator has told him about it," replied Mac, following Sally's train of thought.

"Exactly. I bet I've spoken to a hundred defense attorneys who have told me their client didn't tell them everything. I'm not sure why the senator would be different." Sally took a last drink from her beer.

"Want another?"

"Sure."

Mac got up to get her a beer but didn't stop talking, speaking from the kitchen. He merely spoke a little louder to cross the distance. "So, if I'm hearing you right, what we get tomorrow will depend upon what Hisle knows about the case, and that's probably based on what Johnson has told him?"

"Not necessarily."

"'Not necessarily'? What do you mean?" Mac asked as he came back in and handed her the beer.

"Well, Hisle might get some of his own information. I bet he or one of his lackeys have been working the department for information."

"That would be Lyman," Mac replied, nodding. "He has friends in our department who could feel like they might owe him."

"Why's that?" asked Sally, not understanding his point.

"Lyman's big time, right?"

"Yes."

"But he's also represented a number of cops over the years. He may be a defense attorney, and cops hate most of them, but not Lyman. He's helped out a lot of police, and he hasn't always charged his full fee."

"So ... do you think any cops will talk?"

"If any of them knew anything they might. But to the best of my knowledge Lich, Clark, and Green haven't needed to use Lyman for anything."

"What about the chief?"

"Well, Flanagan knows Hisle pretty well. They're friends. But I don't think he'd give Lyman dick."

Sally smiled. "Well I'd hope not. But what about information?"

Mac snorted. "Touché, Counselor." Mac took a hit from his beer. "Let's assume for the sake of argument that Hisle knows everything we know, or even what we suspect. Everything. The semen, time of death, no forced entry—the whole nine yards."

"All right."

"Assuming all that," Mac continued, "will Hisle let his client talk?"

Sally thought for a minute. "Some."

Mac smirked. "Typical lawyer, won't answer the damned question. I know you think 'some,' but how much? What's he going to tell his client to do?"

"He'll probably allow the senator to answer questions about how he met Daniels and the nature of their relationship. He'll probably allow him to admit they had sex because he'll know we'll probably match semen through DNA. He can't be certain who she might have told about the relationship, so he'll probably answer those questions."

"How about, 'Have you told your wife about your affair with Daniels?'"

"You should ask that question, but Hisle will tell him not to answer. That goes right to guilt and motive. Remember our theory the other day?"

"That Daniels pressured him about his marriage, about a possible divorce, and maybe she didn't like the answer."

"Exactly," replied Sally. "That would be motive right there. I'd be stunned if Hisle allowed Johnson to answer anything near that. He'll say it's irrelevant and all that shit, even though it is." She picked up her beer. "The only way I could see Hisle allowing him to answer that question is if the senator told his wife he was having an affair and she didn't care or something like that. I can't imagine Gwen Johnson going for that."

"No," Mac replied nodding. "From what I've seen, she doesn't seem like the type to put up with that. Plus, she wouldn't have to testify on that point anyway, would she?" Mac asked.

"That's right. Marital privilege."

"Anything else Hisle won't let him answer?"

"You guys might go down the path of encouraging the senator to come clean, basically cop a plea. It wasn't intentional. It was a heat of passion type situation—the manslaughter path." She took another drag of her beer, "However, if you get to that point, Hisle won't allow him to answer. He'll shut him down. We'll have to charge him before he entertains that. Again, that's if the interview goes that way."

Mac sat thinking for a minute, running this all through his head. "Okay. I've got a good feel for what happens if Hisle has all the info he needs. But what if he doesn't? What if he's flying blind?"

"Hisle wouldn't fly blind. If he were *that* blind, he wouldn't have called the chief."

"Maybe he's not completely blind, then. The senator'll have given him *some* information. But you said it yourself—Hisle's probably calling around the department, but he can't get any information."

"You're assuming he hasn't gotten any," she replied.

"True." Mac leaned forward in his chair. "But let's assume he doesn't."

"Then, he won't let his client answer any questions until you tell him what you have."

"I don't have a problem with that. I'd be happy to tell them," Mac quickly replied. "What will Hisle do then?"

"At that point, he'll decide whether his client has anything to say." Sally looked away for a moment, and then continued. "He'll ask for some time to confer with his client."

"And then they'll decide if he'll answer any questions."

"Right."

"And if he doesn't say anything?"

"Then we'll decide what to do. Charge him, continue to investigate, whatever. You can give them the standard line that this is his chance to get in front of this, but Hisle will tell him not to answer. If so, we'll just have to see ..."

"But ... we'll know a lot more after tomorrow," said Mac, finishing the thought.

"Yes."

Lyman and the senator enjoyed a fine meal of steak, potatoes, Caesar salad, and red wine at Lyman's house on the St. Croix. Following dinner they retired to the library to have a brandy, a cigar, and talk about the case.

"So, how do we handle this tomorrow?" the senator asked.

"We'll have to find out where they're coming from, Mason."

"What if they won't tell us?"

"Don't worry about that. They will. They want you to talk. Like I said, when I called Flanagan, he was getting ready to call you."

A frown came down the senator's face, "If I read between the lines here, they have me in their crosshairs."

"Perhaps," mused Lyman. "But they haven't charged you. They haven't put your name out there. Heck, my contacts in the department don't even know who they have for a suspect."

The senator was skeptical. "These contacts, would they even tell you if they knew?"

"The people I've called, yes. They owe me for previous services rendered."

The senator took a sip of his brandy. "So, if we find out what they have, what do I say?"

"We'll see. I may not have you answer questions at all."

"Lyman," he growled, "I can't do that. I do that and I'm done. I'm Gary Condit. The media'll have a field day."

Lyman knew his friend. He was concerned about his career. He didn't necessarily see beyond that, and that had to change if Lyman was going to help him. "Mason, I'll do what I can to protect your career. But we have to see what they have."

The senator had a panicked look. "What? What the fuck are you saying, Lyman? What, you ... you think I did this?"

"NO!" snapped Lyman. The next part would be difficult, he knew, so he took a long drink, a slow drag on his cigar, and walked towards his friend and put a hand on his shoulder. He exhaled slowly and spoke. "Mason, I'm with you, but we have to see what the police have. You didn't do it. I believe you," Lyman said, looking him right in the eye. "But look at the evidence they likely have. You *were* there that night. We have to assume they have the guy who saw you. Otherwise, how do they link you?"

"Yes, I was there. What does that prove, Lyman?" the senator growled, taking a chair.

Lyman sat down next to his friend and continued. "In and of itself, nothing, but they'll have your semen. It wouldn't even be worth a fight on the DNA. They'll get it." Lyman took a drink. "Now, like I said—in and of itself that means nothing, but ..."

"But what *would* mean something?"

"Time of death, forced entry, and if there was a robbery. If there's a robbery or forced entry, and time of death is 4:00 a.m., you're in the clear. You merely help them with their timeline. If this is the case, then the police say thanks, and nobody ever knows you were involved."

Mason Johnson looked hopeful for the first time. Lyman reassured him, "Your name came up. They have to talk to you. Simple as that. But if the evidence doesn't point to you, you'll be fine."

The senator sighed and nodded. "Look. I didn't do it. I need to say that."

"And I may let you. But first, we need to see what they have."

Mac and Sally finished up with how to deal with Hisle and the senator around ten. Mac offered one more beer, and Sally accepted. She was easy to talk to. They talked about sports, politics, and lawyers. They had similar interests. They were both career focused. She wasn't stopping at assistant district attorney. She had higher aspirations.

Mac could feel his attraction to her growing. He hadn't felt this way in a long time, and it was a nice change. He had ignored women since the divorce. It wasn't that there couldn't have been some. There had been plenty he could have taken home from the Pub. More than one had sauntered on up to make a pass at him, and he almost took a couple up on it. Sooner or later, he figured he'd finally break down and do it. But it never seemed right.

Sally was interested. She was attractive as hell, with pretty dark-brown eyes and a bright smile. She was intelligent and liked to laugh, yet she had a little edge, some street to her—which he liked.

She'd been checking out the Springsteen print all night. "So how'd you get Bruce to sign it?"

"You like the Boss?"

"Is there anyone better?"

"No. I've never seen a better live performer."

She got up to look at it more closely. "So, how did you do it?"

"A buddy of mine, Wren Frane, runs the non-hockey events at the Xcel Energy Center. He got me backstage for the second half of a concert. It was pretty unreal. I saw Bruce, Clarence, Little Steven come off the stage, and it was cool just to see them. Anyway, the arena had emptied, and Wren and I were the only ones left backstage. We're just talking, concert's been over for an hour, and here comes Springsteen out of the dressing room, looking to see if they can get a few more beers. Most everyone's gone, but Wren scares up some brews, and the Boss says thanks. He sees the poster and asks if I wanted it signed."

"No way!" Sally replied in disbelief.

"Oh, yeah. Pure luck, but I met the man."

They transitioned to Helen Anderson. "She can't be easy to work for," Mac said.

"That's somewhat true. She's demanding of everyone's time and efforts. But at the same time, she generally lets you do your job."

"Probably because she never did it herself," Mac intoned.

"Well, there might be some truth to that," Sally replied, smiling. "She's more a politician than a lawyer."

Then they got to Lich. "By the way, where's your partner?"

Mac chuckled, "Dickey boy is on a date with Dot."

"Who's Dot? Should I know her?"

Mac shook his head. "No. I just met her this morning. She's a rather, shall we say, buxom waitress at the Cleveland Grille."

"Ahhh. So, your partner's on the dating scene, huh?"

"That he is. I have to give him credit. His last wife absolutely cleaned him out." Mac just shook his head.

Sally looked around the apartment. "It would appear you didn't get cleaned out?"

"We parted amicably." Mac didn't want to talk about his divorce. He caught his ex-wife having an affair with a married partner in her law firm. Mac threatened to expose the affair unless he got the better of the marital assets, which he had. To change the topic, he got up, picked up their empties, and asked, "One more?"

Sally looked at her watch, 11:30 p.m. "I'd like to, but it's late."

Mac looked at his watch. He'd lost track of time, "Geez. You're right."

They walked to the door, and Mac grabbed her coat, helping her put it on. She said, "Thanks."

"I'll walk you down."

As they were walking down the stairs, Sally said, "So, you're ready for tomorrow?"

"Yeah," Mac replied enthusiastically.

Sally picked up on it. "You're looking forward to it, aren't you?"

Mac looked at her. "You're surprised by that?"

"It's a murder case. Yeah, a little."

"Tomorrow's why you do this job. Cases like this don't come along too often. I probably won't sleep much tonight. But, yeah, as morbid as it sounds, I can't wait. I can just feel the adrenaline flowing."

They were at her car. Mac stayed back a few feet. She reached in her purse for her keys and opened her car door before looking back. They stood awkwardly, staring at each other for a moment.

Mac finally spoke. "So, I'll talk to you tomorrow?"

"Yeah. Let me know how it goes."

"I will."

He held back. It didn't feel right yet. Sally smiled at him and got in the car and started the engine. Before she closed her door, she said, "Good luck tomorrow, I'll be thinking of you." She closed the door and backed away from him, turned, gave him a wave, and drove off.

10

"GOOD COP. BAD COP."

Mac, along with Lich and Captain Peters, climbed into Mac's Explorer, headed out of the Department of Public Safety ramp and worked their way quickly to Interstate 35E, driving north out of downtown St. Paul on their way out to Hisle's place in Stillwater.

The morning had been a blur, spent in a number of meetings. It started with a meeting with Captain Peters, which then moved to the chief's office for his daily briefing. Sylvia Miller sat in on that one to discuss what to do if the media showed.

Before they left for Stillwater, Mac finally had time to meet with Lich about last night's meeting with Sally. They discussed her theories about how Hisle might handle their interview with the senator. Lich snorted, "In other words, she acted like a typical lawyer and didn't really answer your question."

Mac had to chuckle. Given his divorce terms, Lich had caskets of animosity stored up for attorneys. "She was a little evasive. Yes, but that's because we don't know what Hisle's going to do anymore than he knows what we'll do."

"So," Lich said, grinning, "how evasive was she?"

"Evasive?"

"Listen, son, you put the wood to her or what?"

"Jesus," said Mac, giving Lich a disbelieving look.

"Sheesh, you really are out of practice."

"Well, how'd you do with Dot?"

"A hell of a lot better than you did," Lich said with a big shit-eating grin.

Mac winced, suddenly developing a bad mental picture of bald old Lich and big-breasted Dot flopping around. "Spare me the details."

Mac exited 35E, onto Highway 36 for the drive east to Stillwater. The drive would have been a lot prettier three weeks earlier when the leaves were orange, red, and yellow at the peak of the fall colors. Now, the ride out towards Stillwater was strewn with leaves blowing across the highway, the trees barren, waiting for the coming cold and snow of a Minnesota winter.

Stillwater, a burgeoning suburb twenty miles east of St. Paul, was located on the St. Croix River, which also served as the border between Minnesota and Wisconsin. Up on top of the bluff over-looking the St. Croix was "new" Stillwater, with big-box retailers and various other suburban amenities. The amenities were surrounded by suburban homes with large yards and three-car garages. The part of Stillwater sitting two hundred feet below the bluff and right on the St. Croix was the quaint old downtown. A lumber town, Stillwater had morphed into an elegant tourist trap of old red-brick and stone buildings full of little antique stores, restaurants, and marinas for river boats.

Lyman lived just north of Stillwater, with a place on a little cliff overlooking the river. Once off the road, Mac took a long driveway that might have been a hundred yards long that circled in front of the house. The house itself was a sprawling prairie-style rambler, the back of which overlooked the river. Lyman undoubtedly had a groundskeeper of some sort in the summer, as there were flower beds and trimmed bushes appropriately scattered over the grounds. The flowers were now in hibernation, but the bushes were all in well-trimmed condition, rounded and squared appropriately. It was impressive.

"Representing criminals pays, don't it, Mac?" Lich commented.

"Yeah, but Lyman's a good guy."

"Maybe I should have hired him for my divorce."

They dropped the Explorer just past the front door. As they approached the house, Lich asked Mac, "Just thought I'd ask, you know, so we're prepared and all, how are you going to handle this?"

"My guess is the senator isn't going to be so impressed with a young buck detective running things. If so, you look at me when we start, my look will let you know. Let's play on that and see if we can't get him riled up."

"Good cop, bad cop?" Lich said.

"Exactly."

Lich smiled and moved to push the doorbell. Before he could, Hisle opened the door. "Good afternoon, Detectives. Please come in."

They entered into a large open foyer. "I thought we'd head into the library," Lyman said, pointing down a hallway to their right.

The library was exactly that. There were windows that looked out over the river. The rest of the walls were built-in bookshelves, with an impressive collection of works. Mac saw an old collection of Charles Dickens tales. There were a few shelves with old legal treatises. Lyman also liked more modern fare, with many bestsellers.

In the middle of the library was a long conference table with four high-backed leather chairs on either side and one on each end. The floor was wood, but a large Persian rug sat in the center under the conference table. As they entered the library, Mason Johnson stood looking out the window. Casually dressed in tan slacks, he also wore a navy blue sweater and white button-down collar shirt. Handshakes were exchanged, coffee poured, and they moved to the conference table. Johnson shook Mac's hand, held it briefly, gave him a long look and smirked just slightly as they sat down. Inside, Mac smiled. *So, the senator isn't exactly impressed with me.* Mac sat down next to Lich, smiled slightly, and nodded. *Let's go with the game plan.*

Lyman opened. "Marion, how should we proceed?"

"It's McRyan's case," Peters said, nodding towards Mac.

Lyman looked at Mac and asked, "Well?"

Mac, pleasant to start, said, "I appreciate your and the senator's willingness to meet with us. We were hoping the senator might be able to clear up a few things for us."

"Like what, Michael?" Lyman asked.

"For example, was he at Ms. Daniels's place the night she was killed?"

The senator looked at Lyman, who nodded. "You know I was."

"What time did you leave?" Mac asked.

"Around 1:30 a.m."

"Why were you there?"

"I was seeing Claire."

"Describe 'seeing,' senator," Lich asked.

"Claire and I were ... involved," Senator Johnson responded evasively.

"In other words, you were having sex with her," Mac said bluntly. It was a statement, not a question, intended to push.

"Yes," Johnson replied tersely.

"Did you use a condom?"

"No." That made DNA less of an issue.

"How long had you and Ms. Daniels been sleeping together?" Mac asked.

"A couple of months."

"How did you meet?" Lich inquired pleasantly. The senator spent fifteen minutes detailing his relationship with Daniels, where they had met, and how the relationship had grown over time.

Mac thought about asking whether the senator's wife knew about Daniels, but because Sally had said Hisle would likely shut that down, he decided to wait. Instead, he asked, "Were you there two nights before Claire was killed?"

"Yes, I was."

Mac, gratuitously, trying to push just a little, "Getting a little action that night as well?"

"I'm not sure it's any of your business," the senator replied sharply. Lyman grabbed his arm. Mac smiled. The senator didn't like him.

Lich, good cop, jumped in all calm and respectful, "What time did you leave that night?"

"Similar time, around 1:30 a.m."

"I was wondering ... how did you get in the last night at Daniels's place?" Lich asked.

"Claire let me in."

Lich, conversational, "Was that always the case? How about the other nights, how did you get in those times?"

"Claire would let me in or I'd use a key she left under the front doormat."

The senator relaxed a bit, so Mac decided to push a little again, "How'd Claire like it?"

Senator Johnson stared at him. "Like what?"

"Having sex. A little rough perhaps? Kinky?" Mac asked.

"What's that got to do with anything?" Johnson growled.

Lyman jumped in. "My client isn't going to answer that."

"Fine, Lyman," Mac replied, then turned back to the senator. "Ms. Daniels seeing anyone else besides you?"

"No."

"No?"

"No. Only me."

"How can you be so sure? Did you ever ask her if she was sleeping around?"

"Yes, I did. She said I was it. I had no reason to doubt her."

"She tell anyone she was sleeping with you?"

"No. She understood that it had to be kept quiet."

That comported with what they'd learned about Daniels. Nonetheless, Mac kept the heat on, pushing, digging. "Yeah, because if word gets out about this, that could play havoc with your political career and the little missus at home." Again, it was a statement more than a question. The senator glared at Mac but didn't respond.

Lich, good cop, stepped in. "Did Daniels ever mention any problems she had with her neighbors, ex-boyfriends, people she reported on or with, anyone prowling around her place?"

The senator, turning away from Mac and towards Lich, replied, "Not that I recall."

"You ever see anyone hanging around that didn't look right? Anyone suspicious? Weird?"

"No, not at all."

Mac took over. "And the night Daniels was killed, you left at 1:30 a.m."

"Yes."

"Anyone know you were at Claire's that night?"

"No."

They worked the facts for another half hour, working through the details, time of arrival, how the senator entered, the nature of the relationship, time of departure. Senator Johnson held tightly to his story, finishing with, "Like I said, I left at 1:30 a.m. and went home to my condo downtown."

Mac paused, folded his arms, and stared at the senator for a moment. He had been there that night, admitted leaving at the right time, and didn't force his way in; they'd cemented everything, including his departure at the time of death. So, how did Daniels die? Time to ask. "Senator, I have a feeling you're not telling me everything."

"What?" the senator snapped, disbelieving.

"You're not telling me everything. You're leaving things out."

"Listen, Detective, when I left Claire's place, she was alive."

"I don't think so," Mac replied, arms folded, rocking in his chair, a smirk on his face.

"Maybe I wasn't clear, Detective McRyan," Senator Johnson replied angrily. "She was alive when I left her place. I'm here to help you guys, and now you call me a liar." He looked at Peters and pointed towards Mac. "This is the guy you have running the case?" Mac smiled inwardly.

Lyman put his arm in front of his client, and spoke to Peters. "Look, the senator is concerned because his friend was found murdered. He came here in good faith, to help you out. He's been cooperative." Pointing towards Mac, he continued, "McRyan is out of line, and if he continues in this fashion, we will be done here."

"Sorry, Lyman," Mac replied flatly. "But before you try to pull the plug, let me tell you what we've detected thus far." Mac flipped his notebook back a few pages. "Daniels was found dead Tuesday morning in her bed by her housekeeper. Her windpipe was crushed. There was extensive bruising around her throat. Someone got on top of her, straddled her, and pressed down on her throat like this," Mac put his hands out in front of him, thumbs pointing up, demonstrating the grip.

He took a sip of his coffee, pausing for effect, and then lowered the hammer. "Time of death, confirmed by autopsy, occurred between 1:00 and 2:00 a.m." Mac looked directly at the senator, who sat back in his chair at the comment on time of death, his eyes going wide, a look of horror replacing the one of derision. Mac expected more of a worried look and wasn't quite sure what to make of this. He hesitated for a moment, then continued. "She'd had sex the night she was murdered. We have a single male semen specimen of which we will be doing DNA testing. It undoubtedly belongs to you, Senator."

Mac stopped briefly, took another hit of his coffee, and while looking at his notes, continued, "We have no evidence of forced entry into her home. We have no evidence of robbery. Nothing is missing. The house wasn't ransacked or disrupted in any way. The house-keeper confirms that. Whoever killed her had a key or was let in." Mac paused, waiting.

A barely audible, "Oh, my God," escaped the senator's lips. Mac noticed the look of horror replaced with disbelief.

Lyman lightly grabbed Johnson by the arm, and quietly asked, "Anything else?"

"That's what we have," Mac replied, then looking squarely at the senator, ticking off his fingers. "I have you leaving her place at the time of death. I have your prints and will get your DNA. I have no evidence of forced entry or robbery, but you had easy access. I have a murder victim dying a violent death, strangled by someone of obvious strength. I have you, tall, strong, and physically capable." Then back to Lyman, "I'll agree with you, the senator's been cooperative. The only thing he hasn't confirmed is that he killed Claire Daniels, but the evidence says he did." Mac folded his arms and sat back in his chair, "So, at this point it would seem that Senator Johnson might want to think about helping himself, not us."

The senator, flushed, glaring at Mac, growled, "I don't fucking believe this."

"Believe it," replied Mac flippantly, pushing, pouring gas on the fire.

"Mason, quiet," Lyman ordered in a sharp voice.

Mac smelled blood, pressed, leaning across the table, getting as close as he could without leaving his chair, a little extra gravel in his voice. "I've got you leaving her place around the time of death. I have prints all over the place—yours. I've got semen—yours. You killed her, Senator. Fess up."

With the senator looking as if he was going to jump across the table after Mac, Lich jumped in, putting his arm in front of Mac and pulling him back. With a calm, smooth, respectful voice, he said, "Look, you'll have to excuse my partner here. He could stand to dial it back a little." Lich shared a knowing look with Mac. Then, conversationally to the senator, "But, the point he's so indelicately trying to make is that this is an unfortunate situation. If it was an accident, now's the time to get out in front of it and give us your side of the story."

Lyman tried to stop him, but the senator, raging, was not to be controlled now. He plowed right through. "What side? Seems like you guys, especially your little prick partner here, have pretty much already decided what happened."

Lich, in his even tone, said, "Senator, tell us what happened Monday night?"

As the senator opened his mouth, Lyman both ordered and pleaded with his client, "Don't answer that, Mason."

Senator Johnson was having none of it. "Nothing. She was alive when I left. I got there just after 11:00 p.m. and left at 1:30 a.m. She was alive when I left. I had not one thing to do with Claire's death."

"Well, Senator," Lich said, his arms spread out, leaning back in his chair, "given what we've found thus far, we have good reason to suspect that you did kill Ms. Daniels."

Lyman grabbed the senator's arm firmly and, with a sharp biting voice, said, "Don't respond to that."

Senator Johnson had already opened his mouth, but he listened. He sat back in his chair, calming some.

Mac stirred the pot again. "Your wife know you were fucking Daniels?"

"Michael!" growled Lyman.

"You arrogant little fuck," replied the senator.

"I'll take that as a no," smirked Mac, adding, "There's motive right there, along with everything else."

Lich, back in the old calm pro, said, "Look, Senator, the question really is, did your wife know about your relationship with Daniels?"

"Mason, you will *not* answer that question," ordered Hisle.

Lich kept going, talking over Hisle, "Say she doesn't know, maybe the more relevant question is, did Claire ask about it?"

The senator leaned forward, wanted to answer, about to answer, but Hisle stopped him, "Don't."

"That's okay," Lich continued conversationally. "But what we were wondering is if perhaps Claire started putting on some pressure, for a divorce or something like that?"

"Or, better," Mac, combative, interjected, "if you don't tell your wife, maybe she will. Claire's sick and tired of being your bed sheet. So, she puts the wood back to you: tell your wife or she will." His voice rising, "Now as these things go, that's not good for a husband cheating on his wife. All you want is a little something on the side, especially something as hot as Claire Daniels. But you can't have that little something stirring up problems at home. It wouldn't be good for the political career." Mac pointed at the senator. "And we've seen time and again how that political career, that power, that ambition outweighs everything else."

Lich back in, calm. "So, you two naturally start to argue. But it escalates. It gets physical. It goes too far and, before you know it …" And then quietly, "You didn't mean for it to happen, Senator. It was an accident."

Captain Peters, having admired the performance of his two detectives, spoke directly to Hisle, "Manslaughter. Work with us and the district attorney will go that direction."

The senator rolled his eyes. "Helen Anderson? I bet she'd sign off on this and file for my office the next day."

"Mason, enough," growled Lyman, obviously upset with his client. To the detectives, "You will excuse us."

With that, Mac, Lich, and Peters headed out of the library and stepped outside.

Lyman and Senator Johnson headed downstairs to his game room. The senator was about to speak, but Lyman waved him off. This conversation would require some courage. He went to the bar, grabbed two glasses and put them up on the counter. He snagged the bottle of Wild Turkey off the back shelf and poured each glass a quarter full, shots. The senator sat down on a barstool, grabbed his glass, and knocked it back. Lyman did the same. Lyman looked at his glass and thought for a moment, another one? He decided the better of it. "Mason, we have issues here."

"I'm sorry, Lyman. I spoke too much, but that little punk—"

"Did a number on you. And so did his partner."

The senator jumped back in his barstool, thought for a moment, cognizance dawning. He nodded. "Yeah, they did." He lifted his glass and Lyman poured him another small drink. He slammed it. "What do we do now?"

Lyman gave his friend another long look. "They've got you nailed pretty good, my friend. Do we need to discuss the offer made upstairs?"

The senator gave Lyman a quizzical look. "You think I did this?"

Lyman ignored the pleading voice, his own voice deep, hard. "I'm asking you this once, do we take the deal?"

The senator didn't hesitate. "I did *not* do this."

Lyman gave him one last long look and decided he believed his friend. Even if he didn't, so what? He was the lawyer. He now had a job to do and a big one at that. "Okay, then, my friend. First thing you'll do is shut the fuck up." He couldn't say that to most clients. Mason was his friend, and he needed a serious dose of reality. He couldn't act like a United States senator anymore. He needed to listen to, instead of give—hell, ignore—direction. He'd also have to give some thought to giving up his seat, but that wasn't Lyman's call. That was one for the political people. Johnson just nodded, and Hisle continued. "I'm going to tell the detectives that we're done."

"They're going to arrest me, aren't they?"

"Yes."

"When?"

"Soon. You were there that night. You admitted you had sex with her. And we learned a few more things."

"Like?"

"No forced entry, nothing stolen, and, most importantly, time of death between 1:00 a.m. and 2:00 a.m."

The senator pinched the bridge of his nose. "Can we beat this?"

"Don't know yet," replied Lyman honestly. "We have a lot of work to do to create reasonable doubt."

"Reasonable doubt?" growled Johnson. "Shit, reasonable doubt ain't going to cut it. My career. Shit. My life is fucked if we don't find who did this."

"We'll try, Mason," Lyman replied.

"I've been fucking set up."

"Like I said, we'll try, but you better think about something else right now."

"What's that?"

"Gwen."

They stepped outside, and Peters closed the door. Still standing on the steps, he took one long look at Lich and McRyan, smiled, and stated, "Boys, that was good work in there."

"Shit," replied Lich, laughing out loud. "Mac, just so you know, I wouldn't expect a Christmas card from the senator."

Mac smiled. "No, I don't imagine I'll make the list."

Peters, chuckling along with his detectives, said, "Jesus Christ, Mac. 'Your wife know you were fucking Daniels?' I thought he was going to lunge across the table."

They all shared a brief little laugh, and then Mac, back to business, said, "What's next?"

"Well, much to your enjoyment, I'm sure," replied Peters lightly, "you'll be working with Sally Kennedy on writing up the summons and complaint."

Mac wanted to say, "Fuck you," but one didn't respond that way to a captain. "You think we're ready to go?"

"Yeah, I do." Peters was going to say something else, but looked beyond the two of them out to the road, "Ahh, shit."

Viper had followed them out from St. Paul. Once they'd reached Hisle's, he'd scoped out his current position, half a mile away, standing in a park on the bluff, two hundred feet above. There were swing sets, slides, and sandboxes all over, abandoned since kids were in school and the cool weather of November had rolled in. He was by himself, looking down from the bluff with a pair of high-test binoculars. He would have been able to look inside Hisle's house if the shades weren't drawn.

Once he found his spot, he made the call. The boss wanted the heat turned up and fast. The first call was to Channel 12 and then to Daniels's Channel 6. Once the call was placed, it took the Channel 12 news truck forty-five minutes to get out to Stillwater. Just as he saw the truck coming out of downtown Stillwater, the detectives walked out the front door. He was briefly concerned, would the media miss them? No. They weren't leaving. Rather they were loitering around in front. The one Viper had learned was named Peters was standing on the front steps, facing him while McRyan's and Lich's backs were turned. Peters had a smile on his face, and it looked like the group was enjoying a laugh. Things must have gone well inside. Viper moved his head to the right and down slightly, picking up the van as it pulled up. He looked back up to Peters, and saw his smile vanish when the news van pulled up. He could read Peters's lips, and while his smile may have vanished, a small one creased Viper's face.

The front door opened, and Viper saw Hisle look out. Hisle saw the news van as well, and a grim look overtook his face. The detectives and Hisle went back in the house. The Channel 6 van pulled up just then. A reporter and cameraman got out. All four of them stood around talking, waiting for something to happen. They didn't have to wait long.

Hisle carefully closed the front door before he turned to the three men. "When did they get here?"

"They just pulled up," Peters replied.

"I guess it was inevitable," said Hisle, and then a little suspiciously, "How do you suppose they found out?"

Peters gave Lich a little look. Did you talk? Lich gave a little shake of his head. No. "I don't know, Lyman. They didn't follow us, we made sure. I don't know how they found out."

Lyman shrugged. It was all going to come out anyway. "What will you say on the way out?"

"I assume that means we're done?" asked Mac.

"Yes, it does. You'll do what you have to do. Again, what will you say to the media?"

"For now, nothing," replied Peters. "But we'll be charging the senator, and that'll be news. I'm sure the department and district attorney'll have something to say."

"I imagine so," said Hisle with a wry smile. "I can't imagine Helen Anderson missing time in front of the camera."

Everyone shared a knowing smile. With that, the three of them left. Mac took the circular drive back out towards the main road. The media stood in the middle of the road. As he pulled up, Peters let his window down from the backseat. The blonde reporter was from Channel 12. Mac had seen her many times but couldn't remember her name, Polly something or other. She stuck her microphone inside. "So what are you doing out here, is Senator Mason Johnson a suspect?" she asked.

No we're out here enjoying the fall colors, Mac thought.

"We have no comment right now," replied Peters.

Channel 6, a brunette, yelled, "Will you be arresting Senator Johnson?"

A better question, thought Mac.

"Again, we have no comment right now. You can contact Sylvia Miller later today. She'll have something to say." With that, Peters put his window back up, and they pulled away, heading back towards St. Paul. The media futilely yelled questions at the Explorer as they drove off.

11

"THE CROSS FILES, RIGHT?"

The media was waiting for them when they got back to St. Paul at 5:00 p.m. Mac understood the attention that was coming. This was a big story: a United States senator implicated in the murder of a news reporter. It was going national as a story and would turn into a circus before all was said and done. Mac called Sally on the way in to let her know what had happened. They would be working late, he thought.

Once back, they headed up to Chief Flanagan's office. Sylvia Miller met them in the hallway. They knocked and headed in.

The chief saw them come in and didn't wait for them to sit down, "Tell me."

"He did it," said Peters.

"He admitted that, of course," the chief replied wryly as he came from behind the desk and waved everyone towards the couch.

"Oh, yeah, all the way down to crushing her windpipe," Lich chimed in as he found a spot on the couch to sit.

"Good, just in time for the media cabal out front."

Everyone laughed a little. Sally Kennedy and Helen Anderson walked in just then and joined them over by the couch. The chief, down to business, asked more seriously, "So, what really happened?" Peters nodded to Mac.

He gave Flanagan the run down for the next several minutes. He stuck strictly to the facts. Peters, pimping his detectives, jumped in a couple of times to talk about the good cop, bad cop routine Lich and Mac had put the senator through. At the end, the chief was smiling. Mac liked Flanagan and so it was good to see a smile crack his face. It had been a long week for him.

"So," the chief asked Mac, "we have our killer, do we?"

"I guess so."

"You guess?"

Mac hesitated, "No. Probably our guy."

The chief pressed, "You don't seem so certain, boyo. What gives?"

Mac thought for a moment and decided, what the hell, he'd play devil's advocate. "It's too easy."

"Hah," Lich bellowed. "What's wrong with easy? I love easy."

"That explains Dot," replied Mac with an evil grin. Lich scratched his nose with his middle finger. Kennedy saw the juvenile display between the two of them and giggled.

"Who's Dot?" Peters asked, clueless.

"Nobody," replied Mac. "I still can't get over the fact that a guy this smart did this. It just doesn't make sense."

"When does murder ever make sense?" replied Lich. "I've spent twenty years dealing with it, and very few have ever made any fuckin' sense."

Mac nodded, "I know, I know. But something's bothering me about this, and I can't for the life of me put my finger on it."

"Shit," replied Lich dismissively. "The senator looked guilty as the day is long."

"Agreed," said Peters.

"I agree with you both for the most part," Mac replied, scratching his head. "But there was a couple of times during the interview where I almost felt like he was ..." he was grasping, "... I can't explain it."

Sally gave it a shot. "You felt like he was telling the truth?"

Mac pointed at her. "Yeah. Something like that. It was just a feeling I had a couple of times. That he had genuine emotion, not of guilt, but of loss. I can't even tell you what triggered it."

"Son," the chief interjected, "I've seen guys who murdered their wives, girlfriends, best friends. After they did it, they felt a sense of loss, but you know what? They were still murderers."

"And, Mac, if he didn't do it," Sally said quietly, thoughtfully, "who did?"

"Well, that's the issue now, isn't it?" Mac said. "Like I said, it was a feeling I had. I have no evidence, zero, zip, nada, to point at anyone else. It's probably silly to even have brought it up." Mac sat back on the couch, exhaling, wishing he hadn't said a thing about it. Lich was probably right. What's wrong with easy?

The chief picked up on his disappointment, "Don't feel bad about it, boyo. Senator's been a convincing guy for a long time. You're just reading a little too much into things, which happens." The chief then smiled. "Bottom line is you and Lich have done a hell of a job here."

Helen Anderson jumped in, "So, we charge him?"

"Mac?" Flanagan asked, prodding.

"We'd be idiots not to."

"Agreed," replied the chief, shooting Mac another big smile. "Helen, I think Ms. Kennedy, Mac, Lich, and Marion here need to get together and write it up."

"I've already started, but I need the detectives to fill in some blanks," Sally replied. "Who's going to arrange for the senator to come in?"

"I'll make the call," said the chief. "We'll work it out so that he can turn himself in voluntarily. Shall we make it tomorrow?" he asked in a hopeful voice.

"Yes, later in the morning," replied Sally.

"Good," and to Mac, Lich, and Peters, "You boys off with Ms. Kennedy. I'll call you with the particulars on when Johnson'll be coming in."

"Any chance you'll have to go and arrest him?" Anderson asked.

"Nah," replied Peters. "That'd only add to the media attention. Johnson'll want to start working the jury now."

"Which means that he'll be ever so cooperative," added Sally. "Let's get this thing written up."

The chief said, pointing to Mac, Lich, and Peters, "You heard her, go to work."

"What about a statement for the media?" asked an excited Sylvia Miller. "We could make the 6:00 p.m. news."

Mac couldn't blame her for being excited. It had been a rough week for her as well.

"We can talk about that, Helen. Why don't you stick around as well," the chief replied. "Boys, good work."

Viper and the boss had been watching from his office, sitting on the couch, having a drink. The boss had a bank of seven televisions mounted into a built in cabinet—a large screen in the middle and three smaller screens on each side. They had on all of the local stations, plus CNN and FOX News. Senator Johnson's impending arrest for Daniels's murder was on every television. The media circus began in earnest with Viper's little tip to news stations earlier in the day. The media had footage of the detectives leaving Hisle's place in the Explorer, as well as pulling into the Department of Public Safety. "I wonder why they didn't just follow them with a van or chopper," said the boss.

The highlight, at least for Viper and the boss, was the joint statement of Sylvia Miller and Helen Anderson that they would be arresting the senator for the murder of Claire Daniels. Anderson was particularly giddy, loving the attention. She apparently was prepared for the press conference as she was immaculately dressed in a blue power suit, her hair perfectly placed with just the right amount of makeup. She was good on camera, not a parsed word in her statement. Sylvia Miller, on the other hand, just looked relieved, which probably was the view of the entire department. Between the Daniels case and the serial killer, it had been a rough week for them, Viper thought.

"It'll be crazy tomorrow," mused the boss.

"Yes, sir, it will."

"Will we rest easier now that the senator has been charged?"

Viper thought for a moment and replied, "Not just yet."

The boss nodded, "The Cross files, right?"

"Yes."

"Where are we at on that?"

"We've been searching. We can't find them, assuming the original files are still out there somewhere."

"We need to assume they are."

"Yes, sir." The Cross files could hang them all. They mistakenly fell into the hands of the company's CFO, who had been dealt with as well. They had a copy of the Cross files, but the originals had proven elusive. The concern was that the originals had been shared with or were in Daniels's possession.

"The files were not at Daniels's place. I looked everywhere."

"And what about our dearly departed CFO?"

"Nothing. I went through her place twice, both before and after and found nothing. We have checked through our contact at her bank—no safe deposit box. There was nothing on the laptop or work computer. We searched her mother's place in Arizona and her sister's place in Florida; nothing. We searched her house and have been tracking her mail; nothing."

"So, where are they?"

"I don't know, sir. We'll keep looking."

"What about Channel 6?"

"We had someone there the night we took out Daniels, two nights before and every night since. He's on the cleaning crew," Viper answered. "If we assume there is a file or box with 437 pieces of paper in Daniels's work area or somewhere around the station, he would have found it by now," he added, shaking his head, skeptical. "He's going to try again tonight, but I think it's a dead end. If they had the files, they'd have used them. If someone found them and was trying to make sense of it all, we'd have heard about it."

"You think they don't exist?" the boss asked with a raised eyebrow.

"All I know is we are looking everywhere and haven't found anything."

"Well, all I know," replied the boss irritably, "is that we better find those damn documents before someone else does or we're dead. Until they are found, we keep searching everywhere."

Viper shared his boss's irritation. If the files existed and were found by the wrong people, he would be on the run for the rest of his life. He prepared for the eventuality of that. He had plans in place to be on the run for years, both while in government service and out. These were options he didn't want to exercise. Living somewhere in South America would be tolerable. Someplace warm and sunny would be fine. But, he liked his home in Minnesota, the winter retreat in the Caymans, the Vette, and his hefty salary. He hated to have to give all that up.

"We'll keep looking."

~

It had been another long night spent with Sally. They finally got started putting together the complaint around 7:00 p.m. Mac reflected on the fact, that despite his reservations, they had an awfully solid case. They had charged, and obtained convictions, with far less. Of course, Lyman Hisle usually wasn't on the other side. Nonetheless, seeing it all laid out on paper made him feel more comfortable. The chief was probably right; he was over analyzing the situation. It's like Lich said, "What's wrong with easy?"

Speaking of easy, Lich was the first to leave. Dot paged him, and he was raring to go again. He left around 9:00 p.m., quietly promising Mac that he owed him big time. Captain Peters hung around. He'd been through this a thousand times and made several useful suggestions about putting the complaint together. Sally had done this many times as well. Mac was, by comparison, a little green with the process and humbly realized he still had plenty to learn.

Around 10:30 p.m., with the complaint pretty much done, Captain Peters left. "You two get going soon. It's going to be a big day tomorrow." Sally said she wanted to go through it one more time, and Mac, being the most familiar with the case, stuck around to answer any questions. Convenient how that had worked out, he thought.

"Tomorrow will be exciting," Sally said, while typing away, making a few changes. It had been fifteen minutes since she had said anything. Mac remembered how a law professor once said that a legal document is never written until it's been edited and polished five times. Sally was proving that axiom a couple of additional times over. Focused and intense, the flirtations of the night before were suppressed. She was all business, and well she should be. Much of Mac's work was over, but hers was only beginning. Not to mention that she would be going up against Lyman Hisle and Senator Mason Johnson. She had best get her game face on now.

"Yes, hopefully I'll avoid much of it," replied Mac.

"Not gonna happen. This is your case. You'll be front and center."

He sighed. "I imagine so."

"Read through this one more time for me," directed Sally as she left the office.

The State of Minnesota vs. Mason Johnson. The complaint laid out their evidence, and the case looked solid. Mac wondered what Lyman would do to create reasonable doubt.

Chief Flanagan called to let them know that the senator would turn himself in voluntarily at 10:30 a.m. Mac and Lich were to be there. He would be processed like any other suspect. After that, a bail hearing was set for 3:00 p.m. The chief and Helen Anderson had also decided to do a perp walk. Mac didn't like that.

You did a perp walk when you wanted the public to see that you had arrested someone. This would involve walking the senator out in cuffs, putting him in an unmarked car, and driving the five blocks from the Department of Public Safety Building to the Ramsey County Courthouse. Then he'd be walked into the courthouse in cuffs and would appear in front of the judge. The whole process would be on the news. There would be pictures in the paper, and the media would yell questions at the senator while he was cuffed. It would be a spectacle.

Mac understood why the chief was doing it. It had been a hard week on the department and on Flanagan. Although he wasn't good himself in front of the media, he knew that his department needed some good press. Especially since the serial killer had yet to be caught. Sylvia Miller probably would have pushed for the whole thing even if Helen Anderson hadn't already approved it.

Sally reappeared, and Mac got a little whiff of perfume. Was that for him or the result of a long day and wanting to smell fresh? "This looks good," he said.

"You feel better about the case now?"

Mac nodded. "Yes."

"You should," Sally replied, and then shifting gears. "I wish I could have seen the interview today."

"You know, this shouldn't be the case, but ..." Mac hesitated.

"But what?"

"It gave me a charge, getting to the senator the way I did."

"That's nothing to be ashamed of. I heard he called you an 'arrogant fuck.'"

"That he did."

Sally nodded. "I get the same feeling on a good cross examination. You get someone to admit something they didn't want to or you box them in, and it feels good. You get a high from it."

"Exactly," Mac replied.

She took one last quick look at the complaint. She looked satisfied with it. "What time is it?"

"Twelve fifteen."

"Holy cow. I've got to get some sleep."

"Me too." He helped her put her coat on. "Where are you parked?"

"I'm across the street in the Vincent Ramp." The Vincent Ramp, despite the efforts of its owners, was the darkest parking ramp around, with low ceilings, lots of pillars, and plenty of places to hide. It wasn't the safest place in the middle of the day, let alone after midnight.

"I'll walk you to your car."

The crisp, cool November air greeted them outside. It felt good after a night in Sally's cramped and stuffy office. The Vincent Ramp was kitty corner from the courthouse. They took the elevator up to level four where her Camry was parked close to the elevator, under a light.

"Where are you parked?" Sally asked as she unlocked the car.

"Back at the department."

"Jump in. I'll give you a ride."

They made small talk as they circled down to the ramp exit. It would be a short ride, five blocks. She took a right onto Wabasha and stopped at the light on Sixth, and her demeanor changed instantly. "So. Did my little outfit last night throw you for a loop?"

Mac bolted upright from his relaxed position. It had then, and now she'd done it to him again. He did some quick mental gymnastics. He didn't want to say no, since that would turn her off and he didn't want to do that. He didn't want to come off cheesy either. He decided she was back in flirting mode, so why not join in. "Let's just say I noticed."

"Did you like what you saw?"

No screwing around obviously. "Yes."

A little smile creased her lips. "I thought so."

She turned left and the Public Safety Building was on the right with the parking garage just ahead of them. Unfortunately, a lot of uniform cops were hanging out front. Mac knew them all. Wherever this little conversation was heading, it would have to wait. If they got close here, he'd never hear the end of it. She pulled past all the cops and up close to the parking ramp entrance. Mac didn't give her a chance to go any further. He opened the door and swung his leg out before he looked back. "I'll see you tomorrow."

Sally was smiling at him, the kind of smile that said you're not going to get away so easy next time.

12

"WHERE DO YOU SUPPOSE HE'S GOING?"

Mac and Lich stood on the front steps of the Public Safety Building and watched as Hisle's limousine pulled up punctually at 10:30 a.m. The media was punctual as well, having been camped out since the crack of dawn. The arrest was a national story, with all the networks and cable news channels present and accounted for. The local channels were there as well, battling as best they could for space. FOX politicos like Fred Barnes and Mort Kondracke were already opining on what impact the senator's involvement would have on party politics. Mac could never remember seeing so many microphones and cameras or so much hairspray in all his life.

Mac and Lich and a couple of uniform cops walked down to the curb. The senator would require an escort, not because Mac wanted any airtime, although Sylvia Miller kept saying it would be good for the department to be seen on camera arresting the senator, but more so because, if they didn't, the media might crush him.

Hisle got out first and issued a perfunctory, "Good morning," to Mac and Lich. He examined the crush of media forming around them.

"Sorry, Lyman, not much we can do," Mac said as he leaned down into the open door to see the senator sliding over to get out. He looked back at Hisle. "Are you guys going to say anything to the media on the way in or—"

"Just get us in," Hisle replied.

Mac looked back down at the senator, who was obviously not happy to see him. Mac ignored it. "Senator, when you get out, we're just going to plow through them. Keep your hands on my back. Lyman'll be on your side and Detective Lich and the uniform cops'll be behind you."

The senator nodded and climbed out of the limo. Everyone looked ready, so Mac turned and headed up the steps, everyone right behind him. They plowed through the media. Mac was hit a couple of times by microphones, and he pushed a camera guy from CNN a little harder than he would have liked, causing him to fall to his knees, hearing a, "Hey, man," as he pushed past. They eventually got inside, the doors closing the media out.

"This way, Senator," Mac said, pointing to an elevator that would take them down to booking. Johnson and Hisle had a brief discussion, and Mac heard Hisle say, "I'll see you in a couple of hours." That would be the arraignment hearing.

The rest of the process, including pictures and fingerprints, took a good hour. Since the senator was going to the arraignment this afternoon and was likely to get bail, they didn't put him in jail clothes. Once the processing was complete, Mac and Lich walked the senator to an isolated jail cell away from the rest of the general populace. He entered the cell and stood with his back to them, hands on hips, surveying his new temporary digs.

"We'll be down for you in a couple of hours," Lich said.

Mac and Lich took the elevator back upstairs. "I want to see if I have any messages," Lich said. Mac chuckled, figuring Lich was looking for something from Dot. Old Dick Lich had a definite spring in his step the last two days. Instead of complaining about his divorce, he was focused on work and had been masterful the day before with the senator. Mac was starting to see why people said Lich had been a good detective. Lich's new-found vigor caused his mind to briefly drift to Sally. She had been flirting again last night, and he'd basically admitted his interest. Bill Clark snapped him out of his daydream, handing him a pink message slip.

"This guy just called in," Bill said. "He lives in an apartment along the alley behind Daniels's place. You left your card for him."

Mac searched in the back of his mind for a moment, "Oh, yeah, out of town or something."

"Right. Anyway, he called."

"Say anything?"

"Nope. He just said you should call him."

Mac dialed the number.

The senator sat on the bed and looked at the floor. Two days before, he had been lunching in the Senate dining room. Now, he was sitting on a bed in a gray cinder-block jail cell, with no window to the outside world, accused of murdering the woman he loved. How had it come to this?

Somebody set him up. They would have to figure out whom. He realized his political career was probably over. Even if he was acquitted, the taint would never go away. If Lyman could actually prove he was innocent, well that might be a different story. However, at the moment, he feared that he might not be able to do that. But if he could, it might help save his career for some future point in time. Of course, if he ever did run again, this whole thing would be brought up. And, even proven innocent, it would be known that the woman who died was his mistress; at least that's how the public would perceive it. He was cheating on his wife, caught red-handed. While not fatal if already in political office, it would make it a hell of a lot harder to get back in.

Lyman set him straight the night before. For now, he had to forget about his career. They needed to focus on keeping him out of jail. He was looking at a life sentence. This was what had to be avoided. This would be Lyman's focus. Hisle had already hired a private investigator to look into other possible killers.

Mason leaned back on the bed, his head against the cold cinder block, closed his eyes, and thought about his last night with Claire. He'd never been with a woman like her—beautiful, energetic, passionate. She said she was probably coming to Washington. He had been so happy.

Telling his wife about all of this had been awful. He suspected Lyman heard her screaming from the other end of the house. Not only did she find out that her husband had been cheating on her— no, that wasn't bad enough—but her husband, having embarrassed her in that fashion, was now implicated in the murder of the woman. Not only that but Mason waited too long; she heard it first from a reporter and not him.

He admitted to the affair; no sense hiding it now. He had intended to ask for a divorce. The timing just hadn't been right to do it. "Don't you worry, the divorce will be coming," was her response. There would be no supportive wife through this.

He just had to get through this somehow. He had plenty of money put away. Between what he inherited from his parents as an only child, and his private sector and Senate earnings, he was in good shape. Gwen earned more than he had for years, so the divorce would not be financially crippling. Upon reflection, if he could beat this, he could go somewhere far away and live. It would not be the life he envisioned for himself two days before, but things could be worse— he could be living in a cell like this for the rest of his life. An island somewhere, with the ocean, the sun, and a cocktail; while not the Senate dining room, it beat the alternative.

Get through the arraignment, arrange for bail, and get out of the Twin Cities. He decided to go up to his cabin afterwards. It was only an hour or so away, so if he had to drive in to see Lyman, he could. Better yet, he could have Lyman come out there. He could ice fish, snow-shoe, cross-country ski, and snowmobile. There were other cabins around, but he had ten acres to himself. The isolation would be good. He felt better just thinking about it.

He took his suit coat off, loosened his tie, and lay down on the bed. He closed his eyes and tried to nap. About the time he felt himself dozing off, the steel door to the cell opened, and the older detective, Lich, appeared with another detective he hadn't seen before.

"Time to go, Senator," Lich said.

"Where's your partner?" the senator asked.

"He's working on something."

It took Mac a minute to realize that Paul Blomberg was worth a look. Blomberg lived in an apartment building that backed up to the alley that split Daniels's block in half. He had left for Las Vegas on the morning they found Daniels's body and didn't know anything was going on. He returned late the night before and found Mac's card. He wasn't sure what he saw exactly, but it might be easier to show him.

Blomberg was the typical late-twenties single professional living on Grand Avenue. His apartment was like many found in the area, a one-bedroom job, wood floors, built-in wooden buffets, and tiny kitchens. Blomberg had just gotten back—his suitcase was sitting in the middle of the apartment, three days of newspapers and mail stacked on top. Blomberg may have been a professional, but he looked worn out, his hair disheveled, a few days of growth on his beard, and dark circles around his eyes. He was drinking coffee out of an oversized mug.

After shaking his hand, Mac asked, "You always look like this?"

"Funny guy," replied Blomberg, "Vegas for three days'll do this to you."

"I imagine it might. How'd you come out?"

"About even. No good at the craps table, but the sports book wasn't bad."

"Yeah? What treated you good there?"

"The Wild, man."

Mac smiled, "Put a little money on the road win at Colorado, did you?"

Blomberg returned the smile, "Man knows his puck."

"I know a thing or two about the game," Mac replied. "So, tell me about what you couldn't explain on the phone."

Blomberg waved him back to the kitchen. It was small, a little fridge and stove and barely enough counter space for a sink and microwave. There was a side window overlooking a parking lot. A small dinner table in front of the window had a toaster and a wood spire that held four mismatched coffee cups. Mac looked out the window. On the other side of the parking lot was Kozlak Foodmart, where Mac often grocery shopped.

"So?"

"Well, she was killed when?"

"Monday night or Tuesday morning."

"Hmm. I wonder," Blomberg said.

"What did you see?"

"It was 2:45 to 3:00 a.m., and I was up. Just couldn't sleep. Wish I could have that night, too, because there wasn't much to be had in Vegas," Blomberg said, and he paused, his mind obviously back on the Vegas trip again.

"Yeah, so?" Mac replied.

"Anyway," Blomberg said, sipping his coffee, "I decided I'd make a piece of toast and have a glass of milk, figuring maybe that would help me sleep."

"That's nice," a little impatient.

Blomberg picked up the pace, "Anyway, as I'm waiting for the toaster to pop, I see this van pull up in the parking lot, lights out. Kind of odd at that time of night, I thought."

"So the lights are out. What happened then?" Mac asked, peering out the window.

"Anyway, it pulls up, and it looks like the passenger-side sliding door opens."

"What do you mean looks like?"

"If you look out the window, you'll see. The van turned away from me. It pulled up parallel to the guardrail there. As it was turning to go to the guardrail, the door looked like it started to open."

Mac peered down, then looked back at Blomberg. "Then what?"

"Some guy came from across the alley, jumped in, and they pulled away."

"Some guy?"

"Yeah, he just ran from over there on the right, across the alley, and jumped in the van, and they pulled away."

"Did you get a look at the guy?"

Blomberg shook his head. "It was really dark, and he was dressed in dark clothes."

"See a face, anything like that?"

"No. Not at all. Like I said, it was dark."

"Tall, short, heavy, slight?"

"Sorry, man. I couldn't make any of that out."

Mac took a look out the window. The lot had parking spaces on the east and west side, as well as a row down the middle. There was a short guardrail that separated the parking lot from the alley. The guardrail prevented someone from pulling into the lot from the alley. "Let's go down and take a look."

They got down to the parking lot, and Mac walked to the guardrail at the back. He looked up to the apartment and Blomberg's window.

"So the van pulled up here?" Mac pointed to the area in front of the guardrail.

"A little further away."

Mac walked another ten feet, "Here?"

"Yes."

"Now where did the guy you saw come from?"

"I didn't see where he came from really. I saw him come from the alley and jump in the van. The van pulled away pretty fast, and I don't think the door was even closed when they drove away."

"Show me where he was in the alley when you saw him."

Blomberg climbed over the guardrail and stood in the middle of the alley. "I didn't see where he came from. I was watching the van, and I noticed him out of the corner of my eye."

Mac walked over to where Blomberg was standing. He looked back east down to the other end of the alley and the left turn into the back of Daniels's place. Mac walked down the alley towards Daniels's place. The alley was narrow, but there were all kinds of garages along the left side and a few interspersed between the various businesses and apartments on the right. There were several tall trees and a couple of large weeping willows. Mac thought about when he was a kid playing kick the can. He could have hidden forever in this alley.

Whomever Blomberg saw could have come from anywhere, Mac decided. He could have been coming from a party, the Mardi Gras bar, maybe getting a little action from someone in one of the apartments. He could have been robbing one of the businesses. Of course, he could also have killed Daniels. How likely was that? Mac scratched his head, looking around. Blomberg seemed on the level. "What time was this again?"

"Two forty-five to 3:00 a.m. Something like that. I remember looking at my clock when I got up, and it was 2:45. I'm not sure how long I was in the kitchen."

"Why didn't you call it in that night?"

"It didn't seem like that big a deal to me. You see all kinds of weird stuff these days. I see people get picked up in the alley all the time. They're going on a date or getting dropped off from one. Just didn't seem like much at the time."

Mac thought a little more. Time of death was between 1:00 and 2:00 a.m., and they had the senator leaving her place at that time. There was no evidence of forced entry, no evidence of anything being stolen, no evidence that anyone came in the back. Odd though. Mac figured it was probably nothing, but he would have to go back and write it up.

～

Viper and another member of his crew, Allain Bouchard, trailed

McRyan. When McRyan came down with the guy and walked to the guardrail in the back of the lot, Viper got nervous.

He climbed out of the van and walked over to the Foodmart. There was an awning that ran one-third of the way along the east side of the building, offering cover for the entrance. Underneath the awning was a *Pioneer Press* newspaper box. Viper popped in a quarter, took out a paper, and walked to the far edge of the awning. He could see where McRyan was walking around and looking at the alley and where they had pulled the van up on the night they took out Daniels.

He saw the guy point to the exact place they had stopped the van, then climb the guardrail and stand in the alley. Viper had come from the garage on the other side. McRyan joined the guy in the alley and then began walking down towards Daniels's place. Too close already, Viper decided not to follow any further. Five minutes later McRyan came walking back. The guy and McRyan walked back towards the front of the apartment. McRyan didn't go back inside the building, instead stopping on the sidewalk, jotting down some notes.

Viper dropped the paper in the garbage can and walked back across the street as McRyan climbed back into his Explorer, pulled out, and did a U-turn in the middle of Grand, and headed back towards downtown. Viper jumped back into the van. "Follow him."

McRyan dropped the Explorer off at the Pub and walked the three blocks to the courthouse. Viper looked at his watch—2:55 p.m. The arraignment hearing would start in five minutes.

"So, what do you think?" Bouchard asked.

"I gotta talk to the boss."

Mac was late for the bail hearing. He saw Lich and went to sit next to him. Lich said, "It just started. I think the judge is going to knit the flag."

Mac immediately realized Lich was right. Generally, the few times Mac had been to these hearings, the judge would dispense with these motions with little fanfare. Not today. Judge Jedediah Mattingly was in the spotlight, and he wasn't going to waste it. There were media galore in the courtroom. The judge, his hair usually a little unkempt the times Mac had seen him, was immaculately dressed, a sharp dark-blue tie and white dress shirt under his robe. Mattingly introduced the case with great drama, talking about the importance of justice and the seriousness of his role. He then motioned towards Sally, "The prosecution may proceed."

Sally stood up, "Thank you, Your Honor. May it please the court ..." She looked great in a black power skirt suit that formed perfectly to her slender body. Her red hair was swirled perfectly in the back. She looked great. The cameras would be all over her.

Whereas the judge made a spectacle of himself, Sally did not. It was like any other case. She made her arguments in a straightforward manner, emphasizing what Mac thought were the key points. Bail of one million dollars would be in order, given the nature of the crime, she argued. The judge's eyes shot up at that.

"One million dollars, Ms. Kennedy?"

"It's murder one, Your Honor. The state feels that accurately reflects the nature of the offense and the ability of the defendant to pay. The defendant surely has the means to flee. This bail is fair and appropriate."

Sally had told him the judge would never set bail that high, but she wanted to make a point. She thought it more likely that bail would be set at $500,000, only ten percent of which would have to be put down with the bail bondsman.

The judge turned to Lyman, "Mr. Hisle."

"Thank you, Your Honor. The defendant has no intention of fleeing. He has every intention of proving his innocence and will be here for trial." Hisle went on to make several other arguments. Again, Sally nailed it on the head as to what Lyman would do. "Therefore, your honor, we feel bail in the amount of $100,000 would be more appropriate."

Each side made some additional rebuttal arguments, and Judge Mattingly drew it to a close. Before rendering his decision, he engaged in more grandstanding, orating on the seriousness of the case, the fairness of the justice system, and the gravity of his responsibilities. "Auditioning for Court TV, I think," Lich quipped.

"He wants Judge Judy's gig," Mac replied.

With great drama, Mattingly finally, and thankfully, announced, "Bail is set at $500,000." He pounded his gavel, "Court is adjourned," and with great dramatic flair he exploded out of his seat and through his chambers door. Sally had hit it right on the head.

The media, en masse, burst out of their seats to head outside for their news reports. Mac looked at his watch, 3:50 p.m. Conveniently, everything was completed in time for the 5:00 p.m. eastern time news shows. Undoubtedly this would be a top, if not the top, story.

Mac and Lich followed the press out, and someone tapped him on the shoulder. It was Sally. He grinned at her and said, "You were right on the money."

"Seemed like the right number," she said, and then she whispered, "Are you going to the Pub later?"

In fact I am, Mac thought. "Yes."

"See you there?" she asked.

"Yeah, maybe we can grab some dinner?"

"Sounds good," she replied with a smile.

As they came out of the courtroom, the media were swarming. There was a bright glare from the lights. Questions were being yelled from all angles, and there were microphones and cameras everywhere. Helen Anderson was holding court, saw Sally, and waved her over. Helen wanted the attention, but the media probably wanted to speak with the prosecutor who would actually be handling the case.

Mac quipped, "Your public awaits."

Sally replied with a mock flip of her hair, "How do I look?"

Mac whispered in her ear, "I like what I see."

She gave just a little giggle and a smile and walked over to the cameras and microphones. Mac and Lich ducked into an elevator, trying to get away before somebody wanted to talk to them. Amazingly, when the elevator closed, it was only them and a couple of uniform cops. Lich naturally didn't miss a thing. "Won't be long now."

"What won't be long?" Mac replied wearily, knowing what was coming.

"You and Kennedy."

"Jesus."

One of the uniforms, Norb Rodriguez, joined in, "Hell, Mac, I thought you hit that already. She's a looker. You see that suit?" His partner nodded along with a big smile.

Mac just shook his head. "Since when did I become *National Enquirer* material?"

"Hey, us married guys like having something to talk about," replied Rodriguez.

"Face it, boyo," said Lich, doing his Chief Flanagan imperson-ation, "you're a popular guy who everyone likes, and frankly, you need to get laid." Lich held his hands out, "What can I say? People just want to see you happy."

Mac replied, rather lamely, he thought, "I wasn't aware I was unhappy."

Lich rolled his eyes. "You're joking, right?"

Mac shook his head. The elevator stopped, the doors opened, and they walked out. He thought they avoided the media, but he was wrong. Sylvia Miller and the chief were conducting a press confer-ence, and they got dragged in. In front of the cameras, Mac and Lich received the appreciation of the chief and the entire department for so quickly making an arrest. Thankfully, they weren't required to answer any questions before Miller and the chief brought it to a close.

Mac was already taking a lot of shit because of Sally; it would only double now. He could just hear it at the bar tonight, his Uncle Shamus would undoubtedly be leading the ribbing, "Ladies and gentlemen, I bring you the savior of the St. Paul Police Department, a fine Irish lad, Michael McKenzie McRyan." Before Mac and Lich left, Chief Flanagan wanted them to stop by his office. Mac knew happy hour would be getting an early Friday start.

As they walked back to the station, Lich asked, "So what happened this afternoon?"

Mac related what he'd learned from Blomberg. Lich was unmoved.

"It's probably nothing, but you better let Kennedy know."

"I imagine I'll get the chance at some point," replied Mac. "And I'm sure our conversation will appear in the gossip column the next day."

13

"THEY SAY THERE ARE THREE PERIODS IN A HOCKEY GAME."

Mac and Lich spent a happy hour with the chief, Captain Peters, and Sylvia Miller in Flanagan's office. They watched the replays of the evening news, laughed and applauded about what everyone had said on camera. Helen Anderson and Sally had been effusive in their praise of the police department, of Lich and Mac in particular. The cadre hooted at the TV when the senator and Hisle declared innocence, confident that when the evidence was presented, Johnson would be found innocent. Lich was his usual humorous self. "He's guiltier than my second wife."

Everyone had a drink, except the chief, who had at least two. Mac could understand why. Flanagan looked like a great weight had been lifted off his shoulders. That feeling would be short-lived, of course. With the serial killer still at large, the headaches would start up again first thing Monday morning. But that was Monday, and it was Friday —time to celebrate.

After having finished their drink, Mac looked at Lich, who nodded, time to go. They shook hands with everyone on the way out. Flanagan walked them through his door out to the waiting area, obviously happy, "Off to the Pub for you, boys?"

"At least for me," Mac replied.

"What about you, Dick?"

Mac jumped in, "Well, Chief, I think ole Dicky boy here has a hot date with Dot."

Lich gave him a dirty look. The chief was amused. "Haven't learned your lesson yet?" Lich's messy divorces were the subject of many a humorous story, usually told by Dick himself.

Lich shrugged his shoulders, "Chief, I've found that women are the one mistake continually worth making. Something my partner should realize."

Flanagan laughed, a happy laugh, and put his arm around Mac's shoulder, "I'm sure our young friend here will get around to Ms. Kennedy sooner or later."

Even the chief knew about this, good grief. Mac stared at Lich who had another one of his shit-eatin' grins on his face. Pay back was a bitch, boyo. Mac decided to cut his losses and turned to leave, "Come on, Dick Lick, give me a ride to the Pub."

The chief laughed again, patted them both on the back, "You guys have a good time tonight. You've both earned it."

They left Flanagan behind and jumped in Lich's little purple Dodge Neon. Mac laughed every time he saw the heavyset Lich get behind the wheel. He made the Neon look like a toy car. Mac looked in the backseat. It looked as if half of Dick's closet was in the backseat. "Geez, you livin' in the car?"

Lich smiled and said, "I haven't been home much this week."

"Does the backseat maybe turn into a Murphy Wall-bed?"

Lich laughed, "I'll mention that to Dodge. Maybe that could be an upgrade in this thing." Lich dropped him off in front of McRyan's Pub, "Have a good one, Mac."

"You, too."

"Oh, don't you worry, boyo."

Mac closed the car door and Lich was off. He walked in the front door and took in the crowd. Friday night was always a good night for the Pub. Cops always stopped off for a beer before heading home. Beers were cheap for any cop on Friday night, a never-ending happy hour. But this night was different. There were cops everywhere, double—maybe triple

—the normal crowd. Mac could tell immediately that a cloud had lifted over the department. Everyone was in a good mood. Mac tried to reach the bar unnoticed. No dice. Once he was spotted, the place erupted.

As expected, Uncle Shamus made a spectacle of his nephew. There were backslaps all around, and Mac knew he wouldn't have to pay for a drink all night. Of course, there was plenty of good-natured ribbing for being on television. Bonnie Schmidt, who had been at Daniels's the morning they found her body, was in a happy mood. "You looked great on television."

"Thanks, Bonnie, although I'd just as soon avoid the attention."

"That ain't gonna happen."

Mac winced. He didn't want to be some billboard for the department. He shoved that aside; it was Friday night, time to celebrate.

He soaked it up and enjoyed the next hour.

The boss took the news calmly. The operation on Daniels had been planned in three days. They only had that amount of time to conduct surveillance and form a plan. They were lucky that the senator was involved. It had created great cover. But with that narrow of a window, any number of things could go wrong. McRyan checking out their pick up point was one of those things. The unearthing of their pick up spot had not stopped the hearing from going forward. Viper seriously doubted that finding it would have caused that. However, McRyan would make a report of what he had learned, and it would be disclosed to counsel for the senator as part of defense discovery. The defense would obviously investigate other scenarios. Once they started looking, what else might they find?

"You're concerned about this?" the boss asked.

"Yes."

"Do you really think this would be enough to create any sort of reasonable doubt on the case?"

"I don't know. I'm not a lawyer. But once they start looking—"

"Who knows what they will find," the boss finished it for him and took a sip of coffee. No drinks. This wasn't a happy hour. "I think it's obvious what we need to do."

Mac had a few beers and enjoyed himself thoroughly. Backslaps and thanks came one after another. He wanted to advance on merit as a cop. He wanted to live up to his father's name. On this night, he felt like he'd done that. A couple of veteran detectives came up and gave him the, "Your dad would have been proud today," making the night that much sweeter. Any doubts he had about the case had been washed away by the last couple of hours. People a lot more experienced than he were happy, so why shouldn't he be? The beers had given him a little buzz, and he was feeling good.

He was standing in the back when he saw Sally come in the front. She'd dropped her hair down, and her glasses were gone. Nonetheless, she was immediately recognized and swarmed once inside, taking in some of the good cheer from the crowd. She'd said nice things about the police on TV. Any prosecutor who did that would earn goodwill, and tonight, free drinks.

They made eye contact, and she slowly worked her way back to him. She looked at his beer. "Buy me one of those?" Mac looked at the bartender, holding up his beer. Another one appeared immediately. She took a long drink.

"A pretty happy group in here."

"I'd say so." Mac took a quick look around. Lots of people were looking his way.

"You look happy too," Sally said.

"I am. It's been a good day."

They both took a drink. He took a long look at her. She was attractive. She was interested, and he had pretty much admitted the same. Enough screwing around, it was time. "Everyone seems to think you and I are an item."

"So I hear," she replied with a little smile and put her beer up to her lips.

"Well then, why don't we act like it?"

She dropped her beer from her lips and gave him a serious look.

"I'm parked out back."

She nodded and put her beer on the bar. At this point, neither of them cared if anyone saw them leave. They walked down the back hallway, and Mac said, "My place?"

"Okay."

Mac held the back door open, and she walked through. Mac followed, and she stopped, turned around and kissed him, deeply, a long, slow, soft, wet kiss. Months of hurt and frustration were released. They stopped and looked in each other's eyes. He lightly took her hand and led her over to the Explorer, opening the passenger door for her to get in. He went around and got in, and they embraced again.

"We better go," she said after a few minutes.

He pulled out of the lot and made his way over to Ramsey Avenue and across the I-35E bridge and up the hill towards Summit. She leaned over and kissed him on the neck and nibbled on his ear as he drove, sending a shiver down his spine. Turning right onto Summit, he accelerated the two blocks to his place. Once the Explorer was inside the garage, he undid his seatbelt and pulled her to him.

"Take me inside," she whispered breathlessly, her mouth a centimeter from his.

They got out and walked briskly arm in arm to the back door. They made it halfway up the backstairs before they embraced again. Carefully he moved up her skirt and picked her up so she was straddling him, carrying her up the rest of the steps, while she nibbled, breathing heavily in his ear. He dug in his pocket for his keys while she kissed him on the neck. The door opened, and Mac dropped the keys on the table, shutting the door with a back kick. Quickly they moved to the bedroom, where they feverishly took off each other's clothes and fell into bed.

The senator managed to fly beneath the media radar long enough to get away to his cabin on Cedar Lake, an hour west of the Twin Cities. It was a large A-frame cabin that had four bedrooms on the main level and a loft that slept six more. It had been his parents' place, and, since he was an only child, he had inherited it upon their deaths. He arranged to have it stocked with food and drink at all times. Upon his arrival, he went immediately to the liquor cabinet and found an unopened bottle of tequila. He was going to get drunk, plain and simple. Tomorrow, Lyman and his crew were going to come out and start discussing defense strategy. They would be there at 10:00 a.m., but for tonight, he was going to take the bottle of tequila, watch television, and drink his problems away.

He grabbed a glass from the cupboard and the ice bucket from the counter. He filled the bucket with ice, headed for the couch, sat down, and poured a drink. He knocked it back and poured himself another and put that one down as well before grabbing some ice and pouring a drink for sipping.

A classic movie was in order, and he grabbed the remote. A little channel surfing struck pay dirt. To Catch a Thief was on, a Hitchcock classic with Cary Grant and the hypnotically beautiful Grace Kelly. An appropriate movie, he thought, since it was about a man framed for a crime he did not commit. His feet up on the coffee table, he leaned back on the couch and took a long drink from his glass.

Mac and Sally slept for a couple of hours until the sound of the furnace kicking in caused her to wake. She snuggled her head on his chest. She felt good, like a woman again. It had been a long time. A year and a half, she thought upon reflection. She'd let off a lot of pent-up frustration and pain.

The first time had simply been sex; both of them so horned up, ripping their clothes off, struggling with each other on the bed. The first time was always awkward, she thought. Not that she'd had lots of first times. She had some friends who went through a lot more men than she had, who always said the first time was awkward. Her friends said that if the second time was bad, he was probably no good in bed.

She wasn't sure she subscribed to that theory, but she didn't need to worry. The second time, which occurred about fifteen minutes after the first, had been much better. McRyan knew what he was doing; there was no doubt about that. He was an energetic lover. The second orgasm was a result of McRyan bringing her there. She couldn't help herself when it happened. He'd given her a feeling she hadn't had in a long time. She smiled inwardly, she felt good, although her breasts were a little sore, and she realized it was probably beard burn. He'd certainly gone for them time and again.

She felt a little shiver and moved her body a little closer to his. He was warm, and she moved her arm slowly up and down his chest, playing with his chest hair. He awoke. She turned her head to him and gave him a soft little kiss. She stroked his face and looked into his dark-blue eyes. They were attractive eyes. "Sorry I woke you." She didn't really mean it.

"That's okay." He rolled slightly onto his side. "Are you warm enough?"

"I'm fine."

He leaned down and gave her a little kiss. He lingered there, and she kissed him back, holding the kiss, sweeping with her tongue. She was ready for a third time. She couldn't remember ever wanting or even going a third time. "You know," she said as she rolled on top of him, and kissed him a little more deeply, "they say there are three periods in a hockey game."

"Yes, there are," he replied, lightly moving his fingers up and down her back.

"Well, we've only played two," she said as she could feel him stiffening beneath her. She kissed him again while reaching back down to slide him in.

"Let's play hockey."

14

"I'M A REGULAR CRIME FIGHTING HERO."

Mac woke up and looked at the clock: 8:00 a.m. The sunlight blazed through the shades of the windows. Normally an early riser, he couldn't remember the last time he slept in so late. He rolled his naked body slowly to the side of the bed, not wanting to wake Sally.

Sitting up, he rubbed his eyes a little and looked for his boxers. It took a few minutes to find them as their clothes lay everywhere. Finally, he saw them over by the door. Quietly, he pushed himself out of bed, walked over and pulled them on. He grabbed his robe from the hook behind the door.

Looking back at her, she looked wonderful. Her shoulder-length hair falling across her face, the blanket covering only the lower half of her body. The rays of light coming through the shades brushed across her, making her look almost angelic. He tiptoed out of the room and headed for the bathroom, engaged in some morning mechanics and left a new toothbrush out for Sally. Once finished, he headed for the kitchen.

He was tired and exhilarated all at the same time. It had been quite a night. His legs felt heavy—sex legs, they had called them when he was in college.

He started a pot of coffee and went down the steps to the back door to grab the newspaper. The arrest was front-page news, with Mac and Lich pictured above the fold, side by side with a picture of the senator and Hisle. A smaller picture below the fold had Sally and Helen Anderson from their press conference. As he walked back up the steps, he scanned the stories, reading the facts that had already become intimately familiar. Inside the front page, the political wags were frothing at the mouth, discussing all of the possible political ramifications. It was speculated that Senator Johnson would need to resign in the very near future.

By the time Mac wandered back to the kitchen, the coffee was ready. He poured a cup and grabbed the sports page, wanting to see the Gopher hockey score. He had tickets for tonight's tilt and wondered if Sally would want to go. He wouldn't need to wait long to ask.

Sally was up and walking down the hall to the bathroom. He heard her laugh, probably at the toothbrush, and heard the water start running. A few minutes later she came walking into the kitchen, wearing his white dress shirt. She'd managed to fasten a button or two, and the shirt hung mid-thigh, revealing her thin, shapely legs.

"Good morning," he said, handing her a cup of coffee. She leaned up and kissed him, then took the cup.

He handed her the front page, and she went over to the small kitchen table to sit down and read. "We both received front page treatment," he said, pointing out their pictures. They spent a few quiet minutes reading the paper.

"So," she said, looking up directly at him, "what are we doing here?"

"Drinking coffee, reading the paper," he replied, momentarily ducking the question.

"You and me here, buster. Is this a one night gig?"

She was direct, and he rather liked it. It was not a one-nighter. Mac liked her, but he didn't really know her yet. He wanted to change that. "Well, I thought we could go to breakfast," he replied.

She smiled. "That's a start."

"I have tickets to the Gopher game tonight."

"St. Cloud State?"

"Yup."

"I'm game."

"Well, why don't we get dressed, I was thinking of the Cleveland Grille."

"A big, greasy breakfast?"

"I need it, woman, because you wore me out. I haven't checked the bedroom yet, but I think we embedded the headboard into the wall."

She smiled, stood up, and slowly walked over to him. She pulled the string on his robe, allowing it to fall open. She put her hands around him, burying her head in his chest. They silently held each other for a minute. "Last night felt good," she said quietly.

"Yes, it did."

She pulled back, looked up, and kissed him, lightly at first, and then deeply. He undid the few buttons keeping her shirt closed, pushing it open to her shoulders. She pulled her arms back and let it fall to the floor. He admired her beauty. She had a wonderful body and looked incredibly sexy, her hair falling messily around her face. He pulled her close again, kissing her. He picked her up and carried her back to bed.

Two hours later, they were off for a late breakfast at the Cleveland Grille. Mac wanted a greasy breakfast burrito to get some fuel into his system. And he had another reason for hitting the Cleveland.

He saw Dot as he walked in, and he looked to his left. Lich was sitting back in the corner, his usual spot, reading the paper and drinking coffee. Sally looked at Mac with a sheepish smile, and he nodded his head to walk back. Lich looked up to see them coming, a big smile spreading across his face. "Well, what are you two doing here on this fine morning?"

"We couldn't get in anyplace reputable, so I said we'll go to the Cleveland and eat with Dick Lick."

Lich cackled, "Fuck you," and to Sally, "How are you, Counselor?"

"Fine, thanks. Reading your press clippings?"

"That I am. I'm a regular crime-fighting hero. They'll be putting the statue downtown in Rice Park any day now." Lich grabbed the front page and looked at it, pointing at the picture of Mac and himself, "Of course, I'd be a hell of a lot happier if they'd just used my photo. My partner here is just bringing me down."

It was Mac's turn to cackle, "Yes, we all know how big and bald sells papers."

"I'd imagine they're selling tons this morning," another voice piped in. It was Dot. "Good morning, Detective, and I assume this is Ms. Kennedy?"

"And you must be Dot," replied Sally.

Dot flashed her a smile. "What can I get you two?"

Sally took a quick look at the menu. "I'll have a ham and cheese omelet and coffee."

Dot looked at Mac, who had no need for a menu. "I assume you'll have your usual?"

"Absolutely."

"Coming right up." With that, Dot turned and went to hand in their order.

Lich didn't waste any time. He seldom did. "I figured you would finally get together last night."

"Why is it," Sally asked curiously, "that Mac and I have become such a topic of gossip?"

Lich smiled. "Well, Ms. Kennedy, I can't speak for what's going on around your office, but us cops, we happen to like our boy here. We just want to see him happy. This morning he looks happy."

Mac wasn't going to argue the point. The world felt a little different today. Lich was right. Women were a mistake worth making. He planned on making more mistakes with Sally. But first, he wanted to eat.

Their breakfast came, and he and Sally dug in while Lich continued to sip his coffee, reading the paper. They had a good time, laughing, Lich telling old stories. He was funny and could spin a yarn. The last week had given Mac newfound respect for him. He'd worked the case hard and had been masterful in the interview with the senator. Lich was back to being a good cop, working the job, and Mac liked it.

They finished their breakfast, and Mac was waiting for Dot to return with his credit card, when his cell phone burped. He looked at the number. The Public Safety Building. "McRyan," he said, his body going cold. He listened a moment, then said, "You've got to be kidding." That caught Lich's and Sally's attention.

Sally asked, "What is it?"

Mac put his hand over the mouthpiece and whispered, "Mason Johnson's dead." Then into the phone, he said, "Where? How do we get there?" Mac gestured towards Lich, who handed him his notebook and pen. Mac jotted the directions. "Take us about an hour. Right. Thanks."

"What the fuck?" Lich said.

"Hisle heads out to the senator's cabin this morning, apparently to start working on the case. He shows up, looks in the back door and sees the senator hanging there. Suicide. Cabin's out on Cedar Lake by Annandale."

Sally put her hand up to her mouth. "I guess he really did it, didn't he?"

Lich, regaining his composure, "I knew he did, but man, I can't believe this."

"Believe it," Mac replied. "I'm heading out there. You guys coming?" They both nodded.

It took them a little over an hour to get to the cabin. As they drove west, it was apparent the sun wouldn't last long. Clouds were rolling in, and the radio talked of rain mixed with snow later. They stopped in Annandale to grab coffee and cups as they doubted there would be any at the scene. From their stop in town, it took five minutes to get to the cabin. A sheriff's deputy was working the end of the road. Mac let the window down, and flashed his badge, "St. Paul detectives and Ramsey County district attorney."

"They said you were coming." The sheriff's deputy took a quick look at the ID to confirm and waved them through. Mac noticed a news van pulling up behind him as he rolled through.

They took the winding road up to the cabin. It was probably five hundred yards. "Pretty isolated," Mac remarked.

They came to the cabin clearing and found three Chevy Tahoes with the Wright County insignia on them and an Annandale squad car. There were two other vehicles, one probably the senator's and the other likely was Hisle's. Mac parked the Explorer near a Tahoe, and they all climbed out. Mac saw Hisle sitting by himself on a picnic table and walked over to him. Lich and Sally followed.

It was rare you saw Lyman Hisle shocked. He saw Mac walk up, but a blank stare remained on his face. Mac put his hand on his shoulder, "You gonna be okay, Lyman?"

He nodded his head, looking out towards the lake. After a moment he said, "I guess you were right."

"Lyman?"

Hisle looked up to Mac, shock and sadness on his face, "He did it. Why else do this?" he said, gesturing towards the cabin.

"I'm sorry, Lyman."

Hisle just shook his head and put his face into his hands. Lich looked at Mac and tilted his head towards the cabin. He was going to go take a look. Mac silently mouthed, "I'll be a minute." Then he leaned to Sally, quietly saying, "I think Lyman could use a cup. It's chilly out here." She nodded and headed back for the coffee.

After a moment, Lyman, more composed, spoke again. "I gotta tell ya, hell of a shock to find him that way." Sally was back and handed him a cup of coffee. Lyman took a sip, some color returning to his face, some life to his expression. "He had me convinced, though. I thought we were going to trial with you, Ms. Kennedy."

"You were inside?" Mac asked.

"Yeah. He hung himself from the rafters. Stood on a barstool, tied himself up, and kicked 'er out."

Mac looked at Sally and nodded for her to sit with Lyman. "I'm going inside."

As he walked inside, they were lowering the senator's body. Mac saw Lich in the front of the cabin, talking up the sheriff.

"Mac, this is Wright County Sheriff Rick Hansen." Hansen was tall, well over six feet, in his early forties, with a developing pot-belly. He was a jovial guy who warmly shook Mac's hand. "Thank you for your call, Sheriff."

"You're welcome. Saw plenty of you boys on the news last night," Hansen said. "Hell of a deal here. I met the senator a few times. Seemed like a nice enough guy. Guess he did that murder, though."

"That he did," replied Lich.

Mac looked at the coffee table. There was an empty liter bottle of Jose Quervo and an ice bucket, half full of water. A drink glass was tipped on its side. "Looks like the senator required a little liquid courage first."

Hansen walked over, "Yes, he did."

"A whole liter? That's a lot of courage," Mac replied.

"True enough," Hansen replied.

He took another look at the ice bucket, half full of water, "Must not have used much ice." Mac looked at the bottle a little closer, being careful not to touch it. The paper seal for the cap on the neck of the bottle looked freshly opened, "Seal looks pretty fresh, don't you think?"

"Yes."

"Drank this whole thing, huh?" Mac replied a little skeptically. A liter of tequila was a lot of liquor, forty-percent alcohol by volume. "Polishes this thing off and can still get up on the stool?"

Hansen caught his tone. "Yeah, we're going to get a blood alcohol as part of the autopsy."

Mac took a look at the rope, a real hangman's noose with good tight knots. "He did a nice job on the rope."

"Must have been a Boy Scout," Lich quipped.

"Hmpf." Mac nodded and walked over to the bar stool the senator used. "So, he stands on this, puts the rope around his throat and kicks it out?"

"That's what we think," replied Hansen.

Mac couldn't argue with that, the stool was high enough that the senator could have used it. It was lying in the right place on the floor for him to have kicked it out. He probably tied the rope and hung it first, then got drunk on the tequila. Mac got ready to head out. "Thanks again, Sheriff, for the call. Will you send me a copy of the autopsy report?"

"Be happy to."

Mac handed Hansen his card, shook his hand, and headed out with Lich. They walked back over to Lyman, who was talking with Sally.

"Lyman, was Johnson a big tequila drinker?" asked Mac.

"I don't know. Why do you ask?"

"Empty liter of tequila on the coffee table. Looks like he got himself pretty liquored up before he did it."

"He wasn't a teetotaler, I know that," replied Lyman.

Mac nodded and looked around. The wind blew and sent a shiver down his spine. He flipped the collar up on his leather coat and put his hands in the pockets. He took a walk around to the front of the cabin. From the front, it was a flat seventy-five yards down to the shore. There were far fewer trees in the front, as compared to the sides and back of the cabin. They had been cleared out to provide a clear view of the lake. He walked to the edge of the trees and looked back. You could see right into the cabin, see the rope hanging down.

"Yeah, McRyan, you can see right in, can't you?" Viper said under his breath, watching with binoculars from a boathouse across the small lake. McRyan was standing twenty feet from Viper's perch the night before.

"He can wonder about it all he wants. We're clean," Bouchard said. "No prints. The rope's clean, and we used gloves. Nobody touched the bottle or ice bucket. No forced entry that they could detect. He can guess and speculate all he wants, he ain't going to find shit. They'll have no choice but to call it a suicide."

At least Bouchard sounded sure. Viper would wait and see. McRyan eventually wandered back to Hisle and put his hand on his shoulder. Hisle nodded his head, and it looked like he said, "I'll be okay." McRyan didn't go talk to the sheriff again or snoop around any further. Instead, along with Lich and Kennedy, he headed back to the Explorer, got in, and drove away.

"Do you feel better now?" asked Bouchard.

"A little."

They were all quiet for a while as they headed back east on Highway 55 towards the Cities. Sally finally spoke, a tinge of disappointment in her voice. "I guess that wraps up that."

"Yeah, Ms. Kennedy, you lost your shot for the big time," Lich replied.

"There'll be others, I'm sure," she replied wistfully.

Mac just looked at the road ahead, wondering.

15

"YEAH, HE'S A SMART FUCK."

TWO WEEKS LATER

Mac pulled up to the Grand Brew for his usual. He got out of the Explorer and put his gloved hands in his trench coat pockets. Before leaving, he put the wool liner in his coat for some extra warmth. He would need it. The cold, windy November days were leading up to the Minnesota winter to come. This time of year, most days were cloudy, damp, and windy, the sun rarely making an appearance.

These days, he needed his hot caffeine injection to start his day more than ever. Since he started seeing Sally, there had been many late nights, and that was a good thing. Mac often thought the last couple of weeks that a person didn't realize how lonely he was, until he wasn't lonely anymore. Whether it was going to the Pub after work, to dinner or a movie, it was nice to have someone to spend time with again. He was still getting to know her, but it was good to be, as Lich put it, back in the saddle again.

Mac needed his caffeine shot for another reason. He and Lich had been assigned to Riley's detail on the University Avenue Strangler. They started that very morning, and he was perversely pumped. The Daniels case was over and done. A new senator had been appointed with a special election set for the following fall. Word was Helen Anderson was already angling to run.

The serial killer was still at large, and the political and media pressure was once again mounting on the department. Mac, having brought the Daniels case home, was the flavor of the month. This was especially the case after, at the chief's request, he gave an extended interview to the *Pioneer Press* about the Daniels case. After the article, questions began to surface from the media, wondering if Mac would become involved in the serial killer investigation. Flanagan, seeing a chance to take some heat off, put Mac and Lich on it.

Mac was of two minds about it. He welcomed the chance to work the case. Cases like this were why he wanted to be a detective in the first place. It was the kind of case his dad would have loved.

However, Mac worried about his friend Pat Riley, who was heading the serial killer detail. The case was beating the shit out of him, and now they were putting the new hotshot on the case. Thankfully, Riles had made it easy, seeking Mac and Lich out, welcoming them, saying the case could use a fresh set of eyes. Pat gave them both a file, the "Cliff Notes" version he called it, to get them up to speed. They could spend time with the full case files in the days to come.

The short file told Mac that they were dealing with a cold, calculating killer. There had been six deaths to date. The last two had only been seven days apart, and the concern was that the killer was picking up his pace. Mac remembered thinking that the Daniels case would take the heat off the chief for a while. It lasted all of four days until they found the sixth body on the following Tuesday.

The file revealed that the investigators, despite six murders, had little solid evidence on the killer, just speculation.

The one certainty seemed to be the victims. With the exception of one, they were working-class women. They worked shifts that usually ended between 10:00 p.m. and 1:00 a.m. They were physically similar women, nondescript in appearance, medium height, thin, and not physically strong.

Once he had the women, the serial killer strangled and then sexually assaulted them. He used a Trojan condom. Other than that, he left no traceable evidence behind. He wore gloves. He never left pubic hair, and they suspected that he shaved the area around his genitals, or perhaps was using a prop to complete the sexual assault. After strangling and assaulting the women, the asshole would dump the bodies in vacant lots in close vicinity to University Avenue. When he dropped the bodies, the killer left his signature, a balloon with a smiley face—"Have a Nice Day." Riles said it was his way of rubbing their faces in it.

The FBI had been brought in to complete a profile, and their opinion was chilling. Their killer was a white male, since all of the victims were white, and serial killers tended only to kill women of the same race. The killer was of strong build and good agility, able to take the women quickly without being seen or heard. He was likely a loner who lacked social skills and has struggled with women.

The victims were very average or ordinary looking women. The killer likely considered himself to be in this category as well, yet had had little success with such women or women in general. He likely sought out women of this type because of some past stressor or experience in his life with a working-class woman or women. This past experience, likely involving rejection of some kind, had stuck with him, something that he hadn't gotten over, that ate away at him and had finally come to the surface and caused him to seek out and kill these women. Nonetheless, he likely needed to have a woman in his life, despite his failings. In this regard, he might still live with his mother.

The areas where the women were found suggested he was a resident of or worked in the area. The killer, if he worked, did so during the day, as the women generally were abducted at night. His ability to get away undetected suggested he had watched the women for days ahead of the abduction, which required surveillance at night. It was likely that he prowled from place to place, looking for his target. Once identifying the target, he spent nights watching her every move, looking for the best place to take her. He then found privacy, perhaps in a van, or at some other location, maybe even his home, to commit the sexual assault. The dump locations and the leaving of the balloon was a way of feeling superior, pulling off the killing and being able to leave a calling card behind.

The sexual assault provided evidence of someone looking to have dominance over women. Poor, unsuccessful relationships or ones in which he was dominated were likely what caused him to act out in this fashion. In his life, he hadn't been able to get women to do what he wanted. Once he strangled them, killed them, he had dominance over them, he could do what he wanted, however he wanted. Then, once the assault was complete, the final act became symbolic—dumping the body like garbage in a vacant lot, the dominance over the woman complete.

His ability to identify his victims, abduct them, and get away almost completely undetected suggested some level of training, perhaps police or military. The ability to leave no evidence behind also spoke of some level of training or education in this regard.

For Mac, the scariest part of the profile was the opinion that the killer had a taste for the killing now, was perfecting his work, getting better at it. He would not stop. The FBI suggested the killer would keep a diary of the events, preparing to share his work with someone at some point in time. He likely spent time with the diary, reliving his acts, reveling in them.

Having seen the FBI's success with profiling, Mac suspected much of what the FBI said was true. Unfortunately, following up on the FBI's profile had proven unsuccessful.

Outside of what they knew about the victims and the FBI profile, direct evidence on the case was thin. The best piece of evidence they had was that he was probably using a van. Witnesses on two occasions had seen a van in the vicinity where a body was dumped. One witness saw a man run out of the vacant lot and get into a van. Problem was he was at least a block away. He couldn't see plates or any other identifying features of the van, other than the taillights, which flashed and were thought to be for a Ford Econoline. The investigative detail didn't have a color of the van, other than dark, probably black, brown, or blue. It was a van like a thousand others seen on a daily basis anywhere in town driven by delivery or repair guys.

The detail had run Minnesota license plate searches for felons with a history of sex crimes, who owned vans and perhaps had military or police training. There were a couple of hits, but they'd been quickly eliminated. There was more for Mac to read, but the condensed version got him up to speed for at least his first day.

Mac dropped the Explorer in the parking garage and walked into the Department of Public Safety Building. There was a detail meeting set for 8:15 a.m.; it would be his and Lich's first. As Mac walked in, he heard a horn beep behind him; it was Lich. Mac waited, and Lich quickly got out, wearing his old beige topcoat, replete with dirt and coffee stains. Columbo wouldn't have been seen in it. He didn't have it buttoned, couldn't over his potbelly. A gravy brown fedora covered his dome. However, the suit was the prize, faded green, with a faded yellow dress shirt and green tie with large gray stripes. His shirt needed collar stays as the tips flipped up.

Mac shook his head. "You don't let Dot see you like this, do you?"

"What?" Lich replied, holding his hands out.

Mac cackled. "What? What? I shouldn't even be seen with you." Mac wasn't necessarily going to be in *GQ*, but he looked good, dressed in a charcoal suit, gray dress shirt, and dark black tie. The tie was new, his first gift from Sally.

"Dot's only interested in what's on the inside, bitch," Lich replied, grabbing his crotch. Fifty-two, and he talked like he was twenty-two.

Mac shook his head and walked inside. Riley's detail had taken over a large conference room. At one end was a whiteboard that contained notes, facts, and information regarding the case. The detectives assigned to the case were listed, along with assignments. Lich and Mac were listed on the bottom, nothing assigned to them as of yet.

On the other end of the conference room was a bulletin board that included a detailed St. Paul street map. The homes of the victims were marked with blue pins, their work sites with green, and the locations their bodies were found in red. The victims were marked with numbers one through six, and information about each was typed on white sheets posted to the right of the map. In the middle of the conference room was an industrial metal table with old metal chairs that had green vinyl padding on the seat and backs. The conference table had three telephones, three thermoses, and two stacks of Styrofoam cups. There were a couple spare packs of sugar and a nondairy creamer container, crushed in the middle from over use. The room smelled faintly of body odor, the product of numerous hours of work on the case.

Members of the detail, eight strong—now ten with Mac and Lich —started to file in. They walked over and warmly welcomed the two new detectives. Mac had worried about the reception, but he imagined that Riles had laid down the law. As everyone milled around and exchanged pleasantries, Mac looked at the dump spots on the map.

Bobby Rockford, one of the detectives on the detail walked over, "Mornin', Mac." Rock was big, six foot three, two hundred fifty pounds, shaved head, with bright white eyes that contrasted against his black skin. He was scary when he smiled, with a gap you could drive a truck through between his two front teeth. A former Division II defensive tackle at Mankato State University, Rock was not a man to be trifled with. Paired with Riley, who was also at least six foot three, they were a physically imposing pair.

"Hey, Rock," Mac said, then looked back to the map. "Checking out where he's dumped the bodies."

"Yeah, he's a smart fuck," Rock gestured with his coffee cup "Every location has at least three ways out. The asshole probably never leaves the same way he goes in." He took a sip of his coffee. "In each spot, he only has a block or two to get back onto University, where a van—if we're right about that—wouldn't be viewed as being out of place, no matter the time of day."

Mac nodded, "I imagine he probably scouts his drop locations as well. He's probably familiar with the area—who lives there, who drives what vehicle, who's up at late hours."

"Yada, yada, yada," Rockford replied, nodding. "You read the FBI Profile on this guy right?"

Mac nodded.

"They think he might be some sort of ex-military or ex-cop, the way he conducts surveillance, attacks them in ideal spots, leaves nothing behind, and gets away undetected. He's good, the fucking prick."

Mac looked at his watch, 8:25 a.m. He wondered where Riles was.

Just then Riles came in, looking harried and anxious. He looked out to everyone and announced, "We have a balloon. Vacant lot on Myrtle, between Cromwell and Hampden. Let's go."

The air was sucked out of the room immediately. On a cold and blustery November day, number seven was awaiting their efforts. Nothing like baptism by fire, Mac thought.

16

"THEY HAVEN'T CAUGHT A BREAK YET. NOT ONE."

Myrtle Street was located in the industrial end of University Avenue on St. Paul's northwest side. That end of town was dotted with an assortment of manufacturing operations behind small sidewalk stores, ethnic shops, and numerous small bars with names like Ace's Place and Pete's Canteen. Mac and Lich drove over in their department-issue gray sedan, turning left at the GasUp station on the corner of Hampden and University. They went one block and hit a dead end, the only way they could go was right on Myrtle and the vacant lot was half way down on their left. A coroner wagon, two squads, and Riley's unmarked were already there.

The body had been dropped in a vacant lot filled with knee-high weeds and brush. Bottles, cups, rusted barrels, newspapers, an old recliner, and dirt piles littered the landscape. There was one sickly tree and the outline of the old foundation of a house that once had occupied the lot. The uniforms had taped off a large area around the body as well as along the street.

On both sides of the vacant lot were chain-link fences covered with vines, tall unkempt shrubs, and weed trees. The combination of vegetation made it virtually impossible for nearby houses to see into the vacant lot. The back wall of the Hancock Foundry spanned the backside of the lot. There were no windows and one lonesome set of double doors, with a dumpster to the left, one lid up and one down.

Across the street stood old two-story, white, wood-sided houses with steep, pitched roofs. They all had a solid, bland, wood front door and single picture window on the front with a metal awning. All the same style, built some seventy years earlier. The metal awnings and front doors were all different colors, the only thing differentiating the houses. The properties were not well tended, most having untidy yards. It was a poor, working-class neighborhood.

Riley was crouched by the side of the body, taking notes, while two crime scene techs examined the body, one of them speaking into a Dictaphone. Mac and Lich stood fifteen feet away. Mac couldn't make out much about the victim, other than she was nude, wrapped partially in plastic. He could see her legs and she fit the profile—thin, medium height. The balloon, tied around her ankle, bobbed and weaved in the November wind, smiling at him. Jeering.

The rest of the detail arrived shortly thereafter. Riley saw everyone coming and got up out of his crouch. He nodded for them to follow him over to the street. Everyone gathered around. Riles quickly gave out orders. They needed to canvas the area around the lot.

"Who found the body?" somebody bellowed.

Riles looked down towards the other end of the street towards the city workers digging up what looked like a sewer line. "One of the guys came over here to take a piss and saw the body. He's over working with his crew. I'll take Lich and McRyan over to talk to him." Everyone else spread out to take up their assigned tasks of what would likely be another fruitless search for anything on this guy.

A uniform fetched the city guy who had found the body. His name was Myron Dix, a large, rotund African American who looked to be in his early fifties, with a bushy gray beard. He was wearing his City of St. Paul hardhat and orange work vest over his tan canvas work suit, a smoke hanging out the side of his mouth. Mac admired the canvas work suit; it undoubtedly was warm, and he was already chilled. It was forty degrees, but with the wind howling it felt more like twenty.

Dix and his crew had arrived for work at 7:00 a.m. They had gone to work and didn't notice anything right away. "Anyway, around 7:45 a.m. or so, my two cups of coffee hit me, and I needed to piss," Dix said. "I'd usually get into the truck and hit a gas station or something, but with the vacant lot so close, I wandered over there." Never mind the fact that urinating in public was against the law and this guy was a city worker.

"What did you see?" Riles asked.

"Well, there's the one tree over there. I went behind it and did my business. On my way out, I looked over to my right and saw the balloon. That's been in the papers. I got a little closer and saw a leg. Another step or two, and I got the whole picture."

Lich jumped in. "Did you touch the body, anything like that?"

Dix put his hands up and shook his head. "No. No. No. Figured that killer was at it again. They say he dumps the bodies in vacant lots." Dix waved his left arm towards the lot, "This shithole qualifies. I ran back to the truck and called it in."

They went back over it again. Time of arrival, did he notice anything out of the ordinary, any vans in the area, anyone else walking through the lot? Dix had nothing to add. The two other guys on his crew were of no help. As they were walking away, Mac asked one last question, "You guys start today?"

"Naw, man," Dix replied. "Noon yesterday."

Mac and Lich stayed with Riley and continued on with the canvas. It was painful watching him work it. You could see it in his eyes as the day went along. House after house, witness after witness, nobody saw anything. The case was beating down on Riley, and the despair showed on his face, as they developed nothing other than their seventh dead body. Mac overheard a couple of conversations Riles had with the chief. It wasn't pretty.

Midday they learned that the victim's name was Charlene Murphy. She worked at the Hole-in-the-Wall, a diner that wasn't but five blocks away. She left work at 11:00 p.m. the night before, and the diner's morning workers found her car in the back of the parking lot, with her keys lying underneath. The strangler likely attacked her there, dragging her back into the alley and to the van they assumed he had. A canvas had been started behind the restaurant, but it was unlikely anyone saw anything. A ten-foot-high fence ran most of the length of the alley. Not only couldn't anyone see anything, but the fence also created an excellent sound barrier.

At 4:00 p.m., Riles ordered everyone downtown, leaving two men behind to catch people as they came home. Mac and Lich headed for their car. When Mac got into the car and turned the key, he noticed the gas gauge was nearly empty. Lich saw it too. "Let's hit the GasUp on the corner."

Mac pulled up to the line of pumps closest to Hampden Avenue, got out, and started filling the tank. "I'm chilled to the bone, man. Grab some coffee."

"Will do," Lich answered as he headed inside.

As the tank filled, Mac looked out onto University and watched the traffic pass by. Not much going on other than normal traffic for this part of town, delivery trucks and vans, beat up cars of working-class folks, the occasional cab. Not much pedestrian traffic, especially on such a cold and ugly day.

He looked back inside and could see Lich at the coffee pots. The GasUp station was big for the neighborhood, with four islands of gas pumps, four pumps per island. A large canopy with the big orange GasUp sign on it rested overhead. Mac looked up and noticed the surveillance cameras looking straight down on each set of islands. He looked up at the one for his island and it was bent, pointing out towards the corner of Hampden and University.

Hearing the pump pop, Mac looked inside and waved. Lich paid for the gas and the coffee.

Mac got back in the car, and Lich was there a minute later, with a steaming hot twenty-ounce coffee.

"Mucho gracias."

"I'd have gotten you a cerveza," Lich cracked, "but we're on the clock."

Mac took a drink and immediately felt better, the Styrofoam cup warmed his cold hands, and the coffee quickly heated his insides. Taking another sip, he looked up at the camera one more time and wondered. He started the car and instead of taking a right onto Hampden to go to University, he took a left, back towards the dump site.

"Where the hell are you going?" Lich asked.

"To check something out." Mac drove back to the construction site, where the crew was still working, minus Dix, who'd gone downtown to give a statement. The road was dug up completely from side to side and into the yards on either side. The hole was down nearly ten feet where they were repairing a sewer line. It blocked the entire street.

Mac got out and approached the crew. "I was talking to Dix earlier, and he said you guys started yesterday, round noon, right?"

A short guy with a wind-reddened, pock-marked face named Borowicz responded, "Yup, uh huh, that's right. Started right after lunch."

"How late did you work?"

"We were off the clock at 4:30."

"How big a hole did you have going at that point?"

"Pretty good size," Borowicz said.

"What's pretty good size?"

"Oh, we had the street dug up good, you know, you couldn't go past. We had the road-closed sign up on the other side so people on Cromwell wouldn't turn in. She was big and deep."

"You're saying no way anyone could get by."

"Nah, unless they were drunk and wanted to drive through the yards and stuff. Why would anyone want to try that?"

Exactly, thought Mac. "Thanks, guy. Stay warm."

"I fuckin' wish," replied Borowicz, heading back to work.

They walked back to the car. "What the heck was that all about?" Lich inquired.

"I'll show you." Mac backed up and turned back towards the GasUp station. "This morning I was looking at the big map of the city where they plotted out all the locations where the victims were found, right?"

"Yeah, so?"

"Rock and I were looking at it, and he made the comment that the guy always leaves himself multiple routes out. He goes in one way and probably out another."

"So?"

"With Myrtle closed like that, the only way in and out of here is Hampden. We take Hampden in, one block it's a dead end, and you can only go right on Myrtle. Now, if Myrtle isn't closed ..."

"He can go any number of ways."

"Right. He can go straight ahead on Myrtle then right or left on Cromwell."

"But, as far as I know, Riley had the gas station canvassed."

"Right. And there was nothing," Mac replied. "But let me show you something."

Mac pulled back into the GasUp station, this time in front. They got out, and Mac said, "Look at that." He pointed up at the camera he had been looking at earlier, under the canopy, pointing right out to the corner of Hampden and University. There was a large street light on the corner.

Lich, seeing it, turned to look at Mac with a little grin, "Long shot."

"Humor me."

The store manager was taking inventory in one of the aisles, making notes on his clipboard. His name was Harold, a short, curly-brown-haired guy dressed in a white shirt, orange tie, and khakis that had seen better days. He wore glasses with large, round, clear, plastic frames ten years out of style. Mac imagined the job didn't pay enough for new ones. Mac and Lich identified themselves.

"A couple of your guys were in earlier. I gave them the names of our people who worked last night."

"So, the store's open twenty-four hours, right?" Mac asked.

"Yeah."

"Are the security cameras always running?"

"Yeah, far as I know," Harold replied.

"Did our guys ask about those?"

"No."

"How come the one on the far left out there, underneath the over-head, is pointing out to the street like that?" Mac asked.

"Ohh, is that what this is about?" Harold replied, shaking his head, exasperated. "Guy who changes the gas pricing numbers hit it with a ladder the other day. I've warned him about that before, that he could hit it and sure 'nuff, he did," Harold stated, satisfied that he'd predicted it right. "I have a call in to get it fixed, but it might be a day or two."

"Is it still operating?"

"Yes. Why?"

"Mind if we take a look?"

Harold waved them to the back of the store. "Would I have a choice?"

"No, but it's all right for us to let you think you have one," Lich quipped.

Harold took them into the security room. After a store clerk in northern Minnesota was abducted and murdered a few years back, convenience stores started putting in more cameras, and GasUp had gone the whole nine yards. Two monitors that showed eight cameras, four inside and the four outside. "Here's the one you're looking for," Harold said, pointing to the upper left-hand corner of the right screen.

It was camera five, and it was looking right out at the corner. A truck pulled in front of the camera as they were watching. You could see most of the truck and the back end. You could even make out the plate. Of course, it was still daylight and that helped immensely, but the picture quality wasn't bad for black and white. Mac felt his heart skip a beat.

"Harold ... do you mind if I call you Harold?" Mac asked.

Harold didn't mind.

"Do you record?"

"Oh, yes, we keep it back several weeks."

"What do you record on? Video tape?"

"No, no, no," Harold replied, shaking his head with some pride, "We actually have a pretty good system. We record onto these DVDs. You can store a lot more on them and if you need to review them, the quality isn't bad."

Mac and Lich exchanged a look and a little smile. "Still a long shot," Lich said.

"Harold, my friend," Mac said, and right now he was liking Harold a whole lot, "we need to borrow the DVDs for the last week. What do you say?"

"Would I have a choice?" Harold asked, a little smile coming across his face.

"No," Mac replied.

"And in this case, I'm not gonna even let you think you have one," Lich added.

They grabbed the DVDs and signed a form for Harold. He'd been helpful, and they wouldn't want him to get in trouble with GasUp management. Mac could feel the adrenaline running through him as he bounded out the door to the car. Lich picked up on it, but cautioned, "Don't get your hopes up, son."

Mac knew he was right, but he didn't care. "Have you read the file on this case yet?" Mac asked back.

"I read the Readers Digest version Riley gave us last night. Not much there."

"That's right. And you know what? They haven't caught a break yet. Not one," Mac replied. "Well, maybe they just caught one. Lord knows Riles could use it."

Lich picked up on the feeling, "That he could, my friend. That he could."

Mac wasted no time getting back downtown, taking University over to Robert Street into downtown, and pulled into the parking garage. He finally had some warmth returning to his body, having already put much of the twenty ounces of coffee away. Once inside the building, he began to feel human again. They headed for the detail conference room. Riles and Rockford were inside, looking at the map, putting pins in for where the victim lived, worked, and where they'd found the body. Mac assumed the others were working the phones or maybe had already gone back out. Riles saw them and had a slightly perturbed look on his face. "Where have you guys been?"

Mac explained what they'd found. He could see just a little color return to Riles's face. "You're not suggesting we're going to see anything on there? I mean, I'd never get that fucking lucky in my lifetime."

"What have you got to lose, Pat?"

"Only my hair, a clump of which I found in the shower drain this morning. Pretty soon I'll look like Lich," Riles replied ruefully and with his first smile of the day.

17

"THOSE AIN'T PINE TREES."

Mac, Lich, Riles, and Rockford spent a few hours putting together a list of vehicles from the neighborhood and then went to forensics to watch the video.

Riles was pumped. If they were right about the Ford Econoline and that Hampden was the only way back to the vacant lot, there was a chance they would see the van. Could they get anything else of use off the video? Well, that would be another story.

Mac had planned to spend the night with Sally. When he called, she understood and was excited. "Call me if you guys find anything," she said. She had been assigned as legal counsel to the detail. Of course, she managed to torture Mac a bit, mentioning her disappointment that he wouldn't see what she'd bought at Victoria's Secret over the lunch hour. "That's playing dirty," he said.

Linda Morgan stayed to help them, and popped the disk for the previous night into the computer and projected it onto a larger screen.

Rockford, in his best boxing announcer voice, said, "Let the tedium begin."

And begin it did. Black and white video of a surveillance camera pointing out to a street corner—can't get much better than that. They started the video at 10:00 p.m. store time, 8:00 p.m. their time, and let it run real time.

The GasUp station was plenty busy for the first couple of hours, with vehicles coming and going. Many turned on Hampden to get to the GasUp and many then left the station on the Hampden Street exit, turning right and then going either left or right on University from the corner. There were a few dark-colored vans that turned into the GasUp station. None of them looked promising. None of them were Ford Econolines. They took down license numbers anyway. When the vans would leave the station, if they turned left on University they could see the back of the van and, if the lights for the plate box on the back were on, they could just barely see the plate, although not the license number.

"A little enhancement on that and you might make it out," Riley mentioned.

"Possibly," Morgan replied. "It'll be tough."

About midnight on the video, 10:00 p.m. their time, the action started slowing down. They started slowing down as well. Lich was out, sitting in a plastic chair, his head tilted back and snoring. Rock was doing the head bobs of impending sleep. Mac was fine, being a night owl most of the time. Riles was with it as well, desperate for something to break. Yet a fifth pot of coffee was brewing in the corner.

Two hours later, 2:00 a.m. GasUp station time, Lich got up and said he was going home. He would see them in the morning. Rockford woke up as well. He rubbed his eyes and yawned. He stared at his watch.

"Rock, if you want to go, go," Riles said. "We'll let you know if we see anything."

Rock nodded, staggered up out of his chair, put on his coat, and left without saying a word.

Thereafter, the action on the video was almost nonexistent. There was an occasional car that turned onto Hampden and went by the GasUp station. At 2:47 a.m. on the video, 12:47 a.m. their time, a minivan turned onto Hampden and went by the camera. Mac checked their notes. "Didn't we have someone who said they got home between 2:45 and 3:00?"

"Yeah, what was her name? Something funky. Oh, yeah, Lemon-jello Hardy."

"Lemonjello?" Mac replied quizzically.

"Yeah, spelled just like lemon Jell-O, but run together," Riles replied with a tired smile.

"Unbelievable."

"Nope. What's unbelievable is that she has a sister that lives with her, guess what her name is?"

"What?"

"Orangejello."

"No way," Linda replied. Mac just shook his head. First Dick Lick and now the jellos. What next? Someone names their daughter ESPN?

At 3:25 a.m. GasUp Station time, another vehicle looking like a van went by. "Anyone coming home around this time?" Mac asked.

Riles yawned and consulted his notes. "Yeah," he took a sip of coffee and flipped a page in his notes. "Mike Moriarity, dropped off by Kevin McReynolds, who drives a Ford pickup with a topper."

Morgan replayed the DVD and got close to the screen to look at the truck as it went by. It looked like that's who it was. Playing the DVD another minute or two confirmed it as the truck came back out and turned left onto University.

Virtually nothing passed after that. At 2:50 a.m. Riles got up and hit the head. Mac, who had started to nod off a little, sat up and rubbed his eyes. He put his coffee up to his lips when he saw it go by. "Linda, run that back."

Morgan yawned first, and then did as ordered. Mac got up and stood in front of the big screen. The van turned left onto Hampden from University. The headlights were square. The headlights on an Econoline were square. This van had a snout nose on it. An Econoline has a snout-nosed front. He couldn't see the plate at all. The left side of the front bumper looked to be caved in. The time in the lower left hand corner was 4:33 a.m.

Riles came back into the room, "What?"

"Anybody dropped off around 4:30 a.m.?"

Riles flipped through his notes, then shook his head. "Nope."

Mac pointed to Morgan. "Again."

Morgan replayed the video. Riles stood next to Mac and watched the van go by. "That's a fucking Econoline!"

"You sure?" Mac asked.

"Oh, yeah. I've studied those damned vans for weeks. That's an Econoline."

They let the DVD run, checking their watches. It seemed like an eternity. The van came back out at 4:42 a.m., nine minutes later. It came into the screen and turned left onto University Avenue. They could see the back and the license plate holder was partially lit, but they couldn't make out the plate. Morgan took it back and ran it again. But it was too far away, and they couldn't make it out other than the tiny white speck of a box on the dark big screen. She rewound it a third time, and they practically put their faces up to the screen. No dice.

Riley went nuts, pacing around the room, waving his arms, "Fuck, fuck, fuck! That's our asshole, guys. That's our asshole." He kept pacing and waving. "We gotta find someone or something. See if we can enhance that."

Morgan shook her head, "That's going to require a lot of work and equipment we don't have."

"Who does?" Riles asked.

"The BCA," Morgan replied. "Jupiter Jones is the man we need."

"Jupiter," Mac added, nodding and smiling. "He's definitely what we need."

Jupiter Jones was a longtime friend of Mac. He had met Jupiter in a computer science class at the University of Minnesota. While Mac went on to major in business and criminal justice, Jupe kept up on the computer studies. He was a computer genius.

Jupiter and a math wizard friend of his had started a little computer software business after college. Jupiter developed an intelligence program that helped businesses determine what their customers bought, when they bought it and how much they would spend. His math wizard friend was able to add mathematical equations to the program. Within five years of his graduation, Jupe's little company had grown to one hundred fifty employees. However, running the business required long hours and business acumen he didn't have or really care to develop. He sold the company for sixty million dollars, which he and his partner split. After taking care of many of their employees with severance packages, they each walked away with twenty million. Jupe didn't need to work.

What Jupiter had done since he sold his business was explore what could be done with computers and video. He had started another small business that developed programs to convert video into numerous uses, but it didn't eat up a lot of his time. So, to keep busy, he also worked freelance for the Minnesota Bureau of Criminal Apprehension, helping when computer and video skills were needed. Now was such a case.

Mac looked at his watch, 3:40 a.m. "Jupiter's going to love this," he said as he dialed him up. Jupiter answered on the third ring.

"Whoever this is," a sleep-slurred voice said, "it better be good."

"Still wearing Tough Skins?"

Silence on the other end for a moment. "Mac?"

"Jupe, I need a big favor. I need it right now, and I think you can help me."

"With what?"

"Identifying a serial killer."

～

The Minnesota Bureau of Criminal Apprehension (BCA) was located on Maryland Avenue, just north of downtown St. Paul. Jupiter, who lived half an hour away, arrived to find Mac and Riles waiting in the lobby with coffee and a bag of donuts. A smallish man with messy, blondish hair and round glasses, he looked like the computer geek he was.

"This'll challenge all of your skills, Jupe," Mac said.

"Hmpf," Jupe snorted. "We'll see about that," he replied cockily as he unlocked the door into a computer and video lab. Jupe slung a bag off of his shoulder.

"What's in there?" Riles asked, pointing at the bag.

"Some of my own equipment. From what you said on the phone, we might need to independently upgrade the state's equipment to flesh this out." He gave a knowing wink.

Mac handed Jupiter the DVD, and Jupiter put it into his computer drive. He pulled the image up and watched the key section a few times. He kept playing it back and forth.

"Well. It's awfully grainy, but I might be able to clean it up some."

"How quickly, Jupe?"

"It'll take some time."

"How much?" Mac pressed.

"Not sure, buddy. Gimme me six, maybe eight hours, and we'll have a better idea. It's very grainy, and it is from a long, long, *long* way away. As I look at it, you can only really make out the right side of the plate."

They looked at the video. Jupiter pointed, "See, there's a little shading there. I don't think you'll get the left side of the plate. But I might be able to get something off the right side."

"Thanks, Jupe," Mac said yawning.

"You boys are free to sack out here," Jupe pointed to some cots stacked in a corner.

"Thanks, man, I owe ya."

"You kidding, Mac? I live for this shit."

Jupiter sat down and started to go to work. Mac and Riles looked at one another and their watches—5:25 a.m. They lifted down a couple cots from the corner.

"The state, always providing plush accommodations," Riles muttered.

~

Mac woke up startled, momentarily trying to get his bearings. "Oh, yeah, I'm at the BCA," he groaned, yawning and scratching his head. He looked at his watch 12:05 p.m. Holy cow, he'd slept a while. He woke up to find the computer screen showing a program running but no Jupiter. Pat was still sleeping, and Mac let him keep going. Sleep had been hard to come by for Riles as of late.

Just then Jupe came back in, carrying a tray of coffee and some sandwiches. Mac grabbed one of each, and Jupe quietly explained how he had been breaking down the frame that had the best view of the van's plate. He had then been working the area of the picture where they could see the license plate. He was refining the picture, trying to get the most out of the pixels. The last picture showed the plate, and Jupe had been right. They would only be able to see the right side of the plate, which was usually numbers. Right now it was still very blurry, three black, squarish blobs on the screen.

"The program I'm running it through now should clean it up as good as I can do anyway," which was probably as good as anyone could do. "Should take another twenty minutes or so."

Mac took a bite of his sandwich and looked the picture over. Riley started to come alive, rolling off the cot, smelling the coffee and sandwiches. "Anything?" he asked anxiously.

"Not yet," Mac replied.

"We'll know soon," Jupe added.

They talked for twenty minutes. Jupe was interested in the Daniels case, and Mac gave him the run down. Jupe asked about women, and Mac gave him the scoop on Sally.

"She sounds like a nice gal," Jupe said.

"Yeah, she is."

They talked a little longer about nothing in particular. Finally Jupe said, "Let's see what we have." Jupiter maneuvered the mouse and opened a program, and there it was.

It was still a little fuzzy, but it wasn't numbers. They had letters, and they were clear enough to Mac, "F-M-G."

"That's odd" Riles said, "These are reversed."

Mac looked a little closer. He was right; the numbers should be on the left side, "Looks like maybe we can make out a number there."

"What is it?" Jupe said, squinting at the picture.

"It's a five or a six, I think," Riles said, also squinting.

Mac took a closer look at the upper right-hand corner of the picture. Along the top of the license plate, above the letters, was what looked like a grainy circle with a house or, wait, the angling of the roof? Mac pointed to it, "Riles, what'dya make of this?"

Riles looked, moving his head closer and squinting at the screen, "Those ain't pine trees."

"Yeah, looks like a barn and a farm scene," Mac replied, and added, "and the letters are on the right side."

"What in the hell are you guys talking about?" Jupe asked.

Riles and Mac smiled at each other and then looked at Jupe, uttering in unison, "Wisconsin."

18

"THIS ONE LOOKS INTERESTING."

Riley called in the partial plate number while Mac drove well over the speed limit back to the station, his flasher and siren parting traffic like the Red Sea. Jupe had come through big time. They finally had a break. Mac could hear the excitement in Riles's voice as he called into Rockford. Mac also heard the obligatory, "You gotta be shittin' me," rejoinder shouted through the phone.

"God, I hope that plate matches up," Riles said when he hung up. "Rock's already starting a computer search."

Mac and Riles walked into the conference room with Rock and the rest of the detail waiting with an extra bounce in their manner. They had a break, and everyone was ready to go. They practically wanted to reach through the computer monitors to grab the information. The printer was spitting out reams of paper.

"Rock, what've you got going here?" Riles asked.

"Report, Wisconsin Econoline vans with F-M-G and a five or six," Rock replied. "We'll make copies and start working through them."

The printer burped out the last piece of paper. A detail guy grabbed the paper out of the printer and sprinted out of the room. He was back within five minutes with a stack of reports.

~

They got started working through the reports, and Lich chuckled out loud.

"What?" asked Rockford.

"Mac."

"What about him?"

"He's got a horseshoe up his ass."

"Thank God," Riles added.

Mac cringed. "We haven't found anything yet, boys."

"It's there. I can feel it," Riles replied.

"Cases are like anything else. Sometimes you get hot," Mac mused. It was pure luck that he'd looked up at the video camera and noticed it pointed out at the street. It was pure luck that the camera was pointed at the perfect angle. It was pure luck Jupiter could get a partial plate. "I'm seriously considering getting on a plane to Vegas."

"You should at least go out to Mystic Lake Casino," Rockford added. Mystic Lake Casino was an Indian casino in Prior Lake, a southwest suburb of the Twin Cities.

Mac started working through his report. Rock had printed all records for vehicles with F-M-G and either a five or six and Ford Econoline vans. That brought them fifty-three records, which everyone started reading through. Each record contained information such as date of birth, height, weight, eye color, address, occupation, income, and employer among other things.

The reading was tedious. There were a couple of possibilities yelled out, with everyone turning to the specific record. One was an address in Prescott, and another in Grantsburg, both in western Wisconsin. The vans were both lighter colored. One was registered to a woman. They were close enough that they were put into the possible pile.

One of the guys ran across the street to Wang's for take out. Gut bomb Chinese food—nothing better. They emptied out the pop machine to wash it all down. The conference table was full of empty white boxes and soda cans. The coffee machine was started, and a few scattered white Styrofoam cups littered the table. It was not a good diet mix. Everyone was belching, and more than one person asked about Tums.

Then they had a real hit.

Riles shouted, "Forty-six looks interesting."

Everyone started flipping pages. Mac was on record forty-four at the time, turned the page and read out loud, "Forty-six. Dirk Knapp. Age twenty-nine. Resides in Hudson, Wisconsin. Has a 1997 Ford Econoline Van registered in his name."

"What's he do?" someone yelled, not yet to the page.

Mac scrolled down the page with his index finger. Bingo. "He's employed as a driver by Quick Cleaners on University Avenue," Mac answered. He grinned.

That got everyone's attention. Quick Cleaners was a large dry cleaning shop and did a huge volume of clothing and uniform dry cleaning. It would not be uncommon to see a Q Cleaner van anywhere in St. Paul and especially on University. In fact, their main location was on University.

There was a buzz in the room. This was a good possibility. Everyone broke into conversation, people fighting to speak over one another. Mac sat back and took it all in. It was the sound of guys who, after working a case for a couple of months with no success, finally saw a ray of light. They had a lead, and excitement simply took over. Any semblance of order was momentarily lost.

Finally, Riles jumped in, "Hey, shut the fuck up. We have some others to go through here, so let's settle down," then to Mac, "Anything else?"

"Was in the Marines, medically discharged in 2000. No criminal record."

"Medical discharge? Anything on that in the record?" someone asked.

"Not that I see," Mac replied, shaking his head.

"Okay, make a note of that," Riley ordered. "If we need to, we'll see if we can get those records. How many more do we have to go through?"

"Seven."

"Okay. Let's get through them. Then we'll get back to Knapp."

Of the seven remaining records, there was one other mildly interesting candidate from Elk Mound, but nothing as close to what they thought they should be looking for as Knapp. Consequently everyone in the room was keyed up to take a closer look at Dirk Knapp. It was 7:45 p.m., and everyone felt like it was 7:45 a.m. with a full night's rest under their belt.

Rockford said what was on everyone's mind, "Road trip to Hudson anyone?"

Hudson was twenty miles east of St. Paul just across the St. Croix River and into Wisconsin. The Wisconsin counterpart to Stillwater, Hudson was a quaint town, with a main street and old brick-front stores and shops. In the summer, the private marinas filled with river pleasure boats. The shoreline was dotted with numerous restaurants and bars with docks so that people could stop in while boating and have dinner and drinks. Now that it was November, the river, docks, and restaurants were quiet. Knapp's address put his home just north of Hudson, resting along Wisconsin State Highway 35.

They made a convoy to Hudson. All that was missing was, "This is the Rubber Duck and a 10-4, good buddy." Eight detectives made the trek out. More had wanted to come, but Riles held them off, wanting to get a look at Knapp's place before half the St. Paul Police Department camped outside his front door. At 9:30 p.m., they all stopped in the parking lot of an Italian restaurant on the north side of town. A call ahead to Hudson was made and the police chief met them in the parking lot. "Whatever you boys need, let me know. We're glad to help." He gave them a rundown of the road ahead and where Knapp's place was.

Riles, Mac, Lich, and Rockford left the others at the restaurant and cruised Knapp's place, which was another half mile up the road on 35.

Knapp's house sat on the west side, one hundred yards back from the road. There was a bright yard light that illuminated an old white, two-story, clapboard farmhouse, two out buildings and a large red barn. A faint light peered through the front picture window. In addition to the van, Knapp also had a 1999 Grand Am registered in his name. They saw neither vehicle. It looked as if nobody was home.

They slowly drove by, taking a look. There were few trees obstructing the view, and recently harvested farmland surrounded the home. Farm equipment was noticeably absent. There were no homes nearby on that side of the road.

"Should be pretty easy to see him coming and going," Rock remarked.

"If we can find a place to sit and watch. We can't exactly sit at the end of the driveway unnoticed," Mac replied.

"I was just thinking the same thing," Riles added.

A housing development was springing up a quarter mile up the road on the right side, opposite Knapp's place. Riles drove down to the development and turned right. Three homes were under construction on the right side of the street. Between the second and third was a vacant lot that eventually would hold a home. It was a pile of dirt for the time being. Riley turned the van around, and they pulled along the curb. They could see through the vacant lot to Knapp's place.

"Here's one spot," Rockford stated.

It turned out that for now it was the only one that they could find to watch Knapp's place without drawing attention. They drove by the farmhouse one more time then went back to the others waiting at the restaurant. Riley gave the orders for the night. Two would wait at the restaurant and watch from the south, while the other two would take up the spot in the housing development. Riles ordered Mac, Lich, and Rock home.

"What about you, Riles?" Rock asked.

"I'm going home too, I'm exhausted."

19

"THE MILITARY HAIRCUT, THE SPIT-SHINED SHOES."

B *eep, beep, beep.* Mac reached over and turned off the alarm. He sat up and yawned and took a closer look at the clock, 6:30 a.m. Riles had sent him home at 10:30 p.m. He'd called Sally on the way home, and she had him come over. Five minutes after hitting the sack, he was asleep. Never a deep sleeper or someone who required anymore than four or five hours, Mac crashed hard and slept soundly. Several hours of sleep left him feeling refreshed.

He swung his feet out of bed, rubbed his eyes, and yawned. He got up, scratched his ass as he went over and looked out the window. A gust of wind rattled the pane, and the leaves skipped down the street. It was overcast, another typical cloudy, windy, chilly November day.

The shower was running. He wondered if Sally was feeling as refreshed as he was. Mac headed for the shower to find out.

Two hours later, he checked his watch as he pulled up to the Grand Brew. He wanted his usual double latte to start the day, even if he was starting much later than usual. Mac was one for routines, and this was one of them.

As he walked inside the coffee shop, he had a smile on his face as he thought about the last two hours. Sally had indeed been refreshed. While she gave him the obligatory, "Men are animals," when he jumped into her shower, they had quickly moved to the bed.

Later, as they dressed, Mac filled her in on Knapp.

"What are you guys going to do?

"We'll follow him and see what develops. We can't even be sure that this is the guy." Mac took a bite of his toast and, with a half-full mouth, said, "But it feels right."

Sally sipped her juice. "How come?"

"Just does. Instinct, intuition, gut. Whatever it is, this is the break the case needed."

"I hope you're right," Sally said as she bit into her toast. "You guys thinkin' about a search warrant?"

"I'm thinking our case on this guy is a little thin. But I imagine we'll be talking about it," Mac replied. "Before we get that far, we have to see the van first." He took a sip of his juice. "Another thing that concerns me about going for a search at this point is that he's been so good at leaving nothing behind for evidence. He probably has that van clean as a whistle. If we go for the warrant, find nothing, then where does that leave us?"

"I see your point," Sally replied. "So you follow?"

"Yeah. If he sticks to his pattern, maybe we catch him in the act or something."

Twenty minutes later, Mac pulled the door open to the Grand Brew and headed inside. He ordered his usual, paid his usual, and headed out.

Sally got into her office just before 9:00 a.m., turned on her computer, and picked up her phone to check voice mails. Only three messages, which was a pleasant surprise. She punched in her computer password and heard a knock on the door. Oh oh. She turned to see Helen.

"Good morning, Helen."

"Good morning. A light day ahead of you?" The tone in her voice said it all. Sally was late. If Helen Anderson was a stickler for anything, it was being on time. She wanted the impression that her office was working hard, doing the people's business and, by extension, her business. Therefore, she always wanted her people in early and working late. Of course, many in the office grumbled that they did all the work and Helen got all the glory. She did like to be on camera and quoted in the paper. The fact that she knew little, if anything, about criminal law didn't help and pissed people off. But she was the boss, at least for now, a senate run in the offing.

"In fact, yes," Sally replied.

"I see," Anderson said, the tone of disapproval remaining.

Sally needed to change the subject, "I have what may be some good news, though."

"What's that?"

"The police may finally have a suspect in the University Avenue killings."

That perked up Helen's attention, "Really? Tell me."

Sally could see Helen savoring the headlines.

Mac, Lich, Riley, and Rock, along with a few others, met briefly downtown with Chief Flanagan and Peters. Knapp came home at 1:15 a.m. He was on the road again at 8:00 a.m., heading into work at Quick Cleaners.

Knapp's Q Cleaners location was on the northwest corner of Lexington and University Avenue. He appeared for work at 9:30 a.m. His MVR record from Wisconsin said he was employed as a driver. They figured he worked some sort of later 9:30 a.m. to 6:00 p.m. shift, which made some sense based on pick-ups and drop offs.

The building itself was on the corner, with a large parking lot full of vans to the west. Mac pulled his van into a shopping mall parking lot across the street with the back of the van facing the store. He and Lich could look out the tinted windows in the back. They each had binoculars, and a radio sat on the floor. The rest of the crew was spread out around the store, waiting for action.

At 10:15 a.m., the radio crackled with the voice of Dan Patrick, "I think our boy just came out the door."

Mac responded, "Copy that." He looked through his binoculars and saw a tall, lean, white male with short blond hair, almost a military cut. He was wearing a green full-body, zip-up uniform and had a clipboard. Mac noticed his boots, bright black, as if they had been spit-shined.

Knapp got into one of the white Q Cleaner vans and backed it up to a small loading dock where a couple of other men from inside started loading the van with white hangers full of plastic-covered shirts, suits, uniforms, and other clothing for delivery. In ten minutes the van was full. One of the other workers gave Knapp a few sheets of paper that he put on his clipboard. Knapp gave the guy a little wave, jumped in his van, and pulled out of the parking lot, heading west along University.

The detail tailed Knapp all day as he made deliveries up and down University Avenue for nearly four hours, going as far west as the University of Minnesota in Minneapolis, and back east along University, to within a few blocks of the State Capitol. Deliveries were made to homes, offices, factories, a motel, restaurants, and bars. The stops never ventured far north or south of University Avenue. At 3:00 p.m. he stopped at a McDonald's for a late lunch. Mac watched through the binoculars as he wolfed down a super-sized meal.

After his lunch, he did his pickups, hitting all of the same kinds of establishments up and down University. At 5:45 p.m., he backed his van up to the loading dock area at Q Cleaners, and a couple of workers came out and started unloading the van while Knapp headed inside.

At 6:00 p.m. sharp, Knapp walked, almost marched, out of the building and got into a red Pontiac Grand Am. He pulled out and drove west on University. Just past Snelling Avenue, he turned left into a parking ramp. A detail van followed Knapp in. Mac kept going west on University one block to a Burger King where he pulled in and stopped, waiting for a status on Knapp.

Five minutes later Riley popped on the radio, "Knapp's inside Applebee's. Looks like he's going to order dinner. Everyone find a spot and sit tight."

Mac and Lich both looked at the Burger King sign and Lich blurted, "You want fries with that?"

~

At 7:45 p.m., Knapp left Applebee's. He didn't head home. He stopped at three bars along University Avenue. At each stop, a member or two of the detail got out and went inside to observe. At each bar, Knapp would stop in and have a beer or two, usually sitting at the bar. Most of the time he watched whatever game was on TV. At Murphy's Bar, he watched the Wild and Red Wings game. At Pistol Pete's, he engaged in idle chitchat with a group of men while watching the Wolves game.

His last stop was Dick's Bar on the northeast corner of University and Arundel. It was 11:15 p.m. The radio chirped with Riles's voice. "Mac, your turn."

"Copy that," Mac replied. He grabbed his leather jacket and his beat up old Twins baseball cap and opened the door. He stopped and quickly looked back at Lich, who was chewing on a cigar. "Got a spare?"

Dick's was a classic dark hole-in-the-wall bar. On the left side was a long bar that ran forty feet to the back. Along the wall behind the bar were shelves with various unorganized bottles of liquor. Along the right side were booths, with red vinyl seats, hacked up from years of use and inattention. In the back was a narrow hallway with a backdoor to the parking lot. There were bathrooms along the right side and a small kitchen on the left.

Dick's was a working man's bar. No suits, no ties. Instead people wore shit-kickers, dirty pants, work coats, and ball caps. As Mac listened to the conversations, every other word was "shit," "fuck," "asshole," or "cocksucker." A smoky haze muted the dim light. Along with the bottles along the back wall one could get a pack of smokes, a cheap cigar, or some beef jerky. A quick count told Mac there were twenty-five customers.

Knapp sat in the middle of the bar, looking up at the TV that hung over the far end of the bar. A hoops game was on ESPN. Mac looked up in time to see Shaq nearly pull the basket down to the floor with a massive dunk, which caused someone to yell, "Jesus Christ!"

Mac picked an empty stool at the corner of the bar, next to the pull-tabs, just inside the front door. He could sit and look straight down the bar at Knapp. The bartender turned towards him to serve a customer between Knapp and Mac. She took his order, looked towards Mac and flashed him a smile.

The bartender was not what you'd expect to find at a place like Dick's. She was attractive as hell. She was a petite blonde wearing a tight white Dick's T-shirt, no bra, and her nipples were in full bloom. The dirty old boys in here must love it. She had short, kinky hair, kind of spiked on top and a hundred-watt smile that she flashed constantly. No wonder there were a few folks in here. Mac wondered what the heck she was doing here. She could be working a lot of other places.

She sauntered on over to Mac, flashed him a bright-white smile, "What can I get ya, hun?"

"I'll take a bottle of High Life and a book of matches."

"Sure thing," she replied with the smile, heading back to get the beer. Along with the tight shirt, she was wearing snug jeans that hugged her slender legs and little ass. Steady boy, Mac said to himself. He checked out Knapp, who was eyeing up the bartender as well, making a little conversation with her while she reached in the cooler for Mac's beer. She flashed Knapp a smile as well and then wandered back to Mac. "$3.25."

Mac handed her a twenty. "I'll take fifteen on the pull-tabs. Keep the rest."

She grabbed a basket, put the pull-tabs in, and wandered off to wait on the rest of the customers. Mac took a pull off his beer and winced a little at the taste. He wasn't a real High Life fan, but it was a working-man's beer, and he was in a working-man's bar. He lit his cigar and started to slowly work his pull-tabs, a uniquely Minnesota form of gambling. Pull-tabs were small cards, smaller than playing cards with three tabs. You pulled away the tabs, and if you had a match all the way across on any of the three tabs, you were a winner. On the fourteenth card, Mac hit $100 with a line through three cherries; his lucky night. He caught the bartender's eye, holding up the winner.

She walked back over casually, flashed him another little smile, "Lucky you." She went to the cash drawer for the pull-tabs and came back with his winnings. "Here you go."

"Keep twenty for yourself."

"Thanks." Another smile. She was cute, in a dirty girl sort of way. She pocketed the money.

Mac took another look at Knapp, who was staring in a different direction. At the far end of the bar was another woman. She was more ordinary looking. She too was small and petite. But whereas the bartender was attractive as hell, this one was less so. She had long, straight, black hair, which she pushed behind her ears to keep it out of her face. The bartender had her face done up; this one was a plain Jane. She had slender legs, but you couldn't see her ass. It was hidden by an oversized Dick's Bar sweatshirt. The bartender was the epitome of "Hey, look at me," but this one was the "Don't notice me" type. She approached Mac with a crate of glasses and proceeded to stack them under the bar, near the ice bin. She wasn't unattractive, Mac thought. If she worked a little, she could probably do pretty well. She just seemed more shy and reserved. And Knapp was checking her out. Mac made a little small talk.

"Could you grab me a glass of ice water?"

She looked up at him quizzically. "Don't get a lot of requests for that in here."

"I don't imagine you do. Just a little parched."

"Sure." She filled the glass up with ice and squirted some water in from the gun. He casually looked beyond her to see Knapp locked in on her. "Here you go," she said as she put the glass in front of him.

"Thanks. What's your name?

"Linda."

"Thanks, Linda."

"No problem." She sauntered back down the bar and past Knapp, who eyed her all the way. He was sly about it, but he was looking.

"Hmpf," Mac thought. He looked at his watch, 11:30 p.m.

For the next half hour, Mac kept his eye alternately on Knapp, Linda, and whatever was on the TV. Knapp watched Linda intently as she came and went. He hardly paid attention to the cute bartender, which made him entirely different from everyone else, including Mac. Linda came in and out of the bar area. She delivered food, took care of the various supplies, and mixed an occasional drink. She was a combo bar back and bartender. The hot bartender just worked the patrons.

Knapp watched Linda the entire time. Mac gave him credit. He had some skill. No way did Linda know she was being scoped.

The hoops game ended at midnight, and Knapp settled up, leaving a nice tip behind. Mac imagined that the hot bartender made nice tips, especially if she dressed like that every night. He would have to get her name at some point, so he did not keep thinking of her as the hot chick. The crusty guys in Dick's weren't going home to anything like her.

Mac watched Knapp head out the back, bumping into Linda on the way out. Wonder if that was intentional? There was some small talk, and Knapp continued out the back door. Mac pulled out his phone and buzzed Riles. "He's on the way out the back."

"Got him. We're meeting in the Gas & Shop lot in five minutes. The second shift will put Knapp to bed." Riley clicked off.

Mac took the last drink of his beer. The bartender saw him and wandered back down to him.

"Can I get you one more, hun?"

"No thanks. That'll do me for tonight. But let me ask you, what's your name?"

"Sheila."

"Well Sheila, my first time in, and I appreciated the service."

She flashed him the 100-watt smile and said, "Well, you come back now."

Mac smiled. He had a feeling he would.

They met in the parking lot. Riley started things off. "So what do we think?"

"He don't look much like a serial killer," Dan Patrick said.

"True enough," replied Rockford.

"It's not like he's going to have a sign hanging on him—'Hello, I'm your neighborhood serial killer,'" quipped Lich.

"I know, Dick," replied Patrick, "it's just that usually those guys have a look about them. This guy looks normal."

"Ted Bundy was normal looking," Rockford replied. "Hell, he was good looking, woman were drawn to him."

Riles looked at Mac. "What do you think?"

"I think he knows University Avenue and the surrounding neighborhoods like the back of his hand. He was up and down it all day long, in and out of all of those businesses. Then after work, he's at Applebee's and three bars, all on University. He's in and out of all those streets. And these guys are right, he's normal looking, so he isn't likely to draw suspicion."

"I was thinking the same thing," Riley replied. "Looks like he works hard for his employer; I mean, there was no dickin' around on those routes today. He was in and out of all those places quick."

"Yeah. Hard-working guy," Mac replied. "We go around asking people where the victims worked, anyone suspicious hanging around. Everyone says no. If it's this guy, he's doing nothing to raise suspicion. He's in and out. I suppose he might throw a little line of bullshit at the ladies. I watched him do that at Dick's Bar just now with the bartender. But she was a hot little thing so that's pretty normal."

Lich jumped in. "He's strong too. He's got that lean body you can tell is strong."

Rock agreed. "He carries a lot of that laundry in on those hangers, over his shoulder. I mean there were some pretty big loads. It's awkward, hard on your hands and arms, and he seemed to be doing it without breaking a sweat. He's gotta have strong hands."

Riley jumped back in. "He walks around like he's still in the military, almost as if he's marching. That straight posture, arms swinging at the side with that clipboard."

"The military haircut, the spit-shined shoes," Mac added. "Do we have someone trying to get his military file?"

"Sally Kennedy is on it. Says we should have it tomorrow."

"Medical discharge, right?" Rockford asked.

"Yeah, that's what we got with the Wisconsin records."

"Wonder if he whacked out or something. I mean, he's walking and working okay."

"We'll find out when we get the file," Riley said, stifling a yawn. "Let's meet at the Cleveland in the morning, and we'll go from there."

"One other thing," Mac stated. "He's got his next target."

"*What?*" everyone replied in unison.

"Bar back, bartender, whatever you want to call her, at Dick's. Her name's Linda."

"How do you—" Riles started.

"—Know?" Mac described the bar and what he saw between Knapp and Linda. "He was practically ignoring this hot bartender and focusing solely on this Linda, and he had this look in his eyes, like a hunger. He was subtle about it, but I could tell. And the woman, this Linda, she fits the profile from what I've seen: smaller woman, working class, not overly attractive."

"A little early to draw that conclusion, don't you think?" Rock asked.

"Absolutely," Mac replied. "I'm just saying, from what I saw, I'd be willing to go down to the casino and put a $100 down that she's the target."

"Anything else?" Riley asked.

"No. Just that you guys are all going to want to take turns going inside Dick's. Let me tell you, that little bartender in there is smokin'...."

~

Viper saw McRyan's Explorer pull into Kennedy's driveway at 1:15 a.m. He and Bouchard were parked a block down. They had another van parked at McRyan's place, but Viper figured he would go to Kennedy's.

"Looks like you were right," Bouchard said.

"I figured."

"How come?"

"They're both fairly recently divorced. They're back in the game again, and they're all hot for each other. Were I McRyan, this is what I'd be doing."

Viper thought he was done with McRyan. But then they'd gotten word he broke the serial killer investigation open. With McRyan having worked the Daniels case, they feared he'd make the connection between that case and how they used the serial killer to cover their tracks.

"So what's the plan?"

"We follow McRyan to see what he and that detail are up to."

"And."

"We may need to find a way to take this Knapp fellow out before they get to him."

20

"HE'S DOING THE RECON ON HER NOW."

The detail trailed Knapp for another five days. By Monday they knew he was their guy and who his next victim would be. Mac was on the money.

On workdays, the pattern remained the same. Knapp started at 9:30 a.m. and did his deliveries up and down University Avenue. He'd eat his lunch and then do his pickups. After work, he would go out to dinner and then hit the bars along University Avenue. Each night he hit Dick's Bar. Each night he'd closely watch Linda. Each night another cop would come out of the bar and tell Mac how hot the bartender was. After Knapp hit the last bar each night, he made the thirty-minute drive home to Hudson, with the St. Paul police department parading behind him.

In the interim, they got a copy of his military file. Dirk Knapp had been an excellent Marine. He was with a recon unit and received top marks in his evaluation reports until he met a woman named Shirley Warner, who worked in the administrative offices at his base. Knapp and Warner found themselves in a relationship that went bad. He had become very possessive of her, and she broke it off. Knapp took the breakup hard, but he seemed to be holding it together until another member of his unit started dating Warner. Knapp lost it, went to her home, and severely beat the other man in his unit and went after Warner with a knife. The indication was that Knapp suffered some sort of a mental breakdown. He was hospitalized for a number of months and he eventually was granted a medical discharge. That was four years before.

Since his discharge, he'd worked for Quick Cleaners as a driver. Tax records indicated a steady income from his work there. A discreet inquiry uncovered that he was an excellent employee, always on time, courteous to customers, and worked hard. He was a bit of a loner and kept to himself for the most part. He wasn't unfriendly in any way, just not terribly outgoing.

Tax records in Hudson revealed he and his mother owned his home. They'd originally owned forty acres but recently sold thirty-five of them to a developer. Soon, a housing development would start around their five-acre plot. They'd come out well on the sale of the land.

"I wonder why the guy even continues to work?" mused Rockford.

"Mother probably kept it all. Fucking women," Lich growled.

Mac and Lich had Saturday off, but were back on the tail Sunday. Most of the day was spent in the van, watching Knapp's place from the housing development. Even with a day off, the tedium of a stakeout gets to one after a while. Fast food, bags of chips, coffee, sodas, nothing healthy to eat. He was cooped up in a van most of the day with the weather turning cold. There were only so many magazines and newspapers he could read. Only so many radio shows he could listen to. Only so many conversations he could have with Lich, especially when he started to talk about what he and Dot were doing.

"Dick, spare me the details."

"Hell. I'm just hoping you'll tell me what a fine piece of ass that Sally Kennedy is."

Mac just rolled his eyes. "I don't talk."

Lich snorted, "You're a cop. Cops talk. Let's have it."

Mac was going to reply when he saw Knapp walk out of the house and get into his car "Our boy's on the move," and not a second too soon. Knapp pulled down the driveway in the Grand Am. They still hadn't seen the van.

"It's Sunday night, he's probably just going for milk or something," Lich thought.

Mac grabbed the radio. Riley and Rockford were down the road at the Italian restaurant. "Riles, Knapp's on the move."

Lich jumped behind the wheel, and they followed him. He wasn't just going for milk. He was heading west, back towards the Twin Cities, to Dick's Bar. Knapp pulled into the parking lot behind the bar and went in the backdoor.

They pulled the van into the Dairy Queen parking lot kitty corner from Dick's on the south side of University Avenue. Everyone else spread out, finding different parking places along the way.

Mac jumped on the radio, "Riles, what is this, four out of five night's at Dick's?"

"Yup."

"Who's going in?"

"Rockford."

"Copy that."

Fifteen minutes later, Mac's cell phone went off, it was Rockford. "What's up?"

"My dick! You weren't kidding about the little bartender chick in here. She's the shit."

Mac had to laugh. Rockford's wife wasn't much to look at. Of course, neither was Rock.

"Our boy isn't focusing on her, is he?"

"No. He's all over the bar back."

Knapp went home at 12:30 a.m., followed by the second shift of followers from the St. Paul Police Department. Mac, Riley, and the rest of them met at the Gas & Shop again. Mac and Lich were waiting when Riley's van pulled up. As Riley got out of the van, Mac said, "I'll bet you the $100 I won in pull tabs in there last week that the bar back is the one he's after."

"No bet."

"Anyone disagree?" Mac asked. Nobody did.

They knew for sure Monday night. After Knapp finished his Monday shift, he went to dinner at Applebee's. After his dinner he went to Dick's, arriving at 8:00 p.m.

Riles got on the radio, "Mac, you go back in tonight."

"Okay." Mac slipped on an old softball jacket and stocking cap. His razor stubble and glasses topped off the ensemble.

Mac got on his cell phone and called Riley.

"Where's our boy?" Riley asked.

"Sitting in the middle of the bar again."

"Where are you?"

"End of the bar, by the entrance."

"How's our boy look?"

"Fine. Focusing alternately on the TV and on the bar back. I can't imagine how he doesn't get distracted by the bartender. I am," Mac said, admiring Sheila again.

Knapp left the bar at 1:30 a.m. Once he jumped in his car, he didn't drive away. Rather, he sat and watched from the back parking lot, well down from the back door of the bar. He watched well past the 2:00 a.m. closing time. At 2:10, the cute bartender came out and got into her little sports car. A couple of lights remained on. At 2:45 the lights inside went out, and the bar back, Linda, came out the back door, by herself. She walked thirty feet to her Chevy Trailblazer, jumped in and drove away.

Mac, Lich, Riley, and Rock kept watching as well. They weren't leaving until Knapp did, which was at 3:00 a.m., slowly driving by the back of the bar, stopping briefly to scan the backdoor area. Then he left for home, with the second shift falling in behind him three blocks east on University, as he headed back to Hudson. Knapp had marked his prey.

Viper, Bouchard, and the rest of their merry band had been following Knapp as well. Viper, disguised with a beard and ball cap had followed McRyan into Dick's. This was the third time he had gone in following Knapp, a different look each time. One time he had a mustache. Another time he wore out-of style dark-rimmed glasses and false teeth. He never went in with the same look. This time, he sat in a booth with a good view of Knapp.

The bartender came over to serve him. She was an attractive little thing. Viper ordered a Budweiser. When she left him, he whispered into his sleeve, "Come on in. I'm in a booth."

Bouchard appeared five minutes later and sat down. Sheila came around again and took his order. Knapp didn't follow, and Viper wondered how he couldn't. Instead, he kept his eye on the less-attractive woman behind the bar. To the trained eye one could see the hunger in Knapp's eyes. She was the one.

Viper watched as Knapp got up from his stool and headed down the back hallway. He always hit the can once a trip, good cover to check out the back hallway.

The bartender and bar back, as it turned out, were the co-owners. Dick had been their dad, and they'd taken over when he died. They both ran the bar and worked the late nights. They were making a boatload, a good six figures a year, according to tax records. They kept the overhead low, working most nights by themselves, with one guy working the kitchen. That was it. A cleaning company came each day. There were no other workers or staff. They would probably work it for a few more years, then sell and leave for better environs, Viper thought.

The bartender, Sheila, came from behind the bar again to serve Bouchard his Bud Light. As she walked back to the bar, Knapp came back down the hallway and retook his stool. Viper looked down the hallway for a moment. "I'll be right back."

The men's bathroom was all the way down the back hallway on the right. Viper pushed the door in and found himself in a small hallway that after five or six feet turned left, down a longer hallway, a little more than ten feet that ran into a wall that contained the sink and mirror. To the immediate left was the toilet stall. Wrapped around behind the stall was a wall with two urinals. Viper took a piss and listened. He couldn't even hear the sounds of the bar. It was as if the bathroom was soundproofed. It had potential.

When Knapp left at 11:30, McRyan followed a few minutes later. Viper and Bouchard waited an additional fifteen minutes to leave. They got into a van and left the area, then switched vans and worked their way back towards Dick's. They knew where the four police vehicles were located and steered clear. From their perch well east and behind the bar, they could see Knapp's car, him in it, and the back of the bar.

"You know, he's getting the hunger to go for her. He's doing the recon on her now. It's not gonna be but two or three nights more, and he'll go for her," Bouchard mused.

"You're right, and there are cops all over the place out here."

"They're on him day and night."

"You have Kraft evaluate going after him at the farm house?" Viper asked.

"Yeah, but two things. First, there's almost no way to approach the place without being seen. Day or night. Second, he's a former Marine and a damn good one until he went haywire. Who knows what kind of security he might have set up. He's got to be thinking he might have to run at any moment, and he could have some sort of security signal or trigger that'd let him know if someone's been in or out of the house. That's Kraft's speculation anyway. So, you better think of something else."

"I did get one idea tonight. We might have to do it in the bar."

The group met at the Gas & Shop at 3:15 a.m. This time Riley was there first. "What do you guys think? Maybe two or three more nights, he'll go for her?"

"That'd be my guess," Lich replied.

Everyone else nodded in agreement. Mac confirmed it for them, giving a run down of how Knapp was staring her down in the bar. "It's not an obvious thing, unless you are looking for it, but he's getting hungry. You can just see it. It's in the eyes." Mac rubbed his eyes, stifled another yawn.

Riles jumped in, "The chief wants to meet tomorrow. We're all going in at 10:00 a.m. Mac, I'm thinking one thing, though."

Mac knew, "We gotta talk to Linda, right?"

"Yes."

21

"ABORT! ABORT! ABORT!"

It was Tuesday morning, chilly, and the weather forecasters on the morning news had uttered something about snow. If the newsies weren't talking about snow, they were talking about the University Avenue Strangler. Last night, Channel 6 had gone with an in-depth story about the investigation. The morning show then played excerpts, which Mac caught. He'd seen more flattering depictions and, in an ominous tone, Channel 6 was promising an additional installment tonight.

Sylvia Miller was getting butchered. She'd had enough, demanded an update, and the chief acquiesced. That's why Mac was rubbing his eyes as he exited the elevator on the way to Flanagan's office. He'd gone to bed at 4:00 a.m. and it was 8:00 a.m., the meeting with the chief was moved up two hours.

When Mac walked in, Miller and Flanagan were waiting, along with Helen Anderson and Sally. Mac had fitfully slept at home. Sally, with a full night's rest, looked like a million bucks by comparison. The chief nodded to the couch where Mac grabbed a seat and poured himself a steaming cup of coffee. He drank it as fast as the roof of his mouth would allow. As he poured himself another cup, Riley came in, and the meeting came to order.

The chief started everything off. "Riles, where ya at on Knapp?"

Miller jumped in with, "Who's Knapp?"

Riles smiled tiredly. "Sylvia, let me tell you about our serial killer." He flipped open his notebook.

The chief jumped in before he started. "Sylvia, you can't repeat any of this. At least not yet."

Riley gave everyone the run down. When he finished Flanagan looked relieved, Anderson looked excited, and Miller was just plain incredulous. Sally knew all about it, pillow talk of the strangest kind.

"How long have you been on this guy?" Miller asked.

"A week now," replied Riley.

"How have you kept it so quiet? I haven't heard even a whisper of this."

"Because if anyone did, they wouldn't have a badge," replied the chief. "And, Sylvia, you can't talk about it either."

"I know. I know," she replied, the relief showing. "I'm just glad to know you're getting somewhere. That this thing might come to an end. I assume you think he'll hit soon?"

Mac jumped in. "Next couple of days. Everyone agrees who's seen him inside the bar, watching the woman. The hunger's building."

"Have we seen the van yet?" asked the chief.

"No."

"Doesn't that concern you?" Anderson asked.

"Not really," replied Riles. "We think he uses it only when he takes the women. We think it's stored in one of the outbuildings at his place."

"Are you going to talk to the bar back?" Sally asked.

"Mac and I are going today," replied Riley.

Mac and Riley got to Dick's as Linda was pulling up in her Trailblazer. When Mac got out of the unmarked car, she looked at him quizzically and then smiled.

"A little early isn't it?" a shy smile creased her face.

"It would be, Linda, but that's not why I'm here." Mac pulled out his badge, introduced Riley, and explained the investigation and Knapp. She led them into the bar and to the upstairs office. Whereas the lower bar was a throwback to a bygone era of a hole-in-the-wall bar, upstairs was a well-furnished office with a distinct woman's touch. There was a large tasteful off-white couch and two sitting chairs, which surrounded a coffee table sitting on a Persian area rug that covered a good portion of the wood floor. Two antique oak desks, each with a new laptop computer on them, allowed the women to do business. A thirty-two-inch TV sat in a corner, along with a CD player. The office served as a pleasant alternative to the bar below.

"So, what does your investigation have to do with me?" Linda asked, as she fell into one of the chairs. Mac and Riles took seats on the couch.

Riles, cutting to the chase, "You're his next target."

Linda quickly put her hand to her mouth, a look of horror overtaking her face, her voice stammering, "You're su ... su ... sure ... he's after me?"

"After last night, we're real sure," replied Mac. "He's been in your place the last several nights. We've had a cop in there every night as well as all over the place outside. He leaves the bar and watches from the parking lot until you leave to go home."

"But why me? Why me? I mean, what did I do?" she asked loudly, her voice anxious, full of alarm.

"He goes for shy, reserved women; you're that. He goes for working-class women. I know you own the bar with your sister, but you have a working-class look and manner about you. He goes after women who are smaller physically, which you are," Mac replied. "You fit the profile to a T."

"So when do you think he'll come after me?"

"Any night now."

"Tonight?"

"Possibly."

"Why don't you just arrest him now?"

"We can't," Mac answered. "Without going into the legal niceties, we don't have enough. We're very lucky to have stumbled onto him, so to speak."

"But so are you," Riles added. "So, we need your help."

She didn't look relieved. "What do you need?"

Riles didn't sugar coat it, "Him to make a move on you."

More stammering, "You ... you ... you mean, letting him come after me? What? You want to catch him in the act?"

Riles and Mac nodded.

She excused herself and went downstairs and returned a minute later with a glass and bottle of Beam, no ice. She sat down, poured herself a shot and knocked it back. She poured herself another one and offered the bottle to both of them. They declined. The second shot went down easily, hardly a grimace on her face. "I assume you have something in mind?"

The detectives smiled, nodded reassuringly and laid out their plan.

Viper was wearing yet another disguise, long black hair, mustache, with a duck-hunting cap and coat to finish it off. He was sitting alone in a booth near the back of the bar, facing the back hallway. Bouchard was disguised as well, all in black. Long black hair down past his shoulder, a black leather biker jacket, black jeans, black leather biker boots, a chained wallet, along with a beard and dark-tinted glasses. He was sitting on a stool at the end of the bar. The long wigs covered their earpieces. They had small, extremely sensitive microphones hidden in their coat collars. They were waiting for Knapp.

He strolled in at 8:30 p.m. and sat on a stool in the middle of the long bar, his usual spot. The good-looking bartender sauntered over and took his order. She would draw the desires of any man tonight. Skin-tight blue jeans and a tight, bright-white top with long sleeves that left her midriff exposed. She apparently had never heard of a bra. Not that Viper was complaining. He caught a quick glimpse of the bar back, in her blue jeans, white sweatshirt, and blue turtleneck. How were these two women sisters?

Knapp was watching the bar back and a Gopher basketball game with equal intensity. At 9:30 p.m., almost finished with his second beer, he hopped off the bar stool and headed down the hall. When Knapp went into the men's room, Bouchard waited ten seconds and then casually got off his stool and followed down the hall.

Bouchard pushed in the door to the men's room, turned left, and as he reached the sink, he could see Knapp in the mirror, at the far urinal on the opposite wall. He walked over to the open one. Knapp glanced over and gave him a slight nod, which Bouchard returned, uttering, "I gotta piss like a racehorse."

"I hear ya."

Bouchard unzipped his pants and faked arranging to piss with his left hand. With his gloved right hand he reached in his coat pocket for the switchblade.

Mac figured tonight was not the night. No van. He and Lich were sitting in a van, a block away looking at the back of the bar. Tonight Rockford was inside. He called Mac from the bathroom.

"What's up?"

"My dick. You oughta see what she has on tonight."

Mac had to smile. Linda had told her about Knapp. Sheila probably decided to pull his chain a little. "Is she drawing any attention from our boy, or is he keeping it on Linda?"

"Pretty much Linda, although even he took notice of this chick tonight. There isn't a guy in the joint who isn't undressing her with his eyes, not that they'd have to work hard to do that."

"Who's that?" Lich asked.

"Rock. He's calling from the can. He can't piss because Bradley gave him a woody."

"Speakin' of pissin', I gotta go bad."

Rockford heard the discussion, "Who's that? Lich?"

"Yeah, your call has given him the urge to piss."

"He can switch up for me?"

Mac thought a second and turned to Lich. "You want to cover the bar?"

"Yeah, that'll work."

"Okay, Rock. Lich's heading in."

Lich jumped out of the van and briskly walked the couple hundred yards to the back door of the bar. He opened the door and hustled down the back hall, suddenly realizing he'd passed the men's room door. He stopped and walked back a few feet and pushed the men's room door in.

Viper took a sip of his beer, his eyes never leaving the back hallway. Bouchard should be doing Knapp about now, he thought. Suddenly the back door opened. It was that fat fuck Lich. Viper tensed and then relaxed as Lich walked past the men's room door. Then Lich turned back and went into the can. Shit. "Abort! Abort! Abort!" Viper urgently whispered into his mike.

Bouchard had the knife out of his coat pocket and was ready to pop it open and move on Knapp when his earpiece exploded, "Abort! Abort! Abort!" It caused him to wince, which Knapp noticed.

"You all right?"

"Yeah, fine," Bouchard replied, quickly slipping the knife back into his coat pocket. He glanced right at the mirror and saw the fat detective approaching. Lich, noticing them both, darted into the toilet stall. Knapp finished, walked over to the sink, gave his hands a quick wash, took a quick look at his face in the mirror, ran his hand through his hair, and headed out. Bouchard waited fifteen seconds and did the same.

~

Viper stared at the backdoor. What the hell happened? He got his answer soon enough when Knapp, no worse for wear, came back into the bar. Fifteen seconds later Bouchard shuffled down the hall and retook his stool at the end of the bar.

Bouchard spoke softly into his collar, "Do we bail?"

"Hold tight, we might get another shot."

They didn't. Knapp quickly finished what was left of his beer, dropped a five on the bar, nodded good night to the bartender, and walked out the back, where the eyes of at least ten cops would be on him.

22

"IT'LL BE TOMORROW NIGHT."

Before Knapp went home, he gave them all something to chew on. He sat in his car, not leaving, waiting on Linda. After she left to go home, he waited five minutes and cruised the back of the bar. He stopped, got out, and walked between the bar and the building next door, a small paint store. Mac had walked in the gap earlier in the day. There was five or six feet between the two buildings. It was a weaving dirt path, strewn with weeds, broken glass and crushed beer cans. It was dark, lit only by an occasional second-floor light turned on in either of the two buildings. It was the perfect hiding place.

"That's where he'll wait," Mac uttered into the radio, watching Knapp through a night scope borrowed from the feds.

"You bet your ass," Riley responded.

Knapp got back into his Pontiac and headed home. The second shift followed him home to Hudson and put him to bed.

It was 3:15 a.m. and they were at the Gas & Shop lot.

Riley and Rockford were waiting when Mac and Lich pulled in. When they were getting out of the van, Riley bellowed, "Is he getting ready?"

"I think he *is* ready," Mac replied. "What do you think, Dick?"

Lich shrugged, "Still haven't seen the van."

Riley nodded. "That'll be the sign. We'll know for sure then. The four of us meet with the chief in the morning for an update. He was nice enough to give us till 10:00 a.m."

Everyone nodded. Everyone was exhausted. Everyone headed home.

~

Viper admired the thoroughness of Knapp in stalking his prey. She was always alone when she left at night. The area behind the bar was dark. It was a good spot. Were it not for the police being right on top of him, he'd get away with it. Again.

The police were thorough in stalking their prey as well. Viper, while frustrated by it, admired the tracking job they were doing. They had a large crew and were masterful in following him. There was a different cop in the bar every night. They used different cars and vans every day. They rotated the tail well, never getting too close. The familiarity with Knapp's movements and routes made that easier, but they had done well nevertheless.

It made it difficult for Viper and Bouchard to get at Knapp. They'd missed their best shot.

Knapp left his hiding place, got into his car and drove away.

Tonight's little recon mission left no doubt he was ready to move. It wouldn't be long now and one thing was clear. Viper had to find a way to get to Knapp before McRyan and company did.

Bouchard shook his head, "It'll be tomorrow night."

Viper agreed. They needed to move fast. But how?

23

"JUPITER, YOU THE MAN."

The meeting started at 10:00 a.m., the night crew still with Knapp, was watching him making his way to work. Captain Peters, Helen Anderson, Sylvia Miller, Riley, Lich, Rock, Sally, and Mac were all in attendance. As expected, Channel 6 had run another scathing story on the serial killer and the lack of progress on the investigation. The force was carved in the sweeps story, and Flanagan was seething. Mac had never seen him so mad. He wanted Knapp, if for no other reason, to stick it back in the media's face.

"Pat, where are we at on Knapp?"

"Could be anytime now, Chief."

"Tonight?"

"We hope so," Riles replied, perverse as it sounded, wanting a serial killer to make a move. "Obviously, we can't predict for—"

"I know, I know," Flanagan replied, waving him off. "I'm getting fuckin' impatient. That Channel fucking 6 is skewering us, and I'm sick of it."

"Can't force Knapp to attack, Chief," Anderson said.

"I know, it's just … frustrating. You boys are doing good work here. We have our guy, and then those fuckin' bastards at Channel 6 with this story." City council members and the mayor had already been on the chief, demanding answers, as if finding a serial killer was a political problem one could solve with a phone call.

"I hear you, Chief," echoed Miller. "But when we catch this guy, we can spin this. This Knapp isn't an idiot; we'll make sure that gets out. We'll play the work these guys are doing, how they broke the case, tailing this guy while Channel 6 was putting together its carve job." Then she flashed a vicious smile. "Maybe, we'll give Channel 12 an exclusive, since they've shown some restraint."

"That all assumes we're going to catch this asshole," the chief noted. "Pat, where we at on that?"

"We're good." Riles went over the planning with everyone. "We have the place covered, and air support's set up. I'm inside the bar with Doug Long. Rock'll be next door. Mac and Lich are across the street. Linda Bradley is with us and ready. We'll get him "

"Is it just you five?"

"No, no. We'll have other units in the area, but we have to keep them back until he moves. We don't want to spook him. The guy was a Marine. He's got to be checking behind him from time to time. I don't want to have him abort."

"I don't want him getting away," the chief said, concern in his voice.

"He won't," Riles assured.

"Once we get him, then what?" Rock asked.

"I want this bastard in court quickly. I want his arrest to be public. I want a fuckin' perp walk," the chief said. "Sylvia?"

"I can handle that," Miller replied. "We'll have as early a press conference as possible. We'll set the time for the perp walk so the media can cover it. Riley and Rockford can walk him in. It'll be great theatre."

"How about you, Helen?"

"Publicity? Moi? Far be it from me to stand in the way," replied a smiling Anderson, drawing a knowing chuckle. "We could have him in court the next day, I think. Sally?"

"We can. Detective Riley has kept me in the loop," not to mention

Mac, nocturnally. "I'll have things ready for a quick hearing if need be."

"Good. I want a public spectacle of this thing. The department needs that. Sylvia, Helen, Ms. Kennedy, Marion, I want you to stick around so we can discuss that further. Riles, you and the boys go catch that piece of shit."

～

Viper contemplated his next move while sitting on the boss's couch, drinking a bottled water. They missed Knapp. It was a good plan. Dumb luck really. If Lich hadn't walked in, Knapp would have been gone. Shit happens. Viper didn't explain it quite that way to the boss, but that was the gist of what happened.

"So, what are you going to do?" the boss asked.

Good question. Knapp was going to go for Linda soon, probably tonight, tomorrow at the latest. Problem was, the police detail would have cops all over the place. According to the boss's source, for purposes of prosecution, it would be best to catch him in the act. There would be no shortage of assets in the area. Viper didn't have many options, so he answered straight, "To be honest, I'm not sure."

"The police are on him tight?"

"As a drum. Bouchard and I think he'll go for it tonight, and the cops are swarming this guy."

"Then we'll have to come up with something while he's in custody."

"In custody, sir?"

"Yeah, somehow, some way, we'll have to get at him that way."

Viper, at a loss, said, "How?"

"Let me see what I can find out," the boss replied.

～

Mac and Lich resumed tailing Knapp at an Arby's on University at lunchtime. Knapp had an affinity for fast food, which made him like a lot of people. Difference was it didn't seem to go to his belly. Mac, on the other hand, felt bloated. He hadn't worked out in what seemed like two weeks, causing him to check his waistline for a paunch. There wasn't one. Of course, if he needed to he could merely look over at Lich. He had enough for the two of them.

"Another day," uttered Lich as he adjusted in the passenger seat.

"Another dollar," Mac finished, trying to get comfortable as well.

"So he thinks we have to take him out when he's in police custody?" Bouchard asked.

"Yeah," Viper replied skeptically. "I'm not sure how we do it. Any ideas?"

"Not off hand," Bouchard replied. "I'd think they'll have him tightly guarded. Not sure how we could get close enough to do anything. Especially before he starts talking."

"If he does talk," Viper mused.

"Most serial killers do," Bouchard replied.

"Could always be a first time." Viper's cell phone chimed, it was the boss. "Well, maybe he has some answers for us."

Mac yawned. It was 4:30 p.m., the sun was setting and the night was rolling in. The sports radio station was on low. It was Vikings season and nothing raised the passions of the sporting public in the Twin Cities more than the Purple. The rubes were in full rage, a recent loss to the Bears causing everybody's bile to percolate. The updated weather forecast had rain turning to snow, and soon. *Oh, goodie*, Mac thought. He and Lich were watching as Knapp picked up uniforms from Murray Engineering.

"We've been following him for how long now?"

Lich rubbed his eyes, tired of the monotony as well. "A week, I think."

"So, next will be the dry cleaning at the 801 Building." It was. Mac laid out his next two stops, right on the money.

"What are you now, Columbo?"

They had his pattern down. They knew his every move, when he woke up, what route he drove to work, his route while working, who he talked to, what he picked up, what he dropped off, what streets he drove, where he parked, where he liked to eat lunch, fill up with gas, take a leak. They had it all. But they couldn't relax. They had to stay sharp. This would be the time he'd throw them a curve ball, and Mac would drive a van right into the back of him. Then the jig would be up.

Per his normal schedule, Knapp finished his route at 6:00 p.m. At 6:05, he casually walked out of the building and got into his car. He left the lot and turned left onto University. Then he took an immediate right south on Lexington. He took a left onto the freeway and headed east on 94. This was not part of the normal pattern. Mac and Lich were in the first vehicle trailing Knapp towards Hudson.

"You don't suppose?" Lich said.

"Yeah. Exactly," Mac replied.

Riley and Rockford passed them, driving a white Buick Century. Rockford raised his eyebrows as they passed. They were thinking the same thing.

Knapp pulled into his driveway at 6:45 p.m. Mac and Lich drove past and pulled into the housing development. The rest of the crew were in the parking lot at the restaurant. Mac and Lich watched out the back windows of the van. Thankfully the back of the van had vinyl swivel seats that were moderately comfortable. They could sit and watch Knapp's place through the night vision scope or binoculars. There was little radio traffic. Everyone was on edge. Something was happening.

Then nothing happened.

At 8:30 p.m. Lich bitched, "What the fuck? He takin' a night off?"

A light, cold rain started. Mac felt the temperature drop five degrees in a minute and a shiver go down his spine. After a brief rush of action, the monotony set back in. Mac grabbed a *Pioneer Press* off the floor, and read the sports page for the fourth time, this time squinting in the dark. Lich was passively watching the house, slouched in the seat in back, his arms crossed, lightly rocking, trying to stay warm.

At 10:15, Mac's bladder started barking at him, and he got out of the van to take a piss. He could see his breath in the cool night, the light mist falling around him. Steam rose from his urine as it hit the ground.

"Mac, get in here!" Lich yelled.

"What?"

"I've got the van."

Mac quickly finished and moved for the van, trying to zip his pants at the same time. Parked in front of an out building they hadn't seen Knapp go into all week, was a Ford Econoline van, dark in color, lights on, a large dent in the front bumper and, most important of all, the right license plate. "I'll be damned, Jupiter, you the man," Mac whispered to himself.

Mac jumped into the passenger seat and grabbed the radio, "Riles, do you copy?"

"Here, Mac."

"We've got the van. It's outside, and we confirmed the plate number."

"Copy that. We're moving out now. You follow Knapp."

"Copy that."

"Bout fuckin' time," Lich yelled gleefully, as he fired up the van, did a quick U-turn. He turned left onto County 35, half a mile behind Knapp.

Any exhaustion they had experienced was history. The game was on—finally. The adrenaline was flowing. They'd been waiting a week for this. "Tonight's the night," Mac said quietly.

Riley, Rockford, and the rest made a speed run to St. Paul and the bar to get ahead of Knapp. The highway patrol was clued in, so there wouldn't be a problem.

At their meeting with the chief in the morning, they went over where everyone would be when Knapp moved. For three days prior, they had pored over maps of the area and spoke with the owners of the businesses surrounding Dick's Bar.

Riley would be in the bar. There was a small storeroom in the back across from the bathroom. He'd hang there. When Linda left the bar for the night, he would be right on the back door, which she would only pretend to lock. He could pounce as soon as Knapp made a move.

Rockford'd be in the back of the paint store, less than a hundred feet away. Mac had lobbied for the spot. Rockford was not that fleet a foot, Mac was.

Mac and Lich would be across the street to the west in the back garage of Ray's Auto Repair, at least one hundred fifty feet away. They had spent a few nights watching from there already. Ray had a son-in-law with the force. He couldn't have been more helpful.

Mac would be able to run across the street—less likely Lich, given his body type, girth, and age. Lich said he'd keep the van pointed in the right direction in case they needed a set of wheels. Mac's concern was if Knapp ran—would they be able to catch him? They had to keep the rest of the vehicles a number of blocks back. Who knows what would happen if Knapp ran? He could slip away, get into someone's house, take a hostage. There were risks if he ran and got outside their perimeter. It's why Mac wanted the paint store.

There were already two cops on the second floor of the office building to the north, looking directly down on the back of the bar. They could see the gap, the back door and would have the infrared video camera on the back. Neither man would be of any help if there was a chase.

In addition to Riley, they had Detective Doug Long on the second floor in the bar. He would be able to look down on Knapp as he hid in the gap between the bar and paint store.

Finally, they had Falcon, the St. Paul Police chopper circling at a distance overhead that could swoop in at a moment's notice.

In the van, Mac and Lich were two hundred yards behind Knapp, with another unit an additional two hundred yards further back. The temperature was dropping quickly. The rain was changing to snow.

The wipers were going high speed, cleaning the windshield while they sped into St. Paul.

"I hope Ray left the heat on in the garage," Lich pleaded.

"Suppose you want some coffee too?"

"A man can dream," Lich quipped.

Mac, getting back to business, "With this snow, visibility'll be an issue."

"You're right, boyo. That area behind the bar ain't well lit."

Viper and Bouchard were parked, watching Riley and his crew a block south of the Italian restaurant. Suddenly the two vans and a Crown Victoria pulled out and sped by, disregarding the local speed limit. Two minutes later, a Ford Econoline van came by.

"There's our boy, I bet," Bouchard uttered.

"See if McRyan comes by." He did, thirty seconds later, keeping his distance.

Viper and Bouchard waited and pulled in well behind Lich and McRyan, trailing Knapp back to St. Paul.

"You're comfortable with everything?" Bouchard asked.

"Yes."

"How about Hagen?"

"He said it would be easy. He even showed me how he does it."

"And the getaway?"

"Got it covered. It'll take thirty seconds to a minute at best for them to figure out what happened. By the time they do, I'm gone."

Doug Long was up on the second floor at the bar. His car was parked next to Linda Bradley's Trailblazer. When Knapp was two minutes out, Young, another cop sitting down in the bar, jumped in Long's car and pulled away three blocks north on Arundel.

Unfortunately, as Knapp pulled into the lot, a spot opened right along the back of the bar, three spaces from Bradley. It was not Long's spot. He backed the van in, killed the motor and went inside.

Mac and Lich heard all of this on the radio and skipped the Dale Street exit, going farther west on Interstate 94 to the Lexington Parkway exit and doubling back to Ray's. Lich dropped the van in the parking lot on the west side of the garage, hidden from view of the bar parking lot. They entered the security code to the building and slowly worked their way to the back and to the door looking directly across Arundel into the parking lot behind Dick's. There were no lights on in the back of the garage, and Mac and Lich slowly made their way to the window.

Mac moved to the right side of the garage door, and as if he was peering around a corner, looked out the window. There were a couple of problems. The snow, coming down in large, heavy snowflakes, made visibility across the street and into the parking lot a problem. It was melting as it hit the pavement, but was gathering in the grass between the street and sidewalk. More importantly, Knapp's van blocked his view of the back door. It wasn't on the other side of Bradley's Trailblazer, as they had planned. They wouldn't be able to see Knapp move. They called it in. Riley told them to stay put and move when the call came.

Knapp came out of the bar at 1:15 a.m. and got back into the van. A half-hour later he slowly got out of the driver's side of the van. Mac watched as Knapp slowly walked to the rear of the van and peered around to his left. Seeing nobody, Knapp moved left and disappeared from Mac's view. His earpiece told him that Knapp was to the side of the back door, sneaking a peak in the back to see if anyone was coming down the back hall. He then scooted over to the gap between the bar and paint store.

Knapp was dressed all in black, with a stocking cap. Long, looking down at him from the dark second floor, reported that Knapp was set back about fifteen feet, having leaned against the bar wall, into an indentation where a door used to be. The boys across the street could make him out through the infrared vision on the video camera.

Everyone was in position.

24

"HAVE A NICE DAY."

Patience. A difficult thing to have when waiting for something to happen, when you know it is going to happen and even when it will happen. Mac must have looked at his watch every thirty seconds since Knapp left the van. Radio chatter quieted. Mac noticed a light go on upstairs. Bradley was now up working the books, putting the money in the safe for tomorrow's deposit.

At 2:15 a.m., per normal routine, Sheila Bradley left. She was well aware of what was going on with her little sister. She had been told to drive way away and not hang around. Everything needed to look normal. It seemed like an hour since she'd left. It had been five minutes. Upstairs, Linda Bradley, Mac knew, would be sliding on a neck brace with Long's assistance.

At 2:42 a.m., Mac's earpiece cracked with Long's voice. "She's heading down now."

Mac and Lich moved to the left side of the garage door window, close to the back door. They were glued to the window, not that it did much good. They couldn't see a thing.

Office building: "Knapp has moved to the edge of the gap."

Mac whispered to Lich, "Alarm won't go off when we open the back door?"

Lich, for the fifth time, "Nope, disarmed." He was twirling the keys to the van in his hands. He'd be in the van if Knapp ran.

Long: "She's at the back door."

Mac left the window and went to the back door, hand on the knob, staring at the floor, waiting for the word.

Office building: "She's opening the door ... she's turned her back, putting the key in the lock."

As Mac heard it told later, as she put the key into the knob, Knapp sprung from the gap. He was on her in an instant. The key was still in the lock, and the force of his attack on her had snapped it off. Riley and Long were trapped inside.

Office building: "Go! Go! Go! He's on her! ... He's on her!..."

Mac bolted out the back door, sprinting across Arundel, leaving Lich behind. He heard Riley in his right earpiece. "The door's jammed. We can't get out! We can't get out! Go, go, go ..."

Chaos.

As he was sprinting across Arundel, Mac heard a voice yell out, "Freeze, police." As he hit the grass between the street and sidewalk he saw a black blur to his left sprinting out of the parking lot north on Arundel. Knapp. Mac instinctively planted his left foot to turn, but it gave out underneath him as he slipped on the snow. He fell hard onto the cement sidewalk, jarring his left shoulder. He pushed himself right up and gave chase.

He heard his earpiece blurt. "He's north on Arundel. All units converge."

Falcon dropped from nowhere out of the sky, the spotlight searching for Knapp.

Mac was running north and gaining speed. He saw Knapp sprinting north on Arundel, just about to pass the alley on the block between Sherburne and Charles Streets, when the lights appeared and the sirens sounded, closing rapidly from the north on Arundel. Knapp stopped abruptly and turned left, ninety degrees into the alley, slipping on the wet street, but catching himself with his left hand. He'd lost some momentum. Knapp turned down the alley, throwing a couple of garbage cans into the way.

Mac, at full speed now, half a block behind Knapp, turned left to the sidewalk on the north side of Sherburne, sprinting hard, parallel to the alley, looking to his right through the houses, not able to see Knapp but getting a general fix from Falcon's spotlight. He wanted to cut to his right, get to the alley, but there were too many fences, bushes. He kept running, looking right. Another house. Then a break, a clean shot through to the alley. Mac veered right. As he crossed the back of the house he saw Knapp running peripherally to his right, with Falcon's light painting him. Knapp, sensing things closing, abruptly veered right between two houses on the other side of the alley, losing some speed but also losing the spotlight from Falcon.

Mac, flying, stayed dead straight, on a beeline to the other side of the house, rapidly closing the gap. He lost Knapp briefly behind the house but picked him up around the front, to his right. Mac had the angle on Knapp, as if he was running along the sideline of a football field. Knapp looked back over his right shoulder for pursuers. He didn't see Mac coming from his left.

Mac didn't break stride down the incline to the sidewalk. Knapp, coming from his right, ran behind a parked car. Mac burst in front of the car and at full speed, drilled the serial killer, ran through him, with his right shoulder, a textbook tackle. The tackle took Knapp off his feet and drove him into the pavement, with Mac rolling over him and landing with his back against a parked car, his head slamming into a tire. Dazed, his head pounding, Mac could see Knapp five feet away, starting to push himself up. Mac told his body to move, but he was reacting slowly, not moving fast enough, foggy from crashing into the car.

Knapp was up on a knee, pushing up with his hands, ready to take a step.

Mac rolled to his right, setting his hand on the pavement, trying to push himself up, wanting to give chase.

Knapp, up now, took a step, but only one. A blur from the left wiped him out. Rockford, all two hundred fifty pounds of him, finished the job for Mac, steamrolling Knapp. Subdued by the force of the tackle, Knapp was easily cuffed by Rock, who just might've taken an extra shot or two in the process. Falcon, having caught up, provided a guide for all of the other vehicles and cops, who circled the area now like moths to a flame.

Mac sat back against the tire, breathing hard, his head pounding, seeing some stars. Perhaps not stars, but little flickering bright lights, like used to happen when he got checked hard into the boards when he played hockey.

Riles approached. He squatted down in front of Mac. "You all right?"

"Yeah, just got my bell rung, I think," Mac replied, trying to focus his eyes. "Help me up."

Riles reached his right arm around Mac's left side and helped him up. Mac set his feet underneath him, and while he was a little light-headed, he felt okay. "How's Linda?"

"She's fine. Brace did the trick," Riles responded, smiling, relieved.

Having steadied Mac, Riles walked over to a face-down and hand-cuffed Knapp. Squatting down again, Riles pushed Knapp onto his right side and looked him in the eye.

"Have a nice day."

25

"THERE'S A PIECE MISSING HERE."

The press conference ended at 10:30 a.m. Mac, Riley, Rockford, and Lich retreated to an empty interview room, found some coffee and relaxed, a few hours of sleep having temporarily refreshed them all. Riles was particularly chipper, the long investigation over, his efforts vindicated.

"What time ya taking him to court?" Lich asked Riley.

"Noon. Rock and I get to walk him in the front door."

"Better you than me," Mac replied.

"You should be there as well. Lich too. You guys broke this thing open."

"Thanks just the same. I'd as soon avoid the media. I had enough of it on the Daniels case," Mac replied.

"Agreed. Besides, I'm not the most photogenic guy," Lich replied, in a huge understatement.

Just then Dan Patrick stuck his head in the room. "Thought I might find you guys here. We're heading out to Knapp's place in Hudson. Guess there's some interesting stuff out there. Anyone care to join?"

"I'd love to," Riles replied, "but I have orders to hang around for the walk over to the courthouse."

"Me too," Rock added.

"I'll go," Mac said. "Dick?"

"Yeah, why not."

"See you boys later?" Mac said to Rock and Riles.

"Yeah, party tonight over at the Pub," Riley replied, "and you all will be there." It wasn't a question. "Anyone who doesn't show will be summarily shot. We deserve a little celebration."

Bouchard slid the card into the reader, saw the light turn green and pushed his way into the tenth-floor hotel room. Hennessey, Hagen, and Skogman were with him and carried in their equipment.

Skogman opened the shades, and Bouchard looked out the window.

Hennessey came up behind and looked out as well. "This should work."

"Agreed," Bouchard replied. "Let's get set up."

Mac had driven by Knapp's driveway many times over the last ten days. It felt odd to finally turn in and go up to the house. The Hudson cops were already there, with the crime scene tape up and lights flashing everywhere. A few curious onlookers were hanging out down on the county road, gawking.

Knapp's farmhouse was maintained to military cleanliness on the main level and upstairs. The furniture was plain, vintage seventies in color and style, but well kept. The personal effects were sparse, except for a few family photos. There was nothing unusual, at least until they went down to the basement.

As they went down the stairs to the basement, it looked and smelled just like a farmhouse cellar. Dark, dusty, filled with crates, boxes, assorted junk with a musty smell, like old potatoes. However, under the steps was an old oak plank door that opened into the back foundation wall. Behind the door was a room underneath the four-season porch. Mac estimated it at fifteen by fifteen. Knapp had kept the room sealed with a combination lock, which now sat on the floor in two pieces, victimized by a bolt cutter.

The room was partially furnished with a television, desk, and computer. Above the desk was a shelf, which contained a half-used box of Trojan condoms, the kind used in each killing. There was also a box with the balloons. Knapp had one of each in the van the night before. However, that wasn't what really caught his attention.

On the left wall was a bulletin board, a monument to Knapp's work. The bulletin board was filled with news clippings, pictures, maps, and diagrams. It wasn't too different from the bulletin board they had in the detail conference room. In a disjointed way, it told the story of what Knapp had been doing for the last couple of months. It was altogether creepy and fascinating at the same time.

Mac started from the left, was a third of the way down, passively looking at the clippings, when Lich came up to him. "Weird, huh?"

"Yeah. Creepy. It's as if in his own warped mind, he was creating his masterpiece or something."

"FBI profile said the guy might keep some sort of journal," Patrick added. "This qualifies."

"I'd say so," Lich replied.

They stood in silence for a few moments, gazing at the wall.

"There's a piece missing here," Patrick said.

"Missing?" Mac asked.

"Yeah, nothing about Jamie Jones."

Mac checked his memory, that was one of the victim's names wasn't it? "Jones ... yeah ... which ... one was she?"

Patrick gave Mac a stern look.

"Hey, Dan, the day Dick and I got on the case, we had the seventh one. I didn't even have a chance to go through all the files. Never really did because we got on Knapp so quick."

Patrick nodded, remembering the sequence of events.

"Tell me about Jones," Mac asked.

"She was the fifth victim. Killed on Halloween."

"Oh, I remember," Mac replied. "That was the day we picked up the Daniels case. So, what was her story?"

"She was the CFO at some local company."

"Really?"

"Yeah. We found her by the Capitol. Just like all the others, though. Vacant lot behind O'Neill's Bar. Balloon tied to her. Sexually assaulted. There was Trojan rubber residue. The whole nine yards."

"Copycat?" Mac asked.

"We kind of wondered about that, but the killing was identical. You can look at the file on it. It had all the characteristics of Knapp's work. It's the same in all the details."

"Everything?" Lich asked.

"Everything," Patrick replied.

"Then why nothing on Jones?" Mac asked.

"I guess we'll have to ask Knapp," Patrick replied.

～

Riles pushed Knapp's head down and eased him into the back of a Crown Victoria and then joined him in back. Rock was in the front passenger seat, sitting next to Frank Franklin, another member of the detail along for a little limelight. It would be a short five-minute drive over to the courthouse.

Rock, never one to allow for a quiet ride, asked Knapp, "Get yourself a lawyer yet?"

"Yeah. Legal aid."

"Thought you weren't going to put up with one of those?"

"Don't expect I'll have to for long. But you all are trying to get plenty of publicity on this, so I don't have much of a choice right now."

～

Bouchard's radio crackled with Hansen's voice. "They just pulled out. Right on time. They're going south on St. Peter."

"Copy that," Bouchard replied, then to Hagen, "Do it."

Hagen was sitting at the desk with two laptops. The laptops had the security cameras of the second and third levels of the Vincent Ramp. A key stroke caused an almost imperceptive blip on the cameras on the left laptop, while the right remained constant. A minute later, Viper appeared on the right laptop, making his way to the southwest corner of the third level of the ramp. The left laptop, which the ramp security cameras were currently seeing and recording, showed the same location without Viper.

Viper moved into position and kneeled down between two mini-vans. The vans, parked in the last two spots on the southeast corner of the parking ramp, provided him cover from anyone driving through the ramp. His position was kitty corner from the front of the courthouse. He had a good field of fire, with an excellent view of the sidewalk area and the forty-foot walk to the front doors of the courthouse.

He took one last look out over the street and to the sidewalk in front of the courthouse. A crowd was gathering, waiting for the arrival of the University Avenue Strangler and his arraignment. All of the local television stations were there, reporters making a last check of their hair, and cameramen doing the same with their equipment. All were kept away by a police barricade, creating a fifteen-foot wide walkway into the courthouse.

He kneeled down and opened his case, which was designed to look like one for a laptop. Inside was his sniper rifle, which he quickly assembled, the last pieces being the silencer and the scope. Three bullets were slid in, two in the magazine and one in the chamber. He locked it in. He slipped a black mask down over his face, which matched his black coat, pants, and thin black gloves. His earpiece came to life.

"They're two blocks out."

"Copy that," he replied. He peered just over the edge, and a minute later saw the parade approach in the form of two unmarked Crown Victorias.

~

"Cripes, what a crowd," Rock stated, noticing all of the media and people in front of the courthouse.

"Lots of hairspray and makeup," Riles replied. "Make sure to smile for the camera as we walk in. Let the media see that big gap in your teeth." An evil grin spread across Riles's face.

"Keep it up, and I'll give you one to match," Rock retorted.

Laughing, Riles got out of the back left of the car, and Rock exited the front passenger side, opening the rear door. Riles leaned into the car and helped lift Knapp up out of the car and onto his feet. "We're just going to head right on in," he said to Knapp, who simply nodded.

"Let's go." Rock lightly grabbed the back of Knapp's left arm and Riles had the right.

~

Lich called down to them. "Hey, guys, come on up. They got it on TV. Riles and Rock are about to walk Knapp into court."

Mac, Patrick, and several others gathered around the TV in Knapp's living room.

"Lots of media," Lich remarked.

"Just in time for the noon news," Mac replied. "The whole town'll be able to see this."

~

Viper had them in the scope as they lifted Knapp out of the backseat. He wanted them a little more to his left for a slightly better firing angle.

He looked through the scope with his right eye, his finger on the trigger. "Don't hit the black cop," he said to himself, training the crosshairs on Knapp. They were moving now, away from the car, the black cop on his left arm, Riley on the right. Forty feet to the courthouse. As they moved towards the courthouse, the firing angle improved, Knapp's head was no longer obscured. The assassin exhaled and squeezed the trigger.

Riles felt something hit the back of his head, moist, he reached with his right hand and felt it. Bringing it around to his eyes it was red, and Knapp was suddenly heavy in his left arm. He looked at Knapp, slumped over now, a large red hole where the back of his head used to be. Riley realized his left side was covered in blood.

People saw it now, the blood, Knapp down. Panic set in as bystanders started screaming, running, or hitting the ground.

"Where did it come from?" Riley heard Rock yell, looking back and to the east.

People were pointing in all different directions, at the various buildings and parking ramps in the area. Chaos broke out as uniforms ran up to Riley checking on him. Others had weapons drawn, scanning the area for the shooter. Riles heard another uniform yelling into a radio for backup.

"Pat, you hit?"

Riles was unresponsive.

"Are you hit?" Rock asked again, grabbing Riles on the left arm.

Riles, getting his head together, "N ... n ... no. I think it's just Knapp's blood." He was coated in it.

"Direct hit," Bouchard said matter of factly, looking down on the area with a high-powered set of binoculars.

"His head's turned to mush," Hennessey confirmed.

"Viper, move. Subject's down," Bouchard ordered into the radio. "Switch it when he gets to the skyway," he said to Hagen.

~

Bouchard needn't have bothered with the order. Viper saw the hole in the back of Knapp's head. Quickly down on a knee, out of sight from the outside, he pulled the rifle apart and put it into the case. He was on the move in ten seconds, a black blur, moving between the vans, across the parking lot, towards the stairway.

Through the stairway door, he was quickly down one flight of steps to the skyway level. He pulled at the Velcro collar on his coat and it opened into a sport coat, with an open-collared white button-down-collar shirt. The stocking cap was off, replaced by a houndstooth driving cap. A fake beard concealed his face, along with a pair of stylish tinted glasses. While walking towards the skyway, he flipped his case over, so the outside looked like canvas. An empty Starbucks cup fished out of the case finished off the ensemble. As he walked out to the skyway, and into surveillance camera view, he blended in and looked like any one of a thousand people walking downtown over the noon hour.

26

"WE GOT OURSELVES ANOTHER LEE HARVEY OSWALD?"

The van pulled up to the curb in front of the Vincent Ramp, and Mac, Lich, and Patrick piled out. It had taken them fifteen minutes to get back downtown from Knapp's place in Hudson. Their fears had been put to rest on the way in, when it was confirmed that other than Knapp, nobody else had been hit. Rock and Riles were okay, which was what they were most concerned about. Riles went back to the station to get cleaned up from Knapp's blood.

The three of them moved up the steps to the third level where they found Rock and two other detectives in the southeast corner of the ramp, looking back towards the courthouse. Rock saw them coming and walked over.

"Christ, what a mess."

"What the hell happened?" Lich asked.

"We think a sniper hit Knapp from the corner area over there."

"Why here?" Mac said, not seeing anything indicating otherwise.

"Somebody claims they saw a muzzle flash from up here."

"Anybody hear the shot?" Lich asked.

"Not that I'm aware of," Rock replied. "Probably had some sort of silencer." Rock wiped his shaved head with his hand. "I gotta tell ya, we're out of the car, walking Knapp in, and next thing I know he's slumped down and Riles is coated in blood."

Mac walked over to the corner between two minivans and looked out over the street towards the courthouse. It was a shot of maybe a hundred yards. The spot provided a good field of fire towards the front of the courthouse. If a person were going to take a shot, this was a pretty good place. Nonetheless, it took pretty good aim and a steady hand to make the shot, Mac thought.

Lich walked up behind him. "We got ourselves another Lee Harvey Oswald?"

"We got someone who was a pretty good shot," Mac replied.

"Don't look that far to me," Lich said.

"Rock, how many shots?" Mac asked.

"Only one, I think." Rock replied.

"One shot from here, not bad," Mac said. "Probably a scope, with a silencer, a pro job?"

"Who knows? Hell, you can get a scope and silencer for a hunting rifle," Rock replied.

"Any of the victims of this guy ... they got family members maybe who hunt or are good with a rifle?" Mac asked.

Rock shrugged, "Don't know."

"How long before you guys were up here?"

Rock grimaced. "Probably three or four minutes at best. It was pretty chaotic. The person who saw the muzzle flash didn't get to us for a minute or two. Then we ran over, but whoever did it was long gone by then."

"Where to? Where do you go from here?" Lich asked.

"There's a stairway to the skyway, there's another stairway down to the street. They might have jumped into a car in the ramp and left. Hell, they could have taken the elevator down, although I doubt it. We're pulling the surveillance cameras. We'll see what we find," Rock replied.

"No rest for the weary," Lich replied. "I thought we were going to get some days off."

"We are," Rock answered. "Chief's already got a whole group

down here looking at it. He says we're off it. We've done enough. If they need to know anything about the families, they'll ask us, but otherwise we're done. We finish up some loose ends tomorrow, then we all get the rest of the week off."

"Fine by me," Lich said.

"Let's go check on Riles," Rock said.

Mac took one last look out over the street and to the front of the courthouse. A large blood spot marked where Knapp went down. Police tape marked the area off, and the crime scene guys were collecting what little evidence there was. He shook his head. Something didn't seem right.

Viper pulled up to the front of the boss's house, parked his car, and walked up to the front door. The housekeeper opened the door, took his coat, and escorted him to the dining room. The boss was sitting at the table, reading some papers, sipping a glass of wine.

"What would you like?" the boss asked, holding up his wine glass.

"One of those would be fine."

Viper sat down while the boss poured him a wine. He waited for the staff to leave.

"How're we doing?"

"Good so far," Viper replied. "I was six blocks away before the police even made it up to the ramp. I was out of downtown within ten minutes. We look clean." Viper sipped his wine, a lovely red. "Did the police get anything out of Knapp before—"

"—his untimely demise?" the boss finished. "No. He immediately asked for a lawyer. That was that."

"So, we should be good then," Viper stated. "Although I have Kraft and a few others keeping an eye on things from my end, just to be sure."

"Good. I'll be doing the same," the boss added. "Now we need to get back to looking for the Cross documents."

"Yes, sir. Now that this is over, we'll refocus our efforts in that direction."

27

"WE MAY STILL HAVE A PROBLEM."

Knapp's assassination didn't dampen anybody's mood. The bastard killed seven women. If someone took his head off, well, that shouldn't have happened, but nobody was going to lose sleep over it. It saved the public some money was a common view held in the Pub. Two months of built-up pressure and steam were being blown off big time. Every cab in St. Paul would be parked outside at closing time, Shamus would see to that. When Mac walked in, someone shouted out his name. Another yelled, "Hey look, it's Ronnie Lott." The room erupted. On his way to the bar, Mac received high fives, pats on the back, and even a couple of kisses on the cheek, which he hoped were from women. When he got to the bar, Uncle Shamus was there with a warm handshake and a cold Guinness.

Mac made the rounds, shaking hands, trading smiles and exchanging wisecracks. He finally found Riley, Lich, and Rock holding court at the end of the bar. Even Dot was there, her first appearance with Dick. What a way to start, Mac thought. There was already a stack of empties developing around the group. It would only get bigger. *If only I owned Tylenol stock*, Mac thought, envisioning the bottles of it that would be consumed tomorrow.

"Mac, my boy," Riles said enthusiastically, acting as if he hadn't seen him in five years, giving him a big bear hug. Riles appeared no worse for the wear from the day's activities. If anything, having not been shot earlier made him all the more ebullient. Or perhaps it was the alcohol, of which Riles already had plenty. Others gathered around to hear Riley tell the story about the take down on Knapp. Riles had it down pat now, probably having told it twenty times already, adding great drama, timing, if not a little embellishment to it. He stood in the middle of thirty people, his arms waving, his voice getting louder, funnier than hell.

"... Falcon's right overhead. The lights and sirens are everywhere. Problem is, nowhere near Knapp. I can see him in the distance, between these two houses. Rock's just ahead of me, but we're prob- ably seventy, eighty yards back, running as fast as our piece-of-shit bodies can go. I see Knapp running into the street between two cars, and just then this blur just comes from his left and wipes him out, takes him off his feet. It's fucking Mac. And I mean to tell you he was going full fuckin' throttle. He practically ran right through him. Cut him in half. I mean, I think his shoes came flying off when Mac hit him. It was a yard sale. NFL films would have loved to have footage of this." Riles took a drink. "But Mac's kind of out of it after the tackle, and we see Knapp startin' to get up. But then Rock kicks it down, finds a gear I didn't know he had anymore, and he finishes Knapp off. Total pancake job." There's laughter all around. "I get there and check on Mac, who's a little woozy. I think you were seeing stars, weren't you?"

"Maybe," Mac replied with a smile.

"Then I walk over and Rock looks like he's gonna puke, he's breathing so hard. I'm not sure if he's holding himself up or if he's leaning on Knapp so he won't fall down."

Mac listened as Riley went on, when someone put a soft, delicate arm around him, slowly walking a hand up his back, scratching lightly. He turned to his left to see Sally, who looked him in the eye and planted a big soft wet kiss on him for everybody else to see. Mac, usually not one for public displays of affection, was caught up in the moment and didn't mind.

After the kiss and some good-natured ribbing from everyone else, he and Sally moved off to the side and out of the commotion surrounding Riley. Mac got her a beer, and they talked for a few minutes when Riles, finally done with the recounting of the take down, came over to join them.

"Case isn't kicking your ass anymore, is it?" Mac said.

"Got that right," Riles replied boisterously and put his arm around Sally's neck, pulling her close and pointing his beer at Mac. "Counselor, did you hear what your boy here did last night?"

"Yes, Detective. I heard your last rendition over there. Of course, I'm hoping I'll receive a more thorough debriefing later," Sally replied, smiling seductively at Mac. He wasn't going to make closing time.

Riles loudly jumped all over the comment, "Ohhh, I'm sure Mac will be thoroughly debriefing later."

Sally laughed out loud. Mac smiled and shook his head at Riles. "Hey, I'm a boxer man. I hate those tighty whitey's you wear, Pat." Mac added, and then in a more conversational tone, "I'll tell you one thing new I saw today though."

"What's that?" Sally asked, taking another sip from her beer.

"I went out to Knapp's place. He had the whole thing on a wall in the basement. Each murder. Pictures, maps, news clippings, the whole shootin' match. I mean right up on the wall. Organized by victim."

"Kind of creepy," Sally replied.

"You ain't kidding," Mac replied. "But that wasn't the really odd thing."

"What was?" Rock asked as he lit his cigar.

"There was one victim missing."

"Really, who was that?" Riley asked casually, taking a drink.

"Jamie Jones."

"Really. Hmpf. Wonder why?"

"Yeah," Mac replied, "I'm thinking I'll take a—"

Before he could finish, Rock stopped him, "Guy was crazier than shit, Mac, killing those women. He probably left Jones out intentionally just to fuck with us. He's dead, case is over—let's get drunk."

Rock was right, Mac thought, at least for tonight. They needed more drinks. "Shamus," Mac bellowed. "Another round!"

The group talked idly for a while before Riley drifted off to tell more stories about the case to anyone who'd listen. Tonight he'd have an audience. More cops were coming in by the minute. Mac managed to stay until 10:00 p.m., when Sally finally dragged him out of the Pub. A day that started lousy was about to come to an excellent end.

Kraft had been sitting in the bar, twenty feet from McRyan, keeping a low profile, just a working stiff having a beer or two before heading home. They wanted to keep an eye on the group, just to be sure all was well. He heard McRyan mention the corkboard wall in the basement and the missing victim. Kraft finished his beer, threw five dollars on the bar and waded through the sea of cops to the front door. In his car, he grabbed his cell phone, punching up Viper.

"Yeah."

"We may still have a problem."

"What?"

"Apparently Knapp was cutting his clippings."

"So?"

"Somebody's missing."

After a pause, "Shit."

28

"EVER HEARD OF BRISTOL, OHIO?"

Mac walked into the detail conference room at 8:00 a.m. and started the coffee maker. He imagined the crew would start coming in shortly, hungover to beat all. Having left the bar at a decent hour, Mac felt good.

It was clean-up day, time to file all the evidence in boxes and then take a few days off. A stack of unassembled bankers boxers already waited in a corner. Mac put a couple together and started working on the corkboard that had the St. Paul map. As he started pulling stuff down, Dan Patrick walked in.

"Good morning."

"Ain't nothin' good about it," Patrick replied, heading for the coffee.

Mac chuckled quietly and went back to work on the board. He got to the pin for the body by O'Neill's Bar, Jamie Jones. She was the one missing from Knapp's board.

"Dan, you got the file on this Jones woman? The one you were so mad I didn't know about." Patrick gave him a "Go fuck yourself" look through bloodshot eyes and threw a folder over.

Jones was the CFO at Peterson Technical Applications, otherwise known as PTA, the single largest business and employer in St. Paul.

They had a downtown headquarters plus research and manufacturing facilities around the state and across the country, and soon around the world. It was a diversified company as far as Mac knew, but their calling card was military hardware and communications-related equipment.

"She was CFO?" Mac asked.

"Yeah."

She was thirty-five years old. "Kind of young for that, wasn't she?"

"She took over last March for a guy. I forget his name now, but he was killed in an auto accident during a snowstorm. Over on Shepard Road." Patrick responded as he threw a couple of aspirin in his mouth and washed them down with coffee. Shepard Road ran from downtown west along the Mississippi River over to the International Airport. For an inner-city road, it was notoriously dangerous in spots. Add a March snowstorm to it, and it wasn't unheard of that a serious accident could occur.

"Let me guess, during the state hockey tourney." Snowstorms during the state high school hockey tournament were an annual tradition in Minnesota.

"Yup."

Mac leafed through the file. It was like the other serial-killer files with a picture of the victim, a couple of pages on the evidence tying her to the other murders and a back page, stapled to the folder, with background information, such as address, date of birth, and next of kin.

Jones came to St. Paul seven years before. She owned a new condo down along the river. Mac recognized the address. It was one of those posh ones in the River Highlands development right on the river, part of St. Paul's effort to take financial, meaning tax, advantage of the river front. Figures, CFO at a company like PTA should be able to afford digs like that.

She was different from the other victims. The other victims were, for the most part, working-class women—waitresses and a convenience store clerk. Even Linda Bradley, though she owned the bar, definitely had a blue-collar, working-girl feel to her. Jones didn't. She was educated, a professional, lived in an expensive neighborhood and worked for a major corporation.

"Dan, PTA have any facilities along University Avenue?"

"Huh?"

"PTA. Do they have anything along or around University?"

"Not that I know of. Why?"

"It's just that she doesn't seem to have much in common with the other victims. How does Knapp stumble onto the CFO of PTA?"

"Don't know, Mac. Some of that occurred to us as well. But, the murder matched all the others down to the letter. Strangled. Sexually assaulted and a Trojan condom was used. No pubic hairs or other physical evidence. Dumped in a vacant lot. Left with a 'Have a Nice Day' balloon."

"Hardly impossible to copycat."

"That's true, except we kept a tight lid on all of the details. Very little got out. Think about it. If the media knew about the Trojan rubber, no pubic hair stuff, the van, they would have run with it. It never got out. We watched that very closely. The only thing that really got out was the balloon stuff, and that was pretty much unavoidable. Point is, we'd have been able to tell if it was a copycat. No dice."

Patrick made a valid point. If it wasn't Knapp, who was it? And if it was somebody else, they had to have the inside scoop to get it just right. Pretty unlikely. Nevertheless, something seemed odd about it all.

Mac touched his belly. Three cups of heavy coffee were getting to him. He grabbed Jones's file and the sports page and headed to the can. The sports page offered little so he put it over the handicap arm lift and reached down for the Jones file. He flipped it open and started reading through the memo again. Jones was strangled with a nylon rope, yellow, might have been a water skiing towrope. She was sexually assaulted post mortem. There was the presence of Trojan condom residue, but no pubic hair or any other piece of evidence left behind. It was a spot-on match.

He flipped the memo up and looked at the background information stapled to the back of the folder. Jones was born in 1969 and raised in Bristol, Ohio. Her mother lived in Sun City, Arizona, now. Dad was deceased. Jones had apparently never married. She was a graduate of Duke University and had a masters from Northwestern. She obviously had brains to get into both of those schools. She worked in Chicago before coming to Minnesota. She had been at PTA for seven years, worked her way up the ladder, becoming a very young CFO.

Mac furrowed his brow. Something on the sheet registered with him, like he had seen it somewhere before, but he wasn't sure what or where. He finished, got up, and went to the sink to wash his hands. The door burst open. His cousin Paddy, in uniform, came in.

"Hey, cuz."

"How you doing, Mac? Hungover?"

"Nah. Early night."

"Ahhh. Sally."

Mac smiled and nodded as he worked the soap on his hands.

"Hell of a run for you, cuz," Paddy said, "catching Knapp the way you did and Daniels ..."

Daniels. Mac bolted from the bathroom, briskly walked down the hall and hit the stairs to the basement and the evidence room. A uniform cop, Jorgenson, was working the desk. "Hey, Mac, great job on Knapp—"

"Thanks. Say, I need to pull some evidence. Everything on the Daniels case."

"Daniels? What'dya need that for?"

"Just want to check something out."

"Okay, whatever you say."

Jorgenson came back with a box with various pieces of evidence. Mac flipped the top off and started digging through evidence bags. And there it was, the 1987 Bristol, Ohio, high school yearbook. He opened it to the page he dog-eared weeks ago that had Claire Daniels, then Claire Miller, graduation picture, first picture on the left, top row. It was on the right page. On the left page halfway down, middle of the row, Jamie Jones. Mac did a rough estimate of the graduating class. There were probably forty or fifty students, a small class.

Mac checked the evidence out and went back up to his desk and started up his computer and did a Google search for Bristol, Ohio. Bristol, south of Youngstown, had a population of just over 1,200.

Mac sat back in his chair and looked up at the ceiling. What were the odds that two women who graduated high school together from a tiny southern Ohio town would be murdered the exact same night in St. Paul, Minnesota?

He got on the phone and called Daniels's mother, who he had spoken to once during that investigation. She wasn't particularly helpful then and was no more so now. It wasn't that she was difficult; she just didn't know much about what her daughter had been doing with her social life. Apparently that was the case for her daughter's high school life as well; she didn't recall a Jamie Jones from Bristol.

Mac had never spoken to Jones's mother, but there was a number for her in the file. Mac introduced himself to Ms. Jones, who spent two minutes thanking him for catching Knapp.

"Ms. Jones, I have one question for you. Do you remember a classmate of your daughter's named Claire Daniels?"

"Claire Daniels ... hmm ... no, I don't recall a Claire Daniels."

Mac kicked himself, "Wait, it was Miller then, Claire Miller. Do you recall a Claire Miller?"

"Oh, I remember Claire. She was pretty popular when Jamie was in high school."

"Were they friends?"

"They knew each other. It's a small town, so everyone was pretty friendly."

"Did your daughter ever mention running into Claire up in the Twin Cities?"

"Ohh, yes. Said she saw her on TV. I guess Claire was a reporter. Jamie said she gave her a call, and they got together for coffee or something."

"Do you know when it was that they got together?"

"No, I don't. I'm sorry. I think it was recently, at least recently before Jamie was killed. But I can't be sure exactly when."

Mac managed to get off the phone before Ms. Jones was able to

ask too many questions. He needed to think. Had he found something or was his mind playing games with him? He got up and walked
over to the pop machine for a Diet Dr. Pepper, popped the top, and
took a long drink, looking out the window over Interstate 94. He
turned to head back to his desk, when he saw Sally walking down the
hall. She saw him and walked over, "Hey." She saw the look on his
face. "You don't look so good."

Mac lightly grabbed her arm and walked her into a vacant interview room and closed the door.

"What's up?"

"I got a bad feeling about something."

"What?"

"Remember I mentioned last night that on Knapp's wall, one of
the victims was missing."

"Yeah."

"Kind of thought it was odd."

"Yeah, so. He was nuts."

"Maybe so. But have you ever heard of Bristol, Ohio?"

"No. Should I?"

"Not really. It's a small town in southern Ohio."

"So."

"It's where Jamie Jones graduated from high school in 1987."

"Mac, I don't see where you're going with—"

"—It just so happens it's also the high school that one Claire
Miller, who became Claire Daniels, also graduated from in 1987."

Sally's jaw dropped a little. "Odd coincidence, I guess."

"It get's even odder. They were killed the same night."

Sally's jaw dropped completely. "What are the odds?"

"Very long, I think."

"It's probably still just a coincidence," Sally said with little
conviction.

"Maybe," he replied skeptically. "But I spoke with Jones's mom,
and she confirms that the two of them had recently gotten together
for coffee."

Sally slipped into lawyer mode. "They're from the same hometown. So what?"

"Murdered on the same night? That in and of itself makes you wonder. But there're other things. I've looked over Knapp's other victims. Jones doesn't fit. She's professional. The others are working class. Jones has nothing to do with the University Avenue area. She lives down by the river and works downtown. How does Knapp run into her? She does no business in the University area, and Knapp never was downtown once in the entire time we followed him."

Sally sat down, looking away at the white, concrete wall of the interview room. Quietly she said, "If you're right, this means the senator—"

"—Maybe didn't do Daniels," Mac said, equally quiet. "And Knapp didn't do Jones."

"So who did?"

"Good question."

29

"THEY CAN'T SEEM TO KEEP A CFO ALIVE."

Viper had been working around the clock, living in a minivan for what seemed like weeks. He was starting to feel all of his forty-seven years of age. Sore, achy, lethargic, and just plain worn out. Kraft's phone call didn't exactly help. They weren't done yet. McRyan's and Kennedy's places would need to remain infested a while longer.

He slept in late, not having set an alarm. Apparently nothing came of pillow talk between McRyan and Kennedy. If anything important had happened or been said, someone would have called.

Viper took a long shower, letting the hot water loosen up his muscles. He slowly massaged the Head and Shoulders through his short hair. He wondered if the police, in particular McRyan, would connect the dots. McRyan, or possibly that fat fuck Lich, could put it together, tying Jones to Daniels.

A full breakfast of eggs, bacon, toast, and juice as well as a chance to read the paper, gave him a feeling of normalcy. But he couldn't get McRyan, Knapp, Jones, Daniels, and Cross out of his mind. He took a look at his watch: 9:45 a.m. He was to meet with the boss at 11:00. But first, some important business, in case the dots started getting connected.

He went to his office and placed a call to a contact in Switzerland. His encrypted phone system prevented tracing. Moving a little over $100,000, he would have that much more money if he had to run. This was in addition to the five million he had in other accounts. This would be a necessary task for the next few days. If he had to run, he wouldn't be able to take much with. His wallet and the account numbers would mean he wouldn't want for much once he was in hiding.

He looked at his watch again. Time to go. On the short drive into the office, McRyan, Knapp, Jones, Daniels, and Cross ran around in his head. Dumb luck all of this had happened really. Cross had been perfect. They pulled the plug on it in time. They made a ton of money on it. In a few years, they would all be retired, living the good life. Then Jones had to go and somehow find out about Cross, and it all started.

Viper parked in the basement and took the elevator up to the top. He waved to the boss's receptionist and walked on in. He declined coffee and sat down in front of the desk.

"So we're in at McRyan's and Kennedy's places?" the boss asked.

"Yes," Viper replied.

"What about following them?"

"We're doing that as well."

"Let me know what comes of that."

"Always."

Mind mapping was something Mac had learned from his dad, who used it when a case got too complicated and he needed to see all the parts laid out to see how they might fit together. The elder McRyan would sit at the kitchen table or at his old roll-top desk with nothing but a pen and notepad. He would put whatever was perplexing him down in the middle of the page and jot all his pieces of information down around this question. More often than not, it worked—one of those little things that made Simon McRyan who he was.

Mac figured if it was good enough for the old man, why not him. He picked the technique up and used it. It had been great for him in school, especially on essay exams. He would lay the issue out in the middle of a piece of paper and jot down, around the page, the points he wanted to make in answering the question. He'd quickly get it all on the paper, number the points in the order he wanted to make them, and then write. Given his grades, it was more than effective as a tool. He hadn't used it much since school, but if ever there was a time, it was now.

So, in the middle of his lined notepad, he wrote, "If not Knapp, who and why?" He wrote Daniels down to the left of the question. He wrote Jones on top and Mason Johnson to the right. He spent the afternoon working it, jotting down notes around each one of the names.

Next to Daniels's name he jotted down everything he could recall about her that seemed relevant. Grew up with Jones in Bristol, Ohio. Had recent contact with her. Investigative reporter.

Next to Jones's name he wrote CFO at PTA. Grew up with Daniels in Bristol. Recent contact with Daniels. Didn't fit profile of other victims.

Under Senator Mason Johnson, he wrote: How'd he fit in? Did he kill Daniels? If not, who did? Did he commit suicide?

Down in the lower right-hand corner, he wrote in quotes, "If someone had the resources to kill Daniels and Jones, in the same night no less, did they have the juice to kill the senator?" He made a note to call the Wright County Sheriff.

What about Knapp? Was his assassination part of this?

Mac got up and paced the homicide division, looking down at the notepad. Occasionally he would stop and jot down little notes as he took his tour. Stopping at the vending machines, he bought a Diet Coke and some Doritos, and walked back to his desk and plopped himself down in his chair. The Doritos were quickly devoured. He slapped his hands together, cleaning them off and took another look at the Jones file. Became CFO at a young age. What did Patrick say happened? The old CFO had died? What was his name, Stephens or something?

Mac pulled his chair up to his computer and did an Internet search of the *Pioneer Press* archives. It took a few minutes, but he found it.

JAMES STEPHENS, PROMINENT CFO, DIES IN SHEPARD ROAD ACCIDENT

James Stephens, 54, died last night in a one-car accident along St. Paul's Shepard Road. Mr. Stephens was returning home from Peterson Technical Applications, where he was the CFO for the past ten years. The accident appeared to be caused by the slick roads resulting from yesterday's snowstorm. St. Paul Patrol Officer Fred Barrett stated that the car apparently hit a patch of ice while traveling west on Shepard, just prior to the stop sign at the end of Shepard and the beginning of Mississippi Boulevard. His vehicle, unable to stop, went through the stoplight, over the embankment, rolling over and coming to a rest upside down thirty feet below on the west bound lane of West 7th Street. Mr. Stephens was rushed to United Hospital and was pronounced dead on arrival. Stephens is survived by his second wife, Yolanda, and two sons, James, Jr., of Washington, DC, and Jeff of Seattle, Washington.

Mac tracked down Barrett. "I tell you, Mac, it was pretty horrific. He went over that embankment, rolled a few times. The car was crushed. He didn't have a chance, even with the airbag deploying and his seatbelt."

"Anything unusual about the accident?"

"Not that I recall. Roads were icy as hell that night, and you know how Shepard gets. He got going too fast in the snow, hit that patch of ice, and that was all she wrote."

It was a dead end. Shepard Road could get nasty, and Mac remembered at least a couple of times when he almost lost it driving along there. He wrote Stephens's name down on the bottom of the page anyway. CFO for ten years at PTA. Jones took over for him. That's how someone so young got the gig.

He kept going around the page, jotting down little notes and theories. Daniels, dating the senator. Maybe he said something to Daniels? But why kill Jones then? Maybe Daniels mentioned something the senator said to Jones. Jones told somebody who didn't like it? Mac shook his head. They'd never get to it if it followed that path.

He looked around the notepad, twirling his pen like it was a baton. How about reversing it? Something Jones said or knew? What would she know? Why would she tell Daniels? Mac stared at the ceiling, running things through his head. Daniels, Jones, the senator. What's the connection? To kill them, you wouldn't do it on a whim, by the seat of your pants. No, it would take planning. To kill all of them you had to have resources, money, people, and intelligence.

He took another look at his page, going around the question clockwise. Daniels, Jones, Johnson, Stephens ... Mac drew a dotted line from the bottom of the page from Stephens to Jones. They worked together at PTA. Daniels was a reporter, specializing in politics and business. Mac thought about the DVDs of her work, white-collar crime and political news. Resources means money and people. Who has resources? Who has money? Who ... has ... people ...? "Shit," Mac said under his breath as it crystallized before his eyes.

He pushed himself out of his chair and walked over to a window that looked a few blocks south to the center of downtown St. Paul. Mac stared at the tall building for five minutes. He admired the combination of glass and stone. He looked at the letters on top of the building, illuminated in the late afternoon dim. It was impressive, holding a prominent position in St. Paul's skyline. He went back to his desk and wrote the letters down in the upper right hand corner of the notepad, between Daniels and Jones. PTA.

He drew lines from Daniels to Jones. Jones to PTA. PTA to Daniels. A little triangle. Resources, money, people. PTA might have that. But why would they do something like this?

Mac took his cell phone out of his pocket and punched up his directory for the letter C. PTA was an economic juggernaut, the biggest employer in St. Paul. Which meant Mac knew about them what everyone else knew. He needed more information, especially financial. Chadley.

If anyone had the 411 on business, it would be Matt Chadley. Chadley was an old roommate from the university days and Mac's financial planner. He worked for West & Palmer, the top brokerage in the Twin Cities.

Mac punched up the number, and the call was answered immediately.

"Matt Chadley."

"Chads, Mac."

"The infamous Detective McRyan. What can I do for you?"

"Tell me what you know about PTA?"

"PTA?"

"Yeah. Financially."

"Well, buddy, I already have you invested in them, and for good reason. They're a Wall Street darling. Total blue-chip stock."

"Why's that?"

"Impeccable books, as close to a sure thing as you can find. They hit their nut every quarter, never short on earnings expectations, almost always exceeding. Audits come back squeaky clean. SEC loves them. They have an active board that watches the money very closely. Closer than almost any board I've ever seen. Enron they ain't. They keep executive compensation within reason, if not lower than normal. People like that. Makes them look responsible. The execs are tight with all the right people in Washington. The president and CEO, Ted Lindsay, and many of the people who work for him, are connected like you wouldn't believe, so the government contracts keep coming. With 9/11, their stock has gone through the roof with increased spending on defense and intelligence, their bellwether areas. Mac, their stock is a must have. Like I said—I have it in your portfolio. It's as reliable a performer as there is out there."

"Ever any hint of financial impropriety, scandal?"

"Negative. I have a pretty good ear out there, and I've never gotten wind of any financial issues. Never. Why do you ask?"

"They can't seem to keep a CFO alive."

"No, they can't. Wall Street loved Stephens. He was top notch. I didn't know a ton about Jones, other than she was considered smart as a whip and followed the rules. In fact, internally they make a huge issue about that at PTA. If there's bad news, get it out there. After Enron, WorldCom ... well, trust became a big issue and PTA has it in spades."

"Never any problems, Chads?" Mac asked skeptically.

"Not that I've ever heard. Why so interested?"

"I can't really tell you. PTA, or somebody there, might or might not be tied into something I'm working. I'm just trying to get a feel for the company and wondered if there might be a financial issue, some impropriety going on."

"Well, man, not that I'm aware of. PTA's numbers are as reliable as anyone's out there. So, if it's financial, it's not because the books are cooked."

Well nothing there. "Thanks, Chad." Mac got ready to hang up the phone, a little disappointed, thinking or hoping he was going to hear something different.

"You're welcome, Mac. One thing, though. If you wanted to talk to somebody on the inside, an old friend of yours recently left the board."

"Who's that?"

"Lyman Hisle."

"Hmpf. Thanks." With that, Mac hung up. He jotted down Lyman's name. He checked his watch, 4:30 p.m.

It was late, and the chief wanted a final briefing on Knapp, after 5:00 p.m. Since it was all good news, there would probably be a drink or two served. Maybe one or two phone calls first.

~

Tired, Sally walked off the elevator and headed to her office, an after-noon of court appearances and plea-bargaining behind her. She carried her briefcase over her left shoulder, a warm half empty Diet Pepsi she bought two hours before in her right hand. Her hair felt like it had lost all of its bounce, and she could feel her blouse un-tucking from her skirt. An afternoon in heels left her feet, ankles, and calves aching.

She sat down at her desk and shook her mouse to wake up her monitor. She had thirty-five new e-mails. She had eight new voice mail messages. "Sheesh. Gone a few hours, and all hell breaks loose," she muttered. Where had the day gone? She and Helen had a meeting with Chief Flanagan about Knapp at 5:00 p.m. Helen would be by any minute. She wondered if Mac was going to spring his little theory. Probably only after he'd had a couple pops of the chief's Irish whiskey to get his courage up.

Mac. She'd spent a lot of time with him in the last few weeks. He was the most perceptive person she had ever met, seeing things others didn't, two steps ahead of everyone else. Cautious, he never over-committed to anything, keeping his options open, evaluating things from every possible angle before acting. Sally was both inter-ested and, at the same time, fearful of what he might come up with.

She knew Mac had doubts about whether Senator Johnson killed Daniels. Nobody else thought that way, but Mac had maintained to her in private what he thought. They talked about the case every so often, and Mac always said, "I still wonder about that case."

She wanted to think about something else, so she started looking at her e-mails. A quick scan told her that only about eight or nine were truly work related. That made her like most other working people—seventy-percent of her e-mails were personal. A knock on the door interrupted her halfway through the first work e-mail. Helen, right on time.

"Shall we go see Charlie?"

Oh, we're on a first name basis now, are we? "We shall." Not wanting to spend another minute in heels, she reached under her desk for a pair of black flats. She took one last drink of the warm Diet Pepsi, left it on her desk, and joined Helen in the hallway.

"So, anything interesting happen today?" Helen asked.

The meeting was short with no real cop business discussed. It was a celebration. Drinks naturally were served, a little Irish whiskey. Flanagan wouldn't have it any other way. With Knapp caught, his big headache was gone, even if the department was being questioned about his assassination. While there was some criticism, there was an undercurrent of "The bastard got what he deserved." So, while the day wasn't perfectly sunny for the chief, partly cloudy was just fine. Mac wasn't about to ruin the day and kept quiet.

"So, it's off to the bar for all of you?" Flanagan inquired.

"Yes, sir," Riles responded. "We're going to have a couple."

"But I think we'll go easier than last night," Rock added.

"Well, good. You boys have earned it."

They all filed out. Sally whispered in Mac's ear, "What are you going to do?"

"I'll tell you at the Pub. First I have to talk to someone."

30

"ON THE TRAIL OF AN ASSASSIN."

They picked up McRyan as he pulled out of the parking ramp, all of them well familiar with the Explorer. McRyan made the short trek over to the Pub, parking in his usual spot in back. They watched him go in the back door from their perch across the street. Another van simultaneously pulled into the parking lot on West Seventh, across the street from the front. Shortly after McRyan had gone in, Kennedy pulled in, followed by Lich, Riley, and Rockford.

Bouchard shook his head, snorting. "Man, these guys do like to drink."

"That they do," Viper replied. "Of course, at a bar owned by ex-cops, I doubt the real ones are paying full price."

"Probably not."

Viper picked up the radio and called to the other van, "Kraft, head in and give us an eyeball."

"Copy that."

~

Mac, Sally, Riley, Rock, and Lich were standing in the middle of the bar, each with a Heineken, talking about the case and how life would be a little dull going back to routine homicide work.

"You say that now, Riles, but I stood here a few weeks ago, and you sure looked like you wanted to go back to mundane police work then," Mac said, playing along.

"That was then, this is now."

"Isn't that a movie title or something?" Rock asked.

Just then, on cue, Uncle Shamus showed up.

"Shamus," Riley said, "to what do we owe the honor?"

"I need to borrow my nephew for a few minutes, but in the meantime, next round is on me." The bartender instantly appeared with another order.

"God, I love this family," Riley said as he put down his empty and grabbed the full Heineken sitting opened for him on the bar.

"I'll be right back," Mac said to everyone and followed Shamus upstairs.

Uncle Shamus had a large corner office in the back of the second floor. On the outside of the door it said, "OFFICE OF THE PROPRI- ETOR." Every McRyan who had filled that role over the years had used the office. It was an impressive room, with high ceilings, crown moldings, polished wood floors, tasteful furniture, and a one hundred-year-old oak desk the size of a dining room table. In front of the desk were two old high-backed, burgundy, leather chairs. Sitting casually in one of them was Lyman Hisle, nattily attired in a gray Italian three-piece suit, a perfect Windsor knot in his black silk tie, even at this late hour. He was sipping an Irish whiskey, neat, when Shamus and Mac walked in.

"Lyman, thank you for coming. I know this seems a little odd." They shook hands and shared a smile.

"I was intrigued when Shamus called. Am I to assume that you don't want others to know of this?"

Mac nodded.

"So, pray tell, how can I be of assistance?"

"This is off the record in my direction, and yours. I need some information."

"About PTA, Shamus says."

"You were on the board?"

"I was."

"Why did you leave?"

"Time mostly. PTA has a very active and involved board, and I couldn't give it the time and attention it needed and deserved," Lyman responded, shifting in his chair to look directly at Mac, one leg over the other, "So, tell me, why would one of St. Paul's finest need to know anything about PTA?"

"I'll tell you why in a minute."

"Very well."

"Tell me about the power structure over there."

"Ted Lindsay is the president and CEO. We brought him in a number of years ago. He's done a fabulous job."

"Where'd you get him from?"

"He was the chief operating officer at Fillmore Electronics, a competitor. He was there two, three years, I think, and did good work. Before that he worked for the government. He was a spook sort of. He held numerous positions in the NSA, then the CIA, where he was deputy director of Operations before he left and went to make his fortune in private industry." Lyman took a sip of his drink.

"He seems to have done well for PTA."

"Sure has. Since 9/11, bad as it sounds, the company has exploded, no pun intended. There's been a renewed emphasis on intelligence gathering. The equipment necessary for that is one of the company's better areas. Even better, Lindsay's connections in the government are amazing. He has friends, contacts—hell, spies—everywhere." Lyman put his drink on the desk and counted on his fingers. "He knows when the military, NSA, or CIA contracts are coming up before anyone else, what the budget is going to be, and who the key decision maker will be. He'll know what he needs to know about the person who has decision-making authority and what buttons to push in that direction."

"I heard he knows everyone in DC," Mac added.

Lyman agreed, "His contacts in Congress are impressive and he's been an aggressive campaign contributor." Lyman creased a smile, shook his head a little, and said, the admiration showing, "If Ted goes after something, he gets it."

Mac, interested, said, "You said spies?"

"Yeah. I mean, he knows people all over the place with information. I wouldn't doubt he's spreading a little money around, which is illegal, but he's a former pro, with a staff of former pros. For them stuff like that is second nature."

"Staff of former pros?"

"Yeah," Lyman said, sipping the last of his drink. "PTA has a security staff that is the size and has the budget of a small army. Old habits die hard, I guess. Lindsay's paranoid and a nut about security."

"This security detail, how big is it?"

"Oh, he's got a couple hundred on staff, spread over all of the facilities. Not to mention the equipment. Hell, they use the same stuff they sell to the government."

"Who runs the security?"

"Webb Alt."

"What's his story?" Mac asked.

"Former spook—although you wouldn't necessarily know it to look at him." Lyman scratched his head, "He isn't particularly impressive physically, but people are scared to death of the guy. He's got a bunch of his old cronies from CIA and NSA on staff here in town."

"Lindsay," Mac asked, shifting gears, "I imagine he's made himself quite a fortune."

"He has, although not as big as he'd like."

"Why?"

"Oh, he thought he should be paid like Jack Welch. The board disagreed. We were sensitive to executive pay before it became a trend. So, there was some bitching."

"Did he threaten to leave?"

"Oh, I don't know if it was that bad for him. There were some whispers, but nothing ever came of it. We upped his pay a little more and threw in a few more options, and the whole thing seemed to blow over. He has it pretty good at PTA. A few more years, and he'll retire with a $100 million in the bank, plus the potential of more with stock options. Not bad when most of your career was in government service." Lyman held his glass out and Shamus refreshed his drink. "So, Mac, what's this all about?"

"In a minute," Mac said, momentarily filibustering. "Has there ever been any financial issues or problems with PTA that you're aware of?"

"No," Lyman replied, shaking his head, "As a board, we went over those books very carefully. Always have. We were very active and not a rubber stamp, something that bothers Lindsay from time to time. The SEC, the company auditors—the board never found any improprieties. PTA's books balance, always have. It's why the stock is such a winner."

"Tell me about James Stephens."

"Came to PTA with Lindsay. He'd been in government service as well, at Treasury and then at the CIA. He left the CIA with Lindsay and went to Fillmore. In fact, Lindsay brought five or six upper-level executives over when he came. It was a shame, that car accident."

"What about Jamie Jones, the most recent CFO?

"I don't really know much about her. She was well regarded and very well liked by Stephens." Lyman furrowed his brow, "Mac, *what in the hell* is this all about?"

"Let me tell you a little story, and you tell me what you think." Mac related his theory.

Lyman didn't react much, sitting back in the chair, his hands forming a steeple under his chin. When Mac finished, Lyman took a long drink, looked away for a moment, and then took another long drink. "Christ, Mac," he said after a minute, shaking his head and pinching the bridge of his nose.

"What do you make of it?"

"Pretty thin. You couldn't go into court with it, as I'm sure your girlfriend has told you."

"I know it's thin, but is it possible?"

"Well ..." Lyman exhaled and looked down, almost sad, "Nothing would surprise me anymore."

"If I'm right, any chance this is going on at PTA without Lindsay knowing about it?"

"No," Lyman replied, shaking his head. "Lindsay knows everything that goes on at that company. Like I said, he's serious about security." Lyman scratched his chin, looked at the ceiling, "I'm certain offices are wired. There are video cameras everywhere that you can see, and I'm sure many you can't. You have to use a personal code to make copies; all e-mail and Internet usage is monitored. Not randomly, constantly. I'm sure somebody eavesdrops on phone conversations." He paused a moment and then leaned forward, his elbows on his knees, "So, if PTA did this, Mac, Ted Lindsay not only knows about it, he ordered it."

"Interesting," Mac replied, stroking his chin.

Lyman cut him short, "But you know what your problem is?"

"What's that?"

"You'll never find what you're looking for."

Mac snorted.

"You don't believe me?"

"There's always a way."

Lyman shook his head. "If Ted Lindsay did this, he would have taken care of all loose ends. He would have left nothing behind. If they did this, they'll have anticipated your every move and covered all of their tracks."

"There's always something."

Lyman snorted. "I have great admiration for your abilities and those of your imbibing friends downstairs. You know that." He squinted and slowly shook his head, "But I have no idea how you get at PTA on what you have. I mean, think about it. You have not one piece of physical evidence, do you?"

"Not yet."

"Then good luck finding it."

"Jesus Christ, Lyman, you act as if these guys are infallible."

"They're pros is what I'm saying, Michael. If they did this, they did it without leaving a trace of physical evidence. I mean, where is your evidence? All you have is a theory at this point, and that wouldn't cut it. Most judges would never let you get to the courtroom with that, and if you did, you'd go down quick and easy anyway. I'm talking an elementary defense here. Your girlfriend would tell you that. Shit, *you* know that. You went to law school."

"Lyman, we haven't started even looking yet."

"If they did this, they have a huge head start on you to cover their tracks." Lyman started ticking his fingers off again. "If they did Jones, they blame Knapp, reasonable doubt. If they did Daniels, they have the senator, reasonable doubt. You think they might have done Johnson, but it sure looked like he committed suicide, reasonable doubt. Knapp? You've got family members of the victims with plenty of motive, reasonable doubt. The only way you get them is if you can find a smoking gun. Ted Lindsay's too good at this sort of thing to leave something like that behind."

The three men went silent. Lyman had given Mac a lot to think about. If PTA had the juice to kill Jones, Daniels, and the senator, they had the resources and people to accomplish it. They'd have the resources and people to stymie them if they tried to go after the books, to look for some financial irregularity, which was the only reasonable supposition as to why to take out Jones. If the auditors, board, SEC, or anyone else didn't find it, how would Mac? What resources would have to be expended to get at the records? What damage would their pursuit do to the department? Would the department even let them go after PTA? Mac's theory looked good when he was mind mapping. But the devil is in the details. How could he go after PTA, without knowing what he was looking for?

The enormity of the task hit Mac. He got up and walked to the back window and looked down at the back parking lot. *You think you're so fucking smart.*

Uncle Shamus, sensing what Mac was thinking, ended the silence, "What are you going to do?"

Good question. But Mac had never backed down from anything in his life, and he wasn't about to now. "Lyman, with all due respect for your view of Ted Lindsay and company, first thing tomorrow I'm going to start taking a look at PTA and a second look at Jones, Daniels, and the senator." Mac hoped he wouldn't be alone. He would have to convince Riles and the others if he was going to have any chance.

"You have any idea what you're looking for?" Lyman said.

"No. The only thing I can think of is a financial issue of some sort. Why else take out Jones. But ..."

"But what," Lyman asked.

Mac met his eyes and held them.

"I'm thinking Jones was killed because she found something they didn't want her to find. Maybe she left it behind or maybe she shared it with Daniels, so maybe that's where we look."

"Well, good luck to you. But one thing," Lyman asked.

"What's that?"

"If you do find anything that harms the company, you let me know. That's the quid pro quo I want for speaking with you tonight," Lyman stated. "I want to know. There are thousands of employees at PTA. If you're right, Lindsay ordered it. That could literally kill the company. So, I need to know so I can inform those who remain on the board. I may be gone from there, but I care about the company. Its health is important to this city."

"Fair enough."

"Mac, why don't you get back to the bar?" Uncle Shamus suggested.

"Yeah, okay. Shamus, I need to use Patrick's Room."

"Go ahead."

"I need to get going as well," Lyman added and gave Mac one last look. "I'll hear from you?"

"Yes."

"Good luck," Lyman said as he shook Mac's hand. Shamus opened the door and patted Mac on the back as he walked out. Lyman would wait a few minutes and leave on his own down the back steps.

≈

Kraft had loitered thirty or so feet away from the door to the office. With his back to the wall, he alternately watched the door, a couple of attractive thirtyish women sitting at the bar, and a Wolves game up on the TV.

As he put his beer up to his lips, the door opened and McRyan came out, with his uncle closing the door behind him. But he also noted legs sitting in a chair. Kraft decided not to follow and waited to see who the other person was. Five minutes later, Lyman Hisle exited the office.

≈

Mac came back down to find Sally listening to Riley, Rock, and Lich talk about Sheila Bradley and her two big assets.

"I'm telling you, they were the size of cantaloupes," Riley was saying, cupping his hands in front of his chest. Obviously the drinks were feeling good as Riles was revving up. "Mac, am I lying?"

Mac looked at Sally, who just smiled. "No, you aren't. I want all you guys to join me in the basement for a minute, I want to show you something."

"What's that?" Rock asked.

"Just come down. Rounds on me," Mac replied neutrally. He grabbed five beers off the bar and turned for the backstairs, joined by everyone. In the basement was the Pub game room with dartboards, pool tables, and a few video games. A couple of big screens added a sports flavor, the Wild game playing in the background. Behind the stairs was a hallway. In the hallway was a built-in cabinet in the wall.

Mac slid open the middle drawer, reached under the ledge and popped a latch. The cabinet, a remnant from the bygone era of prohibition, was the hidden door to Patrick's Room.

Patrick's Room was a conference room, that during prohibition was a place one could get a drink and socialize without fear of trouble with the authorities, as the place was owned by the authorities. Despite its legendary history, Patrick's room was now simply a well-furnished conference room with a whiteboard, conference table, couch, and a TV/DVD, which was used for bartender and waitress training for dram shop liability. Shamus often made it available for cop poker games and Texas Hold'em tournaments. Once inside, everyone grabbed a seat at the conference table.

"So, what's this all about?" Lich asked.

"I want you guys to hear me out on something."

"Which is?" Rock asked suspiciously, noting Mac's tone.

"You ever heard of Bristol, Ohio?"

Riley furrowed his brow, "No. Should I?"

"Hometown of Jamie Jones. She graduated from high school there, 1987."

"I appreciate the local color. So what?"

"Let me ask another question. Who was killed the same night as Jones?"

"Claire Daniels," Riles replied. "But Mac, what does that have to do with—"

"She graduated from Bristol, Ohio, high school in 1987."

The room went quiet. Mac suddenly had everyone's attention.

"How big a town is Bristol?" Lich asked after a minute.

"Oh, about 1,214 people. Pretty steady for the last twenty or so years," Mac replied. "The graduating class for Daniels and Jones was forty-two students."

"How'd you come up with this?" asked Rock.

Mac related how he came to the discovery, Jones missing on the wall at Knapp's place, looking at Jones's file, finding the yearbook at Daniels's, making a couple of phone calls.

"So, you're suggesting that the senator didn't kill Daniels?" Lich asked. "Are you suggesting that we didn't have that right? That we rung up an innocent man." Lich was concerned.

"I'm suggesting it's possible."

"Counselor, you buying the stuff your boy's selling?" Lich queried, still in disbelief.

"Yeah," said Kennedy. "I wish he was wrong, and you guys are the detectives, but I think he's onto something."

"Come on, Mac, isn't it possible that all we have here is a coincidence," Riles pleaded. "I mean, you're talking about your signature case. You're going to tear that down on nothing more than a couple of facts that might fit together sideways. It doesn't make sense."

"I'll grant you that it's a little out there," said Mac, "but Knapp was keeping his headlines. He was taping the news programs. He builds this monument to his work. Everything's there, except this one thing —"

"—Jones," Riley finished, pinching the bridge of his nose.

"Exactly. Nothing about Jones." Mac pushed further, "Don't you find that odd? Aren't you the least bit curious about that?"

"So, he didn't keep clippings of one murder. Maybe it was all part of his grand plan. Guy was crazier than a shit house mouse, Mac," Rock snarled. "You read the file. Wouldn't you agree that the details of all the murders, including Jones, match up perfectly?"

"Yeah, with the exception of one thing."

"Which is?"

"Jones! She doesn't fit with the other victims," Mac asserted. "Think about it, Rock. In all the time we were following Knapp, did he ever once, just once, go downtown?"

"Nope."

"That's right. He kept to the University Avenue area. How would he have run into Jones?"

"Who knows. Maybe she bumped into him at some bar or restaurant. We weren't on him then. He stalks her, takes her down—a new experience or something," Rock argued, his conviction waning.

"She doesn't fit the profile, Rock," Mac kept on. "If I'm right, if you wanted to cover the reason to kill Jones, what better way than to make her death look just like another serial killing. We look in the direction of the serial killer because that's where the evidence points." Mac crossed his arms. "If I'm right, whoever did this got exactly what they wanted."

"But, Mac, few, if any, of the details about what Knapp was doing to the women leaked. We managed that. The only thing the media had solid was the balloon." Riley added, a skeptical tone remaining in his voice, "So, how do they get all the details right?"

"Come on," Mac growled. "It didn't leak to the media, fine. But it could easily leak to someone else, intentionally or by accident. We aren't the damned CIA around here. Shit leaks all the fuckin' time. Point being, it's entirely possible somebody could have copied the murders." Mac sipped his beer, and tacked in another direction. "Of course, we could have tried to ask Knapp about this. We could have asked him about Jones and watched him go blank, deny it, but we can't do that now, can we? That's kind of convenient, don't you think?"

Riley, catching Mac's drift, said, "You think Knapp's assassination yesterday had something to do with this?"

"Possibly," Mac replied. "I checked in with the guys looking at that. The theory is the shooter was on the third level of the Vincent Ramp, right?"

"That's right," Rock replied.

"Surveillance cameras show nobody up there. In fact, nobody on any of the ramp levels."

"Bad surveillance system?" Lich asked.

"I asked. It's okay, nothing special," Mac replied. "But there's another thing."

"Which is?"

"Ballistics. The bullet was for a Russian sniper rifle," Mac let it hang in the air.

"They're sure?" Lich asked quietly.

"They are," Mac answered, then to Rock and Riley, "Anybody with any of the families from Russia, have Russian or Soviet military background, have access to a Russian sniper rifle, have a background indicating they would be good with a sniper rifle? Oh, and then have that rifle available when there's two hours notice of when we're walking Knapp into court and then be able to get away without a trace, not be picked by surveillance cameras?"

Both just shook their heads.

But Lich wasn't buying it—at least not yet. "So, fine, Mac," Lich asked, "you think something is amiss with Jones. But what about Daniels? I was with you when we interviewed the senator. He admitted everything we needed. Frankly, he came off as guilty to me, and to Peters too. So, now you're saying the senator didn't kill Daniels?"

"I'm saying it's possible. Dick, I know this sounds like revisionist history, but I never completely believed the senator did Daniels. It didn't make sense." Mac shrugged, "On the evidence we had, we did what we had to do. But the case always bothered me."

"Why?" Rock asked.

"Politicians, especially ones like Senator Johnson, leave themselves a way out of every situation. Escapability, deniability—it's in their DNA. They don't put themselves in a position like the senator did—if he did. Murder? There's just no escape from that. Even the suggestion of it is a career killer, just ask Gary Condit. Even if Daniels threatened to expose their little affair to his wife or someone else, that's a manageable situation, happens to politicians all the time. It's not a situation to kill over, certainly not with all the evidence left behind pointing at him."

"But if the senator didn't do it, who did?" Riles asked. "On that case, you had no forced entry and a witness having Johnson leaving around the time of estimated death. I mean, that's pretty solid. What evidence do you have that someone else did this?"

"One thing that never came out was a witness I found about the time of the senator's hearing. I got a call from a guy named Paul Blomberg." Mac explained the story of the alley pick up behind Daniels's place the night of her murder.

"This is news to me. Why didn't it ever come out?" Rock asked.

"We never had to disclose it because the prosecution never went any further. It would have been an issue at trial."

"So, the senator doesn't kill Daniels. We prosecuted the wrong man, and he commits suicide over it! Shit, shit, shit!" Lich said, shaking his head, disturbed over the thought. He kicked a chair. "Damn it."

"If he did commit suicide, Dick," Sally said. "Maybe he didn't."

Lich, skepticism in his voice, "What? Now you're saying the senator didn't commit suicide? I mean, I was out there. I saw what you saw."

"Dick, do you know what the senator's blood alcohol was at the time of his death?" Mac asked.

"No, I don't, but I suppose you're going to tell me."

"This afternoon, when I was working all of this out, I spoke with Rick Hansen, the Wright County Sheriff. Remember him?"

Lich nodded.

Mac continued. "Hansen told me the senator's blood alcohol was .32 percent at the time of death."

"Whoa," Riley blurted.

"Exactly," Mac replied, "At the senator's weight, .32 and you're smoked, passed out, not getting up on any stool to hang yourself."

"Not impossible either, Mac," Rock added with a laugh, a little levity. "I mean, there were a couple of guys in here last night that might have pushed to that level, and they were still standing."

"Could they have climbed a barstool?" Mac asked, not laughing.

"I doubt it," Rock answered quietly.

"Exactly. I bet ninety-nine times out of a hundred, a person that loaded passes out long before doing anything, let alone hanging yourself. Besides, if you proclaim your innocence as strongly as the senator and Lyman Hisle did, do you commit suicide that same night? Before going to trial?"

"So, somebody killed the senator? Made it look like a suicide?" Lich asked.

"Possibly," Mac replied. "Follow it all the way out, Dick. If you have the ability to take out Daniels and Jones in the same night, what's taking out the senator a few nights later? It's November, and there are few if any people at the lake. Not to mention the fact that his cabin was isolated and hidden, thick pine trees everywhere. Remember?"

Lich nodded, starting to buy it.

"It was the perfect place to stage a suicide," Mac finished and slammed his beer. He'd shot his wad. But it was comforting to him that an uncomfortable silence overtook the room. The boys were thinking about it. What he'd just told them made some sense.

Riley spoke first, lightly shaking his head, pinching the top of his nose, "Christ, Mac."

"What can I say?"

"You sold me," Riley replied.

"Yeah?" Mac was a little surprised. "What about everyone else?"

Rock and Lich nodded as well.

"I don't suppose you have a suspect in mind," Rock inquired.

"I do, but it's total speculation at this point."

"As if this whole thing isn't?" Rock replied with a rueful chuckle. "Hell, you've gone this far, boy. Don't stop now."

What the hell, Mac thought. "This is not one person acting alone here. Not possible. Whoever did this, if you assume I'm right, had to have money, resources, and people to do this."

"Agreed," Riles said. "If you're right, this is some sort of coordinated effort, and there are some very skilled people—professionals—at work here."

"So, cut to the chase, Mac. Who do you think it is?" Lich asked.

"I don't have a person."

"Mac?" Lich was getting impatient.

"PTA."

Jaws went agape.

"Holy shit, Mac," Riley finally replied, shaking his head. Rock let out a slow whistle.

"What makes you think that?" Lich asked.

"This is where it gets a little thin."

"Ohhhhhh, *this* is where it gets thin," Riley said, a huge smile on his face, causing them all to laugh.

Mac smiled and kept going. "Jones was the CFO at PTA. She took over for a guy who died last year. Stephens was his name. He'd been there a long time, died in a car accident on Shepard Road. Nothing hinky about that. I talked to one of the patrol guys on the scene. It was a one-car accident that happened in a snow storm around the time of the state hockey tournament."

Everyone nodded at that, remembering the storm—over a foot of snow.

Mac moved on. "I don't know. Maybe Jones stumbles across some financial issue that Stephens had managed to bury. PTA naturally wants her to keep it quiet, continue to cover it up. She balks."

"Yeah," Sally added. "She has nasty visions of Enron. She's the next incarnation of Sharon Watkins."

"And she knows Claire Daniels," Riles said, finishing and picking up on the train of thought.

"That's right," Mac added nodding. "I'm guessing Jones talks to Daniels. PTA gets wind of it, realizing they won't be able to control her." Mac tossed his beer bottle into the garbage. "PTA has the money. Maybe they have the resources and the people as well."

Everyone took it all in for a moment, the gravity of what Mac had just laid out for them.

"Anyone else know about this?" Riles asked quietly, leaning back.

"Nope, just everyone in this room and one other person, wholly unaffiliated with the department that we can trust," Mac answered.

"So, where does that leave us?" Lich asked.

"On the trail of an assassin," Mac replied.

"Should we be telling the chief?" Rock asked.

"With what we got? No way. He wouldn't, he couldn't touch this with a ten-foot pole, nor should he." Riles shook his head. "No. We have to protect the department. We keep this to ourselves until we find something concrete. If we do, then we can think about going to the chief."

"And, if we don't," Rock added, "nobody's the wiser."

"So, what's next?" Lich asked.

"We stay covert," Mac replied calmly. "We don't tell anyone what we know or think."

"And?" Sally asked.

"The chief has given us all a few days off," Mac replied. "And I have some ideas of what I'd like to do with the time."

31

"AS LONG AS I ALWAYS GET A THIRD."

Viper tucked McRyan and Kennedy into bed at McRyan's place at 11:15 p.m. The report from Kraft that Lyman Hisle had met with McRyan, followed by the rest of the little detail going downstairs, had him concerned. He became downright worried as he listened with his earpiece to the detective and assistant district attorney discussing PTA prior to moving onto nocturnal activities. Things were not yet over. McRyan and company had to be watched.

The crew dropped Viper back off at his home. He went in the front door, checking the mail on the way in. Mostly bills, one from the gas company, another for the telephone, and one of those annoying credit card offers, all addressed to Webb Alt, Viper's name.

He went to the kitchen and dropped his keys in a little wicker basket on the counter. Having watched McRyan and friends hit the bar left him thirsty for a beer, and he needed to relax and wind down. The fridge was his salvation, providing a bottle of Heineken. He fished an opener out of a drawer, popped the top and went to his den. Grabbing the remote, he clicked on the news and threw himself into his easy chair. Kicking off his shoes, he took a sip of his beer and thought about Cross.

It had been such a sweet little deal. It made Alt, Ted Lindsay,

Bouchard, James Stephens, and select others inside and out of PTA a nice little pile. And until very recently, nobody knew. They needed to keep it that way. McRyan was a concern and becoming a bigger one by the minute. He was connecting some of the dots. They had to keep him from connecting them all.

Ted Lindsay was Alt's and PTA's boss. Ten years before, PTA was a large manufacturing company that was, among other things, a supplier of small arms, weaponry, ammunition, explosives, and communications equipment to the United States Department of Defense. It was a profitable company, with eight thousand employees and operations in Minnesota, California, and West Virginia. It did extensive work for the Defense Department, but little or no work with the CIA or NSA. Ted Lindsay changed that.

In the ten years that Ted Lindsay was president and CEO, PTA went from being one of many companies to being *the* company when it came to contracts with the Defense Department, as well as the CIA and NSA. Lindsay was even starting to make headway with the Department of Homeland Security. The company had grown to more than 62,000 employees with manufacturing operations in sixteen states. It had gone from being a nice little company in St. Paul to being mentioned in the same breath as Microsoft, GE, and Boeing. It was a name people knew. That was due in large part to the vision and work of Ted Lindsay.

Lindsay did two things that made PTA grow. First, at the time of his arrival, the company started developing satellite technology for commercial use, in particular for satellite television. Lindsay understood its potential application to intelligence gathering. He was fully aware of the CIA's movement towards the reliance, if not flat out dependence, on satellites for intelligence gathering. He leveraged his contacts and obtained a large chunk of the CIA's business for PTA. Not long after, he was able to work his way into the NSA as well. PTA became intertwined in the overall defense of the country. It had led to a three-fold increase in their governmental work.

Second, he took the company's expertise in software, communications, and satellite technology into retail. The company was the first company to offer walkie-talkie ability with cell phones. Some of the first personal digital assistants (PDAs) came from PTA. They offered one of the first combination cell phone/walkie-talkie/PDAs. One could buy their products at Best Buy, Circuit City, and Sears. It was a name brand.

After two years and even before the company's aggressive move into retail markets took off, Lindsay had been looking for a big increase in pay. Given what he'd done with the company in his two short years, he felt entitled. He was disappointed with what the company offered. A decent raise and an increase in stock options helped but was nowhere near what he'd expected. He wanted to, expected to, move into the big leagues of executive compensation. However, the board of directors was disturbed by stories about high executive pay at prominent corporations. They did not want criticism in that regard coming their way, especially given how much of the business was based on government contracts. Taxpayers would not be happy to learn that their tax dollars paid a president and CEO ten million dollars, plus stock options and it wasn't enough. Lindsay would have to take what the board was offering.

Lindsay started to look around. Through intermediaries, he learned of potential openings and interest in his abilities. He arranged for that interest to leak to the media. He expected the board would then sweeten his compensation, not wanting to lose the one person who had raised profits and stock prices to new heights. The board, knowing a media leak and power play when it saw one, played hardball and put together their own list of potential replacements and leaked that to the media. Lindsay seriously considered walking.

Then Cross came along.

Lindsay had worked his way up through the CIA over twenty-five years, with his last ten years spent as the deputy director of operations (DDO). That made him Alt's boss. Alt worked as an intelligence officer. Supposedly, after the Church hearings in the 1970s, the CIA was out of the assassination business. That wasn't entirely the case. Alt, and a number of others now with PTA had worked wet operations for years for the CIA. That was how Alt met Bouchard—some joint activities with the French. Lindsay had ordered assassinations and other operations, with Alt integrally involved in many of them. When Lindsay went to PTA, he wanted to significantly upgrade the security at the company. He brought in Alt for that very purpose and made him a vice president. Another person Lindsay brought to the company was CIA numbers genius, James Stephens, naming him chief financial officer.

After two years, when Lindsay was just about ready to walk away from PTA, Stephens and Alt came to him with Cross.

The increase in governmental contracts in Lindsay's first couple of years necessitated that the company go into an expansion, acquisition, and hiring mode. Their facilities were tapped out for space and efforts were made to create as much room as possible to fulfill the contracts. New facilities would be built, but that took time. In the meantime, the company had to ramp up its operations immediately, and they were short of space.

James Stephens had been tasked with evaluating each facility, its equipment, capacity, viability, and needs. Stephens found that at many company facilities there was an abundance of surplus military hardware and equipment, leftovers from previously fulfilled government contracts. It had simply been stored and nobody knew or had ever decided what to do with it. It was largely unrecorded on the company books. Stephens mentioned the surplus to Alt, who in turn started to formulate an idea.

PTA had one facility that was underused. It was an old explosives manufacturing facility outside the small rural town of Cross, West Virginia. Cross was the official address, but given the inherent danger of an explosives manufacturing facility, it was located well outside of the town, completely isolated. It was a facility that had fallen into disrepair, and it was about to be shut down. However, the one thing Cross had, that other PTA locations didn't, was space, and in particular, two empty warehouses. So the decision was made to ship all surplus equipment and materials to Cross. Once there, the company would decide what to do with it all. This is where Stephens and Alt came in with their idea.

Alt, Bouchard, and a few others knew select people with serious money who would jump at the chance to acquire the surplus material. Why? Because these were groups that the United States government did not want to have US military weaponry and equipment. Some were arms dealers. Others were labeled terrorist groups. Still others were in the drug trade, particularly in Columbia. And still others were simply viewed as unfriendly to the US government. They couldn't come to the States and purchase this equipment. However, if the powers that be at PTA were willing to do a little under-the-table dealing, these people would overpay to get their hands on the arms, explosives, and communications gear collecting dust in a remote Cross, West Virginia, warehouse.

Alt and Stephens projected what the take might be. Lindsay said go ahead, "As long as I always get a third," and none of the records included his name.

Alt and Bouchard arranged for the sale and transport of the surplus equipment. They always mixed it up, careful not to get into a pattern for shipment. Sometimes ships were used. A little money to the right stevedore and ship line assured that the goods reached their destination. Other times, the PTA jet had been used, as it travelled the globe for legitimate business. A few extra crates in the cargo hold wouldn't raise suspicion. On other occasions small boats had been used, either out of Chesapeake Bay or down on the Gulf Coast.

And while PTA was making millions selling electronic and surveillance equipment to the CIA, Alt, Bouchard, and others made sure the electronic and surveillance equipment didn't trip up the Cross operation.

With the CIA having moved mostly to electronic and satellite surveillance, the agency didn't have the troops on the ground that they used to. Alt and company took advantage of that weakness. The equipment was always transported in small quantities. Contact was made with the groups through intermediaries. There was no paper or electronic communication ever. Only face-to-face meetings and only cash was exchanged for the equipment. There were no records, except for those kept by Stephens, who moved the money around to prevent its detection, setting up overseas accounts for all involved, under assumed names.

While the original surplus had been older military equipment, as time went on, more current and advanced arms, weaponry, and communications equipment found its way to Cross. While the previous surplus had been accidental, more intentional surplus was created and sent to Cross, where Alt would arrange for its sale. While this made Lindsay, Alt, and Bouchard a little uncomfortable, the money made it worth the risk. And Lindsay, always one to cover all the bases, had a few contacts at the CIA who liked a little side cash, especially when placed in an account somewhere overseas. They would let Lindsay know if the sales were detected. They never had been. For five years, it had been a sweet little operation.

Then, in August of 2001, Lindsay's CIA contacts informed him that some of their arms dealer contacts had found new buyers, including Middle East terrorist organizations Hamas, Hezbollah, and, worst of all, Al Qaeda. These buyers were more dangerous. Lindsay, Alt, and Bouchard decided the risk was getting too great, but it was too late.

The planes went into the towers.

The War on Terror had started.

Lindsay and Alt worried that as the War on Terror progressed, and more intelligence attention was paid to terrorist groups—where their money came from, where they got their weapons—Cross could come to light. If the Cross operation was discovered, charges of espionage and treason wouldn't be far behind.

They shut it down. The Cross facility was shut down all together. The remaining surplus was destroyed. Dummy records were created. Alt and Bouchard hunted down their contacts who had dealt the arms, weapons, and communications equipment to the problem groups and eliminated them. Stephens was ordered to destroy all records. Everyone was ordered not to spend money, but rather to leave it overseas and spread it out as much as possible.

Stephens, having kept all the records and never having had any real operations experience at the CIA, was nervous. Alt wanted to take him out. Lindsay put him off and took a trip with Stephens and his wife, Yolanda, down to the Caymans. On a fishing boat, in the middle of the ocean, Lindsay discussed Stephens's concerns and determined that he had put them to rest. Stephens was on board, although he always made Alt nervous. After all, he'd kept the paper trail. While his accidental death this past March had been tragic, Stephens was the one person who could have reconstructed that paper trail. They didn't have to worry about that anymore. Everyone else involved was a hardened intelligence officer who knew to keep his mouth shut.

Cross was in the past. Dead, buried, and gone. Alt quietly watched his millions in Swiss and Cayman bank accounts grow and grow. In five years, he would retire to the Cayman's, buy a house on a beach, an eighty-foot yacht, play lots of golf, and live the good life. Nobody would be the wiser.

Then six weeks ago, Cross rudely came back to life.

Jamie Jones walked into Lindsay's office with a banker's box, labeled CROSS. Where the heck did this come from? Jones wouldn't say. The box contained detailed information regarding Cross. Lindsay's name was nowhere to be found in the papers, per his original instructions. Jones assumed it had all gone on without his knowledge. While Lindsay's name was absent, Stephens's, Alt's, and Bouchard's names, among others, were all over the documents. But the kicker was when Jones said that what she was giving Lindsay, was a copy. She kept an original, and she wanted to know what Lindsay would do.

Lindsay filibustered, saying he'd look into it. He looked into Jones instead. Alt and Bouchard started tracking Jones's every move. Her office and home were bugged. E-mail, phone, and cell phone were monitored. She was put under twenty-four/seven surveillance. They needed to find the original Cross documents. They believed she had the originals, since her copier use records revealed 437 unaccounted for copies, the exact number of documents in the box.

Apparently Jones recognized Lindsay's response for what it was and had ideas of her own. She met for coffee with Claire Daniels at

Starbucks on Grand Avenue, a few blocks from Daniels's place. From a van in the parking lot, Alt and Bouchard conducted audio surveillance of the meeting and listened as Jones spilled the beans to Daniels, claiming she had documented proof. That set off the alarm bells. Daniels, in addition to Jones, was monitored and followed. Claire Daniels had proven that she was one reporter you didn't want digging around.

Alt and Bouchard quickly realized two things. They had to get the original documents and take care of Jones and Daniels. Making matters worse, Jones and Daniels were childhood friends from a small town in Ohio. When taking them out, the key would be to do it so that nobody made the connection between the two. Making it all the harder was the fact they had to act fast, something that made Bouchard and Alt nervous. They spent their careers doing this sort of thing—tailing their targets for months, knowing their every move and striking at the perfect moment and leaving without a trace. Setting up one killing in a few days was one thing. Setting up two? How to pull that off without anyone making the connection was the million-dollar question.

Then the solution presented itself.

Tailing Daniels revealed her relationship with Senator Johnson. The serial killer was making headlines daily. Daniels was killed by Alt, and they fingered the senator. On the same night, Bouchard made Jones's death look like the work of the serial killer. Their contact with the investigation provided all the details to make it look like one of the serial-killer murders. With a special detail investigating the serial killer, the same people would not be investigating the Daniels murder. Nobody would make the personal connection between Jones and Daniels. That eliminated the problem of linking Daniels and Jones. They could now spend their time looking for the original Cross documents.

But they couldn't find the documents. It was the last thing out there that could hang them.

Then McRyan came along and made the connection between Daniels and Jones. They didn't foresee Knapp keeping his clippings and that Jones wouldn't be included. That was enough to make someone look, and McRyan started, meeting with Lyman Hisle and talking about PTA with Kennedy. He and his little group of friends were on the hunt. They just didn't know for what.

Alt took a sip of his beer. They had to find the Cross documents before McRyan and company did. Their advantage was that they knew what they were looking for, and McRyan didn't. How long would that last?

Alt finished his beer. He pushed himself up out of his chair, walked back to the kitchen, and grabbed another Heineken. He popped the top off and took a long drink, snorted lightly and shook his head. McRyan. Before he went to bed, Alt would go to his office, check on his money and move some of it. Twenty-four hours ago, he thought he was done. Now, more than ever, he realized he might have to run.

32

"CUT HIM LOOSE A LITTLE EARLY, I GUESS."

Mac put the key into the dead bolt and pushed in the front door to Claire Daniels's place. It felt like an eternity since he'd been here last, although it had only been five weeks. The condo was cold and musty, a product of vacancy. He noticed a thin coating of dust on the once shiny coffee table. Claire would have disapproved. All the furniture and other furnishings remained in place, white sheets draped over most of them. There was a for sale sign out front, and the realtor told Mac a sale was imminent.

Lich, Rock, and Riley followed him in, all clapping their hands or making some other movement to shake off the cold outside air. "So, what are we looking for, Sherlock?" Rock asked.

"Don't know exactly," Mac replied. "Let's go through the place, see what we find."

They didn't really know what they were looking for, although Mac had outlined his thoughts at breakfast. Going at PTA at the moment didn't make sense, even if the chief would have allowed it. They didn't know what they were looking for, and PTA most likely would have eliminated any trace of anything that was within their control. What wasn't in their control was whatever Jones and Daniels might have been talking about. They might have left something behind. Mac figured they had to find that, and then they would have something to go after PTA with. Problem was, they had no idea what Jones and Daniels shared. Mac and the others agreed that it was likely Jones found something she wasn't supposed to and told Daniels about it. It might have been something financial, since Jones was the CFO, but they really didn't know. It was like looking for a needle in a haystack, but not having any idea what the needle looked like. But they were all at the window, ready to place their bets.

Everyone took their coats off and threw them over the railing to the staircase and headed in different directions.

"Surprised they went back to Daniels's place?" Bouchard asked.

"Nope. Nothing there though. We went through that place, what, four times?" Alt replied. They were sitting on Summit Avenue, looking from the north down St. Albans at the front of Daniels's condo. Another van was parked on Grand to the south.

"Yeah."

"And *we* knew what we were looking for," Alt added.

"Pointless exercise, in other words?"

"That's my thought."

"They don't know that."

"No, they don't."

"They're cops. Pretty smart ones from what I've seen."

"I'm not suggesting they aren't. We're here watching them after all," Alt replied. "I just don't think those documents are at Daniels's place."

"Where are they?"

"Heck if I know. We've looked everyplace I can think of. Hell, we're still looking."

"My worry is somebody's going to stumble onto them," Bouchard said, frowning.

"I have the same worry. So does Lindsay," Alt replied. "You ready to bail on a moment's notice?"

"Everything's in place. You?"

"Definitely."

They sat in silence, the wind gusts lightly rocking the van and Minnesota Public Radio softly coming through the radio.

Bouchard sighed. "Going to be a long day watching these guys."

Mac and Lich searched the upstairs while Riley and Rock took the main level, basement, and garage. They all pulled out drawers, sifted through papers, looked at pictures, went through boxes, searched closets and cabinets, pulled plates and dishes out of cupboards, looking for anything about Jones or PTA.

Mac found nothing. He went through every file on her computer. Nothing about PTA. He went through all of her filing cabinets, checked the hallway buffet cabinet, sifted through her closet, pulled clothes out of drawers and off shelves, went through all of her personal belongings. He even looked under her bed. Nothing about PTA. Nothing about Jones. He pulled a chair up in front of the cabinet that held the television. He stared at the columns of DVDs. He'd remembered her voluminous collection. There had to be over one hundred movies including lots of romantic comedies, but some steamy movies as well. *Basic Instinct, 9½ Weeks, Body Heat,* even some of those steamy B-movies that found their way to Skinamax late at night. There were videos and DVDs of her news reporting. He remembered the sports reporter at Channel 6, Joe Elliott, talking about Daniels's perfectionism. She even videotaped her golf lessons, he said. She was a total perfectionist. While an interesting little side note, the perfectionism didn't seem to help here.

Everyone else crapped out as well. "Mac, we've been through the whole downstairs, storage, garage, everything," Riley said. Nothing had been found.

Mac looked at his watch—12:30 p.m. "Let's get some lunch."

They went to Bobby's Bar, along Grand Avenue, six blocks to the west of Daniels's place. On the way, Mac took another look at the Daniels file. Over burgers, they discussed the case.

"So what's next?" Lich asked.

"We go back and re-interview people in the neighborhood," Mac answered. "I called Paul Blomberg, that guy who saw someone in the alley. Lich and I are going to talk to him again, run through what he saw. Maybe talking through it again will bring something." Then to Riley and Rock, "I want you guys to go back and talk to her neighbors. In particular, talk to John Chase. He was next door and saw the senator leaving Claire's place one night. Also, go across the street. Talk to this guy."

"Who's this?"

"Our eyeball witness who saw the senator leaving Daniels's place the night of the murder, one Juan Hernandez."

"Why are we talking to him again?"

"He was pretty observant and Johnny-on-the-spot the night Daniels was killed. I want to know if he saw anyone else hanging around. I'm not sure we asked because he gave us the senator, and we moved on that."

Bouchard and Alt were in the Persian Rug store parking lot east of Bobby's Bar, watching out the back of the van. Bouchard bought a couple of cold sandwiches and cups of coffee from the deli across the street. Hansen and Berg were in the other van parked on Victoria to the south, watching the front of Bobby's.

Alt was reading the paper when Bouchard said, "Here they come."

Fat Lich and McRyan got into the Explorer, while Riley and big Rockford jumped into a Ford pickup. McRyan turned into the Kozlak Foodmart lot, while Riley kept going east on Grand. Alt ordered the other van to follow Riley and Rockford. He and Bouchard would stay with McRyan.

"Déjà vu all over again," Bouchard quipped.

~

Blomberg didn't have anything more for Mac and Lich. He gave his story again, almost word for word what he gave Mac a month earlier. He hadn't seen anyone else in the alley that night or any other night.

"Anything come into your mind since I was here last?"

"No. Nothing. Like I said, I just saw the guy get in the van. He was dressed in dark clothing. I never saw his face or anything. It happened really fast."

Lich showed him a picture of Jamie Jones. "Ever see her around here?"

Blomberg shook his head. "No. Not that I recall."

They ran through it again, but Blomberg simply had nothing more to give. The detectives turned to leave when Mac's cell went off.

~

Alt saw McRyan come out of the apartment building, talking on his cell phone.

"They didn't spend much time inside," Bouchard remarked.

Before Alt could respond, his phone chimed, it was Hansen. "Yeah?"

"We have a problem."

~

Mac and Lich pulled up in front of Hernandez's apartment building. Riley and Rock were standing in the entryway with another man. "He's gone?" Mac asked.

"Yeah," replied Riley. "This is the apartment manager, John Higgins."

"When did he leave?"

"Three weeks ago," Higgins replied.

"What about his lease? Didn't he have a one-year lease?" Mac asked.

"Normally he would, but he offered to pay two-months worth up front and then was willing to live month to month. Anyone I would find to take a one-year lease probably wouldn't take possession for a month or two anyway, so it seemed like a good deal to me. Guy kept to himself, caused no problems."

"Did he tell you where he was going?" Lich asked.

"No. Never heard from him personally. Just found the keys in my mailbox one day. No note or anything."

"Have you rented the unit out as of yet?"

"As of the first-of-the-year I have. Right now I have his stuff boxed up in case he calls for it."

They went up to the unit and looked around. It had been sparsely furnished to begin with and now there were just a few boxes lying in the middle of the floor. There were some clothes, a few dishes, and some papers.

Mac looked back at Higgins. "No forwarding address?"

"No. Like I said. One day he was here, the next he was gone. Didn't say good-bye or anything."

"Anyone come looking for him?" Riley asked.

"Nobody that I know of."

"Was he friendly with any of the other tenants?"

"I don't think so."

"And he paid the two months in full up front?"

"Yes."

"How?"

"Cash."

"As in check?" Mac asked.

"Nope. Cash."

"Mr. Higgins, didn't that strike you as odd?" Mac asked, since it certainly struck him as odd.

"A little perhaps." Higgins shrugged, tilted his head and lazily raised his eyebrows. "Guy offers cash, wants two months. What's the big deal?"

Mac snorted and shook his head.

They looked through the boxes. They found nothing to give them a hint of where he went. The only paper of any use was a check stub from Dynastar, his employer.

≈

"Cut him loose a little early I guess," Alt remarked.

"Where did he go?" Bouchard asked.

"Far away, and they won't find him. He's not in the country. He's not living under the name of Juan Hernandez. He won't be found unless we need him to be found."

"Don't you think it'll look odd that he bailed?"

"A little. They might even suspect we did it. And of course, they'd be right," Alt said lightly shaking his head, a bit perturbed. All things being equal, he thought, this was a hiccup he would have preferred to avoid. Hernandez's disappearance only served to heighten their suspicion. Of course, had the police bothered to remain in touch with Hernandez, Alt would have kept him around. Once they killed the senator, the Daniels case was over. Once he was certain of that, he cut Hernandez loose. Alt lightly sighed, shook his head and said, "They won't be able to find him."

"Nothing to worry about?" Bouchard asked.

"I don't think so."

≈

Mac and Lich went over to Dynastar and spoke with the Human Resources manager. Hernandez left without notice and hadn't picked up his last paycheck. He left no forwarding address for sending the check, and they hadn't heard from him. When hired, he'd completed a W-4 and immigration I-9 Form. For the I-9, he provided a Minnesota driver's license and Social Security card to verify identity and ability to work in the United States. Dynastar did not make copies of the documents, although some employers did, even though it wasn't technically required. Lich called the license and Social Security number information to Riley and Rock, so they could check it downtown.

Mac and Lich interviewed people in the production area that worked with Hernandez. He wasn't at Dynastar long. He had been pleasant enough but kept to himself. He didn't mention where he was going and everyone was surprised when he just stopped showing up for work.

It was dark as they walked out of Dynastar, having found nothing helpful about Hernandez. Riley called. While there were plenty of Juan Hernandezes, they couldn't find any with the Minnesota driver's license and Social Security numbers this Juan gave to Dynastar.

At the Pub, Sally joined them, and they went down to Patrick's Room.

"Not much today," Rock said.

"Hernandez is missing. That's something," Lich replied.

"Guy was probably an illegal. People get a fake driver's license or state ID card, along with a false Social Security number and work as long as they can. If the employer sniffs something is up, they bail and go to the next unsuspecting employer," Sally said. "I have some friends who do employment law and they said their clients run into this all the time."

"His absence seems awfully convenient," Mac replied, not buying it.

"You suggestin' PTA had something to do with it?" Riles asked, a smile on his face.

"Hell if I know," Mac replied. "It seems as if he skipped town after it became clear that the Daniels investigation was over."

"It is convenient," Riles said agreeably. "But that's about it. If PTA did take care of him, he's either dead or paid off, drinking an umbrella drink in a foreign land."

"So what's next?" Sally asked.

"Tomorrow we go over to the Jones place," Mac said. "See what we find there."

"And what if we don't find anything?" Rock asked.

"Let's cross that bridge when we come to it," Mac replied.

Mac turned off the bathroom light and went over to his side of the bed, turned off the nightstand light, rolled over and kissed Sally.

"So, not much today, huh?" she said, snuggling up to Mac.

"Just that Hernandez thing," Mac said, lightly scratching her back. "Daniels's place was the same as I remembered it. Something odd about her place though. I just can't put my finger on it. It's like I'm missing something."

"What?"

"If I knew, I'd tell you. I've looked at something there that's important, but I don't know why yet. I haven't put it together."

"So tomorrow you're going to look at Jones's?" she said, running her fingers through Mac's chest hair.

"Yeah, see if we find anything."

"What'll you look for?"

"You know, anything that ties Jones and Daniels together. Something that tells us why PTA might have killed them. Like Justice Stewart once said, 'I'll know it when I see it.'"

"It was 'I know it when I see it,'" Sally replied, "and he was talking about pornography."

"Speaking of which," Mac replied, sliding her panties down.

"Men are animals," Sally replied, not the least bit disappointed.

"Do we take them out?" Bouchard said, having heard the conversation through the headphones.

"All of them? Including Riley, Lich, and that Rockford?" Alt replied, shaking his head. "No way. You'd have to throw in Hisle and probably that uncle of McRyan's, as well."

"So? Take some time, a few more resources, but it could be done. It might have to be done."

Alt sighed. "You might be right. Start making plans, but only just in case. The idea of being at war with the St. Paul Police Department is not my first choice." He grabbed his cell phone. Lindsay needed to be updated.

33

"STEPHENS WAS A LUCKY MAN."

"I obviously went into the wrong line of work," Rock quipped as they pulled up in front of Jones's place. She'd lived in the new high-end condo development along the Mississippi called River Highlands just southwest of downtown along the river—another of the developments in St. Paul's ten-year quest to take tax advantage of river real estate. The condos had brown stone exteriors, with white trim and black shutters; a colonial look that one might find in Georgetown.

They went through the same drill as they had at Daniels's place, splitting up and looking for something, anything, that would tie Daniels, Jones, and PTA all together. Mac took the upper-level, Lich and Riley worked the main level, and Rock the lower level. Everything was as it had been at the time when she was killed. Her mother hadn't been able to bring herself up to clean the place out.

Mac attacked her office. She was like Daniels, an absolute neat freak. They must have drilled neatness into kids from Bristol. Everything was perfectly organized. Perhaps it was because she had an accounting and finance background. These were usually neat, organized people, and Jones fit that description to a T. Everything in its place, undisturbed for five weeks now, much like Daniels's place.

Mac booted up her computer. Like Daniels, she didn't bother to password protect it, and he was able to search her files. There was little if any PTA information, and he suspected she probably just dialed into the company system from home. He looked through her personal correspondence and e-mails, nothing out of the ordinary or from Daniels. There were a number of unopened e-mails from a fantasy football website. Mac smiled, she played a little fantasy football. He took a look at her team, not bad.

He looked through her file drawers, nothing much. All of her bills were organized, and she paid online. She had a number of invest-ments, all of which seemed to be looking good. Her bank statement showed a large balance. He found no record of a safe deposit box, although he would call and check with her bank. Her bedroom was well organized, her clothes neatly stored in her dresser and closet, her bed neatly made. Everything was perfectly in its place; almost too perfect, "unnatural," he thought.

Mac went down to the kitchen, where Lich was looking at various items posted on the refrigerator. It might have been the only messy place in the house. It looked like a typical refrigerator—photos and miscellaneous notes held up by refrigerator magnets. There was a white erase board with a note "Get Milk." A small paper calendar hanging on a magnetic hook, still on October, had notes on various dates, such as "Workout at 7:00," "Coffee with Landy at 10:00" and "Happy Hour at 5:30." Lich jotted down some notes and squinted at the calendar, scratching his chin.

Riley and Rock came in, caught Mac's eye and shook their heads. They took seats at the kitchen table.

"It isn't difficult to know you haven't found anything with these women. I mean, man, talk about two anal-retentive, obsessive-compulsive people. A place for everything and everything in its place. Except, of course, for the fridge," Riley stated.

"Almost too neat, artificially neat," Mac replied.

"What do you mean?" Rock asked.

"I'm pretty meticulous about my place, but there's always some-thing out of place. But these two women are unlike anything I've seen. I mean, there's a little film of dust around here, but you almost get the feeling they would have required you to walk around with plastic gloves on and baggies around your feet. They remind me of an old neighbor we had when I was growing up. He'd sweep out his garage three times a day and wash his car twice a week. His yard was perfect, looked like the infield at Wrigley and he'd have a shit fit if someone set foot on his grass. He was just nuts."

"Well, all I can tell you is that I didn't find anything that seemed related to what we're doing or looking for," Rock replied. "These women make it easy to look for stuff. It's all organized. I mean, if you were looking for something you wouldn't have to ransack the place, just give yourself time to go through it and find what you're looking for."

"And PTA has had five weeks to do precisely that before we got around to it," Mac replied.

"Assuming they had anything to do with this in the first place," Riley replied. "We sure aren't finding anything this way."

"No, we're not." Mac looked at his watch. Noon. "Why don't we get something to eat and go from there." Rock and Riley nodded and pushed themselves up from the table. Lich was still looking at the fridge. "You coming?" Mac asked Lich.

"Yeah. I'll be right with you." Lich replied as he continued to stare at something on the fridge, his hands on his hips.

Mac joined Riley and Rock outside, holding the key to lock the door. The temperature was back up a little, mid-thirties, a bright blue sky. With no wind, it was comfortable, a trench coat sufficient for warmth. None of them wore gloves.

Lich came out a few minutes later, and they started to file into the Explorer. Mac turned the key asking, "Where should we go?"

"Franco's is five minutes away," Rock replied.

"Yeah," Riley added, rubbing his hands together.

"Franco's it is," Mac replied, dropping the truck into gear. They sat in silence for a few minutes, the sports station playing on the radio.

"Was James Stephens's wife named Yolanda?" Lich blurted.

"Riles?" Mac asked. Riley opened the Jones file and started leafing through the notes. "Yeah, Yolanda. Second wife it says here."

"Is Landy short for Yolanda?"

"Yeah, I think so," Riley replied. "Why?"

"Because," Lich replied, "There was a note on the fridge that said—"

"—coffee with Landy at 10:00," Mac finished it for him. "What was the date on that, Dick?"

"October 25th."

"At lunch I'll give Ms. Stephens a call and see if we can pay her a little visit."

"Probably just a coincidence," Rock added.

"Yeah, but so is this whole case," Mac replied.

After lunch, they made their way over to the Stephens' home, a sprawling two-story stucco mansion in the wealthy Highland Park neighborhood, close to the Mississippi River.

"My, we are jet setting today, aren't we?" Rock mused.

The house was set back a hundred feet from the street, and one could tell that, in the summer, it had numerous flower gardens in the front following a serpentine cobblestone sidewalk from the street. It looked like a home you would find in California, with off-white stucco, red tiles on the roof and tall, perfectly manicured shrubs framing the windows along the front.

A housekeeper answered the door. She welcomed them in and asked that they wait for Ms. Stephens in the foyer. Mac admired the winding staircase up to the second level and a couple of the art pieces on pedestals.

Mac recalled having seen a picture of Stephens. He wasn't a homely guy by any stretch, just kind of an average Joe in his fifties. He had clearly overachieved in his second marriage. The second Ms. Stephens, who had answered the phone "Landy," was a stunning beauty in, Mac guessed, her late thirties. She was tall, with strawberry-blonde hair that fell stylishly to her shoulders. Two words came immediately to Mac's mind—Trophy Wife. No reflection on her intelligence, just that he seriously doubted it was Stephens's magnetism that drew this woman to him.

Landy was ever the polite hostess, seating everyone and offering coffee. She sounded almost excited to speak with them when Mac called. Now she was serving coffee and what not, and he got the feeling that she was happy to have company. He wondered if having the mansion and the money still left her a little lonely. Stephens probably had her running with an older crowd. Now that he was gone, all she had was the house and the money.

"So, Ms. Stephens ..." Mac asked.

"Landy," she replied, smiling warmly at Mac.

"Okay, umm, Landy. As I mentioned when I called, we're following up on some things from the Jamie Jones murder, and we noticed that she had met with you shortly before she died."

"Oh, yes. I remember. Probably a week beforehand."

"Were you and Ms. Jones friends?"

"Yes. I really liked Jamie, and so did James. She was really nice, and we kind of hit it off because we were the same age."

"So, why did the two of you get together on the ..." Mac looked down at his notes.

Lich finished for him, "... the twenty-fifth."

"Oh. I had her meet me for coffee out at the Yacht Club. I had been up to our lake home, I guess *my* lake home, up north on Gull Lake. James had an office up there, and I ran across a banker's box with a bunch of PTA stuff in it. I think it was called Cross or something like that. Anyway, I didn't just want to throw it out. It might be something important. I figured if James had it, it was something financial, and I should give it to Jamie. We met for coffee, and I gave her the box."

"Do you recall what was in the box?" Mac asked.

"No, I really don't," she replied and then looked thoughtfully towards the ceiling. "There was some sort of book, like for accounting, I think."

"A ledger book?" Rock added helpfully.

"Yes. That's right. Thanks." She shot him a warm smile. "A ledger book of some type."

"Anything else?" Riley asked.

"Not that I can recall. Just papers, some folders, stuff like that. Most were in those brown file folders. I don't know much about finance and, like I said, it was PTA related, so I gave it to Jamie."

"After that day, did you talk to her again?"

"No, I didn't."

"When you gave the box to her, what did she say?"

"Nothing much. Thanks, maybe. She might have said, 'I'll look it over'—that kind of thing. We were friends. Giving her the file was just an excuse to get together for coffee."

"Did you discuss anything else?"

"We chatted about lots of things. Her work. What I was doing ..."

"Ms. Stephens ..."

"Landy."

"Sorry," Mac replied, "Landy, did you talk about anything else related to the box you gave her?"

She thought for a moment, then shook her head, "Not that I recall. We talked for an hour or so, said good-bye, and that was that."

"And the name on the box was Cross?"

"I think so. Cross. There was that ledger book and some other papers that all looked Greek to me. That was it."

They went through it one more time, but nothing additional came to light. Mac worried that they were pushing it, but Landy never asked what their questions were all about.

They got up to leave, thanking her for her time. She walked them to the door, saying good-bye to each, with Mac being last. He left her a card and asked that she call if she remembered anything else. She promised she would, giving him a warm smile as he left.

Alt and Bouchard watched from a block and a half north, waiting for

McRyan and Company to leave. Kraft and Hansen were in another van a half block behind, waiting for their cue. Alt had been on the phone with Lindsay. Finally, they had an idea of where the Cross documents might have come from.

"When they leave, you'll talk to her?"

"Yes, sir."

"When that's done, call me. It's time for us to put a stop to this little investigation of theirs."

"Yes, sir."

Alt hung up and turned his attention back to the house. The front door opened, and the cops filed out, McRyan being the last. They all got into the Explorer and drove down the driveway, took a right turn, in the opposite direction from Alt and Bouchard.

"Kraft. They're yours."

"Copy that." He heard the engine start behind him and Kraft pulled by, settling in behind McRyan and company along Mississippi River Boulevard.

"Let's go."

∼

Mac and company headed back downtown to the Pub. Mac called Sally to fill her in on what they had found.

"Is this enough to go after them?" he asked.

"No. You don't even know what this Cross thing is. You have to know about that before we could go forward. Sounds like you're on the right track though. You guys are finding things."

"Yeah, but I'm not sure how long we can keep doing this until people start finding out."

"Hopefully something will pop soon."

"We'll be at the Pub. Come when you can."

Shamus told them to use Patrick's Room in the basement if needed and that seemed like the place to go. They each grabbed a beer from the bar and headed downstairs. Mac closed the unique cabinet door behind them and everyone took a seat.

"So, what do we think?" Mac started.

"Stephens was a lucky man," Lich said, his mind ending up where it usually did.

"Yeah, she was a looker," Riles replied, "but did we learn anything?"

"Cross. We learned that. Whatever *that* is. We need to find out what that means. Is it a place, a name, what?" Mac replied.

"How do we find that out?" Rock asked.

"I know somebody I could ask," Mac replied. "I'm going to go make a phone call." He left the small conference room, found a spot in the corner of the basement and punched up Lyman's number. Mac filled him in on what they had learned the last couple of days.

"Mac, as best I remember, Cross was an old explosives facility out in West Virginia. The company owned it for years, but it's closed now, has been for a while."

"Anything unusual about the place?"

"Off the top of my head, no. It was an explosives facility we had. It was old and out in the middle of nowhere. Nothing like a modern operation. They finally shut it down a few years ago."

"Do you know why they shut it down? Any questions or controversies?"

"I'm not sure. I think we just had more modern facilities for producing explosives. I suspect it was determined that it wasn't worth keeping open, probably because it would have cost a lot to modernize it and what not."

"What was out there, just a manufacturing facility?"

"Pretty much. There was a big warehouse or two, so I don't know, we might have been storing stuff there or something. The place was out in the middle of nowhere as I recall. I was never actually there myself, but I looked Cross up on a map once and it was a little town in the hills. The facility itself was well out of town, being an explosives plant and all."

"Anyone you could talk to about the place?"

"I could try. I still have some friends at PTA." Lyman didn't sound hopeful.

"It's a long shot I know, but I'd appreciate it just the same. We're kind of up against the wall, and this is the only thing we have found."

"I'll let you know."

Mac hung up his phone and headed back to the conference room. When he opened the door, Riley was hanging up his phone. He didn't look happy. "What gives?" Mac asked.

"We have to go see the chief."

"What for?"

"He wants to know why we're looking into PTA."

34

"I'M A COP, NOT A POLITICIAN."

A few days earlier, it had been a happy occasion to come into the chief's office. The Irish whiskey had been out. Smiles and backslaps all around. Not now. One look at Flanagan's face told the boys that he was not pleased. His tie was loose, his hair messed, the dark circles around his eyes had suddenly returned. "Sit," was all he said when they walked in.

Helen Anderson was already sitting on the left side of the couch and didn't look any happier. Her arms were crossed, and she had a stern look on her face. Sylvia Miller sat on the other end and looked pensive. While Mac didn't like making the chief mad or causing Miller discomfort, he could give a shit about Anderson. What did concern him was Sally. She was conspicuous by her absence from this little meeting. Helen knew they were dating and he imagined that if it hadn't happened already, Helen would be asking her what she knew.

As they all sat down and the chief came around his desk, the mayor came in, also unhappy. He'd been their friend a few days ago. One look told Mac, the mayor wasn't here to be friends.

"So," the chief started, "can someone tell me what in the hell you four have been up to?"

Riley started, but Mac put his hand on his knee and jumped in. The investigation was his idea. "Chief, you can put it on me."

"What the hell, Mac?"

"Chief, I found some things a few days ago in finishing up Knapp, that caused us to go back and look at a few things related to the Claire Daniels murder, as well as one of Knapp's alleged victims, Jamie Jones."

"What?" Helen Anderson replied, aghast. "Why in the world, Detective, would you dig up all of that?"

"I'd like to know as well," the chief added, doubt in his eyes.

Mac walked them through the whole story. Flanagan and Miller looked intrigued, Anderson incredulous, and the mayor sick. They all had their individual reasons.

"Hell of a theory, Mac," Flanagan said, with a little smile and shake of his head.

"Yes, sir."

"Pat, you went along with this?" the chief asked, looking over to Riley.

"Yes, sir. We all did," Riley replied assuredly. "Mac's onto something here."

"Excuse me?" Anderson accused. "From where I'm sitting, I don't see it. You have no evidence to implicate PTA in anything. You have a number of coincidences that make an interesting story, perhaps, but nothing that would hold up in court."

"We're not in court yet," Rock replied. "We're investigating ..."

"And who authorized that?" the mayor interjected. "Obviously this is news to the chief."

"Couldn't tell the chief," Lich added.

"Why not?" Flanagan, surprised.

"Sir, we were trying to protect you. If we found something, we'd come to you. If we found nothing, then you'd never know that there were some possible questions, not so much about Knapp, but about the Daniels killing," Mac said.

Riley jumped in. "It's been rough enough for the department as it is, sir. We didn't want to come to you with this, unless we found something to support the theory."

"Well, on that account, I'd say you've failed," Anderson replied.

Mac held up two fingers, "We've had two days! TWO! If we're right, PTA has had five weeks or more to try to cover this up, which puts us way behind. But in two days of poking around, we found this Cross lead and link between Landy Stephens and Jamie Jones. We've already linked Jones to Daniels. And I just can't get past two women, lifelong friends, both from a small Ohio town who die in St. Paul on the same night. Something's going on here. If we keep looking, we might find more."

"If you keep looking, all you'll do is embarrass the department and my office," Anderson answered. "You have a theory that, while I can see where you're going, doesn't have any evidence to support it. PTA's lawyers would make monkeys out of us if we went after them with this. They'll paint you as a bunch of rogue detectives who investigated without authority. It'll be a disaster for you, the chief, the mayor and, yes, my office."

"I thought we were on the same team?" Mac replied, disbelief on his face. "We haven't asked to go to court yet. Who knows what we might find if we keep looking. If we develop a good case, then you can decide."

"I won't take this into court against PTA."

Mac, pissed, raised his voice. "We wouldn't ask you. We'd ask someone who's actually seen the inside of a courtroom, not a chicken-shit politician more interested in protecting her bony little ass and her senate run."

"That's enough, Detective!" the mayor replied angrily.

Mac ignored the mayor and glared at Anderson, not backing down.

"Calm down, everyone," the chief stated, a wry smile on his face. "Let's have a drink and cool down." He got up and went to his desk and grabbed a bottle of whiskey and several glasses. While filling them, he asked, "Mac, what would you and the boys here suggest is your next move?"

"We were discussing that when you called, sir. I don't know that we had decided as of yet."

"I'll tell you what I think," the mayor replied. "You go poking around PTA without more than you have, we'll lose them."

"Sir?" Riley asked.

"I got the call from Ted Lindsay over at PTA. We're currently in discussions with PTA to keep them here in St. Paul. Their lease is up next summer, and they bring over four thousand employees downtown alone. My office is working with the building owner, trying to keep PTA and all those jobs here in St. Paul. If we're investigating them on something as thin as what you've put forward here, we'll lose them, especially if the media gets wind of it. I don't need to tell all of you what the loss of those jobs would do to this city."

Rock, stunned. "Jobs? What about murder? Does that count for anything, Mayor?"

"Yes, Detective, it does," the mayor replied. "I'm no lawyer, but from what you've laid out here, you don't have a case, do you?"

"Not yet," Mac replied.

"Not ever," Anderson interjected. "Ever heard of reasonable doubt, Detective McRyan?"

"Yes, ma'am." Mac replied with a wicked grin. "Graduated summa cum laude from law school." He knew Anderson didn't have any Latin on her diploma.

She only blinked once. "Then you know that PTA's lawyers would have no problem creating reasonable doubt."

"For once tonight, Ms. Anderson, you're right," Mac replied, restraining himself as best he could. "Neither I, nor Pat, nor any of us, though, have asked you to go to court yet. We just want to look into this more."

"The more you look into it, the more likely it is that PTA leaves the city," the mayor jumped back in. "Ted Lindsay said as much today."

Rock, exasperated, said, "Fuck 'em. Just because someone employs a bunch of people in this city means they get a free pass?"

"Not on my watch," Riley added.

"Chief," the mayor replied, "put a leash on your boys here, or I will."

"Mac," the chief brushed off the mayor, "what if we could talk to PTA tomorrow?"

"Sir?"

"If I could put you in a room with Ted Lindsay tomorrow—what would you say to that?"

"Might that be the only option you'll give us for going forward?"

The chief nodded.

"I'm game."

"Charlie, no!" the mayor replied. "We're not going to do that. We're meeting with Lindsay tomorrow to smooth this over. This won't help."

"Tell you what, Mayor. I'm a cop, not a politician. These boys are cops, not politicians. They investigate homicides. Now, I'm not sure they have anything yet. But coincidences like these?" the chief shook his head. "I've been a cop for thirty-three years. If I ran across something like this, I'd like to think I'd do exactly what these boys did." Flanagan took a sip of his drink and sat back in the high-backed leather chair. "Now, if Ted Lindsay has nothing to hide, he'll talk to me and the boys here. If he talks tomorrow and answers their questions, and he provides satisfactory answers, then that'll be the end of it. And my word matters on that, does it not, boys?" the chief asked, looking at Mac and Riles in particular. They both nodded. Flanagan continued, "If Mr. Lindsay doesn't have answers for us, then my boys'll continue to look into this." He took a last sip of the dark whiskey, smiled, and asked, "So what's it gonna be, Mayor?"

Mac smiled inwardly. Chief Flanagan backed his boys' play. That's why they loved him. He was the chief of police, not a police chief, not a tinhorn politician.

The mayor, on the other hand, looked like he'd just choked down a serving of Nyquil. "I'll talk to Lindsay and see what he says. He may not go for it."

"Ask the man. If he has nothing to hide, he'll do it."

The mayor sighed, "I'll see what I can do." He turned and left the chief's office to go make the call.

"Charlie, I'd be careful if I were you," Anderson warned, ever the politician. "You're playing with fire here and not just the department's hide, but the city's."

"Helen, if I gave a shit about politics, you would be right." The chief took another sip of his drink, smiling. "But I don't. Never have. If the mayor and the City Council want to get rid of me, I got a big old cabin up north waiting for me." The chief had some dough; his wife came from a wealthy family. "But I appreciate your concern."

"Well, good luck to you all," Anderson replied. "I may have been a little confrontational. Of course, should something turn up, our office, as always, would work with you," she finished, extending an olive branch.

The chief accepted, "Thank you, Helen."

Anderson left. The chief grabbed the bottle of Irish whiskey and gave everyone another touch. He took a long drink and a little smile creased his face.

"Well, boys. I was all ready to read you the riot act."

"We figured that to be the case," Riley replied.

"But I just can't be mad at you. I still don't know if you have anything here, but, damn, if I don't want to let you have a shot at it."

Alt sat on the fine leather couch, close to the fireplace, sipping water and admiring the shelves of books in Ted Lindsay's study. Seemed like there were hundreds of them, different sizes and colors. They must have all been classics. The boss would have nothing but the best.

Lindsay was on the phone with the St. Paul mayor. This was their third conversation of the day. Alt listened as Lindsay agreed to a 5:00 p.m. meeting at his office. He hung up the phone and strolled over to Alt, grabbing a high-backed leather chair, close to the fire.

"So we have a 5:00 p.m. meeting tomorrow?" Alt asked.

"Yes. The mayor, Chief Flanagan, McRyan, and Riley."

"To discuss ...?"

"They want to discuss with us some problems they have with the death of Jamie Jones and how PTA might be able to help clear them up."

"What do they know?"

"At this point, they know that some documents about Cross exist, based on our conversations with Landy Stephens. I want to know more by tomorrow, however."

"I better go back downtown."

"Yes. I want to know if McRyan and Kennedy talk about this. So, let's see if those bugs'll pay off, shall we?"

"Yes, sir. One question. Why take the meeting tomorrow?"

"Because, according to the mayor, if we meet with them and have answers to their questions, the chief has given his assurance that the investigation will end."

"You believe that?"

"I do," Lindsay replied confidently. "Charlie Flanagan is a man of his word. He's backed his boys, which is why that force would run through a brick wall for him. But if they crap out tomorrow, he's smart enough to know that he can't let them keep going. Even if he suspects something, he knows that if we shut them down on this Cross business, they have nowhere to go, no way to get a conviction, and he can't risk exposure of the department on the Daniels case or letting word slip that this Knapp didn't kill one of the victims. So, if we shut him down tomorrow, we should be rid of the police."

"Plus, we hammer the city with the threat we'll leave if they don't back down."

"Yes," Lindsay smiled. "The mayor's concerned about the loss of all those jobs and the impact on his city. He likes being mayor. So, yes, he'd like to see this all go away. In other words, my friend, let's see that we make the mayor happy, shall we?"

35

"IS THAT WHAT THIS IS REALLY ALL ABOUT, DETECTIVE?"

Mac looked out the window of the minivan as they drove through five blocks of rush-hour traffic to the PTA Tower. The Christmas decorations were lighting up the dark 4:45 p.m. sky of downtown. Green wreaths with bright red bows adorned the street lights. Department store and restaurant windows were outlined with red, green, and white lights. Santas were working the corners, ringing their Christmas bells, looking for donations to the Salvation Army. It all made for a festive atmosphere.

The scene allowed Mac's mind to drift, if only momentarily, away from the task at hand: PTA. It was only for an instant, and then it returned, as it had again and again for the past twenty-four hours. The chief, mayor, Captain Peters, Riley, and he were going to meet with Ted Lindsay, the president of PTA, although the mayor would wait outside. Mac had seen pictures and video footage of him for years. He was a prominent man of the town. Now Mac was essentially going to accuse Lindsay and people who worked for him of murder.

And he was going in with less than a full arsenal. He met with Riles, Rock, and Lich all day, discussing scenarios of how to go after PTA and at the same time protect the department. They went back and forth on a variety of approaches, but finally settled on one that tied one hand behind their back. They couldn't use Claire Daniels. Mac reached the same conclusion with Sally the night before.

Daniels's name might come up, but not in the context that they thought PTA killed her, even though Mac suspected they did. Her name would come up as a reporter that Jamie Jones knew and talked to, probably about Cross, whatever Cross was. But for now, at least, they planned to leave the death of Claire Daniels with the senator. If this whole stunt backfired, they reasoned, they wouldn't have to deal with the mess of putting into play the fact that the investigators of the Daniels's murder thought they got the wrong man.

Despite the fact they were leaving Daniels out, it was, nonetheless, decided they would be aggressive. As Riles said repeatedly, "We probably got one shot at this, so let's not leave anything in the bag. Grip it and rip it."

"Damn straight," Rock said, a bull in the China shop if there ever was one. "Let's take our best shot at the bastards. If we crap out, fine, no regrets."

"Mac," Lich said. "Go at him like you went at the senator. Smart-ass young prick detective thinks he knows everything. See if you can get under his skin."

That would be their approach. What made Mac nervous was that when he went after the senator, they had evidence up the wazoo. To say they had less than that on PTA would be an understatement. There were suspicions, but no direct evidence. Somehow they had to prove to the chief and the mayor that PTA was worth investigating further. Lindsay needed to fess up to something or lose his cool. Accomplish either of those things, and the chief might let them keep looking. That was the goal, to keep the investigation alive.

"Go at him with Cross?" Mac said to the group.

"It's all we got," Lich replied. "See what the man has to say."

Mac smiled inwardly. He had a feeling this would be one of those life events he would never forget.

Downtown St. Paul was mostly a maze of one-way streets. The group actually had to drive all the way around the PTA Tower to get to the building's parking garage. A security guard waved to them as they pulled in. He directed them towards another guard standing by a chain-link gate that led to a private parking area. As they approached the gate, the guard rolled it open, and Captain Peters pulled the van through and drove to a spot marked with a VIP parking sign.

As Peters put the van into park, Riley, who was sitting next to Mac patted him on the thigh and smiled. "You know this is probably nothing, a waste of our time."

"Yeah, it's pretty thin."

They both felt otherwise as they got out of the van and a blond guy with a medium build approached. "Hello, Chief Flanagan. My name's Webb Alt," the blond-haired man said as he extended his hand. "I'm the vice president of Security. Mr. Lindsay asked that I meet you all down here and take you on up."

"Alt," the chief replied, taking his hand and then introduced everyone else. Mac shook Alt's hand and gave him a look. Was this guy one of those assassins Lyman was talking about?

"We'll go through this door over here and take the private elevator up to the top and to Mr. Lindsay's private conference room," Alt said, and waved them towards the door.

"Hmpf. Private elevator," Riley said quietly in a sarcastic voice.

"Ain't like going over to Dick's Bar, now is it?" Mac replied with a wry smile.

The group followed Alt and filed into the waiting elevator. Mac watched the digital display over the door, which remained blank all the way until it stopped on twenty. It was a private express elevator; it didn't stop on any other floors. As they walked off the elevator, they were in the lobby where the general public elevators came to a stop as well, two on each side of the hall. Straight ahead was a cherry wood reception desk, vacated for the evening.

Alt, sensing they noticed the vacant receptionist desk, offered, "We appreciate your willingness to come at this later hour. We preferred our employees not see someone as recognizable as Chief Flanagan and Detective McRyan walking through the building to see the president."

Riley snorted, elbowing Mac in the ribs. "So, you're recognizable?"

"Guess I'll need a publicist."

Alt led them past the reception desk, towards a set of double doors that led into a plush conference room. There was a cherry wood conference table with ten high-backed leather chairs on either side. Fine crystal glassware sat on a silver tray in the middle of the table. A large credenza on one end of the conference room held coffee and soft drinks. Built-in cabinets on the other end probably concealed a television and projection screen of some sort, Mac thought, based on the configuration of the cabinet doors.

As impressive as the conference room was, the view was even better. From the twentieth floor, the windows looked west out of downtown. Mac walked over to the window, which ran from floor to ceiling. He could see the Xcel Energy Center's large red letters and message board flashing coming events. The height of the building also allowed Mac to look levelly at the St. Paul Cathedral, up on the bluff overlooking the city to the west. It was beautiful, the white stone of the magnificent church illuminated by ground lights, contrasting against the dark-blue, cold, winter sky.

As Mac took in the view, he heard the doors open. He turned to see Alt walking back in with Ted Lindsay and another man, whom he assumed was the attorney. Introductions were made all around. Lindsay skipped Alt, and introduced his lawyer, Larry Zimmer. Mac had heard of him, although he didn't know him. A prominent lawyer with a big firm, the name of which Mac couldn't remember.

The chief introduced his troops. When Flanagan introduced Mac, Lindsay walked over. "Detective McRyan, you have been busy lately, haven't you?" he said, shaking Mac's hand, looking him closely in the eye.

"As have you," Mac replied stoically, not backing down.

"Well, I'm not so sure about that," Lindsay replied evenly. "But why don't we sit down, and you can tell us why Landy Stephens called me so upset last night."

Mac took a seat at the conference table, opposite Lindsay. The lawyer sat to Lindsay's right. Alt, the security guy, stood behind Lindsay, leaning against the wall with his arms folded.

Mac began, "It's funny you should say that Ms. Stephens was so upset."

"Oh, why would that be?"

"Well, Pat," Mac said glancing over at Riley, "she didn't seem too upset when we were invited into her home, did she?"

"No, she didn't," Riley replied.

"No. In fact, she served coffee and invited us into the living room of her home."

Lindsay smiled. "Landy is a very nice lady. But when four officers show up on her doorstep, I'm sure she was taken aback. I'm sure she felt that if she was pleasant and nice, you'd leave much sooner."

"Perhaps," Mac replied. "Of course, we didn't just show up at her place. We did call and ask if we could stop by. Did she mention that?"

Lindsay didn't reply.

Mac forged on. "Because she couldn't have been more pleasant. So you can imagine our surprise to find out that she was so upset that we'd been to her home and that we were harassing her."

"Detective, I can only convey to you the phone call I received from Landy," Lindsay replied calmly. "Her late husband was a dear friend. I feel a responsibility to look after her. When she called upset, well ... I felt it necessary to investigate." Lindsay leaned forward, elbows on the table, "Especially, when she mentioned all of the questions you were asking about Jamie Jones."

"Mr. Lindsay, I can say that we did not harass Ms. Stephens," Mac replied. "You know, it's funny though. It didn't take long for us to get called on the carpet about going to her house."

"Detective, I'm a man accustomed to getting quick results."

"I'm sure you've gotten to where you are because of that," Mac replied, "but it was so quick, I mean almost as if someone saw us leaving her place." Mac didn't know if that was the case, but Lyman said he wouldn't be surprised if PTA had been watching them. He threw it out there to see if Lindsay would react. He didn't. The lawyer jumped in.

"Detective, why don't you get to the reason you were visiting Mrs. Stephens."

"Good idea, Counselor," Mac replied flippantly, opening his notebook. "Mr. Lindsay, I'm going to tell you a little story, and then I'll have some questions. Sound fair?"

Lindsay nodded.

"As you know, we recently arrested a serial killer named Dirk Knapp. He's alleged to have killed seven women in the area around University Avenue. We captured him last week, as I'm sure you recall."

"Yes, I do, Detective." Lindsay replied. "As I recall, you were the officer who apprehended him. To that we owe you many thanks, since the bastard killed our Jamie."

"Yeah, we thought he killed her, too."

"But ... you don't think so?" Lindsay asked, his brow furrowed.

Mac shrugged his shoulders, "Maybe not. As we all know, Knapp was assassinated the next day. Looked like a pro job. So, we never got the chance to ask him about the killings."

"Unfortunate for you guys," Zimmer replied, "but I don't see how this has anything to do with my client."

"Patience, Counselor," Mac replied dismissively, waving Zimmer off while keeping his gaze on Lindsay. "So, anyway, the morning after we caught Knapp, I went out to his place in Hudson. In the basement he had been keeping his clippings in great detail about all his handiwork. He had a display for all of his victims, except one. Who do you suppose that was?"

Lindsay sat back in his chair, folded his arms, but didn't reply.

Mac kept going. "Jamie Jones. Now we thought it odd that she'd be missing. We would've asked Knapp about that, but lo and behold …"

"He's dead," Riley finished.

"Guess you should have done a better job protecting him," Lindsay replied, pushing back just a little, but his face remaining neutral.

"No doubt about that," Mac replied. "But I'm still curious about

Jones missing from Knapp's collection. I mean, he took all the time to cut all the clippings about the other victims and to tape the news shows, but he completely ignored Jones. Well, we thought it was odd. So, I took a look at our file on Jones and noticed some differences between her and the other victims."

"Such as?"

"Knapp's victims were blue-collar, working women. Jones was not."

"So what?" Lindsay replied.

"Serial killers pick out one kind of victim and stick with that," Mac answered. "They don't stray."

Riles picked up the thread. "So, we took another look at Jones and found some things that caused us to look in the direction of PTA."

"What would that be, Detective?" Lindsay asked evenly, unrattled.

"While we were looking through her apartment, and we noticed Ms. Stephens's name on a calendar on the refrigerator. She met with Ms. Jones six days before she died on Halloween."

"That's hardly unusual, Detective. It's no secret that James and Landy were good friends with Jamie."

"As Ms. Stephens told us. They got together for coffee, apparently something they did every once in a while. Of course, on this occasion, Ms. Stephens gave Jones something."

"Which was?" Lindsay asked.

"A banker's box full of PTA documents for something called ..." Mac looked at Riles.

"Cross," Riles finished.

"Is that what this is about, Detective McRyan?" Lindsay asked, "I can assure you—"

Mac cut him off, "There's more than that, I assure you," an intentional taunt in his voice, pushing at Lindsay. "We also know that after she met with Ms. Stephens, Jones met with Claire Daniels." They hadn't been able to confirm exactly when that meeting took place, but they were pretty sure it had.

"I didn't know that," Lindsay replied, a surprised look on his face. Mac didn't believe him or the surprised look, but they already decided they couldn't use Daniels much more than that at this point.

"Really?" Mac replied skeptically. "Somehow I doubt that." Then he continued. "Anyway, between Stephens giving Jones the banker's box and then meeting with a noted investigative reporter, well, that all seemed fairly suspicious to us. Especially since Jones didn't fit the pattern of Knapp's victims. Certainly you can see why this would be of concern to us."

"Knapp must have taken a shine to Jamie somehow," Lindsay replied.

"I'm not sure how that would be," Riley jumped in. "I led the detail on Knapp. He ran into all of his victims through work and driving around the University Avenue area." Riley shook his head, "In the time we followed him, he never went downtown once."

Mac jumped back in. "And, as far as we can tell, Jones never had any reason to spend much time along the University Avenue corridor. PTA doesn't have any facilities over there."

"Could be a copycat," Zimmer added, wanting everyone to know he was still in the room.

"We think that's entirely possible," Riley replied. "But if the Jones murder was a copycat, it wasn't pulled off by some ham-and-egger. It was the work of a professional."

Mac nodded, adding, "Every detail matched to what Knapp was doing. Except, of course, for the profile of the victim. Jones doesn't fit."

"So that got us to thinking: who else would want to take her out?" Riles said. "And it seems that the only other thing Ms. Jones had going in her life that would cause someone to pick her out, was the fact that she was the CFO for a prominent company."

Mac finished the thought. "Maybe PTA had something to hide."

"Our financial records are impeccable, Detective," Lindsay replied angrily. "There is no financial malfeasance here."

"We'll see," Mac replied, continuing, cocky. "But I'm not done. In PTA here, we're not talking about just any company. We're talking a wealthy company with tremendous assets. A company with a large security force." Mac looked over to Alt. "People tell me that there's more than one professional working for your firm."

"A professional could do a copycat killing and make it look like the work of someone else, it's one of the things they're trained to do," Riley added.

"Heck, a professional could have picked off Knapp from the third level of the Vincent Ramp. Isn't that right, Mr. Alt?"

"I wouldn't know," Alt replied.

"Riiiight," Mac slowly replied, then continued. "So this all leads us back to Ms. Jones and PTA. In particular, we were wondering what this banker's box full of documents Ms. Stephens gave Ms. Jones might have to do with all of this?"

Lindsay, a confident smile appearing over his face, answered, "Is that what this is really all about, Detective?"

36

"THEY SURE WERE SMOOTH."

Alt, with his back to the wall, had listened to McRyan thunder away at Lindsay. He was cocky, intentionally so, which was expected. They knew that he would want to piss the boss off, get him to bite. Lindsay wouldn't, Alt thought. Too smooth, been through something like this too many times. If the Senate Intelligence Committee never got him to buckle, why would some young Irish detective from St. Paul have any luck? Nevertheless, Alt admired the kid. He was on the right track, more than he even really knew. They had suspicions, good ones for sure, but they had no hard facts, other than the Cross file, and they didn't have the file. McRyan would ask about the banker's box full of documents on Cross. They knew he would. They knew his whole strategy. They were ready. This is where Lindsay would end it.

"Is that what this is really all about, Detective?" Lindsay said. From where he was standing, Alt couldn't see the boss's face, until he turned in his chair to him.

"Webb?"

"Sir."

"Could you grab that box of Cross documents that Jamie brought in?"

Alt went back out the double doors and into Lindsay's office. The box was sitting next to his desk. This was their cover, recreated to look like the copies Jamie had given them. He picked up the box and brought them back to the conference room and set them down on the table. As he set the box down, the lawyer was whispering in Lindsay's ear. Lindsay replied out loud. "No, I want them to see it. I want them to see there's nothing to it." Then Lindsay looked across the table, "Now gentlemen, this is what Jamie brought to me, what Landy Stephens gave to her. You're free to look through these documents to your heart's content. I think you'll find there's nothing in here of concern to us."

McRyan and Riley didn't show much emotion, but Alt could see the disappointment. It was their body language. Their backs weren't so straight, nor the shoulders so broad. Their bodies sagged slightly, as if a slow leak had started. Riley grabbed the ledger book and started flipping through it while McRyan thumbed through some binder-clipped documents.

Lindsay went for the jugular. "Now, what you have here is a box of documents that, for whatever reason, James Stephens had at home. They relate to what we were doing a number of years ago at our Cross facility." Lindsay conveyed how they put PTA surplus out in Cross and then systematically had it destroyed.

"Now, Jamie did raise the issue of why we didn't try to sell the surplus materials. Since the weapons, communications gear, and things of that nature would be coming from PTA, they would fetch some money. We might have been able to make maybe twenty-five to thirty million if we'd done that. She thought we should have considered it."

"Why didn't you?" Riley asked.

"I'm a patriot, Detective Riley. If I build it for the government, they're the ones who get it."

"So how did you end up with surplus?"

"Sometimes, it doesn't cost as much to produce a product as you think. In some cases we were more efficient, and sometimes we manufacture a surplus in case problems or errors arise. It happens in all industries, I think. But I didn't exactly want to admit this to the government either," Lindsay answered casually, then turned more serious, "Now, if putting a stop to all of this nonsense you have been engaging in will require me to do that, I certainly will."

"Of course, we don't really know if this is what Jamie Jones had, do we?" McRyan stated.

"This is what she brought to me," Lindsay responded reasonably. "You can believe me or not. That's up to you."

"Convenient that she's not here to verify it," McRyan accused.

"I think that's enough, Detective," Zimmer shot back.

"Shut up, Counselor," McRyan snapped back, the disappointment now out in the open.

"Would it be unusual for Mr. Stephens to have had these documents at home?" Riley asked.

"It would," Alt replied. "Our security is very tight here. For obvious reasons, we have strict rules that company-related documents are not to leave the building."

"So how does Stephens end up with the documents at home?"

"Couldn't tell you," Alt replied, although he knew why Stephens had the originals at home—because they told a completely different story. "What can I say. Executives don't always follow all the rules."

"Webb is, I think, correct in that statement," Lindsay added. "That isn't to suggest we would look the other way, but sometimes those of us who write the rules don't always follow them to the letter." A frank disclosure, one to further make the boss appear forthright and reasonable.

"So now, Detective, can I make you a copy of the documents?"

They were at a dead end, and Mac knew it. To save face he'd take a copy of the documents. Problem was they wouldn't tell him anything, and he knew it, knew Lindsay would never give him anything of value that easy. He knew the documents were fake, a whitewash meant to paint the story Lindsay wanted told. There would be no smoking gun in there. "Sure, we'd like a copy to look at."

"Is there anything else, Detective?" Lindsay asked.

"Not right now. We might be back," Mac replied.

"I think not," the lawyer, Zimmer, replied.

"I don't think that's for you to say, Counselor," Riles replied harshly.

"It will be my decision as to whether my client submits to this witch hunt again, Detective," Zimmer replied acidly, getting on his high horse, pointing at Mac. "This is bullshit, and you know it. You haven't put one piece of hard evidence on the table." Zimmer waved his arms wildly. "You have these wild suspicions and have accused Mr. Lindsay, or someone who works for him, of murder. Yet you have not one, *not one*, solid piece of evidence. It's beyond belief that you're here with this, accusing this company, and its president, a pillar in this community, of this. I tell you what, if the media got a hold of this, I wouldn't want to be in your shoes. I'd advise my client to pull all of their business out of this city, just to start."

"Your client has had weeks to cover his tracks," Mac replied. "We're only getting started."

"You keep going with this garbage," Zimmer said, hot, standing, fists on the table, "and I'll take whatever action I deem necessary to defend my client."

"What would that be, Counselor? Don't we have enough dead bodies at this point!" Mac said, immediately wishing he could take it back.

"Detective!" Zimmer yelled and then pointed at Flanagan. "Chief, you may want to reconsider this detective's position with your department."

"Relax, Counselor," the chief replied, standing up, putting his hands up. "Everyone just calm down. I think it would be a good idea at this point, if Mr. Lindsay and I had a little discussion in private."

"Sir?"

"Mac, you, Pat, and Peters wait outside with the mayor," the chief replied, in a tone that suggested he had seen enough.

"Yes, sir," Riley replied, lightly grabbing Mac by the arm. Mac didn't say anything, trying to conceal his disappointment and probably doing a poor job of it. Along with Captain Peters, they went back through the double doors and out into the lobby area. Mac and Riles left Peters to the mayor and went into a small copy room.

"Fucking Zimmer. What a piece of shit," Mac mumbled under his breath.

"Piece of shit got under your skin," Riley replied.

Mac just nodded and exhaled. He rarely lost his cool. It generally only happened when he lost at something, and he felt like he just lost.

"We're done, buddy," Riley said.

"We didn't get much in there, that's true, but there's something going on here, Pat."

"I agree. But at this point, the chief is thinking we can't get them."

"We don't know that."

Riley snorted. "Shit. What do we have? Nothin' solid. They have an alibi, an answer for everything, and you and I both know it." Pat slowly shook his head. "One hundred dollars says that, when the chief comes out, he's going to tell us to go to the Pub, have a beer, and come back tomorrow, ready to get back into the rotation because we are done with this."

Mac didn't have a response. Instead he grabbed a rubber band off the counter, started twisting it with his hands and walked around the small copy room, looking at the postage machine, the ten different three-ring binders with various office procedures, and then meandered over to the copier. It was new and rather large, with a flat screen touch-pad control panel. On the wall behind it were various procedures for copying, requiring you enter an employee code and project number. There were further instructions for printing from a desktop computer, how to set up large print projects or scanning documents into the system and sending them to your own computer. On the bottom of the instructions, it said, "Think Paperless." PTA must have been making a corporate move to a paperless office.

Mac heard a door open behind him, out in the lobby area. He

heard the chief ask for them. "Let's go," was all the chief had to say when he stuck his head in the copy room.

"What are we doing?" Riley asked as they climbed into the elevator. The mayor was staying behind.

The chief waited for the doors to close. "We can talk about it downstairs." They rode down the rest of the way in silence. Once in the parking garage, Flanagan said to Captain Peters, "You take the van back, the boys and I here are going to take a little walk."

They walked out of the garage and onto the street and back towards the Public Safety Building. "I wanted to wait until we were away from the building. Who knows—they might be listening," the chief said. "You boys are done, you know that, right?"

Riley sighed. "Yes, sir."

"Mac?" the chief asked.

"Sir, if we kept looking ..." Mac started.

The chief put up his hand and then after a few seconds, "Your dad said something to me once."

"What's that?"

"We only catch 'em when they make mistakes. These guys," the chief said, looking back at the PTA building and lightly shaking his head, "they haven't made any mistakes. Sometimes, people simply get away with it."

"So, you think they did it?"

"They're up to something. What? I'm not sure."

"They sure were smooth," Riley said.

"Too smooth," the chief replied. "I don't know. They seemed to know what was coming."

"So, what did you talk about with Lindsay?" Riley asked, shifting gears.

"We stop investigating, and they say nothing of the little conversation we just had. That was the deal."

Made sense, Mac thought. The department had had a rough go with Knapp. The tumult surrounding that had died down now. If word got out that internally the department questioned the deaths of

Claire Daniels, Jamie Jones, and possibly the senator, the department would take another hit. The chief didn't want that to happen.

"So what's the mayor doing?" Mac asked.

"Once Lindsay and I struck our little agreement, he wanted some time with the mayor to talk about issues of interest between PTA and the city."

"Meaning, PTA's willingness to stay in St. Paul?"

"Yup."

They quietly walked for a block. Mac finally broke the silence, "If they don't make mistakes, how do we catch them?"

"I asked your dad that once," the chief answered. "He said, we build a time machine and go back and catch them in the act."

37

"WINNING ISN'T EVERYTHING, IT'S THE ONLY THING."

ONE WEEK LATER

Alt went in the back door, dropped the keys on the counter and scratched his head, late on Thursday night. He was beat, tired, and very much wanted—but knew he couldn't have—a vacation. He thought that when they had taken care of McRyan the week before, everything would die down some and Lindsay would stop worrying about Cross.

Instead, Lindsay had pushed for them to make renewed efforts to find the missing documents. They had to be somewhere. He was relentless. "I want no loose ends. I didn't tolerate them when I was at the agency, and I'm not about to start now," he said. "Go back and retrace your steps. You missed Landy Stephens's name on Jamie Jones's refrigerator, so you probably missed something else. So go back. I want those documents found. You have complete freedom to do what you need to, spend what you need to spend, but find those documents."

So they spent the week looking, everywhere. They had made late-night raids on both the Jones and Daniels places yet again. It was worthless, Alt thought. This was the fifth time through. But the boss ordered it, so they did it. Different people at each location, and they found nothing. And these were people with experience finding items that were never intended to be found. Not a hint of the documents at either place.

They tapped into the systems at Fed Ex, UPS, Overnight Express, and any other package delivery service they could think of, to see if Jones had sent the documents to someone other than Daniels. They checked local delivery services to see what had been delivered to Daniels at her home address. Nothing.

They searched everywhere at the PTA building in St. Paul and at the various company manufacturing facilities in the area. Perhaps Jones thought they would never look under their own noses. Nothing. They tore her office apart. Nothing. Tore her assistant's office apart. Nothing. They tore all of accounting apart. Nothing.

Through the use of her PDA and computer calendar, they tried retracing Jones's steps during her last few weeks. Any restaurant she went to. Any place where she shopped. Any people she saw. They searched three of her friends' homes. Nothing.

She was a member at the University Club, where she had a locker. Nothing.

They searched her mother's place again and delivery records for her. They hacked into her mother's bank records to see if she had been to Jones's safe deposit box at any time in the last few months. Nothing.

They did the same thing with Daniels. They went through her place again, through every closet, every set of drawers, computer, files, office, basement, kitchen, built-in cabinets, car, everything. Nothing.

They searched Daniels's mother's place again. They checked her mother's bank records, no trips to a safe deposit box. No deliveries of any kind. Nothing.

In a new twist, they went through Senator Johnson's St. Paul residence, office, car, and even the cabin. Nothing.

They were back searching at Channel 6. Alt was certain the documents weren't there. But the boss wanted someone there every night until the documents were found.

One solution that had been implemented was that they had very carefully arranged through a sea of paperwork to purchase both Jones's and Daniels's places. They would take possession of both after the first of the year. If the documents were still there, they'd be found because every wall in either place was coming out. Maybe they should be x-raying the walls. That was a thought. Alt would evaluate that one tomorrow.

He reached into the fridge and grabbed a cold beer and thought of McRyan. He'd gone back to regular police work. Alt had stopped following him, especially after he'd made a less-than-subtle remark about being followed.

His group continued to monitor McRyan's and Kennedy's places. Nary a word about Cross. McRyan had scared them. But the investigation, if that's what one would call it, had been shut down. Surveillance since then revealed McRyan and Kennedy were going to take a vacation together. Alt was about ready to shut that part of the operation down altogether.

Alt strolled to the den, dug around in the dark, found the remote, and turned on the television. He dropped into his easy chair, flipped off his shoes and sipped his beer. He surfed through the channels until he found *Indiana Jones and the Last Crusade*. He wasn't a big movie guy but he always liked the Jones flicks. The movies reminded him of going to the movies as a kid, the good versus evil storylines, the heroes, a simpler time. He'd seen this Jones movie a hundred times, which was the case these days, all the cable channels running movies into the ground.

He turned to it just before one of his favorite parts, where Indy is in the old library in Venice, uses his dad's Holy Grail diary, discovers the sequence of roman numerals in the library, and the entrance to the Knight's Tomb, which is in the large Roman numeral X on the floor, and Indy says, with a sheepish smile, "X marks the spot." This was, of course, after he previously said to his archeology class, "and X never marks the spot."

"That's it," he thought. The original Cross documents are buried in a hole somewhere. They just had to find the treasure map and where X marked the spot.

~

Mac grabbed four turtlenecks out of his dresser drawer and threw them into his suitcase. He already packed fleece tops, long johns, socks, jeans, shoes, and his toiletries. His skis, boots, poles, coat, gloves, and goggles were laid out in the living room. He had two ski coats, plus his leather coat he liked to drive in, laid out on the couch. He shook his head—too much stuff. He always over packed when he traveled. Never a Boy Scout, he followed the motto anyway, "Be Prepared." He had everything he needed for a long weekend, and he needed a long weekend away.

Since the showdown at PTA fizzled, Mac was a grump. He never took losing well. He always thought Lombardi had it right, "Winning isn't everything. It's the only thing." He lost. He didn't like it.

The case gnawed at him, and he'd decided it wasn't just because he lost, but because PTA got away with it. Because of jobs, money, reasonable doubt, and politics, a deal had been struck. The chief and the rest of them were pissed about it, sure. They knew PTA got away with something, but they could all rationalize it, live with it, move on from it. They'd all seen it a hundred times before and would see it a hundred times again. "God damn it, Mac, look at O.J.," Lich said one night at the Pub, "he was guiltier than my first wife, but now he's hunting for Nicole's killer on every golf course in America. It's over, OVER, deal with it. Now pass the beer nuts."

Mac understood the deal; he just couldn't rationalize it like everyone else. Maybe he wasn't cynical enough or, on the other hand, maybe too idealistic? In his view of the world there was right and wrong, and there was justice. In his mind, the pursuit of justice didn't include calculating bank balances, economic impact, or political power. No, for the victims, the dead, justice must come for them, no matter the cost. The deal that was struck with PTA was the antithesis of that.

So the bitterness sat with him, percolated inside him, depressed him. Two women and a sitting US senator were dead and the guilty parties were simply going to walk away just like that. And the worst part about it was that Mac still felt like he'd missed something. That there was still something out there to be found. Daniels, Jones, their homes, the senator—all of it kept rattling around in his attic, nonstop, pestering him, like a fly that would hover around his head and wouldn't go away no matter how many times he swatted at it.

That he couldn't put the case out of his mind was not lost on people. The sour mood, lack of concentration, sullen expression all told the story. So Sally and the chief intervened, and now he was packing for a ski vacation up in Lutsen, Minnesota's finest ski resort. At first Mac wasn't sure he wanted to go, but then Sally told him about the place, which belonged to a friend of hers. Isolated and private. Ski in and ski out. Fireplace. Satellite television so they could watch the Vikes game Sunday night. A hot tub. A lofted bedroom with panoramic views of the ski resort on one side and Lake Superior on the other. It was all good. Mac's mood started changing, and he was looking forward to getting away. A little trip away seemed like a good next step for them.

With everything loaded in the Explorer, he drove over to Sally's place. Realizing he needed to get cash and gas, he stopped at the Super America. He jumped out and put the nozzle in and set it to pump itself and enjoyed the mild winter night. The temps up in Lutsen, five hours to the north, would be in the twenties for skiing. Great weather. Mac heard the nozzle pop, took it out, and headed inside.

He got his cash, grabbed a bottle of water and went to the cashier. As he paid, he noticed the security television, showing all the pumps, and thought of Knapp. That had been a lucky strike, noticing that camera, he thought. It was always those little things that broke cases. The security camera could have easily been missed, and they might still be looking for Knapp. Instead, he noticed it, and Knapp was history.

Knapp and the surveillance camera got him back to thinking about PTA. He'd missed something on that case, he just couldn't figure out what. There was an overlooked detail somewhere. Mac hadn't spoken to anyone about it, lest people think he was obsessing, which of course he was. But he thought about the case morning, noon, and night. *Enough already, Mac. Let it go!* he said to himself as he climbed into the Explorer and drove to Sally's.

They stayed up until 10:00 p.m. and then went to bed. Mac lay in the dark room, spooning against Sally, her body warm. Mac never had been one for going to bed early. Carefully reaching over Sally, he grabbed the remote off her nightstand and powered up the TV. He liked spending time at Sally's place because she had full cable, plus some premium channels. She was a big sports fan and liked movies as much as he did. Flipping through the channels, he caught the end of *Ocean's Eleven*. A fun movie, the actors all looked like they had a good time making it.

Mac flipped around some more. He caught a late edition of *SportsCenter*, catching some Timberwolves highlights. While not a huge hoops fan, he followed the hometown club. They'd won, beating the Bulls.

Mac tried some more channels and came to *Indiana Jones*. He loved Indy and once dressed up as him for Halloween, with the fedora, leather coat, whip, the whole nine yards. Indy and Marcus were in the library, looking at the roman numerals. Mac smiled, he loved this part.

38

"WHO ARE YOU?"

Alt awoke stiff and sore. He'd fallen asleep in his easy chair and had overslept. He wanted to be into the office by 8:30 a.m. That was the time he woke up. A hurried shower, shave, and change of clothes put him downtown by 9:15 a.m.

He walked into the operations center, and Bouchard and Hennessey were waiting for him. Alt saw it immediately—they were agitated. "What's up?"

"At the front desk at Channel 6 we found a log book, the receptionist completes it. We missed it the other times we were in," Hennessey said.

"How?"

"It's usually in a locked cabinet. For some reason, it was left out last night."

"Yeah, so?"

"It records packages dropped off and for whom. There's one for a CD, October 26th, a large package from an outfit called Flash Local Delivery. Note indicated it was a large box. The signature looks like Daniels's."

"Have we checked this Flash whatever's records?"

"Hagen's giving it a shot right now," Bouchard responded and led them to the computer whiz.

"What did you get?" Alt asked.

Hagen looked up at them through pop-bottle glasses, "They don't have any sort of system that I can crack into. They don't exist in cyberspace." If Hagen couldn't crack them, they didn't have a system, or at least one that was tapped into the outside world.

"Where are they located?"

"Over in South Minneapolis. Address puts them in a residential neighborhood."

Alt thought quickly, and then said to Hansen and Hennessey, "Take the big van. You might need some tools. We have to know if that's our package."

Mac slept soundly, well after his normal waking time. He rolled over to find Sally standing at the end of the bed, dressed, with wet hair. "You makin' breakfast, big boy?"

Mac smiled, "After a shower." A quick shower, some jeans, and a black mock turtleneck, and Mac was downstairs firing up the coffee and mixing some quick eggs. The TV was on, and he had it on the Golf Channel of all things as Sally walked into the kitchen, her hair now dry and styled. She looked like a million bucks in blue jeans and a white turtleneck with her shoulder-length red hair. She walked over and gave him a warm kiss, and looked at what he was mixing. "Scrambled eggs, yummy. Did you find the cheese and ham?"

"Already shredded and chopped," he replied, pointing to the center island.

"Looks great." She poured herself a cup of coffee and sat down at the table to watch TV. "What's with the Golf Channel?"

"I like it. This is one of those segments where the pro teaches an amateur. I learn a few things watching these."

"I understand, but we're going skiing."

"This isn't Colorado. We don't have a ski channel. Besides, you like golf. You might learn something."

Sally watched as the golf professional showed video of the amateur's golf swing at a driving range. Then they cut back to the studio where the pro, amateur, and host were standing on some fake grass with a net, ready to do some sort of live demonstration. The host asked the softball question about the value of video. The pro responded, "There isn't anything you can't improve through the use of video."

"Ain't that the truth," Sally said.

"What's that?" Mac asked.

"Pro says there isn't anything that can't be improved by video."

"I suppose that's true."

"I mean, video tells you everything," Sally said. "Don't you remember in law school, when they videoed us making oral arguments?"

"Vaguely," Mac said as he poured the eggs into the pan, adding the ham and cheese.

"I sure do. I learned a ton about myself watching that. I keep some of those lessons with me today."

"I know what you're saying. I remember in college we watched tons of video of our games and of the opposing teams. Learned a ton about myself, picked up tendencies of the other side. So, yeah it helps," he replied. "You know who else was a fanatic about video?"

"Who?"

"Claire Daniels," Mac said as he moved the scrambled eggs around the pan.

Sally shot him a disapproving look. "Aren't we done with that, yet?"

"I'm just saying. When we went through her place, she had DVD copies of all of her reporting, videos of herself working out and playing golf, just like this guy on TV. She was anal about it. I remember the sports guy at Channel 6 saying she was a total perfectionist, super hard on herself, vain in that respect. She critiqued every report she did. It's why she was so good, I guess."

"I imagine so," Sally said. "We're not going to talk about that case all weekend are we?"

"No. I promise."

~

Flash Local Delivery was located in a residential neighborhood on Oakland Avenue in South Minneapolis. Quick research by Hagen found it had been incorporated six months earlier by an Everett Flash, hence the business name. A Yellow Page ad indicated same-day delivery, personal pickup, and confidential service with a personal touch. No kidding, it was being run out of the guy's house. Hansen and Hennessey found Flash working in an office on the side of a detached garage. As they went in the door, Flash was on the phone, writing down some notes on a legal pad. A laptop was plugged into the wall, no phone line. No wonder Hagen couldn't get in.

Flash hung up and asked, "What can I do for you gentlemen?"

"We want to see if you remember a package you picked up on October 26th and delivered to Channel 6," Hansen said.

"Did you send it?"

"No, a friend of ours did."

"Well, I'm sorry. I could help your friend," Flash answered, "but I can't tell you anything about it."

"I'm sorry," Hennessey replied, "but our friend was killed shortly after she sent the package. We're trying to track some things down. It would really help if you could provide us with some information."

"I protect the confidentiality of my clients," Flash replied.

"Well," a menacing look overtaking Hennessey's six-foot-three-inch frame, "we would appreciate your cooperation on a voluntary basis. But I assure you, cooperation we will get."

Flash gave Hennessey a look, and then one over to Hansen, equally big, who could give an intimidating look with the best of them. Flash was going to give them what they were looking for, whether he liked it or not. "So, you say your friend was killed?" Flash replied, having sized up the situation.

"That's right," Hennessey replied.

"Well, in that case, I guess they can't complain, can they?"

"No, they can't," Hansen replied, relaxed now, a pleasant grin replacing the menacing look.

Flash started through his records.

Mac and Sally jumped into the Explorer to start towards Lutsen. He turned onto Grand Avenue and drove east towards Snelling, where he would take a left and get to Interstate 35 to head up north. It was 10:00 a.m. and they would get to Lutsen by 5:00 p.m., with a few pit stops and lunch figured in. Sally was talking on Mac's cell phone, checking in with work. She hung up and handed it back, "Thanks."

"What was that all about?"

"Oh, they have a new copier at work that does scanning now."

"Scanning?"

"Yeah, it's like a copier, except it scans the document into the system and saves it as a Word document. All part of an attempt to become a paperless office, which will be virtually impossible. However, it'll allow me to put some documents on CDs to bring home and work on—"

"Wait a minute! Scanning? Could you scan the documents onto a disc, you know, a CD?"

"Sure."

"The discs, now you would copy onto say a CD right?"

"Most likely."

"And the CD, those disks also look a lot like a DVD right?"

"Yeah. Mac, why are you suddenly so interested in this?"

"I wonder," Mac mused, intrigued.

"Wonder what?"

"It's probably nothing," he mumbled, thinking.

"What?"

"Something you said just triggered something in my mind."

"Which was what?"

"Something I saw when we were at PTA last week?"

"Which is?"

"They had a scanner like you were talking about in this copy room Pat and I were in."

"I'm not surprised," Sally replied. "But what is this triggering thing?"

"You mentioned putting documents on CDs, right?"

"Sure, so I could take work home."

"Daniels had a bunch of CDs and DVDs we never really looked at."

"Fine. But I don't see where you're—"

"Going with this?" Mac finished. "It's probably nothing. But we never looked at these CDs and DVDs because the station gave us every report she ever made. But now I'm wondering if Jones could have scanned the documents Stephens gave her onto a CD and given that to Daniels. I never thought of it until now. Maybe there's something on those CDs and DVDs Daniels has."

"But I thought you reviewed those Cross documents that Lindsay gave you guys last week."

"We did," Mac said, shaking his head. "But those documents were bullshit. They said this Cross place was an explosives factory with some warehouse where they destroyed surplus arms and weapons. They shut the place down in October '01. But what I think really happened was they got to Landy Stephens, and she told them what she told us. Banker's box full of documents, with a ledger book. So, they trot out this banker's box and ledger book, and we go home with our tails between our legs. But we have no real way of knowing those documents were real."

"But Mac, you guys never found the documents either, in all that searching you did."

"That's true," Mac replied, "but maybe we were looking for the wrong thing. Perhaps the documents were put onto a CD or DVD or something."

"Of course, to check this out, you would have to go ask the chief."

They sat in silence for thirty seconds. Mac skipped the turn onto

Snelling to get to the freeway and cocked an eyebrow, "Maybe I don't."

"Huh?"

"I still have a key."

"To Daniels's place?" Sally replied in disbelief.

"Yup," Mac replied smiling.

"How?"

"Never turned it in," Mac answered. "Sooo ... the chief doesn't need to know."

"Then let's go," Sally quickly replied, smiling.

"Really?"

"Yeah. There's probably nothing to this. But I know that if we don't go look now, you'll just be distracted all weekend."

"Probably."

"Well," Sally said, smiling seductively, "I don't want you distracted. I want your focus on me. Completely on me. I'll have that once we don't find anything."

Mac turned left onto St. Albans and pulled up in front of the condo. He hopped out and fished his laptop out of the back compartment. The whole thing was a long shot, but for his own sanity, he wanted to check it out.

They made their way up to the second level. Mac set his laptop down on Daniels's desk and picked the first CD out of the tower. Sally started walking in the DVDs from the cabinet in the sitting room across the hall.

Flash found the record. "I remember this one now."

"How come?" Hansen asked, fearful of the answer.

"Big order, and I was dropping it off at Channel 6. It was a banker's box, heavy. She wanted it boxed up, wrapped and delivered same day. Which we do all the time."

So, Daniels had it. But where? Hansen stepped outside and placed a call to Alt.

~

"Is this the last one?" Mac asked disappointedly.

"Yup," Sally replied.

Mac shook his head, the disappointment obvious. He hit file, open, and tried to open the last disk as a document. Nothing. He moved it to the DVD drive, opened it up and it was a recent news report from in front of the Minnesota State Capitol. "Shit," he said quietly under his breath, lightly shaking his head.

Mac sat with his hands in his face. The whole thing had been a wild goose chase. He looked up to find Sally so he could apologize. She was in the other room, flipping through the movie DVDs. She pulled one out and was looking at it. It wasn't like the others, colored, with movie graphics. It was blank. "What you lookin' at?" Mac asked.

"Just looking through the movie cases here and ran across this one inside the *Basic Instinct* box. It's blank on the front, which is odd."

"Let me take a look." She handed it to him. Looked like all the other CD and DVD disks he'd been looking at. He handed it back to her.

"What? You're not going to look?"

"Are you trying to add insult to injury here?"

"No, asshole, I'm trying to help. It seems odd this blank-fronted one is in this case. Check it out."

Mac sighed, "Okay." He opened the CD drive, popped it in. He hit file and tried to open it as a Word document. The operation failed. He clicked to video. He figured it was just another movie or news report. It wasn't.

"What the heck?" Sally said, peering over Mac's shoulder.

The video was of a man and woman having sex. The woman was on top and leaning into the male, who was obscured due to the high angle of the camera. The woman looked to be Claire Daniels. "What? Daniels liked videotaping herself having sex?" Sally said.

"I guess," Mac replied. He looked at the date in the lower right hand corner: 10.29. He then looked up, and the video showed the woman leaning up and arching her back now. It definitely was Claire

Daniels, and the male was now identifiable. Mason Johnson. They were on Daniels's bed, and the camera was looking down on the right side.

"What was Daniels doing with this?" Sally asked.

"I don't know," Mac replied, getting up and walking to the bedroom, leaving the video to play.

"I mean, I can't believe the senator would allow her to do this. Was he that stupid?"

"I don't think he knew," Mac yelled from the bedroom.

Sally left the video and followed him, "What do you mean, he didn't know? How could he not know?"

"I mean, I don't think she asked his permission."

"Why do you say that?"

"The camera angle on the video."

"What about it?"

Mac was looking at the dresser now, "It's too steep to have been sitting on the dresser here or on a tripod or anything. It's almost as if it's an overhead shot."

"But from where then?"

Mac surveyed the ceiling above the right side of the bed. All he saw was a smoke detector. Then he looked further to his right and saw another detector in the ceiling just over the French doors leading into the bedroom. Now that was odd. "Can you tell me why someone would need two smoke detectors in one room?" Mac asked rhetorically as he grabbed a sitting chair and placed it under the detector to the right of the bed. He climbed onto the chair and pushed the button to check if the detector worked. Nothing. He pushed it again, no response. Hmpf. He put both hands up to it and started to twist it. It was like all other smoke detectors, hard to remove, but then he heard a hard click and it pulled free and there it was. "Lookey here," Mac said, as he pulled on a cord, with a glass piece on the end.

"What's that?" Sally asked, moving near Mac.

"A camera, I'd say," Mac replied. "Before we go any further, I'm going to make a call."

"To who? For what?"

"Backup. In case we find anything." Mac placed a discreet call. Paddy was on patrol in the neighborhood and would know to keep the whole thing quiet if nothing panned out.

"What do you think all this proves?" Sally asked while they waited.

"Nothing yet, but ...?"

"But what?"

"We never found any equipment like this when we were searching the place the other times."

"So?"

"It's concealed somewhere we didn't know about. What else is in there besides the equipment?"

Sally shrugged her shoulders. Five minutes later, Paddy showed up with his partner, Mike Remington. Mac gave them a quick rundown.

"So, what ya going to do, cuz?" Paddy asked.

"Let's find out where this camera leads too," Mac replied as he pulled the chair into the closet and underneath the hatch to the crawl space in the ceiling. "Paddy, you might have to give me a boost." Putting his right foot into Paddy's cupped hands, he was pushed up into the attic. Mac called down, "Hand me your flashlight. And your gloves, I don't want to touch the insulation."

Paddy handed both items up. Mac pointed the flashlight towards where he thought the smoke detector was. He carefully walked on the joists and saw the black cabling for the camera, probably six or seven feet away. The cable had been run along a joist to a support post ten feet away, up the support post to the roof and then away from Mac and over towards what he thought was the hallway and perhaps the bathroom. He maneuvered his way over to where the cable came back down and went back into the ceiling, buried under the insulation. Pulling the insulation back, he pointed the flashlight down at the hole where the cabling went through, but he couldn't see anything. He looked back to the opening to the attic. It was at a forty-five degree angle away from him. Carefully, he walked back across the joists to the opening and jumped down.

"What did you find?" Sally asked.

"It leads back that way." Mac pointed in a forty-five degree angle to the hallway, towards the bathroom. Inside the bathroom Mac stood scratching his head. The bathroom was long and narrow. The vanity and toilet were along the left side, but that was the wrong angle he thought. To the right were the bathtub and a small narrow towel cabinet, which contained nothing but towels. He walked back into the hallway where there was a narrow built in wood buffet, which had shelving on the top, a middle drawer and a cabinet on the bottom. The cabinet held some extra towels and nothing else. The shelves had books, a picture, and a wood Roman numeral X. Hmpf. "Has to be right in this area," Mac said.

Mac walked back into the bathroom and looked at the tub. Then he looked back to the hall. He paced the length of the bathroom off, which was five yards or fifteen feet. The bathtub was six feet. The towel cabinet was maybe another foot. That was seven feet, where were the other eight? He went to the hall and looked at the built-in cabinet, it was maybe a foot deep. Looking around the edges of the built in, he noticed a small gap between the molding and the cabinet. "I wonder," he said out loud.

"Wonder what?" Sally asked.

A smile creased Mac's face. "Paddy, where have you seen a built-in buffet like this?"

"I don't know, cuz."

"If there was a plaque here on the right side, then would you recognize it?"

Paddy studied the buffet for a minute then also smiled, "In the basement at the Pub."

"Yeah and down there it's—"

"—the door to Patrick's Room," Paddy finished.

Mac opened the middle drawer and reached under the lip. He felt with his hand, and he hit it, a small metal latch. He pulled on it and heard a click and felt the cabinet push in.

"What the hell, a secret room?" Sally asked.

Mac shook his head, smiling. "Kind of. People had these types of built-ins put in during Prohibition—a good place to hide booze. You've seen the one down at the Pub. It leads into Patrick's Room down there."

Pushing the cabinet in, Mac saw two things: a small television with a DVD recorder and a banker's box with Cross handwritten on the side, resting on the floor. "I guess X does mark the spot," he said as he walked into the hidden room and pulled rubber gloves onto his hands. Mac flipped the top off the box and started looking through the documents. Having studied what Lindsay had given them a week earlier, he immediately recognized that these documents were different. There was a ledger book, which he flipped open. There were entries with names and dollar amounts handwritten in red and black ink. He started running down the names with his finger when Sally spoke up.

"Mac, take a look at this."

Mac stood up and went to the shelf where the television and DVD recorder sat. There was also a rack of DVDs with just dates on them. He went to it and hit the open/close button. There was a DVD inside.

"Paddy and Mike, start writing all this down."

Mac looked at the DVD and then at the rack, and the generic DVD cases all had sporadic dates on them going back what looked like a couple years. There was one unlabeled DVD case, which was empty. He looked back to the one in the machine. Seeing a remote, Mac picked it up and pushed play. He turned on the little television.

The video starts and the view is from the right side of the bed. Daniels and the senator come into view on the left-hand side of the screen, embracing one another, kissing and undressing. There must be some switch that she hit to start it. They fell onto the bed. The video and sound were clear.

"Look at the date?" Sally said.

"Holy shit, October 31st." Mac grabbed the remote and did what most men in this situation wouldn't do, he advanced the video forward. When it stopped, they were to the point in time where the senator had his back to the camera, now clothed, working his tie. Daniels was lying on the bed, naked, smiling and talking. It lasted for a few minutes, some casual talk. Then, finally dressed, the senator leaned down, kissed her, and walked out of the room. Daniels rolled over and had her back to the camera, the nightstand light still on. She lay still, looking as if she had fallen asleep.

Then he came from the left, a black streak. He was dressed in all black, a ski mask over his head. He jumped on the bed and was on top of her in an instant, strangling her.

"Oh, my God," Sally croaked, putting her hands to her own throat.

Daniels flailed away at the killer, hitting him in the face, the arms, kicking with her legs, but he was too strong, never releasing the grip. After a minute, the flailing slowed down, less strong, the life slowly leaking out of her body. Finally, the arms slowly fell down to the bed, and Daniels was gone. The man in black checked her pulse, nothing.

"Who are you?" Mac uttered in a hushed voice, putting his face close to the screen.

The man in black got off her and stood on the far side of the bed and rubbed his jaw through the mask. Then he took off his gloves and pulled the mask from over his head.

"I fuckin' knew it!" Mac yelled.

"You know who that is?" Sally asked.

"Yeah. Webb Alt."

"Who's he?"

"Vice president of Security at PT fuckin' A. I knew it. I knew it!" Mac yelled, a wave of satisfaction rushing over him.

He pulled his cell phone out and started dialing, and looked over to Paddy, "You guys get all this down. You're key witnesses now." They both nodded, furiously scribbling into their notebooks. The chief's secretary answered, "This is McRyan. I need to speak to the chief."

"Mac, he's in a meeting, I can take a message."

"Charlene, put me through on this. When I tell him what I have, he won't care."

He waited and then a minute later Flanagan got on the line, agitated, "Mac, what the hell."

"Chief, we got 'em."

39

"LET'S ROLL."

A lt took the elevator up to the top. At least they knew who had had the documents, Daniels. Taking her out had been the right thing. However, the question was: what did she do with them? They'd been through her place a number of times and hadn't found anything. They would be going back again.

He got off the elevator and walked right in and told Lindsay what they found.

"How did we miss it at the station?" was his first question.

"The log book was in a locked cabinet, sir. Last night it was lying out, and they were able to get a look at it. In fairness to those guys, I ordered them to spend their time looking around her work area and where the station stored documents and not the receptionist area. It wasn't until this week that we started looking at delivery companies. That triggered them to take a closer look up front, where a delivery of this nature would come." He didn't have a better answer than that.

"So, what are we doing now?"

"I'm sending Hansen and Hennessey over to Daniels's place now. I'd prefer to wait until it's dark to send them back in. There is a lot of traffic in the area. They'll sit tight until I give them the go ahead."

"What about moving up our possession of the condo?"

"Already working on it. I've told the real estate guy to do whatever needs to be done."

"If nothing else, have him get us in there today for another look around."

"Absolutely."

"Where else could she have put those documents?" Lindsay asked. He knew they had looked high and low for them.

"I don't know. There's some place out there we're not aware of. However, we know now that it was Daniels who has them. So, now we focus on her completely."

"What about the delivery source?"

"We'll take care of him later."

Mac followed Paddy in the squad in front, with another behind them, lights flashing, as they headed downtown. The box and DVD player were in the backseat.

As Mac drove, Sally was looking through the ledger book from the box. "Mac, these guys were up to something with this Cross place."

"What are you seeing?"

"Huge money going to a lot of people. Stephens, the guy from the video Alt, someone named Bouchard, a Hennessey, Hansen, Kraft, Thompson, Skogman, probably about twenty in all. The biggest money goes to someone who's only marking is an X."

"What kind of money?"

"Millions, Mac. Millions."

"Whatever they were doing, Stephens was keeping the records. He was the money man, after all. Stephens dies in the accident. The records are up at the cabin. He dies, Ms. Stephens finds the box and gives it to Jones. She looks through it and realizes what's been going on. She does two things. She likely confronts Lindsay with it, and she also talks to Daniels. PTA figures this out and takes them both out."

"Why take out the senator?" Sally asked.

"Because if he walks, we might look elsewhere. If it looks like he commits suicide, nobody ever bothers looking. And I'm thinking they took out Knapp too."

"Why would they do that, Mac?"

"He wouldn't confess to killing Jones, because he didn't. Again, if he's dead, everyone assumes he killed Jones, and nobody goes looking."

"And even if anyone does, you could never charge them. No hope of a conviction because they had all kinds of reasonable doubt."

"'*Had*,' Counselor. They don't now."

"Let me use your cell. I have to call Helen. She's going to love this."

"More headlines for her."

Sally made the call and informed Helen to just get over to the chief's office, and she'd tell her more there. She handed the phone back to Mac.

"Boy, we sure ended up taking a circuitous route to find this stuff, didn't we?" Mac said, a Cheshire cat smile on his face. "We go looking for documents scanned onto a CD, and we come away with the actual documents and the video to boot."

"Unbelievable. Amazing. I mean, I don't know what else to say," Sally replied, a huge smile on her face. Mac was definitely out of the doghouse.

"What's amazing to me is to find the video," Mac said, as they came over Cathedral Hill and drove towards downtown. "I wasn't counting on that."

"I agree," Sally said. "Women usually don't do that sort of thing."

"That's true," Mac replied. "But I could have seen it."

"How? How could you have possibly seen that?"

"She had tapes and DVDs of all of her work, workouts, golf swing, all this different stuff. She was a perfectionist at everything. It's not that much of a leap that she wanted to be a perfectionist when it came to sex. I could have seen that. I could have looked for that. She had all these racy videos with some of the hottest sex scenes. She made a sex tape with a boyfriend in college. I could have connected it. I *should* have connected it, but I didn't."

"Geez. Don't beat yourself up over that," Sally said, still shaking her head in amazement. "That would be a big, intuitive leap."

"I remember Joe Elliott, at Channel 6," Mac said, recalling the conversation now. "He'd hooked up with Daniels when she first got to town. He said at the time that she was amazing in the rack. I think he said it was as if she was 'perfect' at sex. Now we know why."

"To have it taping that night ..."

"Yeah, lucky for us on that one. The chief said we only catch them when they make mistakes. They finally made one."

Hansen and Hennessey pulled into the Mardi Gras parking lot and saw the commotion.

"This can't be good," Hennessey said.

"How many squads you think?"

"Four or five, plus a few Crown Vics."

A crowd started to develop, and crime scene tape had been put out to keep them back. They got out of the van and walked over to the crowd. It was clear the police were inside Daniels's place.

"Tell me if you see McRyan anywhere," Hansen asked.

They looked for five minutes and didn't see McRyan or any of the other cops he'd been running around with. Odd.

They shared a look and walked back to the van. Hansen placed a call.

Mac pulled into the parking garage and a spot near the door. Riley, Rock, Lich, and Captain Peters were all waiting as they pulled in. Mac had a big shit-eating grin on his face.

"What the hell did you find?" Riles asked.

"PTA did it, Pat. They killed Daniels, which means they killed

Jones, and we got a different set of Cross documents," he replied, pointing over to Sally who was holding the banker's box.

Everyone grabbed something from the Explorer, and they rushed to a waiting elevator and up to the chief's office. A television was wheeled in. Mac quickly hooked up the DVD player and started the video. The chief, Captain Peters, Riley, Rockford, Lich, a few other high-ranking officers, and Helen Anderson quietly watched as Daniels's bedroom came into focus.

The room was dead quiet as they watched the senator getting dressed. "Look at the time in the upper right hand corner," Mac said. It showed 1:16 a.m.

At 1:31, the senator kisses Daniels and leaves the bedroom. She rolls over and starts to fall asleep.

At 1:37, Alt attacks. Not a sound is made in the room as he strangles Daniels. Once she's dead, the killer rolls off the bed and pulls off his mask.

"Look familiar, Pat?"

Riles snorted. "Amazing," was all he could say.

"This is unbelievable," croaked Helen Anderson.

"It is at that, but I'll be damned, Mac, you were right all along," Flanagan said.

"So, what are we going to do about it?" Mac asked.

"Get me warrants for Ted Lindsay and Webb Alt for starters," the chief ordered. "Helen and Sally, help them out on that."

"We're on it," Anderson said.

"Are we going to take them at the PTA building?" Riley asked.

"Yes. These guys could run at the drop of a hat. We need to move quickly. Marion, get the Critical Incident Response Team ready," the chief commanded. "These guys are pros. We want some heat of our own."

Alt rushed back upstairs to Lindsay's office. They may not have much time to move. The call from Hansen had been unnerving to say the least.

"What's going on?" Lindsay asked urgently as Bouchard also walked in.

"Cops are all over Daniels's place. We don't know if there was a break-in or what. But there are four or five squad cars. A couple of unmarked squads and Crime Scene is there. The scene's tight and secure, and cops ain't talking. Hansen and Hennessey are there monitoring."

Lindsay nodded and went to his desk and took out a cell phone. "Let's see if I can find out what's going on."

The chief led the meeting. A CIRT commander was present. Mac, Lich, Riles, and Rock all put on vests and Windbreakers that said police on the back, their badges now hanging around their necks. Weapons bristled. A crude drawing of the PTA building lay in the middle of the conference table.

The plan was to secure the parking garage and the private elevator, as well as the front entrance. Officers would cover all four sides of the building. Alt and Lindsay would be pinned inside and have no choice. Mac wasn't sure whether they'd throw down, but he didn't want to take any chances. At this point, all they needed was the warrants to be finished, and they were ready to go. Besides everyone around the table, there were numerous other people in the room, talking on cell phones, getting things arranged.

Just then Sally came back into the room with the warrants and handed them to Mac, whispering softly in his ear, "Be careful."

Mac nodded. Anderson came back in the room, a cell phone to her ear, followed by Sylvia Miller and Captain Peters, both hanging up their cell phones.

The chief spoke. "Mac, you and the boys will go in the front. You get to put the cuffs on Lindsay and Alt. CIRT Team 1 goes up with you guys. Team 2 will work to secure the garage. Everyone understand?" Everyone nodded. "Let's roll."

Lindsay hung up his cell phone.

"Where's the chopper at?"

"Took two VPs up to Duluth," Alt answered. "Why?"

"We need to get the hell out of here."

"What's going on?"

"They're coming for us right now. They have the Cross documents, and they have you killing Daniels on video."

Alt, stunned, was slow to follow Lindsay, who came back to grab his arm. "Let's go."

They got into the elevator and headed to the basement. Lindsay spoke, "Apparently Daniels liked to video herself having sex. There was a hidden camera in the room, and it was running the night you took her out. Think back. After you killed her, did you take your mask off?"

Alt nodded.

"Well, they have it on video. Plus they have the documents, which hangs all of us."

"How did they find it?"

"McRyan found it. I don't know how, but he did."

Alt recovering now, thinking about getting away. "McRyan. I should have known."

"I underestimated him, Webb. You didn't, but I did. He's coming for us."

They hustled off the elevator. "Sir, we aren't caught yet."

Skogman and Thompson were waiting for them. They had a minivan running. Automatic weapons and rounds were loaded inside. They all jumped into the van, and Bouchard got behind the wheel.

They pulled up to the exit and took a left onto East Sixth Street, a one-way.

Mac, Riley, Lich, and Rock climbed into Mac's Explorer and the two CIRT Teams followed. Mac was going to pull up in front of the main entrance to PTA, which was on the west side of the building along St. Peter Street. Team 1 would follow them. It would take Team 2 a few minutes to get to the garage as they had to drive all the way around the building on the one-way streets.

Mac crossed East Sixth and pulled in front of the building, his front left tire up on the curb. Team 1 was a half block behind, caught at a stoplight. "We should have had them running with lights," Riles muttered. The police radio blurted that Team 2 was still three blocks away, caught up in traffic on Cedar Street.

"We'll have to wait a minute," Mac said.

Alt made the call immediately when they had turned left out of the parking garage. A CIRT truck was at the stoplight, and it was clear that the driver and man in the passenger seat saw them come out of the garage. They had no choice. Alt let his window down. Skogman behind him opened the sliding door. Thompson was doing the same, looking to the south.

40

"HOW DID YOU KNOW WE WERE COMING?"

The sound was unmistakable—automatic weapons fire. Mac saw it first, the black minivan, coming to the corner to the north on East Sixth. The side door was coming open, and he saw the barrel, "DOWN! DOWN! DOWN!"

Mac hit the pavement and rolled to the entryway of the PTA building. Shots flew over his head, causing glass to rain down over him. People were screaming. He looked quickly back to the Explorer. Lich was down low, hiding behind a cement holder for a garbage can. Riley had rolled to the front of the truck and had cover. Rock was down on the sidewalk, hit in the thigh, exposed.

Mac quickly got to his knees, leaned around the corner of the entryway, took a look at the background and returned fire, emptying his clip. Lich grabbed Rock and pulled him behind the garbage can.

The black minivan veered left, cutting in front of Mac and through a diagonal intersection, in front of the PTA building. Mac gave chase, running behind, firing at the van, shattering the rear window glass. The van turned right onto East Fifth. It was half a block to Washington Avenue. There was construction on the corner of East Fifth and Washington. The van could only go left when it hit the corner.

Mac burst across East Fifth and flew into Rice Park, popping another clip into his Glock. The van turned a hard left onto Washington, tires screeching. Fifty yards away, Mac fired at the side of the van, this time low, at the tires. Shots came from behind him to his right, Riley, firing high. They both connected. Mac got the front left tire, Riley spraying the driver's side windows. The van veered hard right, across the sidewalk, crashing into the corner of a brick wall on the east side of the Convention Center.

With the van stopped, steam coming from the radiator, smoke from underneath, Mac and Riley cautiously moved through the park towards the vehicle, weapons still drawn. Then Mac saw it, someone was out of the passenger side, running. Alt.

"Check the van! Check the van!" Mac yelled while he took off after Alt, firing on the run.

⌣

Alt kept his head low in the front passenger seat, as the van was pelted from behind. They turned sharply left, and the glass on the driver's side started shattering all over, shots flying over Alt's head. He felt the left side of the van abruptly drop and then buck hard to his right. He looked up in time to see the van heading into the corner of a brick wall. The left side of the front of the van took the brunt of the impact, causing the van's back end to buck slightly on impact. It threw him into the passenger side door and most of the airbag missed him when it deployed.

Alt looked to Bouchard, who was slumped over the wheel; a bullet hole through his head. The others in the back were bloody, probably dead. Looking out the driver's side he saw McRyan and Riley slowly approaching from the east through the park.

He jumped out and ran west towards the northeast entrance to the Convention Center. Shots hit the sidewalk around him as he ran for the doors. Once inside, he had two options. Straight was a long hallway, angled upward towards the hockey arena. There were convention-goers walking along the way. Too open.

He turned left through another set of doors into the east end of the Convention Center. There was an escalator one hundred feet away that went up to the second level on the south side of the Convention Center. He had his assault rifle and two clips in his coat. Hitting the escalator running, he got to the top, stopped, and looked back.

Mac carefully approached the double doors, crouched, squinting inside, the tinted glass making it difficult to see. He didn't see nor sense any movement and went in. He quickly scanned the hallway straight ahead. Nothing. Alt went left. As he turned left, the shots came. He dove to his left behind a wall, as glass, cement, and ceramic tile shards fell all around him. The shots stopped, and he heard screaming in the distance from Alt's direction.

Mac pushed himself up and sprinted towards the escalator. He was up the first half of the escalator two steps at a time, and then crouched, peering over the right side as he approached the second level. Loud screaming was coming from the hallway to his right. As he came off the escalator and moved to his right, he saw Alt well down the hallway, convention goers screaming and running. Mac also drew screams when he rushed into the hallway with his weapon drawn. His "Police" vest and dangling badge were useless. Panic all around.

Alt missed McRyan when he came through the doors. He turned to his left and ran down the long, forty-foot-wide hallway between the meeting rooms. A few exhibitors were milling in the hallway while the convention sessions were taking place. They screamed as they saw a man running down the hall, brandishing an AK-47. He came to the open area at the west side of the hallway and heard screams behind him. He turned around and saw McRyan at the other end.

~

"Get Down! Get Down! Get Down!" Mac yelled when Alt spun around. Mac jerked a woman to the ground and ducked behind an exhibitor booth. The shots went high, shattering the Sheetrock of the walls above him, dust and debris cascading all around. The shooting stopped, and Mac rolled to his left, looked to the other end of the hallway, still seventy-five yards behind Alt. Alt was rushing away again. Mac pushed himself up and chased. Alt veered hard left, taking an escalator back down to the first level and the main Convention Center entrance on Kellogg Boulevard, fleeing outside.

Mac sprinted through the crowd to the escalator and frantically looked down. Alt was going out the doors. Mac quickly bolted to his right, where it was fifty feet to the indoor skyway that served as a bridge over Kellogg Boulevard to the Convention Center parking ramp on the other side. In the skyway, he could get on top of Alt, he thought, maybe surprise him on the other side. Down ten steps, he threw his shoulder through the door and turned left. He was on the skyway.

~

Alt didn't stop to find out if he hit McRyan. He jumped onto the escalator to his left, took it down two steps at a time. At the bottom, he turned right and burst through the doors out onto Kellogg Boulevard and heard the sirens ringing out all over downtown.

This wasn't much better.

He had to get out of sight and out of downtown. He needed a set of wheels. There was little traffic coming from the east, stopped from the commotion caused a few blocks away. As he quickly looked back to his right, he saw the stoplight turn green. A single car was coming his direction from the intersection of Kellogg and West Seventh.

~

Mac, running across the skyway, looked left and saw Alt rushing across Kellogg at a forty-five-degree angle away from him but only to go through the break in the median dividing the east-west lanes of Kellogg. Alt's diversion allowed Mac to close the gap. Alt got through the gap in the barrier and then looked back in Mac's direction, but not up at him—back up the street past him. Mac looked right and saw it.

Alt moved towards the car, the assault rifle pointed at the driver. The car stopped, and Alt stood right in front of it. "Get Out! Get Out!"

The driver, frightened, with his right arm in the air, began to open the door with his left hand, when Alt heard glass breaking above him. McRyan was at a hole in the skyway glass he'd just shot out. Alt unloaded the rest of his clip up at the skyway thirty feet above the street.

As he fired, the car pulled away. Alt turned to give chase, but Riley came around the corner of the Convention Center. The assassin quickly popped in a new clip and fired at Riley, who dove away. Alt quickly turned to his right and sprinted for the parking ramp.

Mac was down on the floor of the skyway, lying in a pool of glass. He'd gotten two rounds off before Alt fired. The shots had stopped. Mac got up on one knee and peered over the edge just in time to see Alt going through the doors and into the parking ramp.

Mac pushed up and scrambled twenty feet to the end of the skyway. He veered left and threw his shoulder through glass doors to a thirty-foot stairway. He jumped sideways onto the middle hand railing and slid down on his fanny. Took two strides through another set of doors into the parking ramp and saw Alt at the bottom of a runway, fifty feet away, turning to go further down into the ramp. Mac fired.

The shots sailed over Alt's head as he turned to go lower. The assassin sprinted down, past the second-level elevator lobby, turning back east, hustling to the third parking level. He turned again, going down to the elevator landing between the third and fourth parking levels. Passing the elevators, he continued part way down the walking ramp to the fourth parking level and stopped.

Mac ran down the first runway and could hear the echoes of Alt running a level below him. Mac turned at the first parking level and ran down the ramp back west to the second elevator level, turned back east down the ramp and stopped about two thirds of the way down, looking directly right, into the third parking level and down the ramp and listened. He didn't hear Alt running. He'd stopped.

Cautiously, Mac moved slowly down now, shuffling his feet sideways to the left, scanning the cars and trucks. He got to the bottom of the walking ramp and urgently scanned the lot again. He took a cautious step forward and his heart jumped as something broke to his right.

Alt heard McRyan coming down the ramp right above him and then heard him slow down. Now he didn't hear anything. Alt calculated he was scanning the cars, thinking he'd gone into the parking ramp.

Gingerly edging his way back up towards the elevator lobby, Alt moved to improve his firing angle. He stepped back with his right foot, the rifle aimed up at the parking landing. As he stepped back, he could see more of the landing. He stepped back again and could see even more. As he stepped back once more, he saw McRyan's hands and weapon pointed out towards the parked cars scanning the ramp.

One more step back. He planted his right foot and heard glass crunch under his feet. He fired.

~

The bullets ripped at the loose right sleeve of Mac's windbreaker as he dove back to his left, and the shots flew over his head. His service weapon was a popgun next to that damn assault rifle. The shots stopped, and he heard running again. Alt was going for the bottom. He had to be, it was the only way out.

Mac gave chase, hitting the third elevator level, and pausing briefly. He could still hear Alt running a whole level below him.

He kept after him, going back east to the fourth parking level and made the turn at a sprint back down to the last elevator landing. He turned to his right and stopped. In twenty feet he would be exposed coming down the last walking ramp. Alt was already in the cars, he thought, waiting in ambush for him.

Mac quickly assessed his options. The sirens were way in the distance, although it was hard to tell eighty feet below the main street level now. He looked at the last thirty feet of walking ramp. At the bottom on the right side of the cement half wall was a large square pillar. If he could reach the pillar at the bottom, he'd have cover. Mac stuffed the gun in his pants and crab-walked sideways down the walking ramp, staying below the top of the half wall.

At the bottom, Mac lay on his belly and pushed himself to the edge of the pillar and peeked around the corner.

~

Alt got down to the last level of the ramp and ran straight into the sea of cars and trucks. He needed to find something to hot wire. A white Chevy Impala was in the far row, near the exit for the ramp, the perfect car to boost. But McRyan was coming, and Alt had to take care of him first. He got to the third row of cars and ducked behind a Ford F-150 pickup with a camper top. The position left him a good angle at the walking ramp. McRyan had to come down, and he'd hit him when he did. He heard McRyan get to the last landing. Then the running stopped.

Alt trained the rifle at the walkway, waiting for McRyan to come. But he didn't. The assassin edged out a little from the back of the truck, looking at the ramp, scanning from the pillar at the bottom, back up the walking ramp and then back down to the pillar. Where was he?

Mac saw the feet move, black dress shoes, next to a pickup truck with a camper top. He quietly pushed himself back and rolled to a sitting position. He set his gun in his hands and pushed himself up, his back against the pillar. He had more protection if he turned to his left, the half wall protecting his lower half, and he could duck behind it if need be. If he turned right, he would be totally exposed. He exhaled, turned to his left and fired.

The shots hit the camper top. Mac knew he missed, but he had position now and could wait him out. "Alt," he called out, "there's no way out of here."

Sirens in the distance were louder now, zeroing in on their position. "The cavalry'll be here any minute."

Alt was trapped. McRyan knew it too and was calling out to him.

Then he heard it to his left, to the west, and he had new life. A hundred feet away a car pulled into the ramp.

Alt took off at a full sprint, his weapon up, pointed at the car, a hostage, and keys—a way out.

Mac saw it too and was out from behind the pillar, running at a full sprint, firing at Alt, missing wildly. He got off three shots before his clip ran out. He reached with his left hand into his back pocket and grabbed his last clip, looked down briefly, popped it back in and raised his gun again looking for Alt. The killer had stopped and was facing him. Mac dove away, but it was too late. He took a round in the left shoulder.

~

Alt knew he'd hit McRyan. He pivoted to run towards the woman again. Then to his right, another vehicle came down the spiral ramp, McRyan's Explorer. Riley was in the passenger seat, a gun drawn, scanning the garage. Alt fired at the Explorer, causing it to swerve left and careen into a parked car. Then a shot came from the right. Alt pivoted back that way.

~

Mac pushed up with his right arm and fired. His first shot missed. As Alt turned back towards him, Mac's second shot caught Alt in the left shoulder, jerking his body hard to the left. Mac took a step forward and fired twice more, double tap, into Alt's chest, sending him flying backwards against the trunk of a parked car.

Mac moved quickly towards Alt, his gun pointed at him the entire time. The assassin was slumped back against the bumper of the car, blood oozing through his white dress shirt, the assault rifle lying by his feet.

With his gun still pointed, Mac approached Alt and kicked the rifle away. The blood was dark, coming from the area of the heart. The sirens in the background would not come soon enough for him. The assassin was still conscious, but his breathing was labored. His head was drooping, but his eyes were looking up at Mac.

~

The rifle was by his feet, but, while his mind told his arms to move, they wouldn't. Looking down at his chest, he saw the blood flowing through his shirt. It was dark purple, from the heart. Alt could barely get his breath now. It wouldn't be long.

The assassin looked up to see McRyan approaching him, gun pointed straight at him. He kicked the rifle away. "How did you know we were coming?" McRyan asked.

Alt smirked, beaten by some Irish flatfoot kid. McRyan asked again, louder, kicking the inside of his right leg, "How did you know we were coming?"

Alt was fading now, things started to blur.

"How did you know we were coming?" Mac shouted a third time, but there was no answer. Alt's chest stopped heaving, his breathing gave out, and his head fell to the left, resting against the bumper on the car. Mac checked for a pulse. The assassin was dead.

Mac winced in pain. He'd been hit on the top of his left shoulder, where the vest provided little protection. *You won't be lifting weights any time soon,* he thought, although it didn't look too bad, a little blood; it was worse than a graze, more like he was just nicked good. Lich and Riley were walking gingerly toward him, weapons drawn, although there was no need now. He looked beyond them to see his shot up Explorer. Cripes, what a day.

They all walked towards the driver of the car Alt had intended to hijack. She was shaking and crying. Lich opened the back door to her car and helped her sit down. Officers were coming now from both the bottom and top of the ramp. He turned to his friends. They had just saved his life, and he thanked them. "Took you guys long enough."

"Hey, better late than never, boyo," Lich replied.

"Yeah, and nice driving too," Mac replied as he walked to his now totaled SUV.

"Christ Almighty," Riley hooted. "You save the guy's life, and he bitches about his precious SUV."

Mac smirked as he grabbed a turtleneck from the back compartment. Guess the trip up north was out of the question. As he fashioned a sling for his left arm, he reached into the front seat, moved the now deflated airbag from the steering wheel and grabbed his cell phone, wanting to call Sally. "Dick, could the airbag even deploy against your girth?"

"Fuck you," Lich replied, rubbing his knee. They all shared a pained smile and small laugh. They'd survived.

"Tell you one thing that wasn't a joke," Mac said. "They knew we were coming. I tried to ask Alt how they knew, but ..."

"Yeah, well we still may have someone who can tell us," Riles responded.

"Guess who survived our little shootout?" Lich added.

"Who?" Mac asked.

Riley grinned, "Want another shot at Ted Lindsay?"

41

"I KNOW WHO TIPPED THEM OFF."

Mac was transported to United Hospital. His wound on the top of his left shoulder required thirteen stitches. He wouldn't be able to use his arm for a week or two. The Emergency Room doctor told him to take it easy, keep his arm in a sling, and he wrote a prescription for pain medication and ordered him to start a physical therapy program in a week or so, once the wound had healed.

Rockford was going to be fine, although he would be laid up for a while. He was raging about the shootout. "Find the mother-fucker who tipped those assholes off," he said at least a half dozen times.

Two CIRT officers were in surgery and would be for several hours. The doctors were hopeful, but they both had been hit hard. Several others had been wounded, and the ER was a busy place. Having seen all of his fellow officers lying around with multiple wounds, Mac didn't feel too bad about his little hit to the shoulder.

Paddy offered them a ride back to the Department of Public Safety Building. As they walked to Paddy's cruiser, Mac pulled out his cell phone, and cleared the last call, the one Sally had made while they were driving downtown a few hours earlier. She answered on the first ring. She was calm on the other end, but Mac could hear the relief in her voice.

"You won't believe what we have been finding!" she said excitedly.

"What?"

"I'll show you when you get here. But one thing I will tell you is that those guys at PTA had electronic surveillance on both your place and mine."

"What? You gotta be shittin' me."

"I'll tell you all about it when you get here."

Mac was pissed again. Well, the boys at PTA wouldn't be bugging any more places. Mac was sure of that. They pulled into the parking garage and the chief and Peters were waiting for them.

"I sure am glad to see you boys in one piece," the chief said, shaking each of their hands. "Well done. Well done." He took a long, concerned look at Mac in his sling. "Boyo, you sure you should be here?"

"I'll be fine, Chief," Mac replied, holding up a vial of pain medication. "Where's Lindsay?"

"We've got him in an interview room, waiting for you. I figure you guys have more than earned the first shot at him. But first, why don't you see what we've found."

They took a waiting elevator up to the chief's office. When they entered, Sally saw Mac in the sling and came to him. She touched him lightly on the left arm and looked him in the eye and gave him a little smile. Mac smiled back, his look telling her he was okay.

"Let me show you what we've found," she said, taking him by the right arm. A long folding table had been brought in. The documents from the Cross file were spread out onto the table.

"They've been watching you guys for a while," she said to Mac, Riley, and Lich. "When the police searched the PTA building, we found this room down in the bottom of the parking garage. They had surveillance equipment, computers, listening devices, you name it, and they were watching, especially Mac, and even me," Sally said to everyone. "We found a few guys down there who were part of the operation. We have them in custody. They've also given us the names and aliases of a few others. The department, the state police, and the FBI have that information, and we're on the lookout for all of them."

"Holy cow," Riles replied, a look of amazement on his face.

"Yeah, pretty amazing what they were up to. But they had good reason to be watching. They were up to some nasty stuff with this Cross business." She laid it out for everyone. Cross had been an operation run out of a facility in West Virginia. Lindsay, Alt, and company were selling arms, ammunition, communications equipment, and other military hardware out the backdoor. The FBI was already looking at the log, and it appeared the hardware had been sold to groups who weren't exactly friends of the United States.

"They made millions on this stuff," Sally said. "It looks like they shut it down around the time of the September 11th attacks."

"This file is what Landy Stephens gave to Jones then?" Lich asked waving to the documents on the table.

"We think so," Sally replied. "Jones either wouldn't play ball with them, or they didn't give her the chance to."

"So, they took her out," Riles replied.

"Yeah," Mac added. "But before they could, she shared this information with Claire Daniels, so she had to go too."

"Did they kill Senator Johnson?" Lich asked.

"Yup. We found a computer guy down in that little room, and he's singing. Says they killed Jones, Daniels, and the senator. He also worked the surveillance system at Victory Ramp so we couldn't see that Alt guy shoot Knapp."

"The senator was just a patsy in all this, then, huh?" Lich asked.

"Yes," Sally replied. "What a plan. They kill Jones, making it look like the work of Knapp. They kill Daniels and pin it on the senator. Before the senator can clear his name, they kill him and make it look like a suicide. They kill Knapp before we can talk to him, thinking he'll never have the chance to deny he killed Jones."

"Except Mac found this file and that DVD system at Daniels's place, and we got 'em. Hell if you weren't onto it all along," the chief replied, a smile on his face. "Your dad would have been proud today, Mac, very proud."

"Thanks, Chief," Mac replied quietly, trying to keep his emotions in check.

"So, are the feds going to come in and louse this up, prosecute these guys for espionage or something?" Lich asked.

"We'll work all that out," Flanagan replied. "You boys don't worry about that stuff. Ms. Kennedy and I will handle that."

"There's still one thing we don't know," Mac said. "These bastards knew we were coming. I want to go see Lindsay and find out how."

"Have at him, boys," the chief replied.

Ted Lindsay was sitting in a cinder block interview room. There were no windows, just a bright overhead light. He was sitting in a metal chair, his right arm handcuffed to the table. He was still in his dress suit, but it was rumpled now, with blood spattered on his lapels and white dress shirt. His tie was off kilter. He had a fat lip and bruising over his eyes and along the left side of his face.

Captain Peters joined the three of them in the interview room, carrying a plastic bag that contained Lindsay's personal affects. There was a wallet, watch, keys, and his cell phone.

Mac sat in the center of the table, Lich and Riley on either side of him. Peters stood behind them. Mac thought back to the interview with Lindsay from a week before, when the bastard had a smirk on his face and answers for everything.

"Tables have turned here a little bit, haven't they, Mr. Lindsay?" Mac quipped.

Lindsay didn't respond.

"We've got you, at a minimum, for the murders of Claire Daniels, Jamie Jones, Senator Mason Johnson, and Dirk Knapp—and those are just the ones we know about. So we have you for that. And the feds?" Mac shook his head, taunting. "They're not real happy with you right now. They're going to want to spend a lot of time with you. I doubt we'll have any objection to spending the rest of your life at the federal pen in Marion. Selling your country out with that Cross business—not too good for you there, Teddy boy," Mac said in a semi-mocking tone. Lich and Riley just stared at Lindsay.

"Lawyer," was Lindsay's response.

Mac grabbed for the plastic bag of belongings while Peters jumped in. "Later. First you're going to tell us how you knew we were coming."

"Lawyer."

"No!" Riley howled. "Tell us who tipped you off."

"Lawyer."

Lich snorted. "Boys, he looks like he was roughed up riding around in the van today, don't you think?"

"I do," Riles responded. Peters nodded. They all moved around to Lindsay's side of the table.

"I don't think anyone would notice if we added a few more bruises."

Fear overtook Lindsay's face. He pulled at his handcuffed arm, trying to get away. It wouldn't be a fair fight.

Mac ignored them and looked at the last call made on Lindsay's cell phone, 11:34 a.m., just before they left for the PTA building. The number was familiar to him. He'd seen it somewhere. He sat back in his chair, looking at the number, and ran it around in his head. He pulled out his own cell phone, pressed menu, and looked at the previous calls made on his phone. A smile creased his face.

"Boys," Mac said.

They ignored him or didn't hear him, moving in on Lindsay.

"BOYS!"

They stopped and looked back at him, annoyed, fists still raised. "What?" Peters asked.

"I know who tipped them off."

42

"YOU HAVE THE RIGHT TO REMAIN SILENT."

Chief Flanagan and Sally joined Mac, Riley, Lich, and Peters on the ride over to the Ramsey County Courthouse. A squad car was leading in front of them and two were behind. They pulled up onto the curb and filed out of the van. The chief led them through the doors inside, where the crowd that was milling around stopped what they were doing to watch. Given the day's events, Flanagan and the rest of them were immediately recognized.

They took the elevator up to the tenth floor and the district attorney's office. Sally led them through and past the reception desk. The receptionist started to say something, but then just watched them go by.

Sally walked them right to Helen Anderson's office. Anderson was at her desk, on the phone when they barged in. She looked up to see them. Then held up her hand for them to wait while she finished her call, oblivious to what was happening. Mac walked over to her phone and cut the call off.

Anderson looked up at him, astonished, "What do you think you're doing?"

"Let me see your cell phone," Mac replied coldly.

"What?"

Lich, Riley, and Peters moved to take position around Anderson. Mac asked again, tersely, "Let me see your cell phone."

"Why?"

"LET ME SEE IT!"

Anderson cowered back into her chair, looked to her purse on the credenza behind her desk, and pointed weakly.

Mac rifled through the purse, finding her phone. He hit menu and looked at the call record. There was Lindsay's cell phone number, as well as his own from earlier in the day. He turned to her.

"Is your cell phone number," he said, reading the number on her phone.

"Yes," she replied quietly.

"Sally called you earlier when we were coming downtown today, letting you know what we'd found."

"So?"

Mac produced Lindsay's phone from his pocket and held it so she could see it. "This is Ted Lindsay's cell phone. Let me show you who he called at 11:34 a.m. this morning." He showed Anderson the number. The district attorney slumped back in her chair, knowing she'd just been nailed.

The chief took over. He probably hadn't slapped the bracelets on anyone in years, but he remembered Miranda, "Helen Anderson, you have the right to remain silent. Anything you say can and will be used against you in a court of law. You have the right to an attorney ... and you're going to need a good one."

Mac plopped himself down on the couch in the den at Sally's place. She was on the phone, still working.

It had been a long day that was supposed to have been the start of a little mini-vacation for them. That was out of the question now. There would be tons of follow-up work to do. Sally was going to be swamped with the prosecution of Lindsay and the remaining PTA people who'd been working in their little unit. Some were still at large. The FBI, Homeland Security, and the CIA were on the case as well. They seemed confident they would find all of them. Just in case, two squads were parked out in front of the house.

His cell phone had been going berserk. He finally shut it off after he had a chance to speak with his mom, sisters, Uncle Shamus, and various other family members. He didn't want to be at home, knowing the media would be calling him.

He took his pain medication. His shoulder was sore, and the sling would be an annoyance in the days to come. Putting on a clean shirt had been a five-minute ordeal that he might not have accomplished without Sally's help. What Mac really wanted was to have a beer, but it wouldn't mix well with the meds. Sally made him some apple cider, and that wasn't too bad. He reached for the TV remote.

All of the local stations were doing special reports regarding the events of the day. A lot of issues had been resolved and the department came out looking pretty good. They were up against professionals, with resources Mac could hardly imagine, yet those PTA professionals had been beat by a little bunch of locals. Mac's name was coming up quite a bit, but he was unavailable for comment. That's the way he would like it to stay, but the chief ordered all of them down to a press conference that was to be held the next morning, no exceptions.

The two CIRT guys were out of surgery and remained in serious condition. Riley went back down to the hospital, and word was the doctors were optimistic they would make it. Damn Helen Anderson. She was getting hers on the news now, and she likely would be doing some time. Turns out she'd been dating Lindsay and feeding him information. She thought Lindsay would help her get to the Senate.

Mac flipped to the cable news networks. They were covering the story as well. PTA was a nationally known company, and Senator Johnson was a national figure. Those issues were being covered, debated, and bloviated about on all the talk shows. Lyman Hisle had called Sally to thank her for the heads up. He was able to get with the board and Minnesota's congressional delegation. PTA would take a hit, but the politicos thought they would be able to limit the damage and save most of the government contracts. There was nothing faulty about PTA's products, just some of its leadership.

Mac had heard enough about the day and flipped over to Minnesota Sports Channel. The Wild were on, a good diversion.

He thought about his dad and wondered what he would have thought of the day's events. Somehow, Mac knew the old man would be proud.

Sally finally came in, having changed into black cotton sweat pants and one of Mac's Golden Gopher sweatshirts. She leaned in and kissed him lightly. Then carefully she sat to his right side so he could put his arm around her. She carefully cuddled up against his chest. They watched the game in silence.

"Sorry about our vacation," Mac finally said, trying to lighten the mood a little. It didn't work.

"I'm just glad you're okay. I heard all that gunfire and ..." her voice trailed off.

"It was pretty crazy."

They sat for another few minutes, just watching the game.

"Were you scared?" she asked.

"At the time it was all happening, no. It happened so fast, the shots, the chase, everything. I wasn't thinking. I was just reacting. I don't think I was really scared until it was all over, when I realized what I'd just gone through. Then it hit me."

"I was in the chief's office, and there were radio reports that you were chasing Alt, and he was shooting at everyone. Then when you went into the parking ramp and were out of sight for so long, nobody knew where you were but people could hear all this gunfire. It must have been ten minutes before someone got on the radio and said you were wounded but that you were okay. I was just so scared."

"Is it going to scare you away from me?"

She sat up and looked him in the eye. "No. But you have to know that if we're going to be together, I will worry about you. I'll tell you that I worry about you. You'll have to understand that I'll feel that, every time you walk out the door, it might be the last time I see you.

You will have to understand that that is what I'll have to live with. So, there's one thing you'll have to get used to."

"What's that?"

"That every time you walk out the door now, I'm going to tell you that I love you."

Mac smiled. "I can live with that."

A note to my readers...

Thank you for reading and I sincerely hope you enjoyed *The St. Paul Conspiracy*. As an independently published author, I rely on each and every reader to help spread the word. If you enjoyed the book please tell your friends and family and if it isn't too much trouble I would really appreciate a brief review.

The next standalone thriller in the McRyan Mystery Series is *Deadly Stillwater*. I've also started a second series called the FBI Agent Tori Hunter Series and the first book is *Silenced Girls*.

Thanks again and I'm always writing a new book so look for Mac in the next mystery! To stay on top of the new releases and new series please join the list at www.RogerStelljes.com and I'll let you know when the next one comes out.

ALSO BY ROGER STELLJES

MCRYAN MYSTERY SERIES

First Case - Murder Alley

The St. Paul Conspiracy

Deadly Stillwater

Electing To Murder

Fatally Bound

Blood Silence

Next Girl On The List

Fireball

The Tangled Web We Weave

Short Story

Stakeout - A Case From The Dick Files

Boxsets

First Deadly Conspiracy - Books 1-3

Mysteries Thrillers and Killers - Books 4-6

FBI AGENT TORI HUNTER

Silenced Girls

For new release alerts get on the list at

www.RogerStelljes.com

ABOUT THE AUTHOR

Roger Stelljes is the New York Times and USA Today bestselling author of the McRyan Mystery Series. He has been the recipient of several awards including: the Midwest Book Awards - Genre Fiction, a Merit Award Winner for Commercial Fiction (MIPA), as well as a Minnesota Book Awards Nominee.

Never miss a new release again, join the new release list at www.RogerStelljes.com

Made in the USA
Columbia, SC
25 July 2020